Praise For RBFE

"Quick but highly entertaining read ... reminded me of Jim Butcher's urban fantasy series The Dresden Files."

— Ian Chung, *Sabotage Reviews*

"Hellboy meets Scott Pilgrim vs. The World, meets Jim Butcher and Larry Correia in this insane pulp-action adventure novella featuring a haunted suicidal anti-hero who joins a rock band and fights evil."

— Paul Genesse, author of
the Iron Dragon Series

ROCK BAND FIGHTS EVIL

VOLS 4-6

THE ROAD TO HELL

Contains three complete novels!

Devil Sent the Rain

This World Is Not My Home

The Good Son

ROCK BAND FIGHTS EVIL VOLS 4-6

THE ROAD TO HELL

Contains three complete novels!

Devil Sent the Rain
This World Is Not My Home
The Good Son

D.J. Butler

WordFire Press
Colorado Springs, Colorado

ISBN: 978-1-61475-570-8

Cover design by Janet McDonald

Cover artwork images by Carter Reid

Kevin J. Anderson, Art Director

Book Design by RuneWright, LLC
www.RuneWright.com

Published by
WordFire Press, an imprint of
WordFire, Inc.
PO Box 1840
Monument CO 80132

Kevin J. Anderson & Rebecca Moesta, Publishers

WordFire Press Trade Paperback Edition April 2017
Printed in the USA
wordfirepress.com

ROCK BAND FIGHTS EVIL #4

DEVIL SENT THE RAIN

CHAPTER ONE

I don't like this place," Mike grumbled. The big guy shrugged deeper into his cracked leather jacket.

Rain thumped angrily on the skylight overhead, rattling the warped old metal and threatening to punch through the glass. Water trickled down the cement walls of the room, prickly-cold from the weather and lit in blue and gray by fluorescent tubes. Jim paced the room like a caged cat, looking into the corners and behind the furniture.

"What's the matter, missing your serape? Don't get thunderstorms like this in Oaxaca? No chiles rellenos in the green room?" Adrian needled Mike. Mike wasn't particularly Mexican, had grown up in Texas or something, but he had Mexico in his family and he was sensitive about it. That gave Adrian all the room he needed to tease him.

The truth was, Adrian didn't much like the club either. It was a dive, and dives got dangerous, even without the hurricane-force storm that was building outside. For that matter, the storm might keep attendance down, and that would create a different sort of problem. Fewer drinkers meant less cash for the band meant less gas for the van, and Chicago was still a long drive away.

The thought of clubs and the dangers they presented reminded Adrian that he still hadn't checked this one for wards or other arcane traps, which was definitely his job. He was, after all, the resident wizard.

He reached into his pocket for his Third Eye—

"We can get chiles rellenos," the club gopher chirped. She was young and cute, in a cream-of-the-math-major-and-gamer-girls-crop sort of way, complete with dark-rimmed square glasses and a ponytail. She clicked on her tablet and typed in a couple of characters, moving in closer to Adrian. Adrian grinned his best wolfish grin and tried not to back away. The gopher kept invading his space in a way that made it hard not to realize she was attractive. It wasn't that he didn't like sex, or girls, but Adrian was a wizard, and he couldn't expend his *ka*-energy or burden his shadow with anything as frivolous as sex. "There's a good Mexican place just down the street."

"What is that, Yelp?" Adrian asked. He leaned over her to look at the map of Kansas City that sprang to life under her fingers. He missed his own app-loaded smartphone, which had been crushed by a renegade angel in New Mexico a few days earlier. Besides, if he focused on the cool toys, it helped him not to think about the girl who was holding them.

"*Chingate,*" Mike swore. "Both of you."

"Ain't nothing down the street but water, anyway," Eddie threw in. "Every direction. I looked." Eddie just had to assert that he was the boss, no matter how much of a second fiddle he would always be to Jim. The guitarist scratched himself under his arm, and Adrian knew he was reassuring himself that his pistol was still there. "I'd take comfort from the forecast that this is going to be a light rain, if I was able to take comfort from anything."

In answer, thunder crashed outside the building. The rain stopped drumming and began to hammer.

"Not literally," Gopher Girl agreed. "But we could send a bike."

They stood in the green room of a club called the Silver Eel. The building had once been some kind of dockside warehouse, squatting low down on the water's edge below a steep hill. The green room and performance space were on the upper floor. The green room was a rectangular slice taken off one end of the top floor, stuffed with ratty armchairs and a card table carrying a basket of candy bars and a huddle of water bottles. It had a door at each end, one leading onto the stage and the other into a stairwell that climbed down to the lower floors—there was a lounge and restaurant on the floor below them, at street level, and stairs that led further down, to space that was presumably at the level of the river. Adrian's arms were still stiff from loading in up those stairs.

"You could send a boat," Eddie suggested. "It'd get there faster."

"Any port," Adrian said, "et cetera." In a storm. Obvious, though, wasn't it? Say something useful, he kicked himself. Say something impressive.

As if to punctuate the lameness of his quip, a flash of thunder through the skylight came accompanied by an immediate *BOOM!* of thunder.

"Jeez," Mike said. "That's close enough, it could have killed somebody in the street."

"Mexican food," Twitch commented, swishing her tail as she turned to look around the room, "but no mirrors? How do you expect a girl to do her makeup?" She fluttered her long silver eyelashes and then winked.

"You're a girl?" Gopher asked, then looked flustered.

"Hypothetically," Twitch said, and Adrian managed not to laugh. Twitch was girl enough when she wanted to be. At other times, she was a horse, a bird or a boy. The sheer strangeness of the fairy, and her magical nature, made her feel safe for Adrian. She reeked of sex half the time—Mab's people had that gift—but it wasn't really sex, so it didn't bother Adrian. And he knew she was happier for the fact that there were no mirrors in the room.

"Grandpa Archuleta fought in the war," Mike was still gnawing away at the chip on his shoulder about his ancestry. "World War Two. He was a gunner in the Navy."

"Yeah?" Adrian raised his eyebrows. Low-hanging fruit. "Which side was Mexico *on?*"

He didn't like the green room much, either. For one thing, unless it was caffeinated, the water was useless to him. He'd need caffeine before the night was over, or he'd be slapping nicotine patches onto his arm. He wasn't sure they helped—he knew for a fact they didn't stop the curse from affecting him one hundred percent—but he thought they had some effect, anything was better than nothing, and it was worth a shot. Also, the candy bars were okay, but they weren't great. Sugar was a nice energy kick for a short burst, and that might come in handy, but a candy bar wasn't karmically perfect. The sugar and the nuts would weigh into his shadow and put a drag on his ka. Some wizards were happy to tolerate the dead weight, because they liked their steak and candy bars and because, honestly, it wasn't all *that much* weight. Adrian found it unacceptable. He was a high performance machine, a two hundred megaton sorcerer, and when he needed to explode out of the silo on full burn, he wanted to be able to really light it up. He needed eggs, preferably organic and free range, but any egg at all would be better than any candy bar.

Thinking of sorcery, he remembered that he needed to check the club for traps. He reached for the Eye again—

"Hey, do you want to double check your pedals and effects on this diagram I made?" Gopher Girl held up her tablet and Adrian saw what looked like a circuit diagram, but in color and three dimensions. The view rotated under her fingers as she moved them in a slow circle. He looked at her fingers and tried to ignore the rest of her.

"Everything worked at the sound check," he mumbled, but he was fascinated by the pictures of his own stompboxes. He pointed at a missed connection. "The drum machine runs through the Fuzz Face."

"You sure?"

"Yeah," he said, "I tested the fuzz beats, they work. I guess you just missed it. But how did you do this? What kind of app are you using here?" His hand slapped in vain at the pocket where he usually carried the smartphone. Damn angels. "May I?" He touched the individual pedal icons and saw little windows with their specifications open up. "Is this homemade? I've never seen anything like it."

"It's the club's," Gopher Girl grinned. "It's proprietary."

"Yeah? I dig proprietary inventions, I'm a tinkerer myself. What other cool stuff do they have?" Adrian saw that the circuit diagram included the fixed elements of the club's sound, too—mixing board, PA, and so forth.

"It keeps track of the play list." She showed him with a tap. "And it checks it against what you actually play, and automatically updates the club's blog."

"Did we agree to that?" Adrian didn't think any of the Infernals used the Internet—that was why he had felt comfortable using a smartphone, once he had carefully disabled certain tracking components inside—but the Legate of Heaven was human, and he probably did. He probably had an email address and a Facebook account, if you knew where to look. If you tweaked your settings just right, you could probably get a date with him on Match.com.

He tried not to imagine what those settings would have to be.

"Not to any recording," she agreed quickly, shaking her head so that her ponytail shook like the horse's tail on Twitch's rump. She pointed at Eddie. "He said no recording."

"Good." Adrian relaxed a hair. If Eddie was going to act all large and in charge, at least he'd gotten it right, despite being from a pre-Internet generation.

"Here's all the site will show." Gopher Girl brought up a page showing the Silver Eel at night, window signs lit and the lights of downtown Kansas City sparkling across the river in the background. The day's date was in the subject line of a blog entry, which announced that the Notorious Gentlemen would be playing, and a set list.

Adrian chuckled. He didn't love the fact that the song titles were listed, but it would be hard for anyone to track them by those, since they issued no recordings and had no Internet presence themselves. Also, the sight of the band's name for the evening amused him, since he'd come up with it.

BOOM! More thunder. Adrian shivered, feeling a little uncomfortable. It was the storm that was making him edgy, he decided. He'd get over it once he hit a hundred ass-kicking decibels with the Hammond.

"Jim?" Eddie asked.

Jim stopped against one wall and nodded. His long black hair was clumped together by the humid air and hung around his pale face like a picture frame.

"He's nervous," Mike observed to Eddie. He pocketed a couple of candy bars and bit the head off a third. The skylight rattled in its frame with a glass-against-metal chinking noise. "Aren't you? Couldn't they give us just a *little* booze?"

"Seeing your cousin again?" Eddie asked the question, so it was sincere, even if it sounded harsh. If Adrian had asked it, he would have been asking in mockery. Even as he asked, Eddie's own eye slid sideways and he shuddered.

"No," Mike said. "But it wouldn't hurt to be a little bit buzzed ... just in case."

Gopher Girl looked confused, so Adrian tried to get her attention back on the tablet and away from the talk of ghosts. A wordless voice nagged him in the back of his mind, telling him he was forgetting something important. He ignored it. When the voices in his head could come up with actual words, then he'd listen to them. "What do you think the odds are of me getting a copy of some of these apps ... what did you say your name was?"

"They call me 'Mouser.'" Mouser smiled. "Like a cat. It's 'cause I handle all the little stuff around here, the mice."

"Curiosity killed," Adrian started, and then realized he might sound like he was threatening her, "er, you know." For a two hundred megaton sorcerer, he knew, he had a real gift for sounding like a numbnut.

Mike charged ahead. "I mean jeez, who wouldn't be nervous, after those flaming, sword-swinging giants smashed up the meat packing plant around us. Plus, the flesh-eating horse, the flying snakes, the lamia ... and ... you know, all of it." He looked sideways at Mouser, like he'd just realized she was there.

Mouser giggled. "You guys are funny."

Adrian shook his head and let her laugh. "You don't know the half of it, sister."

"Yeah," Eddie grunted, "life's a bitch. Let's play, collect gas money and hit the road. Maybe the bartender will give you a free beer."

"Or you could pay me," Mike suggested around a mouthful of nougat.

"Or I could use the money to get us to Chicago." Eddie's nostrils flared. He hadn't gotten the sleeves of his green army jacket replaced, so he looked like Arnold Schwarzenegger in *Commando*, only wiry and black and perpetually pissed off. "You do want to go to Chicago, don't you?"

"Yeah." Mike looked down at his feet. "Yeah, I wanna go to Chicago. *Cagado* flat tire."

"You got a better car?" Eddie snarled. "Last time I saw that Impala of yours, it wasn't going anywhere fast."

"The van's our ride," Adrian agreed. He definitely wanted to go to Chicago. For all the horsepower he had running under his wizard's hood, he didn't have enough. He still worked shackled to his uncle's curse, and that was a serious practical problem as well as a constant humiliation. Eddie, he knew, was anxious to back out of his deal with the devil. Adrian wanted to make one, and Chicago was the place to do it. "Mike's just saying what we all think."

"Yeah?" Eddie glared at Adrian, eyes quivering. He was a bit on edge, and no wonder. "What's that?"

"He's just wishing the van wasn't such junk, so he could afford to have a beer." Adrian grinned a grin he knew would irritate the crap out of Eddie.

"It ain't fancy," Eddie agreed. "It needs a little extra attention, sometimes. Some of it's held together by duct tape, and I haven't pimped it six ways to Sunday like you do to everything, Adrian. But *my shit works*."

"Huh." Adrian didn't really want to get into a fight with the guitarist, who was a combat vet and a karate guy, but he couldn't leave a target that easy be.

"What do you mean, *huh*?"

Adrian shrugged. "I have a different strategy."

"Yeah?"

"My stuff isn't *shit*."

"Aren't we on any minute now?" Twitch asked.

The intensity of the rain kicked up another notch, rattling the skylight in its frame and sending spritzes of cold water down through the gaps in the glass. Adrian pulled his jacket collar up around his neck and shivered. The silver suit was summerwear, really, lightweight and comfortable but not warm at all.

"You can go on now," Mouser said. She smiled and held up the tablet for Adrian to see. "I'll be listening to the songs."

She disappeared out the far door leaving Adrian trying to ignore the faintest hint of perfume she left behind. Jim turned and led the way through the nearer exit, into a haze of cigarette smoke and the pungent biting tang of alcohol on the air. At least here the club owners had replaced all the fluorescent tubes with hooded yellow incandescents, neon signs and other lighting more appropriate to a temple of alcohol service. Rock band, hell, Adrian thought. Really, they all funded their quirky quests to undo their own personal damnations by working as traveling salesmen of beer.

He had the heavy feeling that he'd forgotten something, something that might turn out to be important, but he couldn't figure out what it might be.

Maybe he was just missing his smartphone.

The stage was small; they always were, in the dives this band played in. Jim plucked his microphone from its stand and retreated into the shadows on the stage while the other players took their places. Twitch scooted onto the seat behind her minimalist drum kit and produced her drumming-and-fighting batons while Adrian sat behind his arsenal of sonic devices. With a touch in just the right spot, a door dropped open in a special compartment he had bolted onto the underside of his organ, revealing the stubby little Ingram MAC-11 inside. The subcompact submachine gun was his weapon of choice, when the lead began to fly—it only fired .380 ACP rounds, but it fired an awful lot of them, and it was small enough to hide on his instrument.

Just in case, he told himself.

The hall had a high ceiling and tall windows that struggled to hold back the wind and rain outside, which were starting to sound like a hurricane. Adrian took a moment to edge his volume knobs up. No self-respecting rock and roller could let himself be drowned out by mere *weather*.

Then, also just in case, he bit down on two sticks of nicotine gum.

He'd never been a smoker; he just really, really wanted to stay awake.

"Evening," Eddie doused the polite and slightly high applause that scattered around the room. "We're the Notarized Genuines."

"Notorious!—" Adrian snapped, but it was too late—Twitch had already kicked into the tattoo that launched their opening song, "Kingdom Come."

Eddie shrugged at Adrian, turned his back and staggered into the *A-C-D* chord pattern that made up most of the verse.

"Down on the corner stands a man with his back to the wall," Jim sang. He had a haunting voice, that out of sheer gravitas and charisma sounded like it had reverb in it, even when he talked to you face to face. Which he didn't do often, since he kept his mouth shut other than when he sang, for fear of being overhead by his father, His Lowness Lucifer, High Prince of Hell, the former Messenger of Heaven Azazel.

Adrian played the modest right hand arpeggio that went with the verse, adding single bass notes with the thumb or ring finger of his left hand.

> *He leans on a streetlight he thinks is a tree.*
> *He opens his tired fingers, lets the bottle fall.*
> *To an invisible friend, he says hey, do you see?*

Adrian added a full chord with the left hand, jumping big and powerful into the mix. This was how he liked his music, how he liked everything—Adrian overwhelming and dominating. Even Jim struggled to be heard over Adrian's sound, and shot him a glare out of the corner of his eye that made Adrian back off just a notch.

The crowd must be drunker than he thought; their dancing was an erratic shuffle, and they bumped at each other like they were circling for a fight. Adrian shook his head and made sure he had the MAC-11 close to his hand if he needed it. He had the taser in his jacket pocket, too, repaired by hand as they'd cruised across the nothingness of Kansas, but he couldn't be sure how much charge it had in it. And if he absolutely had to pull out the big ones, he had a candle stub and knew how to summon fire with it.

He was ready for any barroom brawl that might come his way.

He saw Mouser at the back of the room, talking to the big Swedish-looking bartender. She looked like she might be looking at him, so he nodded during the chorus.

> *Whoa, whoa, my kingdom's come.*
> *Whoa, whoa, my kingdom's come.*
> *My kingdom's come.*

By the end of the chorus, the crowd's dancing had become really erratic, but as Adrian dropped away the left-hand power, they cooled down a bit. Not drunk, he decided. Maybe they were stoned, high on something that was twisting their perceptions. He'd done LSD himself, and mescaline, more than once on his climb to power. It hadn't strengthened his ka, it hadn't given him any great insights, and all that toxic stuff, not to mention the weird memories, piled hard and heavy into his shadow, much worse than steak or any carnal romp. It had taken him months of fasting and flushing to get it out of his system when he'd realized it was slowing him down and gone cold turkey. Something like that might be throwing the crowd off-kilter, he guessed, making their movements all herky-jerky.

Jim sang another verse.

> *"In a plywood hotel downtown lies a girl with no name.*
> *"She's got a twelve-year-old body and dry withered eyes.*
> *"She pushes the breath through her lungs and the blood through her veins.*
> *"She stares out a bullethole window at the darkening skies, and she says."*

Mouser and the big Swede seemed to be arguing now, and Adrian frowned a little, without losing track of where he was in the song. She was a cool enough kid, even if she couldn't get her mind off sex, and she'd let him play with her toys, so it bugged him to see her picked on. If, he reminded himself, that was what he was seeing. Besides, it didn't bother him all that much; he didn't believe in liberty and justice for all, and if it turned out such a thing did exist, he wouldn't want it. What Adrian Pew wanted was power.

He kicked his sound up for the chorus again, careful not to drown Jim out this time. Not that he was afraid of Jim, but he respected the guy, and he needed him. Jim was the one who was carrying Azazel's hoof, taped to his belly, and he was the one who would connect them with Hell. Eddie did all the talking, but he was really just Aaron to Jim's Moses.

> *Whoa, whoa, my kingdom's come.*
> *Whoa, whoa, my kingdom's come.*
> *My kingdom's come.*

The second chorus transitioned into the bridge and Adrian pulled out the stops, flooding the stage and the hall with the rotary tones of his Hammond. As the big *A* chord, seven notes strong including a low *A* played by Adrian's foot, blasted out into the crowd, they stopped dancing.

Wrong reaction. Adrian frowned and piled on more notes as he climbed into the *C.*

The dancers straightened. It wasn't a natural movement, they straightened with the stop-gap, spastic motions of a rictus smile, like some unseen power had jammed a rod up each dancer's spine, turning them into grotesque puppets. People in the crowd who'd been sitting slammed their backs upright first, then lurched to their feet like the rod was extending downward through their hips and legs.

Jim, silent during the bridge, backed away from the edge of the stage, and Adrian saw that he was standing close to where his fencing saber hid behind a stack of amplifiers. Mike and Eddie edged back from the front of the stage, but it was small enough that there wasn't much of anywhere for them to go.

Could they *all* be on drugs? Was the water laced?

Or was the shit about to hit the fan ... *again?*

Adrian pushed up through the *D* and into the *E*, Twitch carrying him forward on a thunder of snare drum beats, the dancers straightening their entire bodies though their heads hung limp, like screen doors pinned to the frame by single hinges.

And then they began to vomit.

"The hell with this!" Adrian dropped the chord and grabbed the MAC-11. Twitch stood up, and Mike and Eddie faltered in their playing. Their wall of rock and roll sound slammed once against the back wall of the room and then stilled. The pounding of the rain on the windows became gigantic.

A beer glass, knocked to the floor, shattered like thunder.

Then Adrian realized what he'd forgotten, and plucked the Third Eye from his pocket. It was a lens, a bit of old natural volcanic glass that had been polished into a monocle and worn by generations and generations of sorcerers, pinched into their eye sockets. This was his prize possession—most of the rest of what he did magic with was bits of string and wax, chalk and hair made potent by the knowledge he'd stolen from his uncle, despite his uncle's curse, his threats and the constant fear in which Adrian had lived.

He'd stolen the Eye, too, because it was a powerful artifact. When he looked through it, he saw invisible things. He saw spells that were invisible to the naked eye but that existed as tangled lines of power. He saw through arcane disguises and illusions. He could also focus spells through it, which made them more powerful but tended to make them unpredictable, too, a little trickier to control. He thought he could use it to see even more—maybe much more—only he didn't know how to use it.

He'd stolen it, after all. Plucked it from its hiding place and then used it to blast its real owner into oblivion. He didn't even really know what it was called; his uncle had always called it the *Eye of Agamotto*, but that was obviously a joke. It was a joke Adrian didn't really know how to untell, until he could find a better name for the thing.

He squinched the Eye into place and almost immediately dropped it. Inside the dancers he saw worms. Tall, eyeless, limbless things, limp and boneless but muscular, and the worms wrapped around the spines of the dancers and made them move, like hands inside felt puppets. He saw lines of power, too, a web of many overlapping spells and wards splattered along all the walls, the floor, and the ceiling.

He also saw Mouser struggling with the big Swede; he was worm-filled, but she was not. She slapped him with her palms and clawed at him with fingernails, but he only laughed.

Then the first of the dancers exploded. Adrian nearly dropped the Third Eye fumbling it back into his pocket, and was just in time to see several more explode behind the first. Ribbons and shreds of flesh erupted in all directions as the human beings came apart and collapsed like bloody, discarded cocoons. What emerged from each flaccid heap of flesh bore no resemblance to a worm; they were pure monster, vaguely humanoid with hooked talons and a third set of limbs between arms and legs, that looked like it could function as either. Around the gaping maw of needle-like teeth, Adrian couldn't see anything that resembled a face or even a head. They scuttled forward like praying mantises, four lower limbs propelling them while clawed hands groped to the attack.

"We're in trouble!" Adrian yelled, realizing he was way, way too late. A wave of fatigue swished over him like a slow tide of warm chocolate, lulling him to dark oblivion. He bit his own tongue, hard, right through the wad of stimulant gum in his mouth. The flavor instantly changed from peppermint to blood, but he stayed awake.

"No shit!" Eddie shrugged out of his guitar strap and swung his Fender Toronado like a real ax, slamming the red body of the instrument into the snapping teeth of the foremost of the creatures. Jim bounded past him to hook one of the monitors with the toe of his boot and fling it into the onrushing mass of beasts, pummeling one of them in the chest and knocking it sideways.

In the back of the hall, the Swede exploded and fell away like the meat disguise that he was. The demon inside grabbed Mouser with four limbs, cutting off her shriek instantly.

Adrian raised the MAC-11 and fired.

CHAPTER TWO

The girl!" Adrian shouted. There wasn't any good reason for him to care about her, except that she was the only other human in the room. Heck, she'd distracted him with her toys and her sexual fascination, and that wasn't likely to have been an accident. She'd lured him in. He ought to hate her, and be happy to see her get what she had coming.

Only she was arguing with the Swede, and she was still human. And that made her look like an innocent, a dupe.

"The window!" Eddie snapped back.

Twitched hurled herself past Adrian, shifting shape as she did so into her silver horse form. She pounded aside one of the gnarled mantises and raced for the nearest window.

The demon, slightly off-balance from its jostling with the fairy, let rip a throaty, whining squeal and lurched at Mike. It rose up as it charged, running on two legs and slashing with the talons of all four of its upper limbs.

The bassist, tangled up in his strap and unable to get his gun out of the back of his belt, fell backward, raising his instrument up in front of him—

"*Chingón!*—"

SQUELCH!

The body of the bass guitar planted against the stage floor like the butt of a spear, and the head sank into the monster's chest. Steaming green sludge sprayed Mike and the floor around him. It reeked of bile and Adrian almost choked.

He didn't let it stop him, though. "It's nice to see the bass fighting on our side, for a change!" he shouted at Mike. "Spencer would be proud!" A good joke was worth choking on.

"Spencer?" Mike struggled to kick the dead mantis-demon off his bass with one foot while he balanced on the other.

"The last bass player!" Adrian reminded Mike. Spencer had died impaled on the bass by some nameless thing with tentacles instead of arms, before Eddie had doused it with gasoline and lit it on fire. The bass had been too valuable for a guy with Eddie's packrat mentality to leave behind, and he'd insisted on cleaning it himself.

"*Huevos*," Mike muttered, freeing the instrument and kicking the dead mantis off the stage with a loud *thud*.

Adrian aimed the little Ingram and squeezed the trigger, sweeping the floor ahead of him with short bursts as he ran. *B-rap-p-p-p! B-rap-p-p-p! B-rap-p-p-p!*

Beasts wailed and threw themselves aside or fell under his withering fire. A wave of fatigue dragged at the back of Adrian's eyeballs and thick, warm tendrils of sleep crawled up his legs and chest, beckoning him down into comforting silence.

He slapped himself in the face. Damn his uncle, and his uncle's curse.

To his right he saw Twitch the horse raise her hindquarters and kick at the lower panes and frame of one of the windows. With a tremendous shattering sound, glass and twisted metal exploded into the room, driven with nailgun force by the wind outside.

Four monstrous arms wrapped around Adrian's bicep while he was distracted. Sharkish teeth gaped wide as the thing bellowed into his face, its breath reeking of rotten meat and, surprisingly, cheap gin. Adrian could see eyes, this close to the creature—it had lots of them, tiny, beady little things, arranged in a circle around its muzzle like so many beauty moles on a grotesque, rubbery lip. He planted the muzzle of the MAC-11 against the creature's Adam's apple and squeezed off several rounds. It fell back in a spray of stinking green pus, its talons tearing the skin of Adrian's biceps and the fabric of his jacket.

He hoped its touch wasn't poisonous.

Twitch, now in falcon form with a long silver tail, struggled to try to get out the window, but couldn't overcome the wind and rain that crashed in like a river. Jim sprinted forward to the edge of the stage and threw himself in the fairy's direction, like a stage dive, only he held a naked sword in one hand and the crowd waiting to catch him looked anxious to devour his flesh. Mike and Eddie were both untangled from their instruments and followed Jim at a dogged stumble, pistols out and firing.

Twitch turned away from them and focused on the girl.

The thing that had been the Swede had wrapped its jaws around her shoulder and bit down. Mouser screamed as her blood stained her torn shirt, beating the beast in its circular array of shrunken eyes with the tablet.

Adrian ducked under another monster—it seemed almost too intent on getting to Jim to even notice him, once he stepped out of the way—and raised the machine pistol. Mouser shoved the tablet into her attacker's mouth and wedged it open. It reared up to plunge down upon her again—

"Drop!" Adrian yelled—

Mouser might not have seen him, but she heard his voice, and fell—

b-rap-p-p-p-p-p-p!

Adrian emptied the last of the clip into the monster's funnel-shaped head. It exploded like a watermelon in a Gallagher stage performance, and the creature's body dropped.

Adrian scooted around the end of the bar. He shot a glance towards the stage and saw the rest of the band, backed into a corner around the shattered window and fighting off the swarming creatures. If anything, the wind and the rain seemed to be holding the monsters back as much as the band's weapons, but the weather also made it impossible for Twitch to fly out.

They'd all have to jump, Adrian guessed. Oh well, twenty feet or so wasn't too much of a fall—as long as one of them made it without breaking a leg and could drive the van. If the wind hadn't actually flipped the van upside down, of course. Once they were inside the van, its wards of obfuscation and silence should help them evade pursuit and get away.

The six-limbed thing still trembled and shuddered as Adrian kicked it out of the way, switching to a new clip.

Mouser looked up at him, terrified. "I thought it was some kind of gag," she squeaked, meeting his eyes.

"Yeah, I'm laughing my ass off," Adrian grumbled, now wondering why he had bothered saving her. He grabbed her by her forearm and pulled her to her feet, looking at the cuts on her shoulder. There were a lot of them, and they were bleeding, but they didn't look too deep. He tucked the Ingram under his arm, grabbed a bar towel and wrapped it around her injury.

"The big guy, Fafnir or whatever," she continued, a little hysterical, "he said they were going to play a prank on you with your gear. He promised me fifty bucks if I kept you distracted. He said you wouldn't be able to keep your eyes off a shiny electronic toy." She sobbed, but just once, like a hiccup full of tears.

"Son of a bitch." Somebody knew him too well. But who could that be? And if they knew him well enough to know how much he liked gadgets, what else might they know? Obviously, whoever it was knew how to find the band. They'd set a trap, and the Notorious Gentlemen had stepped right into it. "I'd make a joke about thirty pieces of silver," he snapped, "but even my delusions don't have that much grandeur."

Adrian's heart pounded in his chest and his throat felt constricted. Stay awake! He told himself and slammed his knuckles against the hard wood of the bar. He looked back across the hall and saw Twitch the falcon soaring again, but this time into the center of the room, flying with the cold, wet blast of the wind over her friends' heads.

Squeeeeeeal!

Adrian turned, fumbling to get control of the pistol. He kept his eyes open only long enough to see four flailing talons come lunging at him across the bar—

Knock, knock, knock.

Adrian knew he was dreaming. That didn't make it any better.

"Come in, Ade," his uncle called from behind the cracked door.

Adrian pushed the door open, screaming silently. He didn't want to see his uncle. He tried to look at the floor, but he was only dreaming and he couldn't control what his dream-self did. His dream-self looked up at his uncle.

No! he wanted to yell, but couldn't.

The boy Adrian had never said "no," and had never been able to say what he always suspected: that it had been his uncle who had killed his father. In his dreams, Adrian could only watch his nightmares replay, again and again.

"Don't you want to learn about wards of silence?" his uncle asked. His uncle's head was a wolf's head, but not the head of a real wolf—it was cartoonish, with a long muzzle like a clown's oversized shoe, complete with a slack lower jaw for a floppy sole and a slavering tongue that hung wet and pink and threw hot drops of saliva around as his uncle talked.

No more silence! Adrian screamed inside, but his dream-self was more hesitant. No more cooperation!

"I think I can do that one. C-can we talk about wards of shielding?" he suggested.

His uncle's study was red-ribbed and fleshy, like the inside of a whale. His uncle sat at his desk. Adrian the dreamer knew that if you pulled the top left-hand drawer all the way out and reached under the desk, you could find a small hidden shelf. That was where his uncle kept the Eye, and Adrian knew it because in real life, years ago, he had found the Eye and stolen it. Dream-Adrian didn't know anything about it.

Dream-Adrian was trapped.

Books leered wetly at Adrian from sagging shelves on the walls, flapping their covers open and shut suggestively and chanting in a collective whisper.

Silence, silence, just between us!

"Of course we can." The wolf smiled, tongue bouncing on his chest.

"Now?" Dream-Adrian's heart hammered so loud it almost drowned out the books.

"In a bit."

"What about some combat magic?"

The wolf's eyebrows launched off his forehead in skeptical mockery. "Fireballs and death touches, you mean?"

Dream-Adrian nodded. Run away! Adrian screamed. This wasn't exactly a memory, it wasn't a particular scene through which he had ever lived, but it was the epitome of a thousand scenes from his childhood, and he knew how it had to end. "Or maybe something smaller. Like a stunning spell?"

Uncle-wolf frowned, retracting his tongue slightly into his mouth. "Traditionally, masters don't ever teach apprentices combat magic. Combat spells are things a wizard teaches himself, when he is a man of full powers and mature understanding."

"I didn't know you only did things the traditional way." Dream-Adrian's jibe was so flat and understated, even Adrian couldn't be sure it was really an attack. It was the most passive aggression possible, surrender with a joke so subtle it wasn't even obviously a joke. Adrian cursed his own weakness and wished he could look away.

Silence, silence, this is the way of the wizard!

The wolf patted his knee and slid his wet, pink tongue out to its full length. "I can only do for you what has been done for me," he purred, his voice low and husky.

Dream-Adrian edged closer to the wolf, muscles in his lower back tightening. "Can you teach me everything?" he asked. No, run away! Adrian screamed, tears flowing down his cheeks even though they didn't. "I want to be a great sorcerer, like my father. Even better than my father."

The wolf took Dream-Adrian by the wrist and drew him closer. "I know you miss your dad," the wolf said. He smiled, but his tongue dangled so bright and long out of his mouth that it made the smile horrible to behold. "I'm your dad now, I'll teach you everything you need to know to be a wizard. Then you can become like me."

"Will you?"

No!

Uncle-wolf drew Dream-Adrian down and onto his lap. His tongue lay wet and heavy across Adrian's back and neck. "Yes," he promised. It's a lie! "And I'll teach you everything you need to know to be a man, too."

Silence, silence, who is there to believe you, anyway?

◡   ⌒   ◡

Bang! Bang! Bang!

Adrian jerked awake, spluttering. His eyes felt red and puffy as if he'd been weeping, but they also stung from the splash of alcohol he'd just taken in the face. The vaporous sting of it filled his nostrils.

"Son of a bitch!" he spat.

"If you say so," Twitch agreed amiably. "Now get up."

She was in her man form, which was a bit physically stronger than her woman shape, and she pushed a shoulder under his arm as he dragged himself up the bar to his feet. He was splattered with green goo and had to kick aside the bodies of two six-limbed monsters to get up. When he did manage to clear his eyes and stand, he found Mouser, holding his MAC-11 with a defiant stare in her eyes.

Adrian heard howling wind, pounding rain, demons squealing, and guns going off, but the space around the bar was the eye of the storm. He looked down at the second monster corpse and saw that its head had been sawn clean off by a string of bullets.

"Good job," he said.

Mouser nodded.

"Clip empty?"

She shrugged.

He wiped various kinds of moisture from his face and handed her the taser. "Take this, just in case. You'd be surprised what can get taken down by a good jolt from a taser."

"What about you?"

"Don't worry about our boy Adrian," Twitch told the club gopher. "He's a bottomless well of surprises." The fairy slid up onto the bar and crouched there, ready to leap or fight, a wooden baton in each hand.

Adrian snorted and pulled his candle stub from his pocket.

"You're going to fight with a candle?"

He did his best nonchalant shrug. "It's a very specialized style of kung fu. And I never learned tablet fighting, like you did." He pointed at the mangled device, scratched, cracked and covered in slime, where it lay on the floor.

She giggled, with a slight manic edge to her voice.

"What's the situation, Twitch?" Adrian asked. He shoved bullets into the spare Ingram clip as fast as he could manage, out of a rattling pants pocket.

"They want Jim," the fairy said, shaking a baton like a pointer.

Eddie and Mike shuffled forward, shooting, and as a result, they took their fair share of attacks, but Twitch was right—the brunt of the assault hammered down on Jim with brutal, unrelenting force.

The singer held his own, leaping onto tabletops to make great slashing attacks, and then when the monsters grabbed at his ankles, vaulting over their heads to ride their very backs, but he was slowing down, and there were dozens of them.

"That suggests a plan," Adrian mused. Over the shuffle and scrape of the combat, the pistol fire and the howling of the wind, he could barely hear his own words. "Here, take this." He snapped the full clip into the MAC-11 and handed it back to Mouser, then began reloading the other.

"The windows open over concrete," Twitch told him sourly. "The wind's too strong for *me* and the fall will be unpleasant for any of *you*."

Adrian harrumphed and pocketed the full clip. "That dead end only underscores the awesomeness of my plan."

"Which is?"

"Get to the van and get out of here. Rob a gas station to fill the tank."

"Agreed." Twitch laughed, a laugh like silver water that turned Adrian on a little bit, despite his fear and the waves of exhaustion lapping at his body. The frisson of arousal made him nervous, but only slightly. It was just Twitch, after all. "I was imagining you might tell me some of the intermediate steps."

Adrian pointed. "Get Jim into the green room. These things follow him, we have them corralled."

Twitch didn't even linger long enough to say she approved. She just sprang into the air, horse's tail trailing behind her, and the rest of her body metamorphosing into a silver falcon in a split second. She snapped her wings once and was across the hall, swooping among thrashing monsters and reappearing in her drummer form in a divot of cleared space among her three band-mates.

"Come on." Adrian led Mouser by the wrist to the landing at the top of the stairs. He opened the door to the green room and positioned Mouser facing the hall. In the tumult of struggling limbs he could make out flashes of Jim, cutting his way through the monsters towards the stage and its green room entrance. Then Twitch the horse appeared in the fray, kicking a hole through the mound of monsters with her two hind hooves. Jim, Mike and Eddie broke into a run.

"Get ready," Adrian warned Mouser.

"What do I do?"

"If they head this way, shoot them."

"I can do that." The gopher thumbed her glasses up the bridge of her nose and adjusted her grip on the MAC-11.

"By *them* I mean the *monsters*," Adrian clarified, and then thought he should probably clarify even a little more. "The ones not in the band."

He shot a glance down the stairs. It was quiet—no monster sounds, but no restaurant sounds either, and no music. Maybe all the diners had turned into wormy-twisted-six-limbed freaks, too. He heard the distant echo of storm sounds, and didn't know if the restaurant's doors were open or the wind and rain noises of the hall itself were bouncing back at him up the stairs.

B-rap-p-p-p-p-p!

Adrian snapped his attention back around to see one of the creatures explode into green goo. The herd of them charged at Jim, who stood in the green room door, holding them at bay, while Eddie, Mike and Twitch sprinted down the length of the green room in Adrian's direction.

"Wow, these things are stupid," Mouser observed.

"Good," Adrian grunted.

Twitch bounded out of the green room first, followed closely by Eddie and Mike.

Adrian felt sweat run down his back and his forehead, and his breathing felt tight. Not now, he told himself, not now. He patted his pockets looking for the nicotine gum and couldn't find it.

"We get outta here," the Mexican bass player said, "remind me that I want to sharpen the head of that bass."

"Not sure it needs it," Eddie grumbled. "But it ought to have kill notches carved on the neck, that's for sure."

Adrian felt woozy. "Pinch me," he said to Mike.

"*Carajo*," Mike cursed, but did it immediately. "Don't fall asleep now!"

"Come on!" Eddie yelled to Jim, and stepped out of the way.

Jim turned and ran.

Adrian saw him coming in stop-motion, feeling his own body slow down, and he screwed his entire will, all the force of his ka into one tiny point, the point through which he needed to cast his spell. My shadow is light, he told himself. The valley of the shadow of death is nothing. It's sunshine, I'm awake.

Jim ran head down, his long black hair flying behind him and his blade pointed back. Behind him, racing on four legs at a shocking speed, gnarled and twisted necks extended to point their collective thousands of teeth forward, came the beasts.

The others stepped aside. Eddie reloaded.

Adrian felt Mike pinch his side, again and again, as the walls of the green room seemed to blur and slide away in sleep. That was going to leave bruises. He'd asked for it. He tried to focus on Jim, and on the horde that followed him.

Twitch disappeared from his vision.

Jim dove past him.

"*Per Volcanum ignem mitto!*" Adrian shouted. His uncle had never taught him a single attack spell, not one, but Adrian had taught himself this one, late at night on the rooftop with copies of the spellbook's pages that he had scrawled out by hand, comparing them carefully with a lost (and, by Adrian, *stolen*) book of Pliny the Elder. Combat magic was hard, a lot harder than wards and illusions, especially when you tried to work it in the heat of the moment, but Adrian had learned this one spell by heart.

To hell with the truth. It had been a firebolt that set Adrian free.

Fire erupted from the stub of candle and through the Third Eye, a column of white and gold smashing through the ranks of the creatures. Adrian held it as long as he could, incinerating demonic flesh and obliterating their howls of protest, and when he felt himself slipping into sleep, he let the spell go and collapsed into Mike's arms.

Mike slapped him in the face.

"Stay awake, *chingado!*" the bass player swore at him.

Taking a deep, shuddering breath, Adrian did.

Slam!

Eddie banged shut the door to the green room. "They're not all dead!" the guitar player yelled. "Down the stairs, now! Now!"

Mike turned and half-dragged Adrian and Mouser both down the stairs under more fluorescent tubes, one in each arm. Spencer had been a little guy, like him, Adrian remembered. In that respect, at least, Mike was sometimes more useful. Also, he picked locks and stuff.

As his vision recovered, he saw Eddie fire off three short bursts with his Glock on automatic fire, then turn and pound his way down the steps on their heels.

"Where's Twitch?" Adrian asked, stumbling to his own two feet as they hit the bottom of the stairs and plunged into knee-deep water.

"Really?" Mike was incredulous. "Outta everybody, the one you're worried about is the one who can fly?"

"I'm right here," Twitch called. "Sorry."

In the center of the restaurant, above a wreckage of shattered tables, Adrian saw Twitch. The fairy was in her leather-bar-outfit-clad drummer's shape, and she dangled in midair, in the clutches of a pig-headed, eagle-winged giant. Two more giants stood in the restaurant, to either side. One had the head of a bull, and the other was a centaur. Not a knobbly, ugly, twisted beast with six limbs like the things in the club above—the things behind them, Adrian thought nervously—but a beautiful woman with long chestnut hair and the lower body of a horse. Though the ceiling was twenty feet off the ground, each of the giants stooped slightly to avoid hitting it.

The restaurant was lit by incandescent bulbs hanging from long chains or set into the walls, which illuminated the giants' knees very well but left their heads and shoulders in menacing shadow.

"Yamayol," Jim snarled. "Ezeq'el. Semyaz."

"Shit," Eddie added.

CHAPTER THREE

"Holy crap," Mouser muttered.

Don't get passive, Adrian told himself. Don't freeze.

He snapped his uncle's lens over his own eye and looked through it. The enormity of the things in the restaurant and their names should have given them away, but what he saw through the Eye confirmed their identity; they were Fallen.

He could see angelic forms still, through the Eye, burning bright though their wings were plucked off and the stumps bled orange-white light. Those were the *bas* of the Fallen, their essential personalities. But the Messengers that they had once been struggled to occupy the same space as enormous beasts, which were their *bodies*. Together, they looked like kaleidoscope or funhouse mirror images, shifting from one form to the other by degrees as Adrian moved his own head minutely, or they moved in real space. They were kept together by a web of light at the center of each of them, that Adrian couldn't see clearly—even with the Third Eye—but that he knew must contain the *name* and the *ka* of each of the fallen angels.

Beneath them and about them lay the penumbras that were their *shadows*. In high school, Adrian had laughed so hard he'd fallen out of his desk when some idiot with a Bachelor's degree had tried to explain to him and the rest of the class about the unconscious mind, as if he was saying anything new, true, or insightful. Every wizard for the last five thousand years had known the five parts of every human being: *ka*, *ba*, and *body*, bound together with a *name*, all together casting a *shadow*. Duh. That was the first lesson you learned if you ever wanted to achieve any level of magical power.

Messengers—angels who were not among the Fallen—didn't have five parts, but the Fallen were like humans in this respect. Ka, ba, and body made a person. Name bound it together and therefore the true name of any person was the key to being able to command him to do your will—within the appropriate warding. Shadow was the touch the whole bundle left on the world around it. Other than the body, it was all invisible to the naked eye. Through the Eye, some of it could be seen.

Adrian had heard different stories about the animal limbs of the Fallen—that they were divine punishments, or that Heaven itself had taken to vivisecting the Fallen and experimenting on them in some kind of effort to undo Adam's mistake, or even that the Fallen had for some demented reason chosen themselves to graft animal parts to their own bodies. Adrian wondered if maybe they wanted to be beings of five parts for some reason, but that was speculation. He wondered if Jim knew the truth of it. He didn't really know how old Jim was, after all, though he didn't think the singer had been around before the Flood, when the Fallen had made their play and lost.

The pig-headed one had something else on his chest. It looked like a red rose, throbbing with light.

The Fallen stood in a ruin that had once been a decent little restaurant. The windows were all shattered and water flowed through the room like it was raining *sideways*, and hard. The floor was a muddy river full of splintered wood, shifting and treacherous in the yellow-shadowy light. All that Adrian could see with his meat eyes. Through the Eye, he saw again the lines of power that ran around all the walls and webbed across the windows. They tied together intricately, and he couldn't immediately make out what they did, but he thought there were elements of shielding, restraint and domination in the lines. They were elaborate and very precisely drawn, and they practically throbbed with energy. More energy than he'd ever seen; whatever they did, the wards did it very, very well. He was pretty sure the band was trapped.

Without trying to be obvious about it, he shot a glance past the swishing lizard's tail of the boar-headed giant to the space where he remembered leaving the van. The band's ride was still there, but it was smashed into two pieces, like an enormous tree had fallen down right across the middle of it.

Or an enormous foot.

So much for his mobile wards of obfuscation. Adrian shivered.

A mangled mantis-demon limb drifted past him in the water.

"You're not leaving," growled Yamayol, the bull-headed giant. As if to punctuate his sentence, he flexed his body in a weightlifter's pose, clenching his fists and making the gray scales covering his entire body ripple.

B-rap-p-p-p!

A flash of light and a whiff of smoke beside Adrian told him that Eddie was firing his Glock back up the stairs.

"Call off your minions, Ezeq'el!" Jim yelled.

"Why?" the centauress asked. Her voice boomed, but also purred sweetly. "I think they give you all the right incentives."

B-rap-p-p!

Mike jammed rounds into his .45 as fast as he could and Adrian turned to look up the stairs. The foremost of the monsters rasping down the stairs fell under Eddie's bullets, but there were more behind.

"What do you want?" Jim barked. He looked like the statue of a Viking hero in some Scandinavian port, standing upright and determined with his sword in his hand and the rain crashing off his body. His voice echoed like he was standing on a reverb plate.

"To reign in Hell!" hissed the boar-headed giant, and smashed his lizard's tail into the water, stretching wide his wings to their full span, so they filled the restaurant. That would be Semyaz, Adrian thought. Big shot in Hell, and troublemaker.

"Better to reign," he muttered, "et cetera." Damned if it wasn't a thought he'd had himself, a thousand times.

"Screw you!" Jim hissed.

Semyaz flicked his arm and smashed Twitch into the ceiling. The fairy's blood spattered down in a fine mist, mixed with concrete dust. She yelped, but it was a muffled sound, and after the impact she shifted through several shapes then ended in horse form. Semyaz still held her in mid-air like she was a doll. She whinnied softly, shaking her bloodied head.

Squeeeeeeeal!

B-rap-p-p!

No time for Twitch now.

Adrian whipped around, facing up the stairs just as Eddie's pistol *clicked* loudly, the clip empty. A trio of windmilling monsters leaped into the air, crashing down upon the band like comets. Sleep grabbed the base of Adrian's brain and choked him, dragging him away from the conflict, but he shook it off.

He fell to his knees in the water, raising the candle stub and the lens and aiming up the stairs.

"*Per Volcanum ignem mitto!*" he shouted again, and loosed his entire ka-energy reserve into the candle. The coruscating burst of flame stripped paint off the cement walls, shattered fluorescent tube lights and reduced the leaping creatures to a rain of falling muddy ash—

he passed out—

felt himself plunge into water and rebound off the hard floor—

he came up spluttering. And with empty hands.

"Shit!" he yelled, and plunged back into the water. He heard gunfire around him, but it was muted by the water in his ears, and by the shock. The stream rushed past him, and he realized that, as deep as it was, it was still flowing downstairs and into the lower level of the building. That was an *awful* lot of rain.

A whole dead mantis-thing bumped against him, charred black from the waist up. He cursed and kicked it away.

"Adrian!" Mike yelled. "You got 'em, *cabrón*, you got 'em all."

"Screw that!" Adrian shouted. "I lost the Eye!"

Somewhere, Jim was shouting. "I wouldn't be Heaven's plaything, Semyaz! I won't be Hell's, either!"

"Why do you care?" Ezeq'el the centauress asked. Yamayol and Semyaz just sounded angry and menacing; she sounded curious. Adrian didn't pay all that much attention—he kept pulling up bits that felt like the Third Eye, but turned out to be fragments of crockery, broken plates and glasses.

He chanted his own true name silently under his breath as he groped, slapping himself over and over on the neck with wet hands, and forced his mind through memories, trying to reinforce his body, name, and ba against the shadow, to have something to hold him together and awake. He was a superconductor of a sorcerer, he told himself, but he felt like someone had yanked his plug out of the wall.

He tried to avoid memories of his uncle, and champed his teeth in silent rage when he couldn't. He felt helpless, powerless, bound.

"I'll have nothing to do with Hell!" Jim spat.

"Even to save your friend's life?" snorted Yamayol. "Even if we have ... other things to offer you?"

Even if he found the Eye, of course, Adrian didn't have a plan. With his ka spent, there was nothing he could do magically. Unless, of course, he had another power source. He needed another socket to plug the superconductor into. He spat gritty water from his mouth and let that idea germinate in his brain.

"Humans," Semyaz grunted. "They all belong in Hell." He fingered the object on his chest.

"I'm not human." Jim ground the words out through clenched teeth. "Good-bye, Twitch." He turned to walk away, splashing through the mud past Adrian.

Twitch, in humanoid shape now, grunted.

Yamayol lunged forward. He was gigantic, but he was quick as a snake.

Jim spun, bringing up his sword—

but the bull-headed Fallen rushed past the singer and snatched Mouser.

B-rap-p-p-p-p-p-p-p-p!

She emptied the Ingram into his head. Good girl, Adrian thought, but of course it didn't hurt him. He was material, all right, and the bullets must have stung, but if she inflicted any kind of real injury, the giant didn't show it. Crappy small-caliber gun.

Eddie threw himself forward, but the bull's knuckles punched him in the chest and threw him against the wall. Yamayol raised the club gopher into the air and leaped back, brandishing her like a torch.

Bang! Bang! Bang! Adrian didn't know where Mike's bullets landed, but they did no visible damage.

"Aaaagh!" Mouser squeaked, and dropped the machine pistol.

Jim spat into the water and raised his sword.

"Jim, don't!" Adrian shouted. His hand closed over something round and hard and he knew in his heart it had to be the Eye. Even with fingers numbed by the cold water, he could tell it was more circular, and much smoother, than any of the china shards he'd picked up before.

Jim glared down at him, fury raging in the ice-blue eyes.

"Be cool," Adrian hissed. He wanted to say *stall*, but with ears the size of tent flaps, he was pretty sure the Fallen would all hear him. Instead he *thought* the word really hard, hoping Jim had latent ESP or that some unseen shred of Adrian's ka would carry the message to him.

Maybe it worked, because Jim turned slowly and faced the Fallen. "Which one of you reigns, then?" he challenged them. "Hell has only one Satan."

"But it has many Princes," Semyaz snarled, milk-jug-sized flecks of yellow slobber raining from his lips and tusks.

"That's the consolation prize you offer mighty Yamayol?" Jim laughed, and turned to the bull-headed Fallen. "Yamayol, slaughterer of the Five Kings, victor of the Plains of Shinar ... will continue to play second man, only to a new ... and even uglier ... master?"

Yamayol growled. "I am second to none."

Adrian pulled his hand up to the level of the water and peered into his palm. He had the Eye, all right, and his heart skipped a beat from joy.

"We have come with more than just threats," Ezeq'el said, with all the placating charm of a cement truck shifting gears.

"Ezeq'el, the great pacifier!" Jim snorted. "I didn't take you for a rebel."

"The most effective rebels are the unexpected ones," the centauress said slyly, arching an eyebrow at Jim. "Like Azazel was."

"*Was* ... but *is* no longer?"

Adrian tried to remember how the lines of power wrapped around the room, and prepared himself mentally. It would be like taking the batteries out of the taser and wiring it into the wall socket instead, only he was the taser and the lines of the arcane trap in which the band had been caught were the power lines of the house. Adrian felt in his pocket and found string—that was good—and some chalk that was damp but might still write. He shook his head, trying to get out of his mind the image of young, dream-state Adrian walking docilely into his uncle's arms.

"Heaven is weak!" Semyaz bellowed. "If your father weren't such a coward, he'd rule two great kingdoms by now!"

"Only two?" Jim chuckled. "Why not more? Why not *everything?* Could Mab and Oberon stand against the combined armies of Heaven and Hell? Could the squabbling nations of Earth?"

"Join us!" Yamayol thundered. "We will release your friends." He pointed at Semyaz, and Mouser fainted.

Yamayol stamped in the water, sending up small tsunamis of mud and cold grit, and Adrian raised the lens to his eye. He saw the lines of the wards again, and he was close enough to the wall that he could even see how they'd been drawn—pricked with a pin into wallpaper to keep them discreet. They were wards of restraint and domination, a trap, but he could use the ka-energy pulsating in them. Enough power to blow the entire club into a crater if he wasn't careful—one of the Fallen was an accomplished wizard, or they had someone in the wings doing their dirty work. He imagined how he'd run the lines of power through a new configuration, without touching the trap. The trick would be to take the energy and turn it around, use it to open the trap from which it came.

As quietly as he could, Adrian took that bit of string from his pocket. It was a couple of feet long, which was plenty. He took one end of the string between his lips and swallowed it, getting it down into his esophagus and willing himself to neither gag nor swallow the rest, which trailed out of his mouth and lay floating on the stream of water.

It scratched in his throat. Adrian shut out images of his uncle-wolf's long pink dream-tongue and tried not to think about what would happen if he screwed up this spell. What if he only pulled the noose tighter around them?

"Why not just kill me and take what you want?" Jim asked.

"Don't think it isn't still an option," Yamayol rumbled.

"We want *you*, James," Ezeq'el said, shaking her tail and flicking dirty water in all directions. "With you on our side, Azazel won't have the will to resist."

"You make him sound like he has no power anyway," Jim pointed out.

"Enough!" Semyaz thrashed his tail again in the water, sending up a loud crack and spray. He shouldered into Yamayol and, while the bull-headed Fallen struggled with his balance, snatched Mouser from his hand.

No! Adrian yelled silently. By a supreme act of will, he managed not to swallow the string.

"Don't!" Jim shouted, but too late.

Semyaz raised the unconscious girl to his mouth and bit her head off in one quick motion. Enraged, lips spraying blood, he hurled her body against the wall. It hit like a wet rag doll and bounced into the flood, blood spattering like shaving cream from an exploding water balloon. Her corpse twitched and jangled for several long seconds in the water.

"Damn!" Adrian gasped, choking on the string.

Jim hurled his sword. It wasn't a weapon made for throwing, but Jim was really, really good with it, in some surprising ways. He drew his arm back like an atlatl's throwing-stick of flesh and bone, pommel cupped in his palm, and then launched the blade forward.

Semyaz bellowed, mouth open and blood and hair on his tusks—

and Jim's sword hit him right in the mouth.

Ichor squirted from the wound and Semyaz staggered back, thumping Twitch against the ceiling again in the confusion. He choked and spat, and Jim's sword shot from his mouth like projectile vomit.

Ezeq'el the centauress leaped forward, plunging her hooves into the muddy water to trample Jim.

The singer threw himself to one side, scrambling from pillar to table to pillar and groping in the water for his weapon.

Adrian saw his chance and took it. He jumped to the nearest large nexus of ward lines on the wall, pinned the end of the string to its center with his thumb and chalked four quick glyphs around it. *"Per Mercurium vim extraho,"* he murmured, gagging on the string and jamming the Eye over the top of his thumb for good measure. He had to charge his battery before he could use it to get them out.

Fire coursed through him, making the walls shudder and all his flesh pimple up into tingling prick-points of limbic agitation. He felt his ka fill and then flood like the room around him, and he struggled to direct it, raising the Third Eye and pressing it against the chalk marks against the wall and, for good if somewhat irrational measure, against the candle stub.

"Per Proteum," he choked, hearing gunfire and seeing Twitch fall into the water with a large splash out of the corner of one eye. He wasn't sure exactly what he wanted from the spell, which was a bad deficit when you starting throwing magical power around. Really, he'd be a lot more comfortable if he could be attempting this operation with a little less pressure on him. He needed something shape-changing; something that would transform the trap so that it would restrain the Fallen but not the band would be ideal.

Jim lunged at Semyaz, swinging a length of timber in both hands, and the boar-headed giant snatched him off the ground.

Adrian's own shadow loomed up large, jaws gaping like it wanted to swallow Adrian whole. It was swollen, too—somehow in refilling his ka, he had poured power into other parts of him. In Adrian's head, it was hard to tell apart his looming shadow and the giant Semyaz, holding Jim pinned in his grip.

Adrian chanted his name, trying to catch his balance among the five parts. *"Per Proteum ..."*

Mike slammed into the wall next to him, losing all the breath in his lungs in a single *whoosh* that was painful to hear. The big guy dropped his gun and then sank into the water with it.

Adrian's shadow seemed to him to be another Adrian, only taller and stronger, and grabbing him by the throat.

"Per Proteum insidias," Adrian tried again. He imagined the lines of the wards moving across the wall, reforming to create new wards—

with a sick feeling in his stomach, he realized that the shadow looming large over him, his own shadow, had the head of a cartoon wolf and a long, dangling tongue—

and then the darkness took him—

"Insidias muto—"

And he fell.

◡ ◠ ◡

Dream-Adrian stumbled through the house of flesh wearily. He'd been up all night on the roof, reading Pliny's *De Occultata Historia* again and comparing it to his copy of his uncle's pages. He'd finally managed to ignite the wick of a devotional candle he'd stolen from his uncle's private chapel, but only after soaking the wick in oil first, and that seemed like cheating. Or if not cheating, then useless—you couldn't go into combat hoping your enemy would coat himself in inflammable liquid beforehand.

His uncle certainly wouldn't, and his uncle was the enemy that Adrian imagined defeating, over and over again. Crushing, decapitating, mutilating, and above all, burning to a crisp.

He dropped the pull-down stairs slowly, stopping to give the hinges a touch of oil, as he always did. Only in the dream-state, the hinges were muscular, like the hinges of a jaw, and Adrian oiled them by rubbing them down with his hands. He felt unclean and violated.

Part of him, tucked away, knew that he was dreaming. That part wondered if Adrian was under the river of filthy water on the restaurant floor and beginning to drown. A dream might seem eternal in the few seconds it would take his body to fill its lungs with water and slip into brain death.

The carpet on the floor in the upstairs hallway felt like meat underfoot, squishy and wet, and where his bare feet depressed it, he left behind little puddles of blood. He pushed the pull-down stairs back up into the ceiling and shivered a bit when he heard a *click* that sounded like teeth chomping together. The walls sagged in towards him and ran with rivulets of warm moisture, puddling at the bottom and draining, somewhere, but very inefficiently. The air was thick and humid, and felt already-breathed. Light came from a globe hanging from the center of the ceiling that Adrian knew should be an incandescent bulb behind frosted glass, but instead it looked like a swaying uvula. Adrian ducked to avoid touching it.

Adrian knew to step carefully around the wardrobe, because the floor under it was prone to creaking. It caught him by surprise that the wardrobe doors snapped open and sprang at him, biting with long yellow teeth—

snap! Snap!

He stumbled away and caught himself on the banister around the stairwell down. The wardrobe stayed rooted in its spot, but it gnashed teeth at him and tried to bite, exhaling a nasty mothballs-and-dead-mice smell. The piece of furniture had scaly skin like old, cracked wood that badly needed oiling, only tufts of hair grew out of the cracks.

"Son of a bitch," Adrian muttered, and crept past. The wardrobe hummed, but didn't follow.

The bathroom at the top of the stairs was Adrian's safe place—it was the only room in the house so small that when he was in it, his uncle didn't fit. It was the size of a closet, with the shower head directly over a smallish toilet, and no sink. The loose brick behind the toilet was warm and soft to the touch, so Adrian didn't look at it, folding his precious pages and tucking them inside quickly. It was a damp space, which forced him to recopy his pages every couple of weeks, but it was a hidden one.

Inside the bathroom, he could hear for the first time that it was raining outside, cats and dogs. That made him nervous—he had thought from the light in the attic that dawn might still be an hour away, but with the rain cloud cover it might be imminent. And at dawn, the wards of sleeping that kept his uncle from discovering him would end.

It hadn't been raining when he'd been on the roof, he mused. Sudden storm.

At the top of the stairs he looked where there should have been a window, and saw a membrane. Like an eardrum, he thought, or maybe an eyelid. It was red and thinly veined, but there was definitely grayish light beyond it. The membrane trembled with each raindrop that hit it, and Adrian felt sick. Body, body, everywhere.

"The more things change," he muttered, "the more I still hate them."

He nearly slid down the stairs to the ground level, and there he stopped, his heart pounding. Someone was in the kitchen, with a light on. He turned and crept softly down the hall, not looking into the kitchen door on the dream-magic logic grounds that if he didn't see who was in the kitchen, the person in the kitchen wouldn't see him.

He smelled blood as he passed, and heard the snuffling of beasts.

At his uncle's door he stopped, and his heart stopped with him.

He'd built the wards of sleeping over months, carefully writing lines and glyphs behind furniture, inside closets and even between the sheetrock panels of the walls to keep them out of his uncle's sight. The final line of the wards was a piece he had to put in fresh each night, a length of spider's web that he collected from the basement—he shared his space with many spiders—and painstakingly stretched from post to post in the frame of his uncle's bedroom door.

Now the strand of web was broken, the two ends fluttering in the dank, humid air.

Was his uncle awake? The door was shut, but that meant nothing. Had his uncle observed him? If his uncle knew what

Adrian had been doing, what terrible punishments would he inflict on the boy?

Adrian eased open the door down to the basement, slipped in and padded down the stairs in the darkness. They were muscular and meaty and they gave way a little to his touch. Dream-Adrian was nervous, and thought he'd be caught. Another part of Adrian found the dream even stranger than usual. What exactly it was that made it so eluded him, but he stretched for it, trying to pin it down with his mind as he opened the door and threw himself onto his ratty old futon bed.

The futon wasn't ratty, though, it was warm and wet.

And also, there was already someone in Adrian's bed.

He jumped up and back, preparing for the wolf and his insatiable tongue, and found the cord dangling from the light. It felt like an animal's tail, and when he pulled it, a swarm of flying mites clouding about the ceiling burst into luminescent glow, showing him his tiny underground cell.

The futon lay wet and brown in the center of the room, like a giant rotting tongue. On it lay Twitch, Mike, Eddie, and the girl from the club—Mouser. They wore pajamas like kids ready for a slumber party, but the looks on their faces showed surprise and fear. Especially Mouser's face.

"What new Hell be this?" she yelped. "Leave me in peace!"

"This be a Hell of bad grammar," Adrian shot back. It was a reflex, he couldn't help himself. But the fact of speaking to someone in his dream felt very strange. Usually he stood inside dream-Adrian, or behind him, and shouted unheard warnings.

Was this not a dream, after all?

Eddie sat upright and looked around. "It isn't Hell," he said. "Trust me."

"This is wrong." Adrian shook his head. "This is all wrong."

Then he noticed that the floor of the room was covered in water. He couldn't tell where it was coming from, but it was cold and brown and rising.

CHAPTER FOUR

on't tell me it's *wrong*, Adrian," Eddie snorted, rolling to his feet. "Tell me how we get out of here." Pushy bastard. He slapped his hand under his armpit and ground his teeth when his fingers found nothing but pictures of coiled whips stamped on flannel. The glowing flies scattered as he thrust his head into their cloud. "And tell me where my Glock is."

"I don't know where we are," Adrian said quickly. He reached for nicotine gum and found he was wearing pajamas, too. No gum, no taser, no Eye, just pajamas covered with pictures of little kids ... in pajamas. "Are you really here?"

Twitch groaned and rolled over. Her pajamas were speckled with birds and horses. They were stained with blood on the collar and shoulders, too, and there was blood matted in her hair.

"This is really me." Mike stood up. His pajamas were yellow and covered in whisky bottles and sombreros. Just looking at his pajamas made Adrian feel a little guilty.

"Yeah?" said Eddie. "Prove it."

Mike scratched the back of his neck. "What if I tell you something only you and I know?"

"I'll still think I'm dreaming." Eddie scanned the room, and so did Adrian. There wasn't much here—a single shelf with a few Latin books on it, the futon, and the tail end of the old coal chute, from back when the basement had held a coal-fired furnace and this had been the coal room. Adrian remembered the lingering carbon smell from his youth, but didn't smell it now. Today the room smelled like the inside of a mouth, badly in need of dental work.

"Then you can tell me something different that only you and I know," Mike said, and then trailed off. "Carajo."

"A day late, Mike," Adrian said wearily, "et cetera."

"Yep." Eddie helped Twitch climb to her feet; the fairy leaned heavily on the guitar player, moaning. Her eyes drifted aimlessly and Adrian wondered if she had a concussion. Eddie's eye wandered, too, for a moment, and he shook himself like a dog shrugging off water. "Whatever this place is," the guitarist said, "bad things happened here." He looked right at Adrian as he said it.

Adrian swallowed, his throat dry and scratchy. "Let's get out."

Mouser stood up and balled her fists on her hips. Her pajamas were covered in red roses. "By Jupiter, this is a queer Hell that aims only to bore me."

That didn't sound like Mouser; Adrian stared, but saw only the club gopher's face over rose-printed pajamas.

"Careful who you go calling *queer*," Mike said.

"Sorry our conversation isn't snappy enough for you," Adrian added.

"This smacks of addle-pated Roundhead theology!" she snorted. "What atonement can there be in listening to the yammering of idiots?"

"And that, sister," Eddie agreed, "is exactly why I stopped going to church."

"*Church?*" Mouser harrumphed. "And what gyrating African debauch were you accustomed to call *church?*"

"*Excuse* me?" Eddie glared at her.

A loud *creak* sounded upstairs, and with it, the ceiling of the basement bowed in slightly.

Adrian pulled himself away from Mouser and her bizarre words and poked his head out the bedroom door. He'd passed the cellar on the way down without taking in much, so now he looked more closely. The stairs, sagging against the wall, fell down into a small hall, in which squatted an icebox. Over the icebox hung another uvula-light, this one dim and dark.

At the foot of the staircase was another room, a storage room that had once held the furnace, and beyond the icebox was a third chamber. In real life his uncle had kept animals in there, for experimentation and organ harvesting. Adrian had lain awake at night listening to the terrified clucking of doomed chickens. He stared at the door now and wondered what horrible thing could be there in this twisted version of reality.

"I think you're all really here," he said slowly, "and I think *here* is *inside my dream*, somehow, and I think it's my fault."

"And the idiots yammer yet." Mouser folded her arms and grimaced.

Adrian turned on the woman. "Who *are* you?" he asked.

"I ain't gonna waste time trying to prove anybody's who they say they are," Eddie snapped. "I'm here, dammit, and I wanna be in Chicago. What are the exits?"

"The stairs." Adrian stepped aside and pointed. Eddie looked.

THUMP!

Warm streams of stinking liquid dripped from the ceiling at the noise. Adrian felt a little sick.

"Dollars to donuts that's Semyaz and his bodies, stomping around," Eddie muttered.

"I ought to have known Hell's coin would be Flemish!" Mouser snapped. "Heretics...! What is a *donut?*"

Mike stared at her and chuckled. "I guess getting your head bit off really did a number on you."

Eddie shrugged the comment off. "*She* might be a figment." Then he looked back at her quizzically. "Or she might be someone else. Jim?" he asked cautiously, looking into Mouser's eyes.

"I do not know a *Jim!*" she snapped back. "If you are to torture me for love, get on with it!"

"She should write lyrics," Mike grinned.

"Right." Eddie returned to his task. "Time to search this place for other exits."

Adrian shook his head. "I'm telling you, I grew up in this house. The stairs is it."

Eddie cocked an eyebrow at him. "You grew up in a house made out of flesh?"

"Ah ... not exactly."

"That's right," Eddie nodded slowly. "*Not exactly*. Now let's find another way up and out."

"Okay." Adrian took a deep breath, slowly, so he didn't seem agitated. "Just ... be careful. There's bad stuff creeping around in my dreams."

"That's okay," Eddie told him. "In your dreams, I still know karate."

"What about this?" Mike pointed at the coal chute.

"Cemented shut," Adrian said. His uncle hadn't wanted him sneaking out at night, when he had first moved in and had still been small enough to shimmy through the hole.

"Check it," Eddie ordered.

Mike lifted the opening over the chute, which was limp and fleshy like a flap of skin. Inside was a gnarled bud of meatiness squeezing tightly shut, resembling the inner curl of a clenched fist. "Uh ..." Mike said, at a loss.

Eddie shook his head. "Check it," he repeated.

Mike grimaced and hesitated.

Mouser laughed. "What pusillanimous devils ye be!"

Mike raised his eyebrows and pointed at the coal chute. "You do it," he told her.

Mouser promptly sloshed across the dank bedroom, moving doggedly but without haste, like someone resigned to taking orders. Flaring her nostrils in small defiance, she shoved her arm in the chute, up to the elbow.

"Chicken," Eddie said to Mike.

Mike shrugged. "She practically volunteered."

"What do you feel?" Adrian asked. For his part, he felt like throwing up. Strangely, he didn't feel the slightest bit sleepy.

Mouser shrugged. "I have played midwife to more than one of my father's cows. This is much the same."

"Deeper," Eddie told her, and she shoved her arm in up to the shoulder. "And now?"

"No calf's head," she said. "All womb."

Mike shuddered. "If that had looked like a womb, I'd have stuck my own arm inside."

"Enough," Eddie told the girl, and she pulled her arm out. "Who are you?"

Mouser looked at each of them in turn, her eyes skeptical. "I am Elaine Canning," she said. "Which of the Princes of Hell do you serve?"

"We don't serve any Princes of Hell," Mike murmured. He looked astonished.

"We don't serve *anybody*," Adrian added.

Twitch was standing upright under her own power now, rubbing her eyes.

"You're in Hell," Eddie said. It wasn't a question.

"I am a murderess. Ought I be elsewhere?" She pulled her arm out of the sphincter in the wall and shook off a thick film of yellowish goo.

"What year did you die?" Eddie furrowed his brow.

THUMP!

"Not sure we have time for this," Adrian hissed.

"The Year of Our Lord sixteen hundred forty-five. I was taken by a Roundhead cannonball while walking the ramparts of my family home and watching for the man I loved."

Eddie hesitated. "Did you love a man named *James?*" he asked.

Elaine Canning, or Mouser, or whoever she was, looked like she had been punched in the face.

"Come on!" Adrian lost patience and charged out into the basement, the others following.

Eddie came at his shoulder, silent and thoughtful-looking.

Adrian pointed. "Two rooms."

Eddie kept his voice down—the sound of bodies moving about on the floor above was louder out here. "Mike, Twitch!" He pointed at the room in the corner, and dragged Mouser with him into the room at the foot of the stairs.

Adrian made to follow Eddie, but the guitarist stopped him with a glare and pointed at the icebox. Adrian nodded, his heart falling into his boots as his companions disappeared behind various doors, leaving him alone.

He faced the icebox, squatting ominously in the near-darkness. It hummed, but not with the low, crackling hum of electric devices. Looking at it now, Adrian saw that the icebox didn't have a power cord, anyway. Instead it had what looked like a segmented, vaguely scaly tail, like you might see on the backside of an armadillo, lying in the cold water on the floor. Its hum was the hum of discontented appetite, the belly rumbling of a man about to sit down to a meal that he already knew would not be sufficient. It reminded him, all in all, of the wardrobe upstairs that had unexpectedly attacked him.

There was no good way to die, but being eaten by a fleshy refrigerator in the basement of your own mind seemed like a particularly humiliating one.

Adrian bit back curses, grabbed the handle and yanked open the door.

The icebox didn't bite him, and opened. Warm, wet air washed over him, like the steam from a sink full of dishes billowing into an already dank and hot kitchen. The steam came rich with a rotting stink of meat, and Adrian sucked in air through closed teeth to try to control his gag reflex.

Inside the icebox, in a puddle of water, lay a tongue as long as his arm.

Adrian stared at it and felt like crying. This was no dream. Something terrible was happening, and it was happening to him. It felt like it was happening *inside* him.

The tongue twitched—

Adrian swung the door closed, and it stuck shut with a wet *squelch*.

"*Mierda.*" Mike stumbled out of the back room, Twitch behind him. The bassist held his hand over his face like he was trying not to throw up.

"The room is a latrine," the fairy explained matter-of-factly. "Or at least, the bottom half of one." A cloud of cloacal stink followed behind them.

Footfalls passed over Adrian's head and he froze. They sounded like they were heading for the top of the stairs.

Eddie appeared in the doorway of the third room. "There's a way out," he hissed. "Hurry!"

Adrian shuffled across the floor, really wishing he had shoes on his feet. He was the last into the room, and entering it, he stepped down into deeper water, swirling with warm and cold currents. As he passed through the entrance he saw the door at the top of the stairs crack open. He didn't wait to see who was coming, and shut the door behind him.

He expected this room to be lit by a naked 40-watt bulb, pulled on and off by a chain. Instead, in the warm water in which he stood swam five-foot-long eels whose entire bodies but for their bulbous heads glowed yellow-green in the darkness, casting a sickly phosphorescent glow upwards. Lit from beneath, everyone's faces looked cracked and cadaverous, with hollow pits for eyes above green slab cheeks. Adrian expected twisted steel shelving, stacked deep with jars, cans and boxes of food, all well past their expiration dates and yet months away from being eaten. Instead, there were piles of bodies.

Human bodies.

And he knew some of them.

"Son of a bitch."

"Shh." Eddie pointed up at a hole in the corner of the ceiling. "Old furnace vent," he whispered. "It's got to lead up to the other rooms."

Only it didn't look like an old furnace vent. It looked like an open toothless mouth, just big enough to swallow a human being whole.

Twitch must have read the uncertainty in Adrian's face. "I'll go," the fairy volunteered. She turned to face the vent in the corner, leaped forward—

and plowed headfirst onto the pile of corpses.

"Mab's shiny belly!" she spat.

"Twitch can't change shape." There was a note of panic in Mike's voice.

"Yeah," Eddie said, "and you've lost your superpower of deep insight. This time, you first."

He half threw the bassist across the room and Mike started scrambling up the mound of bodies. His bare feet slipped on bellies and crushed heads, turning their necks away at impossible angles.

"*Fundillo*," he grunted.

Adrian stared down at the eels, tears stinging his eyes. At the top of the pile lay the body of his father.

"Oh, man." Mike lingered at the top of the stack on all fours, staring up into the dark hole.

"Pretend it leads to a womb," Twitch quipped. "If that's your preference."

The staircase outside creaked.

"Go!" Eddie hissed. The guitar player scissor-punched Mike in the butt, pushing him forward into the darkness. Then he shoved Mouser up the pile.

Adrian watched them step on the bodies. He was fascinated, horrified and sick. He recognized faces from his childhood. There were neighbors, kids who had gone missing, a survey taker who had really made his uncle angry one day. He didn't know why their bodies were piled here. Had his uncle actually killed them?

Or was this some twisted invention of his own dreaming mind? Did Adrian wish that he, Adrian, had killed all these people?

But then why was his father on top of the pile?

Twitch stepped onto his father's chest and sprang up lightly into the vent. Adrian couldn't be sure, but he thought the opening of the vent constricted a little bit around the fairy as she went into it, like a mouth closing over a morsel.

Creak.

"You next," Adrian said to Eddie. He wasn't sure he could do it.

"Nope," Eddie contradicted. "I got the karate, remember?" He shoved Adrian up the stack.

Adrian closed his eyes just before his bare foot came down on the shoulder of a woman he recognized. Eyes shut, hands and feet scrabbling up a ladder of flesh and bone, he tried to remember where he had seen her.

In the living room. Once. Early after moving in with his uncle, he realized, and he had an image of the woman and his uncle drinking tea and laughing and then Adrian had gone to bed. He'd never seen her again. Had his uncle murdered her?

His uncle was a villain, a monster for what he'd done to Adrian, but could he possibly be that bad? Or was this just Adrian's suspicion, manifesting inside himself?

Adrian hit a concrete wall with his head and shoulder simultaneously. The stinging force of the blow forced him to open his watering eyes, and he found himself perched on top of his father's corpse, staring into pitted green caverns where there should have been eyes.

His father had been the better sorcerer. He'd known it as a point of pride when he was a small child, and when his father had died in an unspecified catastrophe involving a demonic summoning gone wrong, he'd guessed his uncle had been behind the mishap. Adrian tried to hold himself steady. His father's appearance here was only another manifestation of Adrian's own suspicions, and not proof of anything.

A gurgling from the floor jerked his attention away from his dead father's face. The water was rising.

"This is sick and wrong," he muttered, and pushed himself into the vent.

It *felt* like being swallowed. He almost threw up from the strange, all-embracing *fleshiness* of the experience.

Ahead of him he heard breathing and the tussling sound of flesh kneading flesh. Adrian dragged himself upward and forward as fast as he could, the passage bending around him and carrying him horizontally, it felt, between floors.

Behind him he heard the scuffling sounds of Eddie climbing—he hoped it was Eddie—and then a *creak*. Adrian froze, the sounds before and behind him stopped, and yellowish light trickled into the meaty, esophagus-like crawlspace behind him. Adrian looked back between his knees and saw Eddie, jammed into an elbow of the passageway, lit from below. The guitarist looked coiled and ready to spring.

Adrian decided he'd better follow Eddie's example. He was without tools, but given his native wit, his ka and the ability to speak, no wizard was ever completely defenseless. He reached inside himself to tap into his ka, preparing to cast a spell if he needed it—

and his ka wasn't there.

His heart stopped. What was this place? What had happened to him?

"They're not here!" He felt numb and stunned, but Adrian still recognized the throaty bellow—it belonged to the bull Yamayol. But gigantic Yamayol couldn't get down the stairs into the basement, unless he was crawling. Even then, Adrian couldn't imagine how he'd be maneuvering in the tight spaces.

Unless he'd shrunk. Or Adrian and the others had grown.

"No girl, either!" This was Semyaz the pig.

Of course, this wasn't normal physical space at all.

What had happened? What was this place? Adrian forced his mind to think back and tried to remember the moments before he had blacked out and entered this dream state. He'd been trying to divert power from the wards on the restaurant, he remembered. He'd been battling his own shadow, struggling to stay awake, and trying to modify the wards in which the Fallen had trapped them. His shadow had seized Jim—

He shook his head. That wasn't right; Semyaz had seized Jim, and it had only seemed to Adrian that his own shadow was involved.

Slam!

They were all plunged into darkness again.

Without his ka, Adrian couldn't see how he'd ever get out.

Unless maybe he just woke up. But this didn't feel like a dream anymore. It didn't even feel like a nightmare. It felt like the jaws of death, clamping down.

"We have a problem," he said.

"Yeah," Eddie agreed. "The problem is that if you guys don't move forward, I'm going to lose my grip and fall down."

The line ahead of Adrian dutifully began shuffling forward again, and he followed.

"I can't find my ka."

"I'm going to pass on the easy joke here," Eddie grunted behind him in the darkness. "What are you talking about?"

"I can't do any magic in here," Adrian explained.

"Have you figured out where *in here* is, exactly?" Twitch called back from ahead of him.

"No," Adrian admitted. His chest felt tight and he really wished he had a fistful of nicotine patches. "I'm back to hoping that you're all just dream-figments, and I'm about to wake up."

"No such luck," Eddie grumbled.

"Maybe the Fallen can't do sorcery, either," Adrian said. "That would sort of level the playing field for us."

"Also, they appear to be a lot shorter than usual," Eddie agreed. "On the other hand, I don't know where Jim and the hoof are, and I seem to be trapped inside a house made of cold cuts."

"I didn't say it was *all* good news," Adrian grumbled.

He heard a soft *thump* ahead of him. "I'm out," Mike called back in a whisper.

In short order Mouser and Twitch followed him, and then Adrian tumbled through an opening that looking uncomfortably like rows of teeth above and below an open mouth—he half expected to get bitten in two—and fell to the floor.

Immediately, he could breathe a little easier. He much preferred being regurgitated to being swallowed.

He looked around. Ribs rose to the ceiling like the fleshy groined supports of a cathedral's vault, with teetering rows of books sloping back and forth across the pink walls. Beneath the shelves stretched a broad desk with a luminescent toad squatting on one corner of its surface.

Welcome, welcome, Adrian thought he heard the books hissing inside his head. He tried to ignore them.

Eddie scraped out of the vent and hit the ground behind him.

"So now my torture will be to read," Elaine Canning snorted. "How very like nuns you devils are."

Adrian just stared. This was it, the belly of the whale. They were in his uncle's study.

CHAPTER FIVE

The doorknob to the study's only door turned—

Adrian slapped for his gun, which wasn't there, and then his taser, and then his Third Eye. Snapping his teeth together in frustration at the fact that he was unarmed, he jumped for a corner of the room.

The rest of the band had performed the identical St. Vitus' dance, and they all squeezed into the same space behind the door as it opened, a knot of elbows and knees. Elaine Canning joined them last, a puzzled look on her face.

"Like Scooby-Frickin'-Doo," Mike whispered.

"I do not know that devil," Elaine whispered back.

Eddie bared his teeth and they both shut up.

Adrian was shorter than most of the band, and much shorter than the door, so he found himself staring through a forest of people. Looking up, he saw just ceiling, and a tiny space over the top of the door, and he shivered slightly as he saw the cartoon wolf's ears flip up under the lintel and pass the door.

Uncle-wolf shut the door behind himself. He hung a long wool coat, patched at the elbows, on a coat rack in another corner. Then he turned, all without seeing the crowd hiding in the corner of his office, and sat at his desk with his back to them.

The band looked at each other and shrugged. Elaine Canning opened her mouth to say something and this time Eddie clapped a hand over the lower half of her face, silencing her.

We'll tell, we'll tell, Adrian thought he heard the books say. He refused to look at them.

By gestures the band coordinated movements. The books trembled like living things, so they steered away from them. Twitch took the coat and balled her fists into the sleeves, holding the garment like a fighting net. Mike picked up the coat rack like a quarterstaff, hefting it and twisting his face into a menacing grimace. Eddie held up his hands with fingers curled back into knife-hand posture.

Adrian ... looked around, trying to find something that wasn't a book, trembling in anticipation of more whispered slogans of despair. He felt helpless, and the sound of his uncle's pen scratching away at papers on his desk scraped enormous in his ears. It wasn't quite loud enough, though, to overwhelm a faint and rising noise that sounded like gurgling water.

Knock, knock, knock.

Adrian recognized the three polite taps at the door. They were the ones he had always made, hoping not to be heard, not to be admitted into the chamber of his shame.

"Come in," Uncle-wolf said, not turning around or putting down his pen. His words were slow, his voice was heavy with menace and lust.

Mike and Twitch tip-toe-jumped into the corner, assembling themselves as a spread coat and crouching coat rack once more.

Adrian found himself swept behind the door with Elaine Canning and Eddie again. Eddie held a finger to his lips and glared a silent hush order at the woman in Mouser's dream-shape.

The newcomer left the door open and only came in a step.

"I'm here." Adrian shivered. It was his own voice, in a child's piping tones.

No! Adrian screamed silently, as he had done to his dream-self a thousand times before, to no avail then or now.

"Come in and close the door, Ade," Uncle-wolf growled. "Your friends don't need to see the secrets of wizardry."

What friends?

Ade shut the door.

"Now!" Eddie barked, and jumped to the attack.

But they had already lost the element of surprise. More than that, Adrian thought as he stumbled forward in Eddie's wake and saw the scene in the center of the office; he himself might already have lost his mind.

His uncle sat in his office's swivel chair, patting his knee like he'd patted it a thousand times in Adrian's life and a million in his memory. He wore a red smoking jacket and black silk pants over his soft leather slippers. The wolf's head was gone, and his uncle had his own face back, thin and deeply lined, almost ax-like, with tawny eyes that were brown but streaked with gold. He wore the expression Adrian remembered seeing most on his face, a mixture of sadness and excitement that looked like nothing so much as a man enjoying a guilty pleasure. Young Ade, dream-Adrian, shuffled forward with leaden limbs and sat on the offered lap. The two of them carried out their actions like they couldn't do anything else, oblivious to the rest of the movement in the room.

Behind and above and in front of Adrian's uncle loomed the wolf. It sprang up with its long jaws open and teeth glittering like ice, ready for its unwelcome visitors and leaping to the attack. Its body was man-like, covered in short gray hair and rippling with long, smooth muscles.

The wolf and Adrian's uncle shared the same brown and gold eyes. They had another feature in common, too. Each had a long, wet, pink tongue dangling from his mouth, long enough to touch his own chest, bouncing like marionettes as their owners moved.

Eddie hit the monster first, pounding a barrage of knuckles into its flank that didn't faze it in the least. It pushed him away with a quick paw to the forehead, making his head snap back viciously and sending him tumbling like a child rebuffed by an adult in horseplay. Eddie hit the wall with a thud and a small shower of books rained on top of him, the trembling pages and covers gumming him lasciviously like a toothless hooker.

Then Twitch leaped forward, jumping high in the air and swinging her improvised net down with both hands. A hit might have covered the wolf's head and blinded it, even pulled it to the floor. But with its other paw the wolf snatched the coat in mid-air and spun, hurling Twitch—

crack!—

into the door. She bounced off it and fell heavily to the ground.

"Oberon's teeth!" Twitch groaned, rolling over. She still had blood in her hair from her earlier beating—though that been in the physical world, and not in this weird dream-space—still, any way you sliced it, Adrian thought, Twitch was having a bad, bad day.

He wanted to charge and attack. It wasn't his lack of weapons that held him back, it was the fact that he couldn't tear his eyes away from the other scene that was playing out in the room.

Young Ade sat on his uncle's lap, and then big hands went where big hands shouldn't ever go. Adrian couldn't look away and he couldn't quite watch it, either, so he was grateful for the tears that stung his eyes and partially blinded him.

The crisp *crunch* of splintering wood brought Adrian's attention back to the wolf. With its long jaws it had bitten the coat rack in half, but big Mike still managed to land the first blow on the beast, jamming the jagged end of the wood into the monster's chest.

Rooooooooaaaaaarrrrrr!

The wolf howled in rage, but it seemed like an overreaction—the coat rack had sunk into its ribs, but Adrian didn't even see blood. The creature lunged forward, bounding on all fours and slamming its body into the bass player, hurling him into the corner and pouncing on him.

"Get off, dammit!" Eddie roared, and threw himself onto the beast's back.

With his vision still focused on the space the wolf had vacated, Adrian's eye landed on something else—his uncle's desk.

And he thought of the secret shelf.

Did the Eye exist in this strange place? And might he be able to cobble together some kind of spell, if he had it? The Eye wasn't a power source, but if there were ka-energy here, the Eye would help him find and use it.

Though … wasn't that what had brought him here in the first place?

He lurched forward. His limbs moved slowly and he felt like he was swimming through water, but he pushed ahead. Behind him he heard snarling and snapping noises, and the dull *thumps* of punches connecting with their targets.

He turned to look and saw a tangle of wrestling flesh.

And Elaine Canning. The woman who talked like a crazy person about Roundheads and theology stood unmoving, looking at young Ade and his uncle, and wept.

Adrian stopped sluggishly, turning himself to look forward again. His uncle still sat on his chair with young Ade on his knee. He had one hand inside young Ade's clothing, but he patted his other knee with his free hand and smiled without humor or pity at Adrian, his tawny eyes cold.

"Sit down, Adrian," he uncle said in a withered voice.

This was wrong. This was all wrong. He'd been inside his dreams of this moment many times before, and he'd never been a separate person from young Ade. The boy version of himself stared at him now with horror in his eyes, and pity.

"You son of a bitch," Adrian said. He wanted to bellow, but his voice came out like a strangled squeak. "I should have killed you."

"You did." His uncle's tongue slipped further out of his mouth as he spoke, becoming longer and thicker.

"Not soon enough." The chair was in his way, but there was something else, too. Something he couldn't see, but that felt as solid as a brick wall, stopped Adrian from getting closer to the desk.

"Don't be bitter," his uncle said. "It's just the way of the wizard."

"Like hell it is." With an exertion of his will like a push, Adrian threw himself forward. He banged his knee on the arm of the chair, under his kneecap, and then stubbed his toes, so when he tumbled to the floor in front of the desk his leg hurt with a pain that also made him want to laugh.

He didn't like the fact that his back was turned to his dream-uncle and the wolf, but so be it. Kneeling, he fumbled his way forward.

"Chingón!" Mike yelled.

Whack!

Adrian yanked open the top left drawer and shoved his arm under the desk. His fingers found the shelf, but where he thought he would feel the cool sliver of volcanic glass that his uncle called the Eye of Agamotto, instead there was a warm meatball.

He'd been a sorcerer too long to be easily disgusted. Adrian wrapped his fingers gently around the object and pulled it out.

It was an eye. An actual eyeball, moist and spherical, and it lay in his palm and stared up at him. Its iris was brown, but colored with streaks of gold. It was so wet and lifelike, Adrian half expected it to blink or say something.

"Son of a bitch," Adrian said.

"Don't resist," his uncle answered, and Adrian felt a hand on his lower back.

Adrian bucked. He kicked and thrashed his way out from under the desk, like a dog finding a hornets' nest in its bowl. He smacked his own shoulder and cheek on the desk, and when he had rattled to his feet and turned around, it was to see a changing scene.

Young dream-Adrian was opening the door to leave. His clothing was disheveled and he stared at the floor as he moved, tears coursing down his face. Elaine Canning in the shape of Mouser stood to one side, weeping into the balled fingers of one hand and reaching out in the boy's direction with the other, but rooted to where she stood.

Against one wall of the room, the wolf sank its teeth into Eddie's arm. Twitch and Mike banged on its back with fists and sticks, but it ignored them and Eddie screamed. Where were Yamayol and Semyaz? Adrian wondered. Why weren't they hearing all this commotion? Or were they?

In front of it all, Adrian's uncle stood up. His brown eyes flashed fire and he held out his hand, palm up.

"Isn't it time you joined me?" he asked. His tone of voice mocked Adrian, and a tiny smiled curled up one corner of his mouth. Impossibly, and not even knowing what his uncle could mean, Adrian felt tempted. His uncle was powerful—*had been* powerful, and power was what Adrian wanted.

He ripped his gaze away.

Adrian looked down at the eye he held in his hand. Idiot, he thought, you're looking at it for a facial expression or some other message, hoping it will tell you what to do. But an eye all by itself won't tell you anything. It can't even cry.

Not all by itself.

Adrian reached up and popped the disembodied eye into his own eye socket. It shouldn't have fit, since he already had an eyeball there, but Adrian felt his own eyelids reach out like hungry lips to wrap about the fleshy orb, sucking it into place.

And then he saw the scene differently again.

Uncle-wolf stood tall and tongue-waggingly before him, paw out and ears perked at the ceiling. A pool of shadow trailed out behind him, melting upwards and coalescing into another Uncle-wolf shape, pounding sharp-nailed fists into the other members of the band. The band had all changed. They wore their usual jackets and leather, like they would anytime they went on stage, but he saw them now split into multiple images, like he'd see them in physical space through his Third Eye, but with fewer parts.

Adrian squinted. He saw their bas, he thought, and pools of darkness around each of them that must be their shadows. Each wore a tag on his chest that must bear his name—in physical space, that would have been very hard to read, or would have appeared as just a glow, but with the body and the ka out of the way, Adrian thought if he looked close enough he could see each of the band member's true name. Only they were moving too fast.

They moved too fast because they were fighting. Twitch dove left and right to avoid blows, and Eddie managed to catch a lot of them on his forearms, but Mike was taking a beating.

Adrian's ankles felt cold and wet—looking down, he saw that two inches of water flooded the floor of the study. It sluiced in sluggishly from the vent from which he and the rest of the band had emerged only a few minutes earlier.

On the other side of the room, someone slipped out and the door closed. Adrian couldn't quite make out the figure, but it wasn't young dreamself-Ade, it was taller than that, and it had been wearing rider's boots. Elaine Canning sank to the floor sobbing, and she was totally changed. Mouser was gone entirely; Elaine's ba wore a hoop skirt and a blouse with bell-shaped sleeves, she had her hair wrapped in what appeared to be wire and there were chains wrapped around her body. Chains that glowed red-hot.

Down from the ceiling in the center of the room came a white ray of light. Its presence, invisible before, surprised Adrian so much that it took him a moment to see where the ray went. It dropped through the ceiling, turned in the middle of the room and ended right smack in the middle of Adrian's chest. Now that he could see it, he imagined that he could feel it, too, an electric umbilical cord. The line wasn't his ka, and wasn't itself an energy source, but somehow it was a conduit. Energy flowed through it.

His eye hurt from the strain of seeing these things.

"Son of a bitch," he muttered, and then he felt sleep sloshing over him in thick waves. *"Per Volcanum ignem mitto."*

He stretched out his hand and light and fire erupted from it. The blast struck the nearer half of Uncle-wolf square in the chest and obliterated him, shattering him into tatters of darkness that wisped away in the corners of the room.

The heat in the room instantly became almost unbearable, and it also dried the air out. Adrian felt warm and that made him feel sleepy, though he also felt like he could breathe freely for the first time since coming to this dream-place. His throat and chest were tight, and blackness crowded in around the edges of his vision.

The further half of Uncle-wolf dodged the firebolt, bounding around and under it as Adrian blasted away. The shelves flattened themselves to avoid the beam and the books wobbled into the air like fat, awkward birds, flapping their covers to get airborne. *Don't hate us!* Adrian scorched as many of them as he could, but he couldn't see well and his aim suffered. He swiveled his body and turned his aim to try to catch the wolf.

It knocked aside Elaine Canning and raced for the door. Adrian slammed his firebolt on the door tightly, swelling the channel of power to bursting and filling the doorframe with heat and light. The ka-energy felt good running through him and he wondered where it came from. When the beast turned back on him he was ready, and shot straight for its chest.

At the last moment, it turned to the side and sprang for the wall—

Adrian scorched a furrow of charcoal-burnt flesh out of the wall following it—

and the wolf disappeared with a splash into the wall vent.

Adrian snapped off the firebolt. He rolled back and forth on the balls of his feet and his vision yawed. "*That's* the way of the wizard, bitch."

Then he collapsed.

◡　　◠　　◡

Adrian crashed to the floor in a puddle of cold water and woke up.

"Ungh," he groaned, wiping his face and dragging himself up onto his elbows. "Where am I?"

"*You* tell *us*," Mike said.

His uncle's eye popped out into his palm, and Adrian forced himself to look around without it. Mike, Eddie, and Twitch looked even more mangled than he remembered, and were dressed in kids' pajamas again. Eddie's arm where Uncle-wolf had chewed on him looked particularly bad. Elaine Canning was there, too, looking like Mouser again. All four of them had tired and nervous looks on their faces.

Two things that might have been a top-loading washer and dryer squatted in a small room, opposite a teetering set of shelves. The washer and dryer were pot-bellied and covered with scales, though, and they *literally* squatted on taloned legs, in several inches of water. The shelves that in Adrian's memory held detergent and clean clothing here bubbled with caustic, fiery-looking liquids in glass ampules. The tiny chamber had two doors, and they were both shut. All the light in the room came from a host of bugs, like beetles only the size of Adrian's fist, that crawled slowly up and down the walls.

"Never been in a laundry room before?" he joked.

"We're inside you," Eddie said. "I'm ready for an explanation."

"Yeah." Adrian's eye, his natural eye, hurt like hell. He didn't like getting the third degree from Eddie, but maybe he deserved it. "Me, too. I think we're in my dreams, maybe ... or my *shadow*, if that means anything to you."

"Nope," Mike said, "but it doesn't sound good."

"It doesn't feel too good, either." Adrian rubbed his sore eye.

"I wouldn't beat yourself up about it," Twitch said, grinning, "only we don't seem to have come alone." She hoisted herself up on top of the washer and shook flakes of dried blood out of her hair. The washer shuddered like a living thing, and the dryer next to it started to raise its door like a top-loading mouth—Twitch thumped it with one fist, and it fell shut again.

Eddie nodded grimly. "I was kind of hoping that when you passed out we'd all wake up back in the Silver Eel."

"No such luck," Mike said.

"I take it we came here to hide from the Fallen?" Adrian inferred. He imagined one of the others slinging him over their shoulder and jogging. Good thing he was one of the smaller guys in the band.

As if to answer his question, one of the room's two doors rattled.

"I don't think we're really *hidden*," Eddie observed.

"At least we know which door to take." Adrian grinned gamely. He had no idea how to get out of this nightmare. He was afraid to put the tawny eye back into his head, though it had unlocked his sorcery, at least for one spell—he hurt too much, and he didn't want to pass out again.

Boom!

The other door rattled, too.

"All three of them are here?" Adrian asked.

Mike nodded.

"We were hoping you might know another way out," Twitch suggested, crossing her ankles like she wanted to meditate. Under her, the washing machine-beast grumbled and then emitted a noxious stink.

"*Up*," Adrian said, thinking of the white umbilical cord he seemed to have—assuming the tawny eye itself didn't *create* the connection. Even if it did, surely the light had to go somewhere. "I think the way *out* is *up*. There was a window," he remembered. It had been behind the washing room shelves, as he recalled, and he looked there now. Sure enough, he saw a shadow that could be a window, partly hidden behind a haze of fumes filling the upper reaches of the laundry room shelves. "Too bad Jim's not here. We might have a shot at actually taking them."

The water was deeper, almost up to Adrian's knees. He couldn't see how it was coming in, but guessed it must be flooding up under the doors.

BANG!

Both doors shook again at the same moment, struck heavily from outside.

"Oh, I think James is here," Eddie contradicted him. He turned to Elaine Canning, who stood fretting in the corner. "Isn't he?"

"You truly are devils," she said, frowning deeply. "And this is truly the worst you and your masters have yet devised. Almost, you drive me to regret my acts."

Adrian shook his head, feeling groggy. "What's she talking about?" he asked.

Elaine wasn't done. "To make me watch as my lover was so shamed and assaulted." She shook her head and shed a tear from each eye. "You are low, and cruel."

BOOM!

Both doors shook again.

"Right," Adrian said. "What I don't know, et cetera." Not that he believed it. The thing you didn't know was usually exactly what killed you. "Let's get the window open."

"What's outside?" Mike asked. The bassist helped Adrian begin to gather up the bubbling vials and glass pots.

"Hell if I know," Adrian said.

"Maybe hell if you don't," Eddie pointed out.

CHAPTER SIX

Adrian scrambled up onto the top of the dryer. His feet were wet and numb from the cold water and he slipped, but Twitch caught him. Eddie and Mike stationed themselves one beside each shuddering door, fists clenched. Elaine Canning stood resigned in the middle of the small room.

"Thanks," Adrian said to Twitch. He leaned against the wall, which was warm and slick and gave way with slight elasticity, like the inside of his own cheek. He tried not to think about it. He tried pretending he was just inside a bouncy castle, on a humid day in upstate New York. Which reminded him of the house where he'd been apprentice and prisoner both.

Which reminded him of the room he was standing in. The room that was so much like the inside of a mouth. Hell.

Adrian grabbed a smoking bottle in each hand and turned to drop them into the water.

"Wait!" Eddie barked.

Adrian raised his eyebrows.

"What's in those?" the guitarist asked.

Adrian shook off a climbing tendril of sleep that grabbed at his terrified brain as he asked himself the same question. "I don't know," he admitted. "Something bad ... something inside of me, I think. Poison, acid. A curse."

"Your sins," Elaine Canning said. The water was up to the middle of her thighs, and was choppy with the vibration of the doors.

"Just little ones, though," Mike chuckled.

Adrian looked at the bottles. He thought of the body of his uncle, charred and smoking in his own bed where Adrian had ambushed him in his sleep. Adrian wasn't sure he had little sins.

"Here," Twitch suggested. The fairy stood and bent down to yank open the door-mouth of the washing machine. Inside, stubby jagged teeth ringed the underside of what should have been a washer door, and a pink blob like a tree stump quivered in the bottom of the compartment.

"Hell," Adrian grumbled. "Does everything have to be bodies?"

"The house does kind of give the impression that it's trying to cop a feel," Eddie growled. Adrian struggled to control the shudder of revulsion he felt at Eddie's words, keep it from being noticeable to the other guys.

"It's Mikey's lucky day," Twitch quipped.

"Hey," Mike complained. "Call me *Mike*."

Adrian dropped the bottles inside the washing machine and Twitch let the mouth clamp shut.

Poomf! Acrid, stinging smoke wafted up from the clenched mouth and the machine-beast groaned and squirmed.

"Out of sight," Adrian muttered, "you know the rest." Idiotic cliché. What was out of sight was always in mind. He grabbed other bottles from the shelves, hurling them into the creature's mouth as Twitch yanked it open. The receptacle wiggled and coughed, but whatever had been in the first bottles stunned it beyond any effective ability to resist. Eddie looked resolutely at the door during the process, his bad eye sliding every which way as he did.

When the shelves were cleared, the fairy shut the monster's mouth for the last time and stood on it, concealing a fiery, angry, bubbling mass of goo. The air in the laundry room was hardly breathable for the fumes, and the cheek-like wall was drying out. Here and there beetles lost their glow and fell off the wall, splashing softly into the rising water.

But the window was cleared.

Only it wasn't quite a window. It looked like a sphincter, coiled tight, and big enough that if it could be forced open, a man could crawl through it.

"Huevos," Mike grumbled. "Really?"

"Just imagine it belongs to someone you really like," Eddie snapped.

"Now Mikey will remind us that he's fond of boobs," Twitch insinuated, winking at the bass player.

"Carajo."

Adrian grabbed one of the shelves and yanked it out by force. An oily red fluid oozed from the shelf supports where the shelf had been attached, but now there was a space big enough to allow approach to the sphincter-window.

"I'll go first." Adrian felt like he had to. They were all inside him, somehow, and he wondered how that was even possible. He stepped over thrashing water and scooted up to the "window" on his knees, the tawny eye still held tight in one hand. With the back of his fist, he swiped beetles out of the way, but he missed one and his knee reduced it instantly to a phosphorescent splat on the shelf. The sphincter pulsed once, and he felt sick. "We'd better look before we ... you know," he said. "Maybe this doesn't go anywhere at all. I'll stick my head in and see, and if I signal you guys, pull me out."

"I don't think you're going to be able to yell with your head up ... I mean in ... I mean ..." Mike struggled.

"Why not?" Twitch smiled sweetly. "I've known many people who are fine talkers with their heads all the way up their own—"

"Click your heels," Eddie suggested. "Three times, and we'll pull you back."

"So we can all die here together," Mike complained. The water was up almost to his waist, and he was taller than the others.

"There's no place like home," Adrian said.

His vision grayed at the edges and his breath was shallow; Adrian grabbed at the shelf strut to catch himself, sucked in hot, noxious air and then shoved his head into the opening.

It was wet and tight, and he didn't immediately emerge from the other side.

Scrabbling with his feet, he got purchase with his bare toes on the struts of the shelving and inched himself forward. The opening tightened as he pushed, and Adrian struggled to slip his arm in alongside his head. He couldn't breathe, his heart hammered, he thought he might lose consciousness.

This was a house, he told himself. It was in his shadow, it might be part of his shadow, but it was modeled on the house where he'd learned wizardry, the house of his nightmare. That house had had an inside and an outside, like any house did. This one would have an outside, too. It had to.

Of course, he couldn't be sure what was out there.

Then he got his fist holding the eye up next to his mouth, and the forced passage allowed him to breathe again. He kicked forward, slid, wiggled, groped his hand forward—

pop!

His hand holding the eye poked out into space on the other side. Adrian's head was still in the trembling, meaty tunnel, but suddenly, he could see....

Through the eyeball in his hand.

"Sumfabish," he muttered through tightly clenched lips.

The house of Adrian's apprenticeship had been a nineteenth-century creaker on a genteelly decaying street in upstate New York, gnarled with vines and shrouded from its neighbors by several ragged rows of maple trees. What Adrian saw outside this building was a tempest of color and noise. Streaks of red and gold fell past the eye like lightning, dropping away into darkness, and he felt water.

With a mighty kick of his legs, Adrian pushed his head out.

He filled his lungs with the air outside the building and looked around. He saw the streaks of light and followed them down, looking for ground. But there was no ground where he thought there ought to have been, no carpet of green grass and wildflowers untouched by a mower, no laid path of flat stones circling the house. There was a fall that might have been infinite, for all the perspective that Adrian had, and at the bottom, there was a maelstrom of color and sound. Rain pelted the back of Adrian's head as he stared down into the crimson and gold pinwheel, slowly rotating and crunching with a sound like an infinite rockslide, like a river of stones the size of the Mississippi, grinding together forever.

Adrian wished he had something impressive and witty to say, but he didn't. No one would have heard him, anyway.

Then someone grabbed his ankles—

for a heart-stopping moment, he thought he was going to be dragged back inside by the Fallen—

but instead he was pushed.

"Holy shit!" Adrian yelled, and grabbed for any support he could find. The real house, the house of his subjugation and misery, had been overgrown with strong old creepers. They were the reason Adrian's uncle had made him sleep in the basement—it would have been too tempting, his uncle said, to climb out the window on the vines if his bedroom had been on the second floor. Not that Adrian hadn't been allowed to leave the house, but he'd only been supposed to do it with his uncle's permission and under wards of tracing.

Adrian slammed his empty hand against the side of the house and found a vine. He grabbed it.

Only it didn't feel like a vine. There was no bark, no leaves, and the fibrous cable he gripped was far too straight to be a naturally growing vine. It felt kind of like rope, of a thick and particularly scaly kind. It reminded him of something, but in the panic of the moment as he grabbed at it, he couldn't think of what.

Adrian's feet shot out of the sphincteral passage and spun out into space. He bit off a scream and tried not to let go as suddenly the weight of his body was all on the strength of one arm. His legs arced out sideways and he tumbled once completely around, like a hot dog in a gas station's heating rack, before his body slammed into the side of the building, in a thick tangle of the heavy cable. Flakes of something shook off the wall on impact and fell on him like ash or fake snow.

The building trembled, sending a ripple through the thicket of cables. Adrian smelled a thick animal musk, and suddenly, he realized what he was holding onto.

"Son of a bitch," he muttered. The rope was *hair*.

Adrian lost his breath. His heart thumped once in his chest and stopped. His vision spun and he started sliding.

"No!" he screamed.

By willpower, sweating and trembling, he stayed awake. He clamped his hand onto the strand of hair and stopped his fall. His arm hurt, he ached, his vision pulsed in and out. He cursed his uncle as his consciousness returned. He'd told the band he'd been cursed in revenge for his theft, but that wasn't true. His uncle had been deader than a well-done steak when Adrian had finished with him, and in no condition to cast any curses.

He'd cursed Adrian before. He'd done it at the beginning of his apprenticeship, to cripple Adrian. He'd only taught Adrian weak and watered-down magic anyway, and he'd forced on him this narcolepsy that limited his powers even further, so he wouldn't ever be a threat to his master. He hadn't really wanted an apprentice—he'd wanted a victim, someone he could trap and lure into complaisance with the sorcerous equivalent of candy.

To hell with him, Adrian thought grimly. He'd never underestimate Adrian again.

He shook himself back to the present. He needed both his hands to climb. Adrian looked at the tawny eye in his palm, then down into the coruscating void beneath him. His face throbbed, but he couldn't risk dropping the eye—without it, he didn't think he could perform any magic in this strange place.

With a whimper of pain, Adrian jammed the eye back into his own eye socket. Immediately, even with his head tucked down into his chest, he again saw the umbilical cord of light sprouting from his own body. It pulsed crimson and gold, matching the colors of the maelstrom below.

Just as Adrian looked up again, Elaine Canning poked her head and shoulders out of the "window" above him, her hair wet and plastered to her head under the wire in which it was bound. "Zounds!" she gasped.

"Grab onto the ... vines!" Adrian called.

She heard him and followed his instruction, climbing out onto the wall with surprising agility for a woman in a hoop skirt. The chains wrapped around her looked red-hot and gave off smoke, but they didn't seem to slow her down.

With both hands free, Adrian began dragging himself up to join her. He was cold and wet, and he hoped he didn't have to climb too far this way, but the hair-vines were surprisingly easy to cling to. They were hard to flex, but they were rough, and his fingers found good purchase.

"You're pretty nimble," Adrian grunted, trying to take his mind off the madness around and below him.

Mike's thick black hair and leather jacket punched out of the opening next.

"I can ride a horse and shoot a gun," she snorted, "as well as play the thirteen-course lute. And I can keep accounts in accordance with Pacioli's *Summa de Arithmetica*."

"Yeah?" Adrian grabbed Mike by the collar and helped him steady himself as he climbed out. It was good to see Mike out of jammies and back in his cracked brown jacket again, but Adrian knew he was only seeing it that way because of the tawny eye, and the eye made his head hurt. "You ought to join the band."

"The band of hell?" she asked, as they both climbed slowly up.

"Seems like it sometimes, doesn't it?" Adrian muttered.

"Jeez," Mike grunted, righting himself and clambering after them. "I'm sure glad this went somewhere. We were afraid we might have shoved you into a bottomless gut or something."

"Yeah," Adrian agreed, "that would have been a *lot* worse."

Twitch pulled herself out of the hole quickly. "Oberon!" she shouted, but grabbed a handful of hair without missing a beat and then waited. The sphincter looked more relaxed, and Adrian tried not to think about that. He felt sick to his stomach.

Eddie launched through the opening like a bullet from a gun, missing his catch.

"Dammit!" the guitarist yelled, slapping for a grip—

he pitched forward, tumbling into the void—

and Twitch caught him by the ankle.

Eddie swung out, limbs splayed like he was ready for a cosmic belly flop into the grinding lights below. Twitch grunted—

slid down several feet—

but held on. Eddie reached the end of his arc and fell back against the side of the house, head-down and shouting curses.

"Come on!" Adrian yelled. The void about him spun like the park around a carousel ride and he tried not to look at it. It made him want to let go, fall asleep, and just drift down into the light. Whatever the light was.

He was pretty sure it couldn't be good.

The wall—he forced himself not to think about what it really was, but the slightly quivering surface under all the hair—sloped sharply in now, and he dragged himself onto an almost flat shelf. The rain hit him full force, cold and hard, and he squinted up into it. He could see no cloud, nor anything else resembling an ordinary sky. He saw darkness, streaks of light, a shining cord of light rising into the black, and rain hitting him in the eye.

Adrian grabbed Elaine Canning by her outstretched hand and dragged her up onto the roof with him. "Don't let go," he urged her. "It's moving." In New York, this would have been a shingled stretch of roof beneath a window opening into the upstairs hallway. Here ... well, the building was covered in hair and twitching, and he hadn't yet dared look at the spot where the window should be.

What was this place, and how had they got here? He remembered the wards on the Silver Eel in Kansas City, how he had tried to tap into them and failed. The wards had been a trap, set by the Fallen. The Fallen had seized Jim. Adrian remembered the frantic moments of spellcasting—it had seemed to him that his shadow, the wolf-shaped uncle of his nightmares, had held Jim in his grip, rather than Semyaz the Fallen.

Maybe Adrian hadn't *failed*, it occurred to him. Maybe he had bungled it *spectacularly*. Maybe he had reshaped the wards of restraining and had drawn them all down into his shadow.

It was bizarre, but it held together with a certain logic, in the dream-like analysis of sympathetic magic. Adrian had redrawn the lines of the trap, so that now they were all stuck inside Adrian.

So what had happened to Jim?

Or maybe Adrian had drawn his own shadow up into the club, and made the old warehouse look like the inside of his own psyche.

Was there a difference? He wasn't sure. In the one case, they might all be running around in the Silver Eel, only not seeing it. In the other, maybe they were all lying face down on the club floor and drowning in flood water.

But, in either case, who was Elaine Canning? Where had she come from? And what was her connection with Jim?

It probably didn't matter, anyway. Whatever the exact nature of the trap they were in, the only way out seemed to be the way up, and Adrian's connection to the golden cord. Could he cast a spell to raise them all out of this trap now? It would be easier if he could touch the rest of the band.

He stretched himself out flat and looked back into the abyss. Mike was the slowest, but had had a head start on the others, and as Adrian looked, he reached the edge and started dragging himself over it. Something golden flashed on his chest, and he and Adrian both shivered from the rain. The others were ascending fast, but Eddie had started from below the exit and had just risen above it when their pursuers emerged.

The sphincter spat out light, and then a burning being.

Adrian nearly jumped back in fright. He'd expected something with a bull's head, or a boar's, but instead what crawled out of the passage, grabbing for Eddie's ankles and narrowly missing, looked like an angel.

"Watch out!" he yelled. Angels could fly, and that would make them hard to fight, especially without guns.

Only the angel didn't fly. It lunged, jumping upward, and when it narrowly missed Eddie, it buried its hands in the wall of hair and caught itself. Adrian shook his head in disbelief. The angel had no wings.

And then he realized what he was looking at. This was one of the Fallen, but detached from his body and ka. This wasn't physical space, Adrian reminded himself. This was all … astral … spiritual … karmic … shadowy. A flicker of hope tickled the inside of his chest.

And then a second Fallen crawled from the sphincter. That seemed so appropriate that Adrian would have chuckled, if he hadn't been frightened and off-balance.

"I have hoped for rescuers for centuries," he heard Elaine Canning say beside him. "But now that I see the angels that are sent, I think I prefer my torments."

"Good call," Mike told her. "You wanna hold out for a better offer than *that*."

Adrian felt a twinge of sympathy for the sphincter, imagining what it would feel like to have multiple people crawl through his own body. He burned with vague shame and reminded himself not to get distracted.

Twitch scrambled up to the ledge and threw herself over.

"What have you got, big boy?" she leered at him. "A bit of Vulcan's Kiss at least, surely?"

"Better than that," Adrian cheered himself on. "I'm getting us out of here, as soon as I can touch Eddie." As he said it, he wondered if he was doing them any favors, or if getting them all out of his shadow just put them back into the power of the Fallen in the physical world. There, after all, they had a huge size advantage and could use sorcery. And Adrian had screwed this up before.

He wondered if he could somehow leave the Fallen behind.

"Come on, Eddie!" Mike shouted. "Kick that *pendejo!*"

The nearest Fallen on Eddie's tail grabbed for him again, and Eddie took Mike's tactical advice, slamming the heel of a combat boot into the former angel's shining forehead. The Fallen grunted and slipped, sliding down several feet.

"Everyone touch my body somewhere," Adrian told his friends on the shelf with him, and felt hands anchor onto his back and legs. He willed himself not to be uncomfortable with the fact that people were crowding around and touching him, and mostly succeeded.

What if he didn't have the tawny eye in his head? Adrian thought, feeling the eye's presence like a painful, invasive foreign body. Like a kidney stone in the urethra of his skull. Eddie would appear to have bare feet, then. Would it affect how hard he kicked?

If they were all inside Adrian's shadow, his perception might be *defining* the world for *all of them*, and not just providing the lens through which he himself saw things.

He batted away the thought as abstract and a detour. They needed to get out of this place. He reached out and started muttering incantations.

"Grab the wizard's hand!" Twitch called down to Eddie.

Adrian looked Eddie in the eye and Eddie stared back, concentrating on covering the last feet to Adrian, throwing himself up at a reckless pace, hand over hand and foot over foot. Dangling from Eddie's chest and bouncing around inside the hairs carpeting the wall, Adrian again noticed a tag. It was like a dog tag, only the size of a tea saucer and golden. They all had them, he realized. He hadn't noticed them in the climb because they'd all been covered in the vine-like growth of hair.

The plate bore Eddie's true name.

Adrian didn't need that, but suddenly he wondered about the Fallen. The Fallen had true names, didn't they?

He tore his eyes away from Eddie. The three Fallen dragged themselves up the side of the wall, moving as fast as Eddie moved and maybe even a little bit faster. In New York, this wall had been twelve feet tall, if that. Here it seemed to be thirty, but that was no comfort. They were all bearing down—bearing *up*—on Adrian with alarming speed.

Gold saucers bounced on the chests of the Fallen, too.

Adrian's heart leaped to attention. If he could see those names, he could end this, right here and now. Knowing the true names of his enemies and being the only one—he hoped—with access to ka-power should give him the ability to command them, bend them to his will. Maybe he could force them to help him and the band escape. Or he could escape, forcing them to stay behind. Their ba-less bodies in the physical world would be inert and useless. The band could collect their gear, walk past the Fallen like so many tons of sleeping elephant, and hail a cab.

Okay, a cab wasn't quite their style. But they could steal a car.

"Semyaz!" Adrian yelled, trying to get the Fallen's attention. The two former angels kept climbing and ignored him. "Yamayol!" he tried again, and this time one of them looked up.

Adrian got a glimpse of the Fallen's name-plate and his heart sank. There was writing on it, all right, but it was in one of the

Primals. Infernal, probably, if Adrian had to guess. Adrian had been born after the Tower of Babel and the Confusion of the Tongues—a long time after—and he could recognize Infernal, but he couldn't read it. Much less speak it out loud, which is what he'd have to do.

So much for that hope. Adrian focused on the spell he was weaving. He didn't know exactly what he was doing, so he improvised. He started with incantations he used in setting wards of obfuscation and he reversed them, imagining them as spells of pathfinding, and envisioning the golden umbilical cord as a path.

A path that went straight up into the sky.

He tried to remember the wards inside the Silver Eel's restaurant, shaping his incantations to leave them intact, but let him and his friends—those touching him—pass through.

Without warning, the third Fallen emerged from the sphincter, nearly leaping out, the portal was so worn now. Maybe that one was Semyaz, Adrian thought, and then he saw that the last of the Fallen carried a prisoner in his arms.

It was Jim.

He was as tall and heroic-looking as ever, with his sculpted face and long hair, and he wore his prairie shirt, jeans and rider's boots with flair. But Semyaz carried him tucked under one arm easily, like a small child. Jim snapped his head back and forth, but to no effect. Tendrils of darkness wrapped around his chest like chains, pinning him and leaving him unable to free himself. Adrian felt his chest constrict and his breathing become shallow.

Jim was trapped. Adrian had reshaped the wards of restraint and imprisonment, and in this twisted house of flesh that was Adrian's shadow, he had trapped Jim in the role of dream-Ade, the helpless little boy.

Holy crap.

Eddie lurched forward, his hand slapping into Adrian's. "Go!" the guitar player yelled. He didn't see Jim.

Adrian didn't want to leave Jim, but he didn't know how to save him, either. It didn't matter—at this point, his body and mind marched down the path he had already set for them, and it was too late to make them turn.

He felt like he was watching his own lips mumble from the outside, and he heard his own voice as if from far away. "*Per Wepwawet Mercuriumque semitam sequitor,*" the far-away-Adrian said, just as Adrian had planned.

And then far-away-Adrian disappeared, and so did everything else.

CHAPTER SEVEN

Wet flesh rasped his face, like the tongue of a dog. Like the tongue of a dog so big that Adrian could fit inside its mouth. Adrian tasted bile in the back of his throat.

He opened his eyes. They hurt like needles had been shoved into both of them, but he saw just fine. He was in the long upstairs hallway of the house. Not the real one, the horrible dream-shadow house made of body parts. He saw Mike's and Eddie's backs as they rammed the wardrobe up against the hallway's lone window. The wardrobe snarled and snapped at them, but they kept out of reach of its grinding jaws.

They were wearing jammies.

"Son of a bitch," he groaned. "It didn't work."

"Oh, it worked just fine," he heard Twitch say. Swiveling his head, he found the fairy, standing at the top of the stairs and looking down them with a sturdy meat club in her hands. It might be the shower curtain rod, he thought idly. "You got to miss the nasty part. Again. Well done, Adrian."

Wham!

Eddie and Mike slammed the wardrobe against the wall again. White light shone around the edges, and Adrian thought he saw white fingers slammed under the woody flesh.

Wararargh! chomped the wardrobe, throwing a rain of warm spittle on all of them.

"Adrian!" Eddie barked. He dug his heels into the moist red floor and threw his shoulder into the wardrobe. "A fireball'd be nice about now!"

Adrian patted around on the floor and found the tawny eye. He picked it up and hesitated.

"That's going to smart," Twitch warned him.

"I look that good, huh?" He tried a devil-may-care grin.

"Even better," the fairy said. "You're bleeding out both eyes."

"Nothing ventured," Adrian bluffed. "You know."

He touched his own face. He felt like tenderized steak all over so he hadn't noticed, but Twitch was right. He had blood under both eyes, as well as on his upper lip and trickling down his neck. "Ugh," he groaned.

Wham!

Eddie tumbled to the ground as the Fallen on the other side of the wardrobe hammered against it. Mike jammed his fists into the red rubbery walls of the window well and leaned back hard. Elaine Canning, again looking like Mouser in rose-spotted pajamas, jumped forward to throw herself against the wardrobe with the bass player.

"Mierda!"

Adrian pushed the tawny eye into his eye socket. The searing pain was so intense and so immediate that his whole body contracted in a spasm, and the eye promptly plopped back out again. It stared at him from a puddle of wet fluid on the floor, smeared in guilty, inadequate blood.

Adrian shuddered, almost crying. "I can't do it!"

He grabbed the eye and stood, and his lungs filled instantly with smoke. From the floor he hadn't noticed it, but colored fumes billowed up the stairwell. They stank of sulfur, tobacco smoke, and rotting flesh. The sudden influx burned his lungs and he staggered against the sagging wall, knocking his head against the hanging uvula-light in the process. It swung back and forth, sending all the room's shadows dancing in circles.

"Uh oh," Twitch warned them all. "Stairs."

"Adrian!" Eddie yelled again, and jumped to the top of the staircase. "*Now* would be good!"

Adrian nodded. Eddie was right; now would be very good indeed. He leaned both shoulder blades against the spongy, resilient wall, ignoring the trickles of warm water that snaked down his back, and braced himself.

To hell with the firebolt. To hell with trying to bar the path to the Fallen. He needed to get them all back to Kansas City, and pronto. They'd have to come back for Jim, if they could. And if they couldn't, well, Jim's body had the clipping of Azazel's hoof in Kansas City. Adrian coughed, crouched to get down into cleaner air, took a deep breath and jammed the tawny eye over his own eyeball.

He felt blood spurt out onto his face and winced. A *tun-tun-tun-tun-tun* machine gun pulsing exploded inside his head and his vision blurred and skewed sideways. Adrian grabbed his temples and dropped onto his knees and elbows.

"Aaagh!" his mouth filled with hot fluid and he coughed and spat as much of it as he could onto the floor. He forced his eyes open and found himself staring into a puddle of yellow-gray slime, like bile, or worse.

But he could see the umbilical cord again. "Touch me!" he gasped to the others, trying to wind up the incantations again that he had begun on the ledge of hair outside.

"You've got to be joking!" Eddie, again in his sleeveless jacket and combat boots, kicked and punched at one of the Fallen, who tried to emerge from the stairwell. Adrian saw the angel's nameplate and silently cursed his inability to read the Primals. That was stupid and pointless of course—Adrian would never be able to read the Primals, and it wasn't his fault. Still, the sense of powerlessness and frustration almost overwhelmed him.

The white angel grabbed for Eddie's jacket, but Twitch threw herself in the way, slamming aside long-fingered, lightning-colored hands with her improvised club.

"We're busy!" Mike grunted.

An increase in the white glow from the lower story told Adrian where the third Fallen was. He raised his arms and opened himself to channel ka-energy through the umbilical cord.

"*Per Wepwawet Mercuriumque semitam—*"

With a flash of pain that Adrian saw as much as felt, the eye popped out of his head.

Adrian screamed and dropped to the floor.

His breath tightened and his vision turned black. He fell into a dark, dark pit—

"There must be another way out, yes?"

The voice belonged to Mouser. She knelt over Adrian, dragging him away from sleep. Adrian's spine tingled with discomfort from her being so close, but it helped that she was wearing jammies. It made her look like a big kid, and not a woman.

"Murmph." Adrian spat bile from his mouth and rummaged around until he found the tawny eye again. It looked dented and bruised, a little knocked out of shape from being inside his eye. He heard *thuds* and cursing that told him that his friends were fighting, though he couldn't see it.

"I do not believe you are devils," Elaine Canning said.

"Handsome is," Adrian agreed, and threw up a little more.

"But if we are to flee, we must flee now."

Adrian nodded. His mouth was sour with fluids of his stomach, and as he spat to clear it he pointed at the ceiling. "There's an attic," he said. "And an exit to the roof."

"And then what?" she asked. "We fly away?"

"More or less." Only Adrian didn't know whether he could do it. He felt like he had a harpoon through every opening in his head, which throbbed and shook and oscillated around him like a satellite in orbit. Even in the best of circumstances, he wasn't sure his spell would work—he didn't really know what the umbilical cord was or where it went.

Elaine Canning nodded. "You open the door, and I'll free the others."

"You have some weapon I don't know about?"

"I have a plan," she said, standing. "I would trade it for a good horse pistol, loaded and primed."

Adrian snorted. "Wouldn't we all, sister?"

He lurched to his feet and staggered down the hall.

The trapdoor in the ceiling was easy enough to find. He'd begun this bizarre journey climbing down out of the attic through the pull-down stairs that looked like a jaw, but somehow, they looked much worse when he stood below them. More monstrous, more disgusting, bigger. A loose lip dangled to expose yellow teeth the size of fists and permit a trickle of house-slobber to splatter down on him.

Adrian shook his head and tried not to throw up.

He looked back down the hall. Eddie and Twitch hammered back and forth with one of the Fallen now, and Elaine Canning stood above them, holding something in her hand that might have been a brick or a raw steak. Mike slid slowly away from the window, pushed by the angel beyond it.

The Fallen looked different, not seen through the tawny eye.

They looked like his uncle, only angelic. Down to the glowing white smoking jacket. It all began to make sense to Adrian. He had relocated the Fallens' trap into his own shadow. They were trapped by it as well as the band, now, and all of them were separated from their kas, and Adrian's out-of-control spell had put the Fallen into the role of his dream-uncle, just as it had put Jim into the role of his dream-self.

Knowing what had happened didn't give Adrian any kind of clue what to do about the mess he'd made.

He had to jump twice—he was broken and tired—but he sank his fingers into the juicy, flaccid lower lip of the door into the attic and grabbed hold. Then his weight opened the door, dropping the jaw so that a staircase the color of old ivory could rattle slowly down and into place.

"Ready!" he shouted, but then gasped.

He felt a cold chill down his spine, and wheeled to look behind him.

There was nothing there, only lopsided, irregular doors, staring blankly. They led in New York to rooms with unfinished floors, rooms full of boxes and uninteresting books, rooms that smelled of mothballs and formaldehyde.

But here? Adrian had no idea.

He groped for his taser reflexively, but caught himself before his hand got to where the stunner should be.

"Now!" Elaine Canning yelled.

Adrian spun in time to see the seventeenth-century damned woman hurl her brick of mortar-flesh. The Fallen, struggling with two attackers at the top of the stairs as its comrade reached past to land occasional long-armed licks of its own, ducked—

but not fast enough.

Whack!

The angel took the brick in the face and fell back down with a *splash*.

"Yes!" Without meaning to, Adrian pumped his fist in the air.

He looked into the stairwell and got a clear view of the two Fallen, tangled together and rolling in water that was nearly up to the level of the hallway floor. Neither held Jim, so that probably made them Yamayol and Ezeq'el, with Semyaz banging at the window.

Unless they'd gone ahead and tossed Jim into the void outside.

Could they do that, even if they wanted to? Or would Adrian's spell, that put Jim into his own nightmare role, protect Jim from that horror as it subjected him to others? Magic, Adrian snorted. It might not be an art, but it sure wasn't a science.

Elaine Canning came sprinting up the hall in his direction, jammies flapping heavily in the humid air. Twitch followed, and then Eddie yanked Mike away from the window and dragged the big bassist with him to bring up the rear.

WHAM!

The wardrobe slammed forward to the floor, and over his friends' heads, Adrian saw tattered flaps of a membrane, halfway between a punctured eardrum and a torn fortuneteller's curtain. The membrane glowed pink where it blocked his vision, and through the big, flapping, ragged tear in the center he saw an intense white light, accented slightly with tendrils of darkness, like ivy growing up a column. Wind and water rushed in through the suddenly open window.

Cold water spilled up out of the stairway, flooding the hall floor like an overflowing toilet. The Fallen sloshed and flailed at the banister, trying to drag themselves out of the icy pool.

"Go!" Eddie shouted.

Adrian stopped staring and scrambled up the jaw-stairs. The steps were hard and sharp under his bare feet, and the teeth were slick and difficult to get a good grip on. His blood quickly mingled with the brook of slobber that lubricated the ascent, and he banged both his knees and the palms of his hands. The tongue lying in the middle of the jaw was rough and he pawed at it like a dog running on all fours; his hands found good traction in the squashy pink tissue and he threw himself as far as he could into the attic.

He landed, gasping, on the warm attic floor. Dim light, flashing in various colors, trickled through trembling window-membranes.

The room was dark and close. He heard pounding feet behind him, almost as loud as the pounding rain on the roof overhead, and guessed that the others followed, but he couldn't make his body turn to see or help them. His field of vision darkened and narrowed, his breath tightened, his heart rattled in his brainpan.

You cannot fall asleep now, he ordered himself. Not now.

And then he realized that he wasn't alone.

Soft brown leather house slippers and black silk trousers told him whom he was looking at even through his tiny, straining vision. Adrian coughed and spat on the floor.

He heard footsteps behind him, but they faltered.

"You stole something from me," Uncle-wolf said.

Adrian forced himself to lift his head. His vision cleared a bit, and he could see the smear of blood his own face left on the floor.

"You stole *everything* from me," he said.

Uncle-wolf clicked his tongue and made a sound like purring. "My books," he growled. "My time and tutelage. My patience."

"My freedom," Adrian shot back. He'd never talked to his uncle this way in real life, he'd never really resisted at all. He'd only fought back in secret, stealing spells and teaching them to himself, until the night that he snuck into his uncle's bedroom and incinerated him and his bed in a blazing Vulcan's Kiss.

"The Third Eye," Uncle-wolf said. There was an impatient strain in his voice now, and Adrian forced himself to look up. The cartoonish wolf's head sneered angrily at him, tongue dangling only just barely out of his mouth. As Adrian looked at him, the tongue extended a little further. "You took the Third Eye. Give it back."

"You took my innocence!" Adrian snapped.

Crash!

The floor shook. He heard creaking noises and felt the floor of the attic yaw to one side like the deck of a ship in a storm.

"Adrian!" Eddie shouted.

Adrian lunged up onto his knees and then to his feet. He had to hop to keep his balance, but he managed to stay upright. The wolf towered enormously over him, impossibly so since he seemed taller than the ceiling was high, and jabbed an accusing finger in his direction. Adrian scooted sideways to get out of the way of the blaming finger, winding one hundred eighty degrees around his uncle, and saw the rest of the band.

Eddie, Mike, and Twitch were backed into a corner, fists and fleshy weapons raised. Elaine Canning huddled inside their protective ring. She didn't look frightened, more ... surprised.

And touched, maybe.

Between his friends and the wolf stood arrayed the three Fallen. All three of them looked identical, like glowing white renditions of his uncle. Yamayol and Ezeq'el (Adrian guessed, unable to really tell them apart in their simplified ba-and-name forms) sparred with his friends. Semyaz stood in the center of the room, holding dream-Adrian, the young boy.

That would be Jim.

Tendrils of darkness wrapped around little Ade-Jim like rope, and Semyaz struggled with them, fighting to keep his prisoner. The boy's face was quiet, unreadable, hiding deep secrets. Adrian shook blood from his eyes and susurrating shadow from his head, fighting to stay awake. He looked again, and saw that the darkness of the tendrils dropped into a pool at Semyaz's feet. The pool filled the attic.

The same pool flowed into and rose up in front of Adrian in the form of his uncle, the wolf.

"You took my life." The wolf spoke gravely, and with authority. It was true, Adrian had killed him. Murdered him in his sleep, not even in a fair fight.

Though what fight could ever have been fair between the full-fledged sorcerer and his apprentice?

Fairness doesn't justify anything, he heard himself think. You can't steal things because it isn't fair that someone else has what you don't.

But what about justice?

"You took my father."

Adrian had never known, not for sure. Had suspected it, but never said anything about his suspicions out loud. But the wolf's tongue extended another arm's length as he said it, the wolf towered even taller, and the wolf denied nothing.

"Join me," the wolf urged him. "It's not too late. There is always struggle between master and apprentice. That's the way of the wizard. It only confirms that you're mine."

And Adrian felt that maybe he should. He took a shuffling step forward, and Uncle-wolf blurred. His body became a little indistinct, a little open, like Adrian might step inside him like a hand into a puppet. Or would the puppet be Adrian, and the invading hand the hand of his dead uncle, haunter of his dreams?

But at least he would have power. His uncle had been powerful. Being his uncle would mean never being powerless again.

The Semyaz-uncle looked pleased. He nodded and chuckled, still wrestling with the tendrils of darkness.

Adrian took a deep breath of warm, dank air. "No," he whispered.

He felt like a gear inside his chest had just rotated.

All four uncles turned to look at him. Eddie took the opportunity to kick the nearest glowing white wizard right in his solar plexus, and the angel stumbled back before regaining its balance and rejoining the fight.

"What do you want magic for?" Uncle-wolf asked quizzically. "It's the purest form of power in the universe, and can do anything, properly focused. What wealth do you desire? What person do you wish to destroy? Whom do you want to make a god?" His teeth were long and snaggled. "Tell me, and I will show you how."

His uncle's body seemed to open like a cape. In the dim light, Adrian couldn't tell his uncle's front from his back, his inside from his out. The shadowy form seemed to drift in his direction, and he couldn't tell if he was looking at his uncle's face, or out through his uncle's eyes.

Adrian looked away from his uncle and into the silent, opaque eyes of his child-self, clutched in Semyaz's arms.

"This is just the same crappy deal you offered Jim," Adrian said. He wasn't really sure which of the images of his uncle he was talking to. He felt stoned, and everything seemed to blur together. "It's just a rotten little bribe. I said *no* and I meant it."

Semyaz-uncle raised the child Adrian closer to him, wrapping an arm around his neck. Adrian involuntarily shot a look at Mouser, remembering her … death. She looked horrified.

"Join me," Uncle-wolf said, "or I'll destroy this innocent."

That wasn't new, either. Adrian ground his teeth together. "What I want magic for is to kill creeps like you, you son of a bitch." He straightened his back though the floor continued to sway, deciding that if he had to die, at least he wanted to die with dignity. "Besides, that kid is no innocent. And I said *no*."

The wolf raised himself to his full height—

which suddenly wasn't all that tall, after all. And his tongue disappeared, and his ears and other wolfish features melted away into nothing, until he was just Adrian's uncle.

And suddenly Adrian noticed that his uncle wasn't physically imposing at all. He wasn't a tall or a strong man, no taller than Adrian himself, and a good deal less muscular. He looked like an older Adrian, withered and atrophied by vice.

Against the wall, Adrian's friends' clothing changed, pajamas vanishing in a wink and being replaced by their more normal choices. Elaine Canning once more looked the part of a seventeenth-century lady, too, though Adrian couldn't see the red chains.

And the space in the attic was a good deal less dark than it had been.

The three uncle-angels became three Fallen again, too. For some other observer, that might have been a change for the worse. For Adrian, they were less terrifying in their angelic forms, maybe because they were less familiar. He could resent an angel's intrusion into his affairs, but he had no personal history with them.

With most angels, anyway.

Rooooooowwaaaaarrgh!

Semyaz threw back his head and bellowed, a terrible, frustrated, agonized sound in the attic. He raised child-Adrian over his head, as if he was going to smash the boy to the floor—

but Ade wasn't a child anymore, and he wasn't Adrian, he was Jim—

and Jim the rock and roll singer punched both his fists into Semyaz's neck, just behind the ear on each side.

Semyaz grunted and staggered back. Jim swung his legs up against the ceiling and kicked off, throwing himself down into Semyaz like a hammer.

CHAPTER EIGHT

CRAAACKKK!

Wind and rain blasted Adrian in the face. The suddenness of it caught him by surprise, and it took him a moment to realize where it came from—a chunk of the attic's roof and sloped wall had torn away, leaving a gaping hole. Beyond were darkness and water, and strange lights like something out of deep space in *Star Trek*.

Jim piled into Semyaz and they collapsed to the floor in a rolling tangle of elbows that bounced and headed in Adrian's direction, fists pummeling and feet flailing.

Adrian tightened his grip on the tawny eye and danced out of the way. "The roof!" he yelled. His words were snatched away by the storm and he wasn't sure anyone had heard him, so he yelled louder, "GET ONTO THE ROOF!"

His friends weren't in jammies anymore, but Adrian's view of his ka-umbilical cord had not reappeared—nor had Elaine's chains. He needed to see the cord and be able to tap into its power again if he was going to get them all out of there, but he didn't want to put the eye into his head too early. He'd wait until the last possible second this time.

He skittered aside again as Jim and Semyaz rolled back his direction—

and something slammed him from behind.

"Oooomph!" Adrian hit the floor of the attic, hands out in front of him—

and lost his grip on the eyeball.

He groped after it, missed, watched it roll away from him, felt fingers knotting themselves into his short hair, saw the eyeball fall down through the open hatch of the pull-down stairs—

wham!

His face cracked against the floor. For a slab of warm meat, it was surprisingly solid, and Adrian hurt.

"You had your chance," his uncle told him. Adrian felt a knee between his shoulder blades, pinning his chest to the floor, and he wiggled to try to escape.

He failed.

Wham! His face slammed into the floor again. Darkness slithered all around him like a jar of snakes. He saw Elaine Canning's hoop skirts, slick and shining from the rain and glowing red and green from the psychedelic lights, flash past him. She kicked Semyaz in the head, and then Jim punched the Fallen's eye.

Good for them, Adrian thought, a little hazily. Fighting to the end.

"Weakling."

The fingers in his hair pulled his head back again, and Adrian prepared for the impact. Maybe this would be the blow that finally did it, he thought. He couldn't possibly hurt any more than he did, and it would just be like falling asleep. He'd passed out a thousand times, thousands of times, and the thought of losing consciousness held no terrors for him.

Though if he was going to go like this, he kind of wished he'd eaten a T-bone steak first. And a milkshake.

And wouldn't his losing mean that his uncle had won?

Adrian jammed his forearm under his face.

Thud!

His arm softened the blow. The collision of his head with the crook of his own elbow, together with the image of his uncle grinning triumphantly as he died, snapped Adrian's thoughts into clear focus.

"You were never strong enough to follow the way of the wizard," his uncle snarled softly above and behind him. "I should have seen that from the start."

He pulled back Adrian's head again.

Adrian rolled sideways, hard. His uncle cursed and slipped off, bouncing to the floor in a *swish* of silk and soft leather. Adrian punched his uncle as hard as he could with the knuckles of his left hand, right in his astonished expression. Backhanded and off-balance as the blow was, it couldn't have hurt very much, but it would do; his uncle fell back and let go, a trickle of blood showing at the corner of his mouth.

Adrian threw himself forward and into the hole in the floor.

He didn't need to beat up or kill his uncle. But without the tawny eye, he had no idea how he could possibly escape.

He sucked air into his lungs as he dove, and nearly spat it all back out again when he hit the water. It was like diving into ice, a thousand needles poked him everywhere in his body at the same moment and he felt like the water was flaying off his skin.

He opened his eyes.

The house was gone. There was no hallway, no wardrobe, no bathroom, no windows, no banisters, no staircase, no walls or ceiling. There was a bottomless well of cold, wet darkness. Down beneath him, lights flashed like explosions in the deep, sending up bright colored beams and bubbles of gray smoke. Between him and the lights, monsters drifted back and forth, big scaly leviathans of the deep, with glowing escae before them and misshapen heads and limbs.

Above the monsters, but slowly drifting down, sank the tawny eye.

Adrian spun himself in the water, wishing he were more of a swimmer, and scissor-kicked to move downward. He reached out a hand, almost far enough to close his fingers around the eyeball, kicked again—

whumph!

Adrian squeezed half the air in his lungs out his nostrils as something piled into his back, hard. He closed his fist and felt the meaty orb of the eye pop out between his fingers and drift away.

Hands clawed at his back as he spun around, battering away fingers with his elbows and punching with his forearms at an angry face glowing green in the subaquatic light.

"You could have been great!" his uncle roared, and wrapped his fingers around Adrian's throat.

Huh? How was his uncle talking?

Adrian lost a little more air and struggled to fight back. He brought his knees up between the two of them, managing to get one of them against his uncle's chest. He pushed, and his uncle's sharp fingernails scratched his throat as they were knocked free of their grip.

Adrian turned, trying to find the eye. He could firebolt his uncle and end it once and for all. Or could he? Would Vulcan's Kiss work at all when submerged, he wondered? The water was heavy as well as cold, squeezing him in a death-grip like a python made entirely of ice.

He saw the eye and stretched out his hand for it.

"You won't get me a second time!" his uncle roared. He grabbed Adrian with long fingers, sharp with razor-like nails and more wolf-like every second. Adrian's suit tore under the pressure. It ripped away from his shivering body in great handfuls.

Adrian buffeted his uncle in the face, rocking the older man's body but not knocking him very far. How on earth was his uncle talking underwater? Adrian's lungs screamed at him for mercy, but he had none to give. He reached out for the eye again, and his uncle grabbed his throat once more.

"It's not so easy when I'm awake, is it?" his uncle snarled, his face inches from Adrian's own in the green shadowy soup. The darkness of inviting unconsciousness puddled at the edges of Adrian's vision like warm, sweet maple syrup, and he didn't know if it was his narcolepsy or imminent suffocation that threatened to take him away. At this point, it didn't matter.

His uncle dragged Adrian closer, jaws gaping wide to reveal long teeth that glinted yellow-green in the flashing lights at the bottom of Adrian's dream-ocean.

Adrian's uncle could change shape. He could survive a firebolt, be in two places at once. He could even breathe underwater.

It wasn't fair. Adrian didn't even have his own ka, he was crippled, and his nemesis was some kind of superman.

Something clicked deep inside Adrian's brain as he felt unconsciousness taking him. Hoping it was an epiphany, he struggled to focus on it. His uncle didn't have to play the normal rules of reality ... neither did the house. The house was a person, what person was it?

Was the house his uncle?

That made no sense. His uncle was dead.

Adrian stirred, batting aside a hand at his throat and jamming his fingers into his uncle's mouth. His uncle bit down, and Adrian screamed wordlessly in a column of air bubbles. The pain woke him up, at least for the moment.

Was the house him, Adrian?

That had a terrible, sick logic to it, and a hint of something that felt like the truth. Adrian had trapped himself and his friends—and their enemies—inside his own shadow, which took the form of a house that was the same as Adrian's own flesh. And his uncle was so flexible and fast and so impervious to the logic of physical space because his uncle was a creature of Adrian's shadow.

No, he realized. His uncle *was* his shadow, just like the house was.

He looked again at his uncle's face and found himself staring into his own eyes. Shadow-Adrian grinned mercilessly and opened his mouth to bite.

You're not real, Adrian thought.

The jaws clamped into his flesh and he thrashed, the water warming with the admixture of his own blood.

That wasn't right, Adrian realized. His shadow was real.

You're me, he corrected himself.

You're me, and you can't really hurt me unless I let you.

And I won't let you.

No, he told himself.

And suddenly, his uncle was gone.

Adrian hung stunned in the water, unsure of which direction was even up, for several long seconds. Through the warm, milky cloud of his own blood, he spotted the flashing lights again and realized that he was floating head-down.

His lungs still ached.

And there was the tawny eye, floating just out of reach. He kicked downward, reached out, and closed his hand around it.

The eye felt reassuringly material in his clenched fist.

But that was silly, of course. The eye might be something real, but it, too, was a manifestation of something in Adrian's own shadow. The tawny eye wasn't the Eye of Agamotto.

Whatever it was, though, it worked.

Adrian kicked and thrashed with his arms to right himself again, and looked up. He felt like he'd been fighting and sinking for eons, but a dark shadow above him, with a rectangular sliver of light in the middle of it, looked like it must be the floor of the attic—as if that made any sense—and it was almost within reach.

He clawed towards the light.

A face met him just below the doorway, a slit-nostrilled, fang-mouthed face, flat as a dinner plate and sloping backward to a tiny forehead. A jutting lower jaw trembled, pointing teeth like sabers at Adrian. Behind the face, a long body like a shark's or a whale's stretched out into the murk.

Adrian met the monster's gaze.

It opened its mouth.

"Piss off!" Adrian snapped, and then kicked up and into the attic past the puzzled, hesitating fish.

He should have been gasping for air when he broke through the jaw-pull-down door, but he wasn't. He hurt all over, though, and he was freezing.

"Adrian!" he heard Mike shout, and then the big bass player and Elaine Canning in her hoop skirt and big sleeves, plastered to her forearms by the cold water, grabbed Adrian by his collar and shoulders and dragged him out.

He was careful to pull his feet away from the edge, just in case the fish changed its mind.

"Adrian, how do we get out of here?" Mike asked.

"Is the moment come to fly?" Elaine added.

Rain and wind pelted his body and Adrian struggled up onto all fours. The attic roof was entirely gone and the attic floor floated on a turbulent, choppy sea like a raft of meat. Eddie, Twitch, and Jim battled the three Fallen, but with Semyaz's arms no longer occupied, they were being beaten back. Eddie took punch after punch to his shoulders and side from one of the angels, and especially to the raw and bloody place on his arm where Uncle-wolf had gnawed on the guitarist. Twitch could do little more than dodge the onslaught of attacks that came her way, slapping ineffectively back with empty hands. Only Jim had the strength and athleticism to get any punches in, hammering forward with fists and elbows, and occasionally throwing up a sharp knee. Even he was looking haggard.

"Yeah," Adrian agreed. "It's time to fly."

"Though what we do when we get back to the club is anyone's guess," Mike muttered. "Carajo, over there these guys are twenty feet tall."

"Yeah," Adrian said, reluctantly bringing the tawny eye up to his face, "but over there we aren't surrounded by a sea of ... whatever. So we get out of here, and we run like hell." A cold wave sloshed over him as he spoke, like punctuation.

Mike nodded.

"He who fights and runs away," Adrian said. It was a dumb saying, since he who fought and ran away more than likely just kept on running. His limbs felt like cold lead. "Though I'm sure you've heard that before, and don't give a rat's ass."

"Right now," Mike grinned, "I give every rat's ass I have."

Come on, Adrian told himself. This is all just in your head, and none of it can hurt you. He shoved the tawny eye into his eye socket. And screamed—

"Aaaagh!"—

and fell to the ground, clutching his head. Pain lanced him like bullets, his head forced the eye back out, and he bled. This isn't real, he told himself. It isn't physical. I don't have this much blood in my body. How can I still be bleeding, how can this even hurt me at all?

"Huevos," Mike muttered.

"What aid do you require, sorcerer?" Elaine leaned over him.

"That's it," Adrian laughed weakly, wiping blood from his face and trying to stand. "I need another sorcerer."

"Michael," she said to the bass player.

"Mike," he said. "Well, anything but Mikey ... Michael's fine."

She ignored him. "We have to free James."

James? "Jim?" Adrian asked. A flurry of blinking and a torrent of tears began to clear his eye.

"Follow me!" Elaine Canning turned and charged into the fight.

Shaking his head, Mike lumbered after her.

Adrian stared. The seventeenth-century woman hustled right past Jim and dove at the angel he fought. The angel tried to step sideways and ran right into Mike's tackle, and between the two of them they dragged the white, fist-throwing personage to the ground.

Adrian managed to get one foot under him and rise nearly to standing while Jim hauled off, kicked the fallen angel hard in the stomach, and then grabbed Adrian's elbow and helped him stand all the way upright.

"You look like hell," Adrian said, and Jim only laughed.

"We're in your shadow," he answered. "Can you make the Fallen weaker, or trap them?"

"I don't really have control," Adrian told the singer, "but I think I can get us out."

"What do you need?"

Adrian hesitated. "I don't know," he admitted. "With this eye in, I can see a line of energy running from me up into the sky. I think I can follow it and get us out, but the eye won't stay in my head anymore." He held the eye in his palm to show Jim.

"That's a weird damn sentence," Jim said.

"It's a weird damn experience."

"Is that the Third Eye?"

Adrian shrugged. "I don't know. Maybe an ... analog of it, or something? We're in my shadow here, so it's a version of some real thing."

"Affected by your experience and perceptions."

"Yeah." Adrian held the eye up and Jim took it from him. "Elaine seems to think you know some magic."

Jim pressed the tawny eye to his own socket. Strange as it was to push the thing into his own eye, it was stranger still to watch Jim's eye take the object. The singer's long-lashed eyelids slid forward like the two lips of a mouth and wrapped themselves around the bloody, squashed orb, sucking it in. Jim reeled back, a little unsteady, clenching his eyes shut.

Adrian looked nervously past the singer at the rest of the band. Twitch was down on the ground and Eddie stood over the drummer, fists up defiantly as two Fallen swung at him. He couldn't even block the punches now, but just shrugged into them, trying not to get knocked out or take the blows directly on his biggest wounds. The third Fallen stood, holding Mike by the throat and shaking him like a doll. Elaine Canning clung to his shoulders, biting and screaming, but it wasn't clear she was doing any damage.

Hurry, Adrian thought.

Jim straightened and his eyes opened. One was silver and the other was tawny.

"She's wrong," he said. "I'm no wizard. But I'll do what I can."

"Do you have the umbilical cord?" Adrian asked him.

Jim shook his head. "You do. And it doesn't come from your belly button, it comes out of your mouth."

Of course. "It's the string," he realized out loud. "The string I swallowed as a conduit to the ka-energy of the ward I was trying to hack into."

"So you can follow it back out." It wasn't a statement. It might have been an order.

"Yeah, I think so." Adrian wasn't as confident as he thought he sounded. "If I can see it or feel it."

"Here." Jim grabbed Adrian's hand and pressed it against his throat. Hand at his own Adam's apple, Adrian could feel a soft, warm vibration, like a battery-powered plush toy giggling faintly for the ten thousandth time as its battery died.

"Yeah," Adrian agreed. "Get the others."

He started chanting. Chalk would be good, but he had none in his pockets. Fortunately, he had plenty of his own blood, and in streaky red lines he began tracing some basic wards on the fleshy floor around him.

Eddie was on his knees when Jim hurled himself sideways into the angels attacking him. Adrian didn't know if the whole Cyrano de Bergerac story was true—didn't know what the story was with Elaine Canning, or how old Jim really was, or anything else—but the guy could *fight*. He spun horizontal like a log going down a river through the air. His boots kicked one angel in the face and with his hands he grabbed the long hair of the other and dragged it sideways with him into a muddle on the ground.

"Go!" Jim shouted to Eddie.

Eddie picked up Twitch and stumbled in Adrian's direction. The fairy bled from numerous wounds in her body, and Eddie looked like he'd been chewed on by a pack of dogs. Beyond them, Jim kicked one of the angels out of the way and then drew the other back by its hair to punch it in the face—

and paused.

He squinted at the Fallen's chest. He's seen the chest-plate, Adrian thought.

The third angel jumped Jim.

"Mike!" Eddie shouted. The guitar player tossed Twitch to Adrian's feet in a crumpled heap and lurched to grab the bass player.

Jim staggered sideways, punched in the temple, but Elaine Canning didn't abandon the singer. She lunged into the fray, grabbing the third angel's ankle and dragging it to the ground. Jim kicked that Fallen in the shoulder, flipping it over on its back and staring at its chest for a moment before one of the others grabbed him around the knees.

"Go!" he yelled, falling to the ground.

Adrian sucked in the cold wet air of the storm and tried not to think about even the possibility of passing out. He felt the warm vibration at his throat, visualizing it as the anchored end of the golden cord running into the sky, out of his belly and into the ward in the restaurant of the Silver Eel. He felt ka-energy under his fingertips, and coursing through his being.

"*Per Wepwawet Mercuriumque semitam sequitor*," he chanted, willing himself up the cord and into the Kansas City club.

"I love you!" he thought he heard Jim say.

He gritted his teeth, stayed awake, and passed from one storm into another.

CHAPTER NINE

SPLASH!

Adrian hit the water, deep as his waist, choking. Around him he heard more splashing, thuds and muffled curses. His body was too numb to feel the cold, but on his face the filthy flow felt like ice water, and burned his skin. His hands tightened convulsively as he bumped into the hard floor, and he was a little reassured to realize that he held the Third Eye.

Not the weird-dream meatball of the tawny eye, but the hard glass of his uncle's monocle.

Of Adrian's monocle, dammit.

He retched, gagged, and spit out the string running down his esophagus, then pushed up off the floor and arced out of the water, blowing grit and mud from his teeth like a porpoise emerging from a tank of sewage to spout out its blowhole. Around the rain- and river-blasted wreckage of the Silver Eel's restaurant, he saw others doing the same—the band as well as the three Fallen—everyone regaining his balance in the howling wind and sideways rain of the storm.

The dim and downward-pointing lights of the restaurant, even with a number of them shattered by the weather, were a relief from the shifting, psychedelic colors of attic-roof in Adrian's shadow. Also, none of them looked like bugs or body parts, so that was a serious improvement.

As Mike had predicted, the former angels were once again twenty feet tall and bestial. Semyaz didn't look quite as scary, though, flailing in a muddy soup like a naughty kid taking a bath in a puddle. Adrian almost laughed—

until he saw the headless body of Mouser, the club gopher. The corpse lay with limbs in broken-doll positions against a pile of restaurant flotsam, shattered tables and chairs, pulverized china, ruined table cloths, bits of mantisoid demon burnt extra-crispy, and other junk, all piled into a blockage at the top of the stairs leading down. It was an accidental dam, and Mouser lay dead on top of it. That was why the water in the restaurant was so deep, Adrian realized. He tried not to think about the girl.

Or Elaine. What had happened to Elaine Canning, who had helped him more than once?

Adrian saw his taser on the pile beside Mouser and picked it up.

"Run!" Eddie yelled.

"*STOP!*" Semyaz bellowed.

The Fallen sloshed to their feet, sending up colossal sprays of water.

Adrian snapped his monocle to his eye and threw a glance around the restaurant. The wards were gone, ruined. Probably their energy had been diverted into creating the shadow-trap Adrian had sunk them all into, but that was an academic question at this point. The wards were gone, so the band could leave.

Semyaz and Ezeq'el lunged for Jim at the same moment. He scooted between them, moving himself further away from the rest of the band and the stairs down. Fists pounded into the choppy water around him, and it looked like he was heading out the front door. Where's he going? Adrian wondered. The van is totaled, and the only one of us who knows how to hotwire cars is Mike. Does Jim think he can just outrun them on foot?

Adrian was close enough to help. He raised the taser and pressed its *fire* button.

Fitzzzz. Nothing.

"Hell."

Eddie charged towards Adrian. He jammed the Glock under one armpit and dug in his jacket pocket for shells as he ran, kicking up thick sprays of brown water. "Go!" he yelled, kicking Mike in the direction of the stairs.

"Where?" Mike wiped water from his face and followed. "Mierda, where are we going?"

"Anywhere but here!"

Twitch pushed into Adrian's face, snapping her fingers. "Are you awake, big boy?" the fairy asked him. Adrian felt the sexual allure of her Glamour and grinned. It was familiar and normal enough that it almost felt good.

"I'm awake," he said, and jammed the taser into his jacket pocket. "I'm trying to figure out if I should firebolt one of those big guys."

Together they turned and looked at the action. Jim didn't run out the front door; at the last second he slipped to one side and ran vertically up the steel doorframe, his speed carrying him forward and into the air like Jackie Chan on steroids, despite the fact that his boots were designed for other things and were also soaking wet.

Bull-headed Yamayol lurched forward, grabbing at Jim. He missed, and his barrel-sized fist punched through the steel of the frame, crumpling it—

but Jim was already kicking off and leaping away into mid-air, flying backwards and leading with his head.

Semyaz snapped with his tusks, and missed.

Jim completed a reverse somersault and came down on Ezeq'el's broad back. The centauress reared up, surprised, and rammed her own head and shoulders into the ceiling. Chips of concrete and a cloud of white dust exploded downward and were instantly swept into the flood by the wind and rain. Ezeq'el staggered sideways; Jim held his seat by virtue of having his two hands balled up in the long curls of Ezeq'el's hair that flowed wet down her back.

Adrian raised the Eye and tried to choose a target. He patted himself for the candle but couldn't find it; that would make the spell harder, more exhausting, but they couldn't leave Jim behind. For starters, Jim had the hoof.

"Can you help him?" Adrian suggested to Twitch.

"Can *you?*" the fairy countered, but she leapt forward into the wind, flapping her wings once and becoming the silver, horse-tailed hawk that was her avian form. She circled the fray, looking for an opening.

"Come on, dammit!" Adrian heard Eddie yell. "Jim knows what he's doing!"

"No man!" Adrian yelled, and looked for his open shot. *No man left behind* was a stupid thing to say. They weren't Marines, they were rock and rollers, and not very organized rock and rollers at that. But he hadn't come this far to leave Jim in the hands of the Fallen.

Besides, this was Jim's body, and not just his name and ba. And Jim's body had Azazel's hoof taped to its belly.

Yamayol jumped at Jim, swinging with both fists. Adrian winced, imagining the crushing pain that contact would inflict, and raised the Eye, taking aim at the bull's forehead—

but Twitch plowed into Yamayol's face, clawing at the bull's cheek and eye with her talons and emitting a high-pitched, piercing shriek.

Yamayol stumbled and missed. He fell heavily with his elbows on Ezeq'el's back and pushed her hindquarters down and into the flood. Ezeq'el slapped behind her with both hands. She shook her head, still a bit dazed from punching her head through the ceiling. Jim scrambled to his feet, clinging to her hair and writhing this way and that to avoid being caught.

"Crap!" Eddie yelled. He and Mike opened fire. They'd have to make a ridiculously lucky shot to do any real damage, Adrian thought. Mouser had already tried this and failed—and died for her trouble. Adrian deliberately didn't look at the dead club gopher.

What Jim needed was a little support from the band's big gun. That would be Adrian.

Semyaz charged, roaring. Adrian raised the Eye again, to fire at Semyaz—

Jim jumped. Narrowly avoiding both sets of giant arms grabbing for him, he hurled himself upward and into the porcine face of Semyaz.

Blocking Adrian's shot.

"Son of a bitch!" Adrian snapped. Darkness clouded the edges of his vision and his heart pounded loud in his ears. He shook off the creeping fatigue and focused.

Jim slammed into the Fallen's chest and Semyaz staggered back. Somehow, Jim held on—was he gripping the former angel by his chest hair? Adrian wondered—and rode the collapsing Fallen down like a surfboard on a tidal wave.

Then Yamayol whipped around, fist out like a tetherball. He bellowed like the monster that he was and his head scattered a halo of thick blood as he snapped in a circle—

POW!—

and punched Jim.

The singer sailed through the air in Adrian's direction. The wizard ducked and quickly shuffled to one side, and Jim splashed heavily against the dam of tablecloths, body parts, and restaurant furniture.

Right on top of Mouser's body.

"Huevos!" Mike yelled. The big guy had been taking cover behind the piled up debris, and Jim's landing soaked him again.

Twitch touched down immediately after Jim, and she and Eddie pulled the singer from the water.

"Downstairs!" Eddie barked. "The water's draining, so there must be a way out!"

"Water can drain through a toilet," Adrian pointed out reflexively, and regretted it. However bossy he was being, Eddie was probably right. There was probably a way out on the bottom floor, at the level of the river. Depending on how long the rain lasted, they might not have much time to take advantage of the fact.

Semyaz rolled in the water, regaining his feet. Yamayol wiped blood from his eyes and blinked to recover his vision, and Ezeq'el shook her head. They'd be after the band again in a moment.

"Hey," Mike said, and picked up something from the flotsam of the dam. It was Jim's sword, and he held it out to the singer.

Jim took his weapon and grabbed Adrian by the front of his jacket.

"Can you make wards of commanding?" he demanded.

Adrian hesitated. There was a crazy light in Jim's eyes, even crazier than his normal driven mania. "Sure," he said. "But there's no point, without the true name of the person being bound."

"Get downstairs," Jim snarled. "Do whatever you have to, and turn the downstairs into a ward of commanding. I'll give you as much time as I can, but that will be very little."

"What are you doing, Jim?" Eddie asked. "Let's run."

"I'm not leaving Elaine." Jim's skin was whiter than usual from the cold, and the veins in his temples and the cords in his neck stood out with the effort of speech. He turned back to the Fallen, who were lumbering in their direction.

"And the names?" Adrian said. "For want of a nail … you know." Jim was very tall, and his leaning over Adrian reminded Adrian of his own diminutive stature.

"Leave them blank," Jim told him. "And be ready."

He spun around and bounded back to the attack, sword slashing the air in front of him.

Elaine?

Adrian remembered something he'd glimpsed through the Eye earlier, so he held it up and looked again. It was still there: a pulsating red light on Semyaz's chest, in the shape of a rose. Elaine, when she looked like Mouser in Adrian's dream-shadow nightmare house of flesh, had been wearing pajamas with roses on them.

That was what the Fallen had come to try to barter with Jim. They had his lover, and were offering to give her back. Her presence in the … object on Semyaz's chest, whatever it was, had led to her being trapped in Adrian's shadow with the rest of them.

Adrian had a sudden sick feeling in his stomach that Semyaz's offer was probably really, really attractive to Jim.

No time to worry about that. He turned and ran.

Adrian climbed over the debris at the top of the stairs. On the other side, water poured down the steps in a shallower stream. He shivered from the storm's cold and dug with numb fingers in his pockets.

He had chalk.

The stairs zigged one direction, zagged the other and then the four of them sloshed into a short hallway lit by flickering fluorescent tubes. The water was up to Adrian's waist again, and he noticed with disappointment that the ceiling was plenty high enough for the Fallen to force their way through. Of course it was. *They'd* chosen the location for the trap.

"Mike," Eddie gruffed. "Wait here for Jim."

"Carajo," the bassist said. He snapped the clip out of his M1911 and pushed a few bullets into it. "Why me?"

"'Cause if it's you," Adrian joked, "at least you'll have your brother to keep you company."

"That ain't as funny as it must have sounded inside your head, man," Mike complained. "But maybe a good joke about your uncle would make us all laugh."

Adrian's shoulders drooped. Ah, hell.

"Yeah," he admitted. "Sorry."

"I'm the better sentinel, anyway," Twitch offered. They all looked like they'd been roughed up, but she looked the worst. The hurricane of wind and water weren't enough to wash away the blood from the wounds she'd received when she'd been smashed head-first into the concrete ceiling. Fairies were tough, Adrian thought. If he'd been in her place, he'd have left his brains behind.

"I wish you were better-armed," Eddie said, offering her his Glock.

"Why would a girl need to be *armed*," Twitch asked with a grin, "if she's *winged?*"

"Too much banter." Adrian started off down the hall, looking for a room. He needed to enclose all three of the Fallen in a single circle, if he could, and he didn't trust the smallness of the space. He pushed forward holding the chalk over his head in one hand and the lens in the other, and suddenly it occurred to him to wonder how he was going to inscribe a circle, when the floor was four feet under water.

The sloshing sound of his friends at his heels didn't reassure him. Whatever Jim had in mind, they were all depending on Adrian to get his part of it right. He breathed deeply, fighting back a constricted feeling in his chest. You're the big gun, he told himself. Be the big gun.

Then the hall ended in a large room, and his heart sank.

The ceiling here was lower than it was on the upper floors, but still might be fifteen feet high. It would cramp the style of the Fallen to fight under it, but they'd fit. That wasn't what made Adrian's heart sink, though; there were boxes floating in the water, boxes and shelves stacked everywhere. This must be the Silver Eel's stock room, he realized. However well-organized it might have been kept before, it was a disaster now. Soggy boxes of napkins and crates of frozen beef patties drifted around in the churning water like chunks of carrot in a stew of mud. Alcohol bottles puttered in circles like Sunday afternoon yachts, their labels slowly puffing up from the water. Shelves lay knocked over, with a folding ladder lying across the top of two of them. At the far end of the room, wind gusted in through shattered windows and a door that hung off its hinges.

The water didn't flow out of the stock room, it just eddied in a slow circle. Outside, the water was just as high, and Adrian saw the dingy white hulls of cheap boats drifting in the darkness and the fury of the storm.

"Crap." There were corpses outside, dead animals floating in the water.

"What?" Eddie asked.

"Jim wants me to draw a circle," Adrian explained.

"And?"

Adrian pointed around at the water, the tipped-over shelving and the drifting objects. "The floor isn't clear. Even if it was, I don't think I can really chalk underwater and expect it to stick."

"Can't you draw a circle with something else?" Eddie suggested.

Adrian shrugged. He felt defeated. "Sure. Like what? A line of rolled-up napkins?"

"Does the circle have to be on the floor?" Mike asked.

Adrian snorted his derision.

And then he thought about it. Did the circle have to be on the floor?

"Actually," he said, "I don't know."

He racked his brains. His uncle had only ever taught him to put circles—and other wards—on floors, of course. Preferably flat, smooth floors, because the more perfectly drawn the ward was, the easier it was to power it and therefore the more efficacious it could be. But a ward's influence was in three dimensions of physical space (as well as other dimensions more difficult to visualize), and Adrian realized that Mike's question was a good one.

Why not put the wards on the wall, for instance?

Only on the wall, it would be difficult to chalk a ward that would capture three beings the size of the Fallen. They would have to be within the physical capture area of the ward, after all, and a ward was active in the direction perpendicular to its plane.

"Like, a string, or something," Mike said slowly, looking around.

So the ward could be on the room's ceiling.

"You're a genius, Mike." Adrian patted the big guy on the back.

"*String?*" Eddie sounded skeptical.

"Nope." Adrian pointed. "The ladder."

"Ladder?" Eddie sounded even more skeptical. "Nope, I don't get it."

Splash!

The sound came from the hallway, and it was immediately followed by loud knocking and rumbling noises. That would be Jim hitting the basement hallway, Adrian guessed, and the Fallen coming down the stairs after him.

"Hurry!" he called. "I have to put the ward on the ceiling."

It would have to be quick and dirty, he thought, as Mike and Eddie grabbed the ladder and carried it over to him. Oh, well. Had he ever done it any other way?

"Hold me steady," he urged them, and climbed the ladder.

"Good thing you're a little guy," Mike grunted. He and Eddie strained, chest-deep in the water, but they raised the ladder and put Adrian right up against the ceiling.

CRUNCH!

Sounds of fighting came into the room from the hall.

"Steady," Adrian repeated, and he gestured with his arm to show the area he wanted to encompass. "And walk in the best circle you possibly can."

"Easy," Eddie said to the bass player. "This is just a little stroll in four-four time."

"Says the guy who always comes in early," Mike grumbled. They lifted the ladder and began moving in a wide circle. Metal clanged on concrete in the hall.

"Someday I'll play you a tambourine solo," Eddie muttered darkly. "That'll show you what real rhythm is."

"Sweet," Mike said. "Until then, don't give lectures on timing to the only guy in the band who has any."

"There's Twitch."

"I said *guy*."

"Twitch sometimes has boobs, Mike. That doesn't mean he isn't one of the boys."

Mike looked embarrassed, shut his mouth, and focused on his footing in the deep water.

Adrian chalked as quickly as they walked, inscribing the most perfect circle he could (it was terribly imperfect, maybe disastrously so, he worried) and framing it with suitable formulae in Akkadian and Doric Greek. The chalk was moist, which made it crumble alarmingly as he worked, leaving too much chalk behind on the surface of the ceiling and too little in his hand. He worried the chalk would run out entirely, but in the end it was enough, with a little left. Adrian ended his ward with a conduit on the wall, opposite the entrance, a tail that dropped down into a smaller circle, inside which he would have written the true names of the persons to be commanded.

Per Jim's instructions, he left this space blank, like the cartoon speech bubble of a mute.

"Hell," he muttered, as Mike and Eddie threw the ladder away. *SPLASH!*

Jim and Twitch burst into the room on the crest of a surge of water in the hall, Twitch in her horse form and Jim hanging around her neck, riding and swimming and paddling with his saber all at the same time. Behind them, something huge and heavy crashed through the passage, pushing water and debris ahead of it.

Bang! Bang! B-rap-p-p-p!

Eddie and Mike opened fire into the hallway entrance.

"Get back!" Adrian shouted, and they complied, crouching down behind fallen shelving to one side of the ward with the muzzles of their guns over the top and barking. Twitch transitioned from horse to hawk and swooped around, out of their line of fire, to join them.

Jim splashed straight to Adrian. His eyes took in the ward on the ceiling as he did.

"Chalk!" he snapped, holding out his hand. Adrian saw now that in his other hand, along with the saber, he held a few links of chain from which dangled a glittering glass bulb.

Adrian handed him what was left of the chalk, a soggy nub the size of his smallest pinky bone. "I admit I don't get it," he said. "What are you going to do?" He held up the Third Eye and looked through it to confirm his guess—seen through the Eye, the bulb was a pulsating red rose.

Elaine.

And then his jaw dropped, as Jim began sketching out characters inside the speech bubble.

"You can't ... you ... how can you do that?" he asked, fumbling for words.

CRACK!

Concrete dust and chips exploded in a cloud into the room, and the bull head of Yamayol thrust itself in through the enlarged entrance.

CHAPTER TEN

Jacob!" Yamayol bellowed. He pushed himself forward, his shoulders shattering concrete, and moved into the stock room. He stood, bent over like an adult inside a child's playhouse, but plenty mobile enough to kill them all. If anything, the lower ceiling emphasized the hugeness of the Fallen, and the great swinging car-sized enormity of their heads in particular.

Jim and Adrian huddled by the name-conduit of Adrian's warding, on one side of the room. Their band mates retreated warily towards the far side, holding their fire. Adrian watched Yamayol advance, trying hard to gauge his position relative to the ward in the ceiling without actually looking up, but it didn't escape his notice that Mike pocketed a small bottle of some liquor that floated past him as they moved.

"Jacob?" Mike snorted.

"Call me *Jim*." Jim tossed the bit of chalk aside with a wet *plunk*. He put his fingers inside Adrian's speech bubble, casually, like he was tired and leaning against the wall. He rested the wrist of his other hand on Adrian's shoulder.

Like an experienced wizard, establishing a conduit, but that wasn't the weirdest thing about what Jim had done.

"Jim." Adrian couldn't help himself. "Who the hell *are* you?"

"You know who I am."

"Do I?"

Behind Yamayol, Ezeq'el the centauress moved into the room. She looked less comfortable than the bull-headed Fallen, because she couldn't crouch at the knees at all. Instead, she bent forward even further at the waist and neck. Her arms were long, and her fingers nearly trailed in the swirling water.

"I'm Azazel's son." Jim had an irritated, wary look on his face. Adrian didn't know if the expression was play-acting for the benefit of the Fallen, or if he was really provoking a reaction from the singer. For his part, he really was astonished. "You surprised?"

"You shouldn't be able to read the Primals," Adrian pressed, in a whisper. "No child conceived in a human womb has been able to for thousands of years, not since the Confusion of the Tongues at Babel."

Semyaz ducked to enter the room. Ezeq'el drifted past Yamayol to make space for Azazel's boar-headed rival. She grimaced in discomfort, picked up the ladder from the soupy mess of the floor and leaned on it like a crutch.

Jim shrugged.

"Who was your mother?" Adrian pushed.

"Start the spell," Jim pushed back.

Adrian felt shaken. He had thought Jim was Azazel's son, and had assumed that his mother was a human, that Azazel had repeated back in Cromwell's day, or whenever it was, the naughtiness that had gotten him busted and demoted from the ranks of the angels in the first place. Had he been wrong to think that, being born of a human mother, Jim would be subject to the Confusion?

What other wrong ideas did he have about Jim?

Adrian started chanting. His ka, blessedly, was full and crackled with power, and he pushed the energy through his own body, through Jim's, and into the ward, whispering words of power.

"You've taken my amulet," Semyaz snarled. He stood smack in the center of the circle, and it took great effort not to look up at the chalk markings that comprised the ward. Adrian knew the circle was intact and functional without peeking, anyway; he could feel the ka-energy crackling back around to him, like the electricity in a closed circuit. The leader of the Fallen trio hunched low over the swirling waters, shoulders hunching massively above his own head, drool dripping from his tusks.

"You noticed." Jim slouched, like he was leaning on Adrian for support. He didn't break contact, and Adrian's ka-power continued to flow. Good man, Adrian thought. Just don't throw us under the truck, now.

"And what will you do with it?" Yamayol asked. "Whether you hold the bauble or Semyaz does, the bargain is still the same. The amulet only gives you a glimpse, just a taste of the joy that could be yours. You need our help to free your Elaine from Hell. We will give it to you."

Adrian chanted. He was counting on Jim to step in and say the names of the three Fallen at the climactic moment, but he was only guessing that Jim could speak the Primals—or whichever Primal it was, Adrian couldn't tell—as well as read them. He didn't know that for a fact, and though the room was freezing cold and wet, Adrian felt hot drops of his own sweat trickle down his back and under his arms. For that matter, Jim had denied being a wizard. Was he smart enough to understand Adrian's incantation and step in with the names at exactly the right point? Adrian shut out images of terror and defeat and kept mumbling.

Power. Everything came back to power.

"I don't need anything from you," Jim rasped back.

"Foolish!" Semyaz thundered, pounding both fists to the ground and sending up sprays of mud and soggy napkins.

The spell was nearly complete. Adrian didn't look up, and he didn't look into the Eye, though it weighed a ton in his hand. He chanted, wishing he'd been able to chalk a stronger ward.

"And if I did need your help," Jim continued, raising his head defiantly, "I'd rather die than ask for it."

"*Per Yahweh Sabaoth ego vos jubeo*—"

Semyaz roared in sudden realization of the deception. He lunged forward, hands open and grabbing—

Ezeq'el shouldered the boar-headed Fallen aside with her greater bulk and charged in, sweeping the ladder like a sword at Jim—

Jim shouted three words that Adrian could not clearly hear; they sounded like rushing water mixed with the sizzle of lighting—

ka-energy flared within and through Adrian, shooting into the ward at the moment that the Fallen rushed beyond its capture area—

wham! Ezeq'el's ladder slammed into Jim's chest, hurling him against the wall. The circuit was broken, Adrian staggered away and slipped.

He fell into the cold water.

He'd failed. Darkness swept over his head and veiled his eyes, his skin prickled like he was being hugged by a hundred hedgehogs, and he felt like throwing up. Time slowed for him, and as he drifted down, he used the honey-trickling moments to berate himself. He should have learned more. Maybe he should have stayed with his uncle longer, tolerated what had seemed so intolerable at the time just a little longer so that he could learn more. Maybe he could have drawn a better ward, stronger and less flawed so that the Fallen couldn't break through, or bigger, so they might have still been in its reach when his spell had gone off.

He hit the floor and bounced slowly back up. He couldn't tell if the ache in his chest was from lack of oxygen, or the harbinger of sleep taking him, or just pure regret and bitterness. His head broke the surface, gasping—

Jim was alone, beside the ward's name-conduit. He was bruised and filthy, but standing. In one hand he held his sword, and he looked down into the palm of the other with something like sorrow written on his face.

The world grew dark and Adrian felt himself sinking. Then Eddie was there, grabbing him by the collar of his suit and dragging him to his feet. The water was up to Adrian's armpits, until Eddie pulled him up onto some higher submerged footing. He felt numb and beaten.

He still had the Eye, though.

"Good job, Adrian," Mike said, patting Adrian on the back. "I think."

"Thanks," Adrian mumbled, unsure whether Mike was being sarcastic. "Is there a Plan B?" He looked around—the level of the water had almost reached the tops of the windows, but he could still hear the wind and the rain outside.

"How long can you hold your breath?" Eddie asked.

A bellow louder than a train whistle interrupted them, and they looked back to Jim and the Fallen.

"I told you not to hurt him!" Semyaz roared, turning on Ezeq'el. "If he dies, we waste our time!"

Ezeq'el backed away a step. "You waste your time anyway, Semyaz. You heard him. He won't aid you against his father."

"Won't aid *you?*" Yamayol rumbled. He had a bloody furrow up one cheek and the eye above it was swollen shut and purple. "Whom do you serve, horsewoman?"

"I serve Hell!" Ezeq'el cried. The drama of her declaration was undercut a bit by her hunched posture, but her voice rang loud and clear. "As you would *not* do, Semyaz! Ambition alone qualifies you for *nothing!*"

"You are Azazel's?" Semyaz roared and grabbed for a weapon in the water, coming up with a set of heavy metal shelving in both his hands.

Ezeq'el grabbed the ladder again.

"*Stop!*" Jim yelled.

The Fallen stopped. Their faces twisted into grimaces and snarls of anger, but they froze in their tracks.

"Son of a bitch," Adrian whispered. His body trembled with cold and also with excitement. "I did it."

"I don't believe Ezeq'el would serve Azazel's ambition any more than she would serve yours," Yamayol snorted, shaking his bull's head.

Ezeq'el was silent.

Jim touched his hand to the ward. "Tell us," he instructed her. It might have been the room, but the natural reverb in Jim's voice was even more pronounced than unusual. It gave his order such a hard edge that Adrian almost felt compelled to come forward and start saying true things.

The centauress's eyes burned holes in Jim and she spoke slowly, but she spoke. "You are Lucifer's weakness, Jacob," she said.

Mike hunched forward on the submerged artificial sandbar on which they perched, poking between Eddie and Adrian. "Can he just make them do anything he wants now?" he asked.

"He can't make them do anything they ain't already capable of," Eddie said.

"Says the expert," Adrian shot at him, and then regretted it. Eddie had pulled him from the water more than once today. "Sorry."

"Did he tell you to kill me?" Jim asked the centauress.

Ezeq'el struggled to clamp her teeth shut.

Eddie shrugged, but the noncommittal gesture was a challenge. "Am I wrong?"

Adrian shook his head. "You got it right. Also, Jim has to put ka-energy into the ward to give them commands."

"How much?" Eddie wanted to know. "How many commands?"

"It's like a genie and wishes," Mike said. It was probably involuntary, but as he said it he grabbed the liquor bottle inside his jacket.

"He didn't," Ezeq'el admitted to Jim. "I don't think he ever would. But Hell needs him, so Hell needs you dead."

Semyaz growled, a sound like a dumptruck revving up. Yamayol narrowed his one good eye and looked back and forth between the other two Fallen.

"I dunno," Adrian told them. "There's three of the bastards, and they're big and powerful, so I hope Jim doesn't waste his … wishes … on unimportant shit."

Eddie looked around at the wrecked stock room and laughed. "I ain't sure I know what's unimportant anymore."

Adrian harrumphed. "Anything that doesn't get us out of here is unimportant."

"You were trying to stop Jacob's quest?" Yamayol rumbled to Ezeq'el.

"Who is this chingón talking about?" Mike asked. "Who's Jacob?"

"James, Jacob, Jim," Eddie muttered. "Same name. *Mikey.*"

"Hey," Mike objected.

Ezeq'el somehow managed to look like she was throwing her head back proudly, even though she was huddled forward. She looked imperiously at Semyaz, and Adrian was happy not to be standing in the path of her hooves. "I came to stop *your* quest, Semyaz," she thundered. "I planned to do it by killing Jacob, so you couldn't use him against his father."

Semyaz bellowed and lunged—

"*Stop!*" Jim roared.

With a great splash, Semyaz lurched to a halt. He stood snorting and flexing his muscles.

"You cannot continue this forever, Jacob," he grumbled.

Wasn't that the truth? Adrian thought. The room's windows were now totally submerged, which meant that even if they dove down to get through them, they'd find themselves in the flooding river. He wasn't a bad swimmer in ordinary circumstances, but Adrian was tired, numb, and dispirited, and he didn't really want to drown.

Eddie read his mind. "Let's get out of here, guys," the guitar player whispered, and pointed towards the stairs.

Then Jim started talking gibberish.

It couldn't really be gibberish, because it would take an idiot savant to spew out that much nonsense without missing a beat, but Jim said—shouted—long strings of syllables that not only meant nothing, but were hard to hear.

It was like they slid around Adrian's eardrums without quite making them vibrate. Or the sound waves made his eardrums vibrate, but they distorted the result, so what Adrian heard sounded slippery. It sounded forgettable, and even as Jim was talking, Adrian instantly lost the words.

"Son of a bitch," he gasped, splashing softly into cold, muddy water and dog paddling behind Mike towards the flooded hallway. Jim was talking to the Fallen in one of the Primals. He'd have given an arm in that moment to be free of the Confusion himself, and felt intensely envious.

And a little frightened.

Eddie didn't wait for the singer. He led them swimming up the hall, over unseen debris that Adrian felt with his kicking toes and past assorted floating body parts of the six-limbed creatures that had attacked them in the bar.

At the stairs, Adrian dragged himself out on all fours and climbed to his feet again, teeth chattering. Mike gave him a hand up and he nodded a quick thanks.

"There's no van," Adrian told the others.

"Screw the van," Eddie snorted. "It was junk, anyway. I want my shotgun."

"Someone could ride Twitch," Mike suggested, and then blushed. "I—"

"Oh, yes?" Twitch smiled a smile that was haggard but sweet at Mike. "You *what?*" Not waiting for an answer, the fairy shook her arms to throw off water, then jumped into the air and into her falcon form. With a snap of her broad wings, she propelled herself up the stairs.

"I was thinking you could hotwire a car," Eddie suggested. He pushed himself forward into a dogged jog up the steps, his combat boots kicking up cold water at every step. Adrian and Mike both lumbered after him.

"Yeah, let's do that," Mike jumped to agree.

"Let's do it *fast*," Adrian amended the plan. "I don't know what Jim's up to, but I'm afraid it might not go well."

At the top of the stairs, Adrian forced himself to look at Mouser's headless body. She had been a good comrade in arms, he thought, and then realized he was confusing the club's gopher and Jim's three-hundred-years-dead girlfriend. *Elaine* had been a good comrade in arms, he thought, sloshing through the wind and the flood of the wrecked restaurant towards the street. *Mouser* had been a kid with cool toys, in over her head.

A distraction. She'd been a good one.

Outside, the rain continued to fall, but it came down now as a slackening drizzle. Eddie dug his shotgun out of the wreckage, and boxes of shells.

"What about the instruments?" Mike asked.

"Itching to practice a little more bass guitar kung fu, are you?" Adrian grinned at Mike, and the big guy laughed.

Eddie shook his head, looking up and down the street. The Silver Eel sat among other large buildings, former and current warehouses, factories and other big commercial properties. In the storm, no one had noticed the destruction going on inside the club, and apparently everyone inside had been killed in the initial attack on the band. There were lots of cars of various sorts parked in front of the Eel, including a beamer or two, but Eddie nodded at a beat-up Ford Windstar.

"Really?" Adrian laughed out loud. "We got our pick of rides, and you want the only one that would be a trade *down?*"

Eddie shrugged. "We all gotta fit," he pointed out, and continued digging in the ruin of his old van for things to salvage. "We can't commit ourselves to having to fill two tanks."

Mike moved over to the minivan. "It ain't even locked," he told them. "Huevos, some people. This'll be easy."

"Good." Eddie jammed stuff into his pockets, and Adrian joined him, trying to find his decks of cards, nicotine gum, and the other miscellaneous objects he kept in the back seat. "Assume we have less than a minute."

Twitch swooped down out of the darkness and lessening rain, touching down in her human drummer form. "Jim's coming," she said.

Eddie pumped his Remington shotgun. "Alone?"

The fairy laughed. "He sent them packing, our boy did."

Adrian felt a profound pang of disappointment. Somehow, Jim had banished three of the Princes of Hell. Not *somehow*, Adrian thought, he did it *using my spell*. Still, the fact that the final moment of the face-off had taken place outside of Adrian's presence made him feel cheated.

Even though he probably wouldn't have understood a word of what passed between Jim and the Infernals.

The Windstar groaned into life. The passenger side window slid down smoothly at the touch of a button by Mike. "At least we won't have to crank the windows manually anymore," he called.

"Shall we get the instruments?" Adrian asked.

"No."

The answer came from Jim. He stood in the wrecked doorway of the Silver Eel, a big, broad-shouldered silhouette against the light, naked sword in his hand.

"We gonna rob filling stations for cash, then?" Eddie asked. "Chicago's a ways away, still."

"We're not going to Chicago," Jim said.

"What the hell?" Eddie demanded. "We come all this way, and you go and give the hoof to the first pig-headed giant who asks *pretty please?*"

Jim raised his shirt, showing the bands of duct tape that still held the fragment of his father's hoof there. "Hell knows we're coming," he said, stepping out into the rain. "We'd better take a short cut."

Adrian couldn't hold his curiosity and uncertainty in any longer. "Jim, what happened back there?" he almost exploded. "What was that?"

Jim arched his eyebrows at the wizard. "What was what?"

Adrian didn't know where to start. "You're a sorcerer."

"No." Jim shook his head. "But I've spent a lot of time around them. Enough that I knew when to jump into the spell."

It was Adrian's turn to raise his eyebrows. "Enough to be able to read, write, and speak Adamic?"

"What Adamic?" Jim laughed lightly. "That was some Old Occitanian. France has turned out more than a few decent witches and wizards in her day."

Adrian didn't believe him for a heartbeat. Should he play along? "Which you learned ... by hanging around wizards," he asserted.

Jim nodded, and clapped his hands once. "Our shortcut's going to mean no instruments," he said, "but if you left anything else you want in the building, now's the time to get it."

"And Elaine?" Adrian tried to catch Jim's eye.

Jim stared back levelly, and nodded once, slow and deep. "We'll get Elaine," he said.

"How about the van?" Mike asked.

By way of answer, Jim stepped forward and smashed the side view mirror off the minivan with the pommel of his sword. He picked the mirror up and showed it to the bass player. "This is all we'll need from the van," he said.

"Oberon's teats," Twitch cursed.

"I thought Oberon was the male." Mike frowned as he got out of the van.

"Sometimes, Mike," the fairy said with an affectionate smile, "you have a very limited imagination."

"My pistol," Adrian said. And nicotine patches, and gum. He felt good, in ways he couldn't quite put his finger on, but he had no confidence that he wouldn't fall unconscious the next time he came under pressure. He still needed to undo his curse, still wanted power, was still looking to deal with the devil.

"You're definitely going to need a gun," Jim said. He grinned, but Adrian knew he was keeping secrets, and that made the grin seem less friendly.

"Some things never change," Eddie grumbled. "Come on, I'll help you find your shit."

"It isn't shit," Adrian said, but he followed Eddie into the devastated club.

With the Fallen gone, the Silver Eel was transformed from a menacing trap, a mouth of steel, concrete and storm, into a simple wreck. Adrian picked his way among shattered timbers and severed mantis-demon limbs, hearing a fire truck siren start up somewhere in the city. "Maybe we could get something to eat in the kitchen before we leave," he suggested to the guitar player. "Who knows when we might get our next safe meal?"

"Sure," Eddie said. "That's a good idea. They might not have eggs blessed by the Dalai Lama here, though."

Adrian's stomach rumbled.

"Steak," he said. "I was thinking maybe a nice ribeye."

ROCK BAND FIGHTS EVIL #5

THIS WORLD IS NOT MY HOME

CHAPTER ONE

"Y ou're not thinking of trying to get past Herself, are you?" I ask Jim Throat.

The big guy laughs. He's strapping his sword on him like a knight, like you don't see on the Outside anymore except in pictures and parades. "We're late, Twitch, and out of options."

"Late?" I ask. I'm up to my knees in floating wreckage. We all are. It's hilarious, and it doesn't feel like we're *late*. It feels like we're *too late*. The joke's been told. Not only has it been told, but it beat the stuffing out of us all in the telling. My head hurts, I have blood in my hair, and, judging by the scrapes, bruises, and blood on the others, I might have got off easy from our encounter with the boar-headed Prince of Hell, Semyaz, and his thugs in the Silver Eel.

"The equinox," Jim says. "The Liminal Year." I'm not sure what he means. "If you have a better plan, now's the time to tell me."

Adrian Keys already has stuff in his pockets, but he's cramming in more. There's the Eye he has no idea how to use and candles and string and maybe a dead mouse. And that gum he's always chewing. He's got nice breath, Adrian.

"I don't think I can think of a better one," I admit, "but aren't I allowed to feel sad that our choices are so few?"

"Just don't cry," Eddie Guitar grunts. Eddie has one bad eye, and it slides off in the wrong direction as he's talking. He's got stuff in his pockets too, but it isn't wizard-stuff—no dead mice. It's pocketknives and wire and bullets. In his hands he has his long boomer. "You mean Mab, I guess?"

"Close. Only much worse." I have my fighting sticks; that's all I need. We all wade through the ruined restaurant and bar, picking up our stuff after taking a serious beating from some of the major Fallen. There are dead bodies all around, and parts of dead bodies. Some of them look human. The Infernals are funny, all right, though I sort of feel like I'd like to hear a new joke now and then.

"Stop!" says Mike Bass. He's the big one, and the way he's shoving candy bars and booze into his pockets, he plans on getting bigger. "Just for once, can't somebody tell me what's going on ahead of time?"

Jim Throat nods at me. I guess he's done speaking, and no wonder, if we're going to have any stealth in our approach. I don't know if it's true that Jim's father can hear him talking, but Jim seems convinced of it.

"Sure," I say. "There's a special road our Jim here wants to walk, a very old one. We're going to have to go through the Mirror Queendom to get to it, and we'll have to deal with the guardians. The biggest of the guardians is Herself."

"What road?" Eddie asks.

"Guardians?" Mike adds.

"Creatures that will try to stop us. Herself, for instance, is a sort of reptile. The road is the Crossroads. It's the oldest road, and one of the fixed points of the Queendom."

"*Herself* is Rahab the dragon," Adrian Keys says. Adrian always knows just enough to get himself in trouble, and a good deal less than he thinks he knows.

"Dragon?" Mike Bass asks. "Like Sleeping Beauty?"

"Like Isaiah," Eddie Guitar mutters. "Art thou not it that hath cut Rahab, and wounded the dragon?"

"*Cagado,*" Mike says. "That sounds bad."

"Nah," Adrian tells him, snapping the chewing gum in his mouth, "it's cause to be optimistic. It's a dragon who can be killed."

"Wounded," says Eddie. "And it doesn't even say wounded *how bad*."

"That's right, big fella," I say to Adrian. "It's cheerful."

Mike looks at me with that hurt look, so I show him udders. It's funny to see him go all red in the face and confused.

"No, it ain't," says Eddie. He stuffs even more boomer shells into the pockets of his jacket, which has the sleeves ripped off it. "Rahab was wounded by the Arm of the Lord. Which we ain't got."

"Thanks," Mike mumbles. "That spark of hope I was feeling disoriented me. I needed someone to kill it."

"'And Miriam the prophetess, the sister of Aaron, took a timbrel in her hand,'" Eddie says. "'And all the women went out after her with timbrels and with dances. And Miriam answered them, Sing ye to the Lord, for he hath triumphed gloriously; the horse and his rider hath he thrown into the sea.'"

"'Song of the Sea,'" Adrian says. "The song of Heaven's triumph over Rahab the chaos dragon."

"What's a timbrel?" Mike asks.

"Go to hell," Eddie tells him.

"Don't feel bad," I say to Mike. I swish my tail to be shiny for the big guy. "If we die, we'll all die together."

Jim holds up the mirror in his hand. I hiss, already feeling the Push against my body, but I don't show it. I'm not really sure I'll be able to get to the Crossroads, but it sounds like a good plan, so I'll try.

I still don't know quite what Jim's hurry is.

"I guess you know the way?" Eddie Guitar asks me.

Ah, Eddie. Always wanting to be sure everything is under control. And the great big fat joke on you, Eddie, is that nothing is ever under control. "Of course."

Adrian says a short incantation and touches the mirror. It opens. I feel the Push immediately, like hands all over my body scratching and punching me and trying to throw me away. The Push makes me feel sad. And lonely.

I try not to let my face show anything. The others won't be able to feel the Push because they're humans, or whatever they are, and not Outcasts. There aren't many Outcasts. You have to really make Mab angry to get thrown out. And if you make her too angry, she just kills you. It's a fine line.

Jim doesn't wait. He grabs the hilt of his sword and steps through. At least he doesn't actually draw it; the Rangers will look on us with enough hostility without our actually having bared weapons in our hands.

"Once more unto the breach," Adrian mumbles. "Et cetera."

Mike Bass is breathing hard. "Keep your eye on the ball, Mike," Eddie tells him, patting him on the shoulder. "We're just passing through, and the destination ain't far."

"That reminds me," I tell them both, and also Adrian. "Don't eat anything." I show them a boy, because I don't want to distract Mike so much that he misses my words. Though that might be very funny.

"Why not?" Mike asks. "Is it poison?"

It is definitely funny to leave him hanging. I fight against the Push and step through the mirror into the Outer Bounds.

In the moment of transition, I spare a tiny thought for Pulse. Is he where I left him? I wonder. He must be. He's probably been laughing his head off without stop since we parted ways.

The light changes immediately. From the weaving, unnatural blue light of the long, skinny bulbs in the bar, it switches to the patchy gloom and dull glow of the Outer Bounds, shafts worming through the darkness from every direction and intersecting in a beautiful yellow-white lattice like a spider's web stretching forever in all directions. It's not home, but it's closer to home than I've been in a long time, and I'm going to get closer still.

I feel ... sort of excited.

Two of the Queen's Rangers are already there, leather on their bodies and their legs, tree-and-lightning-bolt symbol on their chests, and weapons in their hands. I know them, and if I didn't, they'd know me.

"Outcast!" hisses the larger one. He's showing a bear, but the tail hanging off his rump might belong to an iguana the size of a horse. Well, getting called names tends to dampen my enthusiasm just a bit. Even if they're technically correct.

"Buzz," I nod to him, and then to his companion. "Flit."

Adrian enters the Outer Bounds behind me, and we both step cautiously aside. We have to make room for Mike and Eddie to join us.

Flit's showing girl to everyone, but she has her fox's tail. Anyway, I'd know her by her face. "You came back once, Twitch Pony," she says. "Mab let you off that time. You shouldn't have come back again."

I shrug, because what else can I do? "Fine."

The Rangers both raise their spears and point them at me. The spears are sharpened wood, so I keep a careful eye on them.

"Fine?" asks Buzz Bear. "We have to kill you."

They both hop from one foot to the other where they stand. They're nervous about Jim. He glares at them, then leans back to rap hard against the mirror out of which we've just stepped.

"You, though," Flit says, pointing her spear at Jim. "You come with us."

Eddie Guitar slides through the gate. He pumps his boomer as he steps into the Outer Bounds and puts on an I-mean-business face. He looks around at the staircases arching overhead and the shafts falling through the floor and the passages that seem to bend away and come back to the same point before Outside geometry would permit them.

"No one's actually shooting at us," he says. "That's nice for a change."

"*Yet*," says Adrian. "Give them a minute."

Mike touches the ground immediately at his shoulder. Mike has his shooter out, too. "I've seen you eat ... human food," Mike says to me. "Why can't I eat ... uh, fairy food?"

The gate closes behind Mike.

"I had to get used to it," I tell him. "The first thing I ate was a Chocodile, and I thought I was going to die."

"No!" squeals Flit Fox. "You don't have a minute, and you can't eat! Abandon the Outcast and the half-devil and get out of the Mirror Queendom."

They know who Jim is. They're scared of him, but they want him.

And they're hesitating. I guess it's because they worry about the Outsiders I have with me. As they should. My Outsider friends aren't just any ordinary companions; they're a rock-and-roll band.

I show the falcon, and I spring high into the air. I find a stone lintel that juts out far enough, and I perch on its edge. The Outer Bounds around me wheeze and scuttle, making the slow groaning sound that comes from so much stone shifting on its thousand, thousand axes.

Flit shows a swallow, and with two flaps of her wings, she joins me on the lintel. It's wide, too wide to be comfortable because Flit shows girl again and points her spear at me. It's lethal, that wood is, not blunted by Outsider hands and smelting. I ease out my fighting sticks and show Flit my teeth. She shows hers back. It might be romantic, except that we're armed and we both mean business.

"We're too many," I say to Flit. "Don't even try it. Do you want to be hurt?" I mean it. I don't want to injure Flit Fox or any of Mab's Rangers. I'm in enough trouble as it is. I just want to get through as quickly as I can.

Flit fidgets. She waits, keeping her spear between us.

Below us, Buzz roars. He lunges forward on all fours, teeth snapping.

Jim is ready for him. The tall singer steps to one side, and he avoids the easy mistake. He leaves his sword at his belt and just kicks Buzz in the muzzle. When Buzz yelps and falls forward onto his face, Jim Throat grabs him and drags him across the chamber. It doesn't pay to underestimate Jim.

Flit stabs at me, and I catch the spear. "Wrong move," I tell Flit, and then I show her the pony. I kick with my rear legs, knocking her wings-over-tail off the lintel. The spear falls clattering to the floor and I fall with it. I slow my fall by showing the falcon and glide to a landing showing girl. Easy. I'm very good at this.

"*Caray,*" says Mike. He's right. This is not a promising start.

Jim throws Buzz Bear down a hole in the floor and waits. When Buzz reappears two seconds later at the edge of the well,

showing lizard and frantically scrabbling for a grip, Jim pounds the
Ranger in the snout with a clenched fist. He knocks Buzz spinning
back down into the well.

"And stay down!" Eddie snorts. He's still standing with his
boomer, looking tough.

"You won't escape the Rangers, devil's son!" Flit Fox yells, and
zips out of sight under a low arch. Her warning is unnecessary.
Buzz's roar has already alerted all the Rangers in earshot, and that's
likely to be very many of them. Flit will be back, and she won't be
alone.

"Which way?" Adrian asks me. He could probably figure it out
if he had to, he's clever enough with languages and magic spells
and secret stuff, but as it happens, I know where to go.

"In," I tell them, and I cut past two false hallways and into a
doorway that they don't see. It's showing wall, but I know it's a
door, and I step right into it.

"Damn," Eddie mutters, but he's smart enough to follow me.

Mike Bass's teeth chatter as he steps in through the door.
"This Rahab," he asks. "Is it in the Moses half of the Bible?"

"Why do you care?" I ask. Silly book. All books are silly, vain
attempts to put pins through reality to make it hold still, when it
won't, might as well pin water to a board. But any book written by
someone who's that desperate for you to see him as the hero, well,
you know it won't be trustworthy.

Mike puts his hand in the pocket of his leather jacket. He's
holding on to one of the bottles he picked out of the wreckage of
the restaurant, I guess. "Dunno," he says. "Everything from the
Moses half just seems meaner."

"If you're hoping someone's going to tell you that Rahab's a
big softy," Eddie says, chewing his words because he thinks
they're so good, "it ain't gonna happen." Even here, his bad eye
slides to the side every few minutes. He sees visions, Eddie does,
and they aren't happy ones.

"I'm just hoping that one thing, for once, will turn out to be
easy."

Adrian laughs. "You're in the wrong band."

I lead them past three archways, each taller than the last. They look tempting, with light spilling down from windows high above into broad courtyards, and I can smell cinnamon, but I know they're traps. I know this place. Besides, I can hear the breathing, and the echoing thumps of feet and paws.

Instead I turn sideways to edge through a crack in the wall. Three arm-lengths in, it opens up, and I find myself standing on a wide mezzanine. A stone balustrade keeps me from a long drop, and stairs roll down, double-wide, to the floor below. Beyond the stairs are a chasm in the floor and a bridge across it.

Massed on the stairs are a dozen Rangers. They crouch fiercely, protected by layers of leather and a bristling wall of wooden spikes.

Flit Fox is one of them. She stands slightly behind the others, raising her spear and pointing it at me.

"Twitch Pony!" she cries. "Outcast! Surrender now!"

Here we go. I ignore her because of the silly things she says. Instead, I show them the falcon and leap into the air.

A rattling storm of wings shakes the Outer Bounds, and many of the Rangers follow. Rooks, starlings, thrushes, mockingbirds, and even an owl fight among themselves for airspace, snapping after me. The room behind me sounds like an enormous cloak having the dust shaken out of it by its giant owner.

I swoop close to the wall, where ornamental columns are staggered in climbing rows. Their pedestals and capitals are leering skulls, stone flames in their eyes and tongues lolling over their crumbling teeth. I'd laugh if I weren't so occupied. Instead, I show girl, kick my heels into the forehead of one of those skulls, and take my fighting clubs into my hands as I spring back at my foes.

This surprises them. I laugh and lay about me, *thump-a-ta-thump-thump!*, a basic, bouncy little rhythm, and Hop Badger tumbles out of his badger-tailed crow showing, hitting the ground with a heavy thud as I land beside him on my toes. I roll forward with the fall, ignoring Hop's groans, and swing around me again. Another of the Queen's Rangers falls, clutching her head, and then I show the falcon once more. I flap my wings and push through a descending hail of feathers to head in the opposite direction, ceilingward, past and beyond them.

Mab's Rangers mostly train to fight Outsiders who get lost and lucky, or terribly unlucky, depending on your point of view, and accidentally come into the Outer Bounds. Outcasts are rare, and Outcasts who try to return are rarer still. The Rangers are well armed, but they're not really ready for me.

They're not really ready for Jim Throat, either. As I swoop above the staircase, owl pecking at my long tail, I see that Jim's taken Flit Fox's spear away from her. He's beating the Rangers around him with it, the wood bruising them where steel would be unable. He could easily be stabbing them with the poky end, so the fact that he isn't means he's deliberately holding back. He doesn't want to anger Mab and Oberon, maybe. The Rangers reassemble showing birds and swarm back at him, but then Eddie Guitar is at Jim's side, raising his weapon.

BOOM!

It's a loud gun anywhere. Inside this stone chamber, it's enough to wreck one's hearing. The slug tears through the cloud of flying Rangers. If they were normal birds, they'd be on the stone and dying, but because they're really Mab's children, instead they're knocked back in the air, leaving Jim free to keep wreaking havoc with his borrowed stick.

Adrian and Mike come up at the rear. The big guy keeps poking Adrian in the ribs, which probably means he's trying to stop the wizard from falling asleep. Adrian doesn't sleep more than other men. He just sleeps at all the wrong times, poor boy. He's looking through the Eye, muttering as he does, and clutching his bit of candle wax. I'll have to stay out of his way if I don't want to get my tail singed. When he comes through, Adrian comes through in a big way.

Jim crashes down through the Rangers. He looks all wrong, wearing his jeans and his loose, long-sleeved shirt almost like a tunic or a blouse. He looks out of place, but he rolls through the Rangers like the Juggernaut. He hits the bottom of the stairs as I circle around the mezzanine again, landing and showing the pony.

Buzz Bear is at the top of the stairs. He's decided to leave the Outsiders alone and face me. He's bruised about the face and his tail is kinked, which is probably why he looks so unhappy.

"You don't belong here anymore, Pony," Buzz growls. "Can't you see that?"

He stabs at me and I rear up, lashing out with my front hooves. I knock him back a pace or two and then for good measure I kick out backward, too. I don't know what I hit, but it yelps.

I quickly switch to showing girl and flash my teeth at him, waving my fighting sticks in invitation. "Why not, Buzz?" I ask him. I spin around and poke Amble Owl in the throat with one of my sticks. He goes down with gargle. Others are with him, and I pound one or two and then spin aside, getting under Buzz's next attack. I throw him into his friends and retreat to the top of the stairs.

"Look at what you're doing!" Buzz's face is purple, he's mad. "You're invading the Queendom!"

"No, I'm not," I say, and I mean it. I borrow Eddie's words. "I'm just passing through. Stay out of my way, and no one will get hurt."

But they aren't getting in my way, not most of them. Most of them are trying to pile on to Jim Throat. I see from the top of the stairs that I've only distracted a few of them, and the rest are after him.

Maybe it's because he's in front, I tell myself, and I take a few quick swipes at Buzz. He shows bear and snaps at me with really big teeth, but I'm too quick for that. I show falcon in a split second, and a flap of my wings takes me over his head. I show boy against the wall and kick off against it, pounding Buzz in the face with my fighting sticks. Girl is more acrobatic, but boy has stronger arms. Buzz is not going to feel good tomorrow.

But maybe it isn't that, after all. Maybe all they really want is Jim.

I shove a stick down Buzz's craw, forcing him back, and I point down at Jim with the other. "You'll never get it, you know," I say to him. "It's his by right, really. Best give up now and get out of our way."

The light in his eyes tells me Buzz knows what I'm talking about. It also tells me he isn't happy, so I show girl and jump back to the balustrade. He lunges, still showing bear. That's a fierce form, all right, with lots of teeth, but I leap high into the air and he misses.

I flip backward. It feels good, so I flip right back over the balustrade and show falcon so I can glide to the ground. Buzz Bear and Amble Owl poke spears at me, but they miss. While they've been drilling in the Queendom's gardens and throwing out wandering apprentice wizards like so many bouncers, I've been dodging Zvuvim and the Fallen. They're no match for me.

They might be a match for Jim, though. Only because there's an awful lot of them.

He charges into a knot of Rangers on the narrow stone bridge. More Rangers rush him from behind, and I see Mike and Eddie ducking out of the way as Adrian raises a handful of his pocket trash.

I show falcon and veer to the side.

"*Per Volcanum ignem mitto!*" Adrian shouts. That one's his favorite. It's big and showy, and it packs a real kick.

A gout of flame explodes out of his candle and the Eye. It knocks down several of the Rangers, and they don't get up. Most of the others run, scattering with singed tails in all directions. My own tail feels warm, and as I land on the far side of the chasm, I check it; its tips are black and crisp.

"Mab's pointy teeth!" I snap.

Adrian has done well, and so now he crumples over. Mike has him by his shiny silver jacket and is trying to keep the wizard from falling into the chasm. That's good, this is a deep one, and Adrian Keys doesn't have a flying form to show. He's more of a stand-in-place-and-draw-circles sort of wizard, who can once in a while let fly a good bang.

I show falcon and cross to the bridge to help. I land showing pony and whinny to get Mike's attention. Mike slings Adrian across my back and steadies him.

Behind me, the Rangers regroup. I hear Eddie pay them some close attention.

BOOM! BOOM! BOOM!

The boomer won't kill them, not unless Eddie's loaded in some strange ammunition, but it'll sting, so they'll duck and try to stay out of the way, and if they get hit they'll be knocked back. I move forward. Adrian's snoring body on my back makes me more aware of the Push that continues to operate against me, shoving at me with every step. It'll get worse once we're out of the Outer Bounds, and again I wonder about my ability to actually get to the Crossroads like Jim plans.

I snort to show I don't care, and I follow Jim.

He slams one Ranger's head against the floor and then flings her into the air. The Ranger shows dazed whooping crane and sags in a descending circle over the crevasse before she manages to crumple onto the stone floor behind me. Jim kicks another Ranger who isn't so lucky and shows basset hound as he goes yipping down into the darkness.

For just a moment, the way ahead is clear.

But then I hear a terrible buzzing sound.

CHAPTER TWO

Nuts!" Eddie barks.

"Again?" Mike Bass asks. "I thought we lost that guy in New Mexico!"

"Might not be the same one." Eddie pumps his boomer.

"How does that make me feel better?"

"Making you feel better isn't my job," Eddie growls. "I just book the gigs and play the chords."

Jim Throat strides out onto the far side of the bridge. Before him is a row of arches, each coming down in a tip like a stalactite, melting and flowing into a stalagmite base rising from the floor. Behind the arches are open passageways, and whipping up one of those is a cloud of flies.

Really big flies. Flies the size of large dogs. With clacking metal mandibles.

"Mab's belly button." We've seen these things before.

Jim draws his sword, and about time.

I realize I'm last, and I look over my pony shoulder. Hop Badger and Amble Owl and the others are regrouping. There's no time to waste.

"This way!" I call to the band. They hear it just as a whinny, but they must see me flashing past and racing into a narrow, shadowed corner of the portico. It doesn't look like a passage because it isn't lit, but I know it's one anyway. I race into the darkness, careful not to let Adrian fall off my back.

I hear pounding feet behind me, which must be the band—they all run too heavy to be any of Mab's folk, and the flap of wings is distant and behind them. Then I hear *BOOM, BOOM, BOOM* and *BANG, BANG*, and the noise is thunder, so loud that the walls of the passage shudder, trying to cover their ears.

Ahead there's an exit. I'm no expert in things Infernal—if I were, I'd have known about their inability to take a joke, and I might have avoided my Gigantic Colossal Mistake and still been welcome in the Queendom. But I remember that Zvuvim are creatures of darkness. They can't take daylight, it melts them right into nothing. Their master-spawner, the Baal, doesn't like it either.

Adrian could get us some light, he's done it before, but he's asleep.

Still, I know the way out. And in the Queendom, it's always day.

Ahead of me is a spiral staircase. I need to get on it and head down, but four Queen's Rangers suddenly come racing up from one side and array themselves in front of me. Two of them show bobcat and raccoon, which don't worry me much. But the others show ape and rhinoceros, and unless I get very lucky, I'm not going to be able to just run past them.

But I decide I'd better try.

I don't want the ape to wrap its arms around me, nor do I want the rhino's horn in my flank. I aim between them, hoping that neither one of them will be able to stop me. Behind me is all *BOOM, BOOM* still, and I lower my head, scraping against the rhinoceros and feeling my side abrade like I'm being rubbed with a file. The ape grabs, but I'm too fast and he misses, and I'm through.

I'm on the other side, laughing and showing boy at the top of the stairs, with a fighting stick in each hand, before I realize that the ape wasn't grabbing at me after all.

He flashes me funny teeth and slings Adrian over his shoulder.

"Ooh-ooh-ooh," he says. It's a joke. He's stolen my wizard, and now he's making monkey sounds to tease me. I have to admit, it's kind of funny, but I don't laugh. Behind him, Mike Bass and Eddie Guitar are getting closer. Jim is behind them, poking flies out of the air with his sword.

I shrug. "Keep him," I say, and I turn to go down the stairs—

Then I spin suddenly. I fling one of the fighting sticks under my arm. It flies straight, like a skipped stone off a flat lake.

Wham! I smack the ape in his eyeball. He hisses, drops Adrian, and then shows skinny green snake as he slithers away.

Adrian hits the floor hard, poor fella. "Mmmmph?" he asks.

I show pony to kick the rhinoceros in the side of his head because he's looking at his buddy, the ape. Then I grab my thrown fighting stick off the floor and I slap the two of them together, on opposite sides of Slip Bobcat's neck, just as she jumps up and tries to kick me. Her kick fizzles out, and she sinks to the floor, choking.

But then Dodge Raccoon lunges at me, and his spear is out. He's clever, he's let the others take the damage and exhaust me, and he's jumping in for the kill. I'm not going to be able to get out of the way, and my sticks are in the wrong position to block.

This is going to hurt.

BOOM!

Dodge flies sideways. The boomer shell is too worked, too man-made to really hurt him, but the impetus of the little hunk of metal is enough to throw the Ranger down the stairs, squeaking.

For good measure I pummel Slouch Rhinoceros in the face several times. He's so stunned he shows girl and then passes out.

"You're almost late!" I say to Eddie. It isn't a very good joke, but it's all I can come up with at the moment. I'm distracted because the Zvuvim are not only following Eddie, they're also swarming at me from somewhere else.

"There's a second Baal here," Eddie grumbled. He blows three of the big flies into black papery shreds with a single pull of the trigger of his boomer. They're thick around us now, and I pound them before I crouch to grab Adrian Keys.

"Down the stairs!" Mike shouts, and fires his shooter. He's right. I can hear the second Baal Zavuv coming, heavy footsteps. The stone shrinks away from his touch, it isn't right for the

Infernals to be here. Not that it's the first time, of course.

Grrrwwaaaaaragh!

The squealing noise makes my tail stand up. It means Jim has managed to poke the first Baal and the beastie isn't happy about it.

"Come on, love," I say to Adrian. I show him lovely girl, warm-peace-sunshine-happiness-and-I-love-you-you-silly-wizard, and I stroke his face. He's not bad-looking, for an Outsider who always shows the same thing. "Wake up now and give us a nice spell."

"Gah." Adrian struggles, but he's forcing his eyes open now.

"What is it, Twitch?" he asks.

"A little light, darling." I show him tender, smiling girl, and he smiles back.

He digs into his pocket and pulls out the Eye. "Easy-peasy," he says, "and so on."

BOOM! Eddie Guitar and his boomer shatter a Zavuv chittering behind my shoulder. Jim's close.

"Now would be good," I suggest warmly.

Adrian grins like it's nothing. And it should be nothing, only every time he tries to do anything that matters, Adrian Keys risks falling asleep. "*Per Isidem Lux*," he says, waving the Eye.

And that's it, daylight. The dark columns and shadowed niches are all suddenly bathed in yellow light like it's noon in the Outer Bounds, where it's never usually anything but twilight. The demon-flies buzz, they're in pain. They swarm this way and that, scattering to get out of the light. Some of them make it. Others don't, and they melt away into nothing.

Slip Bobcat yowls. It might be surprise or it might be a war cry. Either way, big Mike kicks the Ranger and sends her flying down the stairs. She lands on the face of the second Baal Zavuv, just as he's trying to shield his eyes. Suddenly his fly-eyed, pig-tusked head, gray-black and mummified-looking, is wearing a bobcat fur cap. That bites and scratches.

He stumbles back into the darkness, teeming with his fly horde progeny.

"Which way?" hollers Eddie. He's dragging Adrian to his feet. I keep showing girl to Adrian and smiling at him, trying to distract him from the angry buzz of flies and the bellow of a rhinoceros trying to climb to its feet.

"Downstairs," I tell him, and I shrug an apology.

"There's a monster down there!" Mike shouts. *BANG, BANG!* He fires his shooter down the stairs, into the darkness that's alive with flies and their lord.

"Upstairs, then!" I laugh. "It all goes to the same place!" That's not really true, but it's funny to see the looks on their faces, and I have an idea.

The wizard's eyes start to flutter. Eddie slaps him, which only sends him to sleep.

The light snuffs out.

"*Fundillo!*" Mike grabs Adrian and slings him over his shoulder. That's fine, it frees me up.

I show falcon and race up the stairs. I strafe the raccoon and the rhinoceros as I go, raking them with warning claws to remind them that I'm dangerous and that I'll be back, and then I'm wheeling past Mike, who huffs and puffs, and around the staircase. The boomer starts going off again below me.

The stairs up are lit by windows beneath each step, which makes everyone's face look strange and cavernous, gaping eye sockets and mouths. "Don't imagine this light will help you," I call out as a reminder, but of course I'm showing falcon and all the band will hear is a bird's cry.

At the top of the stairs is a long hall. I touch down and show girl, fighting sticks in both hands. Six Rangers charge in my direction across the hall, a leopard and a wolfhound and others I don't immediately make out because they're coming too fast.

"Wake up Adrian!" I yell to Mike as he shuffles to the top, and I run at the Rangers.

They're too many, I don't like the odds. Naturally, I run right for the biggest, fiercest looking one of the lot, and that's the leopard. "Fool!" she snarls.

Two of her fellows are showing boy. I know them, they're Skip Robin and Shudder Mole. They're holding nets and running at the outside of the pack. I can't afford to get into a fight, or I'll get myself tangled up in rope.

I have to keep moving.

The leopard leaps and I leap too. I throw myself at the floor under her feet, and at the same moment I show falcon. The cool stone floor whizzes beneath me just under my feathered breast, and I fly underneath the leopard. Claws slam into the floor on either side of me from above.

I bank sharply to the right once I've passed beneath her, swerving towards the stone wall and then swerving right again.

The wolfhound leaps for me, misses, and then Shudder Mole throws her net. Dog and net together collide into the wall and fall to the floor.

I show girl, which has me running on the wall for two steps before I tumble to the floor and land in a crouch. Jim fights at the top of the stairs with his sword. Dead flies lie around his feet like nutshells or the rinds of eaten fruit, and he stabs at the Baal Zavuv, keeping it from coming out. Fortunately, the stairs are narrow enough and the Baal Zavuv is big enough that only one of them can come up at a time. I think. It's also fortunate that Jim is so good. Good as he is, though, he won't last much longer, even with Eddie at his side pumping boomer shells down the stairs.

I can barely hear myself, even though I yell. "Wake Adrian up!" I point at the wall. My head hurts from all the noise. "Tell him he has to open a hole right *there!*"

I hope that'll work.

And then a net falls over me.

But only over my back and haunches. It doesn't quite cover me, and when I switch instantly to showing pony, it covers me even less. Mike shakes Adrian. I kick back, and I feel my hooves kick into flesh and bone.

I bolt forward. A spear jabs me in the haunch, and it hurts, but then I'm away from the attacker. The net snags on my rump, and I drag it with me.

"Ummph!" yells one of the Rangers behind me. I hear the thud of someone hitting the floor, and I feel weight. I look back. The leopard charges me, and two other Rangers have their hands tangled in the net. They're climbing it like a ladder on the ground, dragging themselves in my direction.

I run. I gallop into a mass of flies, champing with my teeth and throwing my head around like a club. I knock some of them out of the way and keep their mandibles from my face, which is good.

But they land on my back and bite.

It hurts. I can feel myself bleed. Their jaws look like harmless steel, but cut into me like lethal bone.

Into me, and into the rope strands of the net.

I feel the weight suddenly lift as the Zvuvim cut through the ropes and the net disintegrates. Immediately I show a girl and somersault forward. Confused flies bounce away from me, and I slam into them with my fighting sticks, crushing eyes and wings and legs with every swipe.

Eddie backs away from the stairs, reloading shells into his boomer. Jim backs with him, and I see both Baalim squeezing out of the top of the stairs. They're big and gray and man-shaped, like ogres, but they have eyes like enormous flies and tusks like wild pigs. And they reek. Where Jim has cut them or Eddie has plugged them with his boomer, they leak black ooze. In the ambiguous, criss-crossing shafts of light that leave the hall a dull gray, I can see tiny flies bubble in the ooze.

"Now!" I yell.

Spring Leopard charges me with a spear tucked under her arm, its sharp end pointed right at my chest. Behind her come two more Rangers, one on each wing. I brace myself and bring my sticks into position.

Mike punches Adrian in the face. He yells something in Spanish, and it doesn't sound very happy.

I charge. I yell as I go, "Here's Johnny!" I saw that on television once on the lips of a crazy man, and it was hilarious. Also, Spring Leopard won't know what it means, so it might confuse her.

I think I hear Adrian's voice, but I can't make out what he's saying.

I jump and show falcon.

But one of the Rangers jumps before I do. It's the wolfhound, he got out of the net somehow, and his jaws clamp down on my shoulder. I gasp and show pony. In the same moment, he shows boy, and his arms are wrapped around my strong white neck. We fall to the ground hard. I was not prepared for this and I land badly, on my side and tumbling.

Spring Leopard stabs me. Then I roll over the spear and shatter it with the weight of my body. I feel the splinters in my flesh, and then she shows me her leopard. At the same moment the other one shows wolfhound, and they pile on top of me, tearing and biting.

This really isn't funny.

BANG! BANG!

Something bowls the wolfhound away from me. Slugs from Mike's shooter, I guess. I show girl just as Snow Leopard does, and we roll to a stop. I'm on top of her with my hand at her throat, and I punch her right in her button nose.

She lies still. I really hurt.

"Thanks, Mikey," I say to him. He ignores my words and shoots past me, I guess at the other Rangers. The little brass shells from his weapon rain down around me, stinging when they hit my face. I drag myself to my feet. I'll have to pluck splinters from my hip and butt later, but right now I don't have the time.

"Mike," he says. He jams more rounds into his shooter.

"Per Janum portam aperio!"

I see Adrian. He stands, Eye in one hand and looking through it, chanting and waving his fingers at the wall, right where I pointed. As the last of his words leave his lips, the wall parts like eyelids opening. Light streams in, not the gray light coming through every mirrorgate in the Outer Bounds, but the golden-green-blue-red light of day in the Queendom.

Relief. It worked.

Adrian's legs buckle.

"Adrian, baby!" I call to him with my silveriest voice. I show him a girl picnicking beside a stream and shove my arm under his to try to catch him. My rump hurts, and so does my head. I need a long rest in a cool, quiet place, and I don't think I'm going to get one today.

"Twitch?" he says in that woozy voice that means he's not quite asleep yet.

Mike's shooter explodes again in my ear. Zvuvim buzzing around me splatter into wisps of dried carapace and husk, falling apart as the beams of light touch them. The Baalim shriek, outraged. They stagger back. Jim presses the attack, stabbing them with the sword he has in one hand and swinging some wiggling, flailing, unhappy object in the other.

The object complains loudly and changes shape. I see that it is Flit and that Jim has her firmly by the tail as he pounds her into the face of the nearest Baal Zavuv again. Flit yowls. She's having a bad day. Ah, well. I told her I didn't want her to get hurt, and she should stand aside.

"Come on, handsome," I whisper into Adrian's ear.

"I'm awake," he insists, and stumbles towards the light.

I help him get through the opening. It's a circle, just opened up in the wall, so we have to pick up our feet a bit to step through it. On the outside is a rooftop, sloping gently down just beneath the hole. Its tiles are baked clay, and they hold firm as we step onto them. The daylight warms my skin out here, and a gentle breeze tickles me under the ears. The sweet smell of rotting matter fills my nostrils. My bottom still hurts.

"Mikey!" I call. "Mike!" I add, since it's funny to call him *Mikey* but maybe now is not the time to provoke him into doing something stupid.

Mike Bass galumphs our way. He stops at the opening and turns to fire some more. Even standing outside the Outer Bounds, the noise of all the gunfire happening within is still deafening. I look over the edge of the rooftop and see the tops of trees. That's good. Depending on the trees, of course, we might still be a mile off the ground, but it could always be worse. If you force them to, the Outer Bounds go up forever.

Eddie backs up to the opening too. They both smell like the bitter smoke that pours from their weapons.

"Jim!" Eddie yells. I doubt Jim can even hear him over the riot. "Get over here, dammit!"

Mike shuffles out through the opening like an ape. He teeters on the roof and almost loses his balance, which is less like an ape and more like a clown, but then he recovers and sets about putting more ammunition into his shooter.

Eddie is smoother. He takes jerky, deliberate steps, and when Amble Owl gets around a boomer blast and comes at him, Eddie swings the butt-end up the boomer up and clocks Amble right in one of his owl eyes. He shows boy and falls to the floor, crying. Eddie knees Amble in the face and kicks him back into darkness.

I move with Adrian closer to the edge.

"You ready to close the door, sweetie?" I whisper to him, showing him proud lover. I show him this one a lot. It makes him feel powerful, which is what the band usually needs from Adrian Keys.

He nods, adjusts his grip on the Eye.

Mike and Eddie unload a fusillade of thunder into the hole and then pull back. Jim vaults through, lands on the rooftop, and spins to face the threats behind him. He still has his sword in one hand and Flit in the other.

"Now!" I shout, but Adrian is already waving his fingers.

"Per Janum portam claudio!"

A pair of gray arms lunge from the opening and grab Jim Throat. Jim smashes at the bug eyes above them with the hilt of his sword. The Baal shrieks, I don't know whether from the pain of being clobbered or the pain of being burned by the light.

Jim struggles, pounding the basket hilt of his sword against the Baal's knuckles repeatedly. He skins the monster, and black ooze spatters Jim's shirt.

The Baal squeezes tighter. Jim stabs the Baal in the shoulder, twisting the point of his sword in the wound.

Grrrrraaaaaaraaaaaarrgh!

The Baal shrieks, but he doesn't let go. He yanks Jim inside as the opening shrinks. He slams Jim's head against the wall and Jim goes slack, dropping his sword and the trembling body of Flit Fox on the tile before he's dragged into darkness.

Eddie grabs at Jim's boots and misses.

Adrian collapses to the tiles, unconscious.

Then the hole closes and Jim is gone.

CHAPTER THREE

No!"

Eddie raises his boomer to his shoulder and fires into the blank stone wall repeatedly. Sparks fly and he gouges out chips of rock, but the opening doesn't reappear. In the sudden silence the shots are enormous, and birds scatter from the branches nearest the rooftop.

Then I see that Adrian is sliding. "Mike!" I yell, and grab Adrian. I could show pony, which would make me really big and heavy so I could just bite Adrian's pant leg and keep him on the rooftop, but if the tiles give way, we'll both fall. I can show falcon before I hit the ground, but Adrian can't. Especially not when he's asleep.

The Eye *chinks* onto the tile. I grab it with one hand, and with the other I scramble for purchase. I can't hold him, though, he's going over—

And then big Mike Bass is there, grabbing Adrian by one ankle and hauling him to safety with a loud grunt.

"*Mierda,*" Mike curses.

He sounds far away and muffled, like I'm hearing him from the other side of a practicing drum corps. It's sort of funny, so I laugh.

"Adrian!" Eddie yells, and rushes over to shake the wizard. "Adrian, the wall!"

I step out of the way so the boomer's not pointed at me. Eddie's distraught, and I've got enough bruises.

Adrian snores. I can barely hear it over the ringing in my ears from all the gunfire in the Outer Bounds.

I'm not in the Outer Bounds anymore, though. This is the Mirror Queendom proper. This is home, sort of. I look around.

There's no sun because the whole sky is the sun, and it's streaked with every conceivable color that shines. Even black. The black is the shiniest part, not dark at all. The ground's not so far down as it might have been, but I can only see it as shadow among the plants. The trees are tallish but no taller than Outsider trees get. Maybe a hundred feet, and I see places where even mediocre climbers can simply grab a branch and lift themselves into the trees. The climber would have to mind the serpents, of which there are approximately a million, hanging from every branch, but I think the lads' guns will work just fine on the wriggly creatures. We can climb down, no problem.

We'll have to watch out for Wild Things.

Below is a great thicket. I can't see the extent of it, but that doesn't matter here as much as it does Outside. There will be a path, assuming I can overcome the Push. The thorns are long, though. As long as my arm, I think, growing out of branches as thick as my leg. Maybe this improvised exit was better than using one of the regular doors, after all. Except that we lost Jim.

Jim. And the hoof. I turn around.

"Wake up!" Eddie is shouting much too loud. His hearing is probably battered by the gunfire too. He carries earplugs in the stuff in his pockets, I know, because he puts them in when he plays guitar. Maybe he has them in now and that's why he's shouting.

"Eddie," I say, "that's loud."

"Is it?" He yells at me now, and the veins stand out in his neck and at his temples. "Is it too loud for you, Twitch? Maybe it's so loud even Jim can hear! Maybe it's so loud that if you flew around this, this," he flails with one arm at the Outer Bounds, "this building, you could still hear me while you were looking for another way in."

I look up at the Outer Bounds. From this side, it looks like an infinitely tall castle wall. It has roofs and balconies, catwalks, parapets, battlements, gargoyles, rain gutters, and stairs, but it has no apparent upper end. And no windows or doors.

"No," I say, "the ways in are all below us."

Eddie glares at me. "Adrian!" He shakes the little wizard so hard I worry he might accidentally throw him off the rooftop. Accidentally or on purpose. Eddie is very unhappy right now.

Adrian takes no notice. He keeps snoring.

"He's out," I say, "and Jim's gone. We're not going to catch up with him, not that way."

"The Beel … zeboov," Mike says slowly. He's still the new guy. He always will be, until we get a new member; that's how the band is. "What's he doing here?"

Eddie stops shaking Adrian and looks at me.

"It's a good question," I admit. "Do you think they could have followed us all the way from New Mexico?"

"No," Eddie says immediately. "No, I don't."

"I don't either," I agree. "Which means they were waiting here for us."

"Do Azazel and Mab have an alliance?" Eddie looks at me with hard eyes.

"No," I tell him, but I look down at my feet. "No, but there are sometimes dealings, as, you know, there might be between any great powers."

"What are you hiding?" Mike asks.

"Hiding?" It's a bit embarrassing to be caught out by Mike Bass. He's the slow one. No, I remind myself, he's not really slow. He's just new. It isn't the same thing at all. "Ah, look, it's nothing. It's just … well, the reason I'm an Outcast, you see, it has to do with the Infernals. I was a sort of official escort to one of the Princes once, when he visited, and he didn't appreciate my sense of humor."

"Escort?" Mike gulps. "You mean … ?"

"No," I say, "that's not what I mean at all. I mean I was one of the horses pulling Belial's chariot. And I ... I arranged for a special set of trumpets to blow him a welcome, see? And, look, never mind, it means nothing. Only that sometimes Mab treats with Hell, and maybe she's doing it in our case."

"Trumpets?" Mike asks.

"Holy shit," Eddie mutters. He shakes his head. "You were pulling the chariot of one of the Princes of Hell, and you farted at him."

Memories. I try not to smile too big. "A lot of us did, actually. It was pretty funny." So funny that someone had to take the blame.

"But why?" Mike puts his hand in his pocket. He's got it wrapped around a flask or a candy bar, I bet.

I shrug. "I like funny things."

"No, I mean ... why would Belial ... ? I don't get it."

"It doesn't matter," Eddie says. "What matters is Jim."

"Right," I agree. "So isn't it useful that Jim has left us someone to help?"

Flit Fox is groggy. She's so groggy that although she's showing girl, she flickers into fox and back again every couple of seconds. And no wonder, her face looks like it's been used as a club on a monster with a physique like a brick wall. Which it has.

I grab her by her hair.

"Anybody have any cold iron?" I ask.

"What?" Mike is confused.

"True iron. The meteoric stuff. Star metal. Unforged, you know?"

Mike's expression is still blank.

"Newbie," I mutter.

"Check the wizard's pockets," Eddie says. He delivers the line like an order, but he does the searching himself. When he finds a thin, sharp bit of iron, like a razor, and shows it to us, I grin and try not to back away.

I remember the Marked Woman leaning over me, pushing just such a blade against my throat as the tattoos on her face swirled about like threats and curses. That wasn't funny, not the tiniest bit.

"Very good." I show teeth. "Now, follow my lead."

I kick Flit Fox in the belly, and when she sits up, eyes bulging out, I grab her before she can do anything.

"Show your sparrow," I say, "and my demonic familiar here will kill you."

Flit's eyes gape. For a moment I think I've got her.

Then: "That's no demonic familiar. It's just a human, of the kind with lots of pigment! What kind of idiot do you think I am?"

Well, it was worth a try. I carefully conceal my disappointment.

Eddie's boot slams onto the tile next to Flit's head, and suddenly he presses the cold iron up against her face. It's quick enough, and his snarl is ugly enough, that I'm taken by surprise. I feel nervous. "Show your sparrow," he growls, "and I'll kill you anyway. I may be just a human with extra pigment, but I'm from Chicago."

That does the trick. Flit nods and looks very uncomfortable.

"Been Outside, have you?" I ask.

"Some," she agrees.

"There a lot of that going on?"

"More than there used to be. More than when you were a Ranger, Twitch Pony."

"Twitch Pony?" Mike laughs.

I scowl at him.

"Like *My Little Pony?*"

"Shush," I tell him. "You're interfering." It's one thing to be called my full and formal name by one of Mab's other children. It's something else to be compared to a little girl's toy by one of the guys in the band.

"Do you have a brush for your tail, Twitch Pony?" He laughs more. It's annoying, and I try to look stern. "Or sparkles on your bum under that leather?"

"What do you want, Mike?" I ask him.

Mike stops laughing. "You know what I want."

"Right." I nod. "*Mike* it is. No more *Mikey.*"

Mike nods, and the grin vanishes from his face. He points his shooter at Flit Fox and pulls back the part on top to make it ready. This probably doesn't impress Flit nearly as much as the cold iron at her throat, but he doesn't know that. He's trying to do his part.

"Now tell the lady what she wants to know."

"Yes," I agree, and turn my stern face back to Flit. "What are you doing out there?" I ask.

"Scouting," she says. "Gathering information Mab and Oberon want. Following orders, which was never your strong point, Pony."

"Some might say that's because I bred true," I point out.

Eddie slams his fist into the wall, startling me and Flit both. "Jim!" he barks. "Where's Jim?"

"The Baobab Tree!" Flit splutters.

"Well, of course they're taking him to the Baobab Tree!" I snort my derision, as if it couldn't have been any other way. "But why?"

Flit glares back at me, sullen.

Eddie stabs her. It's just a little stab, a poke in the cheek, but Flit screams horribly. I smell the stink of death, like burning trees, and smoke hisses from the wound.

"*Cagado*," Mike says. He's shocked, and lowers the point of his shooter.

Eddie may be shocked, but doesn't show it. "Answer the question," he snarls, "or I poke this all the way through into your brain."

Of course Flit Fox's brain won't be anywhere so obvious as behind her face, but Eddie doesn't know that. And the iron hurts Flit enough that she takes him seriously.

"Belial!" she yelps.

I feel queasy. "What?" I ask.

"Belial wants him!" She's screaming her answer through tears, and Eddie eases off a bit, takes the blade out of her flesh.

"Him?" I ask. "Or the thing he's carrying?"

"Both!" Flit sobs. "Either! We've been watching for Jacob bar Azazel or for his father's hoof for many shifts! Mab said it would be soon!"

"Jacob bar Azazel?" Mike scratches his head.

"Jim," I tell him.

"Yeah, I get that it's Jim," he says. "I just wish the world would hold still for a second so I can focus on it."

"What's the urgency?" I ask. "What's the rush? Why does it seem like every power in the universe is dogpiling on us all at once?"

But Flit only cries.

"I don't know what to do with you, Flit Fox," I muse. "If I let you go, you're duty-bound to run off and tell Mab and Oberon we're here, and what you've told us."

Flit cries some more.

"You can't even promise me you won't, because you've already made a big deal about how good you are at following orders."

I'm genuinely a bit flummoxed.

"I could kill you, I suppose," I say, as if it was no big deal. It is a big deal. It's a big deal because I'm already permanently in trouble with Mab, and it's a big deal because I don't really like hurting my own kind. Especially here. It's one thing to fight the Rangers in the Outer Bounds when they attack me, but it's something entirely different to enter the Queendom and kill one in cold blood. This is my home. I can't do that to my home.

"I have an idea." The voice is Adrian's. I turn and see that the wizard is awake. He's standing up carefully, leaning against the wall and keeping away from the edge of the rooftop. "I mean, loose lips sink, and all that, but I think I could keep our friend's mouth shut as long as we need it to be."

He holds up the Eye.

Flit gasps. "Rahab!" she hisses.

Adrian chuckles. "Worse than that," he swaggers. "I'm gonna go all Vulcan on you."

He kneels over Flit Fox, who doesn't resist.

"Why waste a firebolt?" I ask. "We can just stab her."

"Not that kind of Vulcan." Adrian presses his hand on Flit Fox's face, with his pinky upside her nose and one finger at the corner of her eye. Flit's nervous, and she flickers in and out of showing fox as he does it, but the knife at her cheek keeps her still.

Adrian takes a piece of chalk from his pocket and draws lines around his own hand on Flit's face, including a circle around her mouth. "*Per Thoth te ad silentiam adiuro*," he mutters. He plucks a bit of hair from Flit's tail, and then he backs off.

"That's it?" I ask. He hasn't fallen asleep or anything.

"That's it," he says, and puts the Eye back in his pocket. He carries that thing around like it's a cigarette lighter. He has no idea what it is. I'm not comfortable with my guesses, but unlike Flit Fox, I keep them to myself.

"Talk!" Eddie snaps, and pokes Flit again with the iron.

Smoke sizzles from her cut cheek, she hisses. Her mouth opens and shuts, but she doesn't say anything. She can't.

Mike holsters his shooter. "Look, I don't want to give anybody ideas, but won't she just write down what happened?"

"Fairies can't read." Adrian smirks at me.

I smirk back at him. "Fairies choose not to. Books are overrated."

"Either way," Eddie growls, "what do I do with this one?"

"Throw her over," I say.

Eddie doesn't hesitate. He drags Flit off the tiles. She scrabbles at him with vulpine paws, but he ignores her, and then he hurls her out into space. She falls, snapping her teeth mutely and showing fox. Serpents on the branches bite at her, and she looks like she's going to plunge to her doom on the forest floor below.

But she's not so disoriented as all that. As a snake the size of a cow unhinges its jaw to snap her up, she suddenly shows swallow. A single flap of her wings and she avoids the bite, and then Flit Fox goes winging off into the forest.

"What happens when they break the spell?" Eddie asks.

Adrian shakes his head. "Fairies can't do magic. Not like humans."

"Let me rephrase that," Eddie says. His voice is harsh. "What happens when you fall asleep?"

Adrian grins sheepishly. "Hey, I thought of that." He holds up the hairs from Flit Fox's tail. "We're covered. Just don't lose these."

"We'll be fine," I say. I don't know if it's true or not.

Eddie nods. "Have another stick of gum," he recommends. Adrian takes two.

"Which one is Belial?" Mike asks. "Is he the one with the cow head?"

"No." I remember Belial clearly. "He looks more like a squid. Or a mass of kelp. Or Jell-O with asparagus in it, like they eat in Utah."

"They eat Jell-O with asparagus in it in Utah? *Mierda*."

"Stay focused," Eddie grunts. "How do we get to the Baobab Tree to rescue Jim?"

"We have a stop to make first," I say. "There's something we'll need."

"What kind of a something?" Eddie is suspicious.

"Think of it as a friend," I say casually. I really hope Pulse is where I left him. "Or a witness."

"We get this friend," Eddie thinks it out, "and the friend helps us rescue Jim. And then we go to the road Jim wanted to take us to."

I nod.

"And you don't want to tell me anything else about this friend, do you?"

I hesitate. "It'll be easier to show you."

"And how do we get to him?" Mike wants to know. "Or … her."

"Easy," I tell him. "But first we have to get down."

I show falcon and strafe down along the nearest tree branches climbing up over the rooftop. A scaled viper with long ridges on the top of its head snaps at me, but that's a mistake—I'm a bird of prey, and I eat snakes. I snatch the viper from the branch and hurl it down into the thorns below. A second viper meets a similar fate at my talons, and when a constrictor with stubby vestigial legs tries to coil about me, I show boy and pound it into senselessness with my fighting sticks.

"This way!" I call to the band.

Adrian comes first, followed by Mike, then Eddie in the rear, his boomer dangling ready by a shoulder strap and Jim's sword shoved through a slit in Eddie's jacket to improvise a sort of hanger for it. They're all deliberately not looking at the sky, and I realize that they're not used to anything other than plain, boring blue.

Adrian is a little shaky as he moves. It's not just magic that makes him conk out, I remember. It's pressure. I show him a pretty girl, nonthreatening. "Come on, friend," I say to him. "This is easy. It's a sidewalk."

It isn't a sidewalk, it's one branch under his feet and another clenched in his fists. But it isn't bad, and he takes a few deep breaths and then gets over it. By the time he reaches the thick crotch of the tree, he looks reasonably comfortable.

Mike follows, then Eddie. Say what you will about this ragged band of rock and rollers, we aren't cowards. And we aren't afraid of heights.

I lead the way again, scaring off more snakes, and also a pack of things that look like squirrels but have long fangs. Not Wild Things, just part of the Queendom, like the snakes. Halfway down the trunk, I plunge into the thicket. The thorns are tall here, they groan and they rustle a lot.

At the bottom of the tree, I show girl and look up. The last twenty feet or so of trunk are a bare slide to the ground, but the guys are hesitating well above that. I show falcon and fly up to them. They're all poised just above the top of the brambles, and I perch on the thorn bush branch nearest them and show reassuring, cheerful girl.

"Are you stuck?" I ask.

Adrian's eyes are closed, and he's breathing carefully. Mike Bass clutches his body tightly to a tree limb with one arm and with the other points to the bramble branch beside me.

I look. There's a body impaled on the bramble beside me. Thorns protrude from its chest, and hands stretch in my direction, pleading. The hands are frozen, but the corpse's white mouth works mechanically, opening and shutting.

"Hilarious," I tell them, and laugh.

They don't look amused.

"What?" I say, and I wave at the corpse dismissively. "If this showed up at your doorstep on Halloween, you'd tell it how cute it was and give it candy. Come on, Adrian. You've seen worse than this." I show him stern teacher, his secret crush, and then I drop to the ground.

They follow, mostly with eyes open.

Eddie drops to the thicket floor last, and when he stands, he looks around at the corpses impaled on thorns at every hand, their blood slowly dripping to the ground. "Twitch," he says, "I can't imagine why you would ever want to come back here."

"Home is where you ..." Adrian sniffs and nods. "Whatever."

"I've been to *your* home," Mike snorts. The big guy shudders.

"Well," I laugh lightly, "it's what you're used to, I guess."

CHAPTER FOUR

"How far are we from this friend, exactly?"

Eddie is the only one who can bring himself to look up at the corpses. I suppose this is the sort of thing he's used to seeing all the time, or at least whatever he sees out of that bad eye of his lets him shake this off without too much effort.

I don't take it seriously, of course. It's what the Queendom is showing here and now. It will show us other things later.

"That's not really the right question," I say. I'm almost running but not making much headway. The thorns around me seem to always be the same thorns, the caterpillars creeping away into the darkness under leaves bigger than my body the same caterpillars. The Push is strong on me, and it always presses into my face.

I have to stop for a moment, and I lean against Mike Bass. It helps, and to thank and entertain him for letting me lean, I show him pretty girl. He clears his throat and fidgets. I almost laugh, but I don't.

"Tell me the right question, then." Eddie grips his boomer in both hands. His eye slides sideways, and he grinds his teeth. "I can accept that I'm chasing after somebody's imaginary friend 'cause I've done things that were a lot weirder, but it still ain't my idea of fun. It'd get a little easier if I could at least understand why it feels like I'm running in circles."

"There aren't that many fixed places in the Queendom," I explain. It's painful to be so clear and direct, but I think we need Eddie to hold us together, and it isn't good that Eddie is asking hard questions. "Places that hold still, if you know what I mean. Getting from one to the other isn't so much a matter of following a road or taking a direction as it is a question of knowing where you're going and choosing to get there." There. I've practically told him everything. "And Pulse isn't imaginary. He isn't even properly dead."

"So you don't know where you're going?" Mike guesses. He looks at me, careful not to look around at the thorns. He shakes a little bit. I don't think it's the corpses that bother him. It's the fact that the corpses move and try to get his attention.

"Do you really think that's possible?" I sigh. The burden of having to share is painful. "Something's holding me back."

"What about that?" he asks, and points at a crumbling stone pagoda off in the trees. "Is that a landmark? Or might there be a road there?"

"It's just a remnant," I say, and when they all look confused, I sigh. "It's a piece of an older world," I tell them. "A bit of a ruin. There's lots of that stuff in the Queendom. Some of it is ... is creatures, living things. What we call the Wild Things. But all of it moves. It isn't a landmark, no."

"What do you mean, *older world*?" Eddie squints suspiciously at the pagoda.

"I don't know what I *mean*," I tell him. "I just know what I *said*."

Adrian looks at me through the Eye. "The thing that's holding you back. Does it feel like a hand?" he asks.

"Yes," I say. Why not? "It feels like a hand holding me back."

"It looks like a hand."

"Thank you."

Eddie frowns. "What is it?"

"It's my banishment," I explain. I am humiliated. "It's a physical force, is what it feels like, pushing on me."

"Does it hurt?" Mike asks.

"Am I crying?" I counter. "No, it doesn't hurt. But it pushes me outward. I try to move in, and it holds me in place." I sigh again. "I think that's why we're not making any forward progress."

Mike leans in and whispers. "Can you trick it?"

"What?"

"You know," he continues, "pretend you're going the other way and make it push you where you want to go."

I snort. I'm tempted to show pony and kick him for that. "It's not a person," I tell him. "It's a decree. There's no tricking it."

"There doesn't appear to be any moving forward, either," Eddie adds.

Adrian is still squinting through the Eye, but he's looking past me now, over my shoulder. "I think I can help," he says.

"Oh?" I ask. "You see a path around my banishment through that, do you?"

The wizard shakes his head. "I see a lot of things, though. Tell me what you're looking for, and I'll try to get us there."

"It's a shack," I tell him. "It looks like a skull, and the fence around it is made of gravestones." I hesitate a moment, then add more. "It's a remnant, too, so it moves. Really, most things in the Queendom move around."

Adrian rotates slowly about me. He reminds me of a surveyor, or an artist examining a model. I hold still while he looks past me.

"I can see it," he says finally. "A woman lives there, or an ogre hag. She's big as a truck, talks like a child."

"Buzzard Betsy."

"She's carrying a doll."

My feet feel chilly with excitement. "Yes." That's Pulse.

Adrian pauses. "Eats children."

"Yes, that's Betsy," I agree.

"*Huevos.*"

Eddie pumps his boomer. It's a reflex. "Nice family you have."

"She's not one of Mab's subjects," I protest, "and she's definitely not family. She's just here." *And she's kind of funny,* I want to say, only I don't. "She's a bit of an older world too. I think she might have been a queen in her own right, somewhere, some time."

"I bet that was a great place to live," Mike mutters.

"The hand is pushing against you strongest from that direction," Adrian reports.

"Thanks," I say. "Your Eye is so mighty." I say it sarcastically, but in fact the Eye might be far more powerful than he knows.

"I think I can pull it aside." Adrian schemes. "For just a moment. What do we all need to do, just follow you?"

"Yes," I agree. "But how long is a moment? What if you fall asleep?"

"I'll carry him," Mike Bass offers.

I shake my head. "It was a stupid question. I'll carry him."

I show pony, and Adrian climbs onto my back. Mike and Eddie stand to either side of me, bending their knees like runners. They look silly, especially Mike. He's too big to look dignified doing much of anything except firing his shooter and playing bass.

"Ready?" Adrian asks. He's still looking through the Eye. His face is a little pallid.

I neigh. *Yes.*

"*Per ... per Mercurium ...*"

Adrian weaves on my back. Mike comes out of his starting crouch long enough to pinch the wizard.

"*Per Mercurium manum distraho.*"

I feel Adrian collapse, but at the same moment I also feel the Push disappear. It doesn't go away, it lunges past me, like I've suddenly become slippery.

I take advantage of the moment and bolt forward. The Queendom tries to show me thicker brambles and corpses that grab my ankles, but I ignore it and show it clever pony, dodging and dancing among the obstacles. I clatter over a fragment of road, hoping it doesn't distract Mike. The stones are worn almost to film, it's obviously just another remnant and doesn't go anywhere.

"Shiiiiiiiiiiit!" Eddie swings at obstacles with his boomer, but he doesn't fall behind, and no one takes the wrong road.

And then the brambles and the bodies are gone. We're at the edge of a clearing, and the sky again dazzles me with its many shimmering colors.

I stop at the row of headstones, show girl, and toss Adrian to the ground. He hits harder than I mean him to. I should be grateful, even though it's a little annoying that he basically forced me to admit to everyone that I'm subject to the Push. Okay, I am grateful. I crouch over him and pat his cheeks. He only meant well, poor boy, and he's knocked himself out again for the rest of us.

Eddie and Mike crouch too. They look around, boomer and shooter ready.

"Adrian, wake up." I show the wizard a picnic, with a stream and a basket.

Hyoo-hyoo-hyoo-waaaaoooo!

Hyoo-hyoo-hyoo-waaaaoooo! call the Mockers.

"What the hell is that?" Eddie asks.

"It's Adrian. He wakes up better if I'm gentle."

"No." Eddie points with his boomer at the trees surrounding Betsy's shack. I look and see that they're massive old oaks, bent over under the weight of their own dignity and trailing green evening gowns of Spanish moss. I hear them sharing secrets with each other. I can't hear the words, but the trees' voices are bitter and unkind. "What's *that?*"

"Trees?" I suggest, and then I hear the birdsong again. "Oh, *that*. Those are Mockers. They're imitators, like parrots or doppelgangers. They're Betsy's creatures, sort of her children. Come on, bonny boy."

"They sound like screaming kids." Mike shudders.

"Yes," I agree.

"Tell me this isn't your friend." Eddie looks like he wants to hit me. His eye is going crazy.

Adrian sits up. He's dazed, but I help him to his feet, and he can stand.

"This isn't my friend," I agree. "This is a violent monster. She isn't Mab's friend, either. She isn't anyone's friend. She's here because after Herself was chained, all the bits of the old worlds washed up here, ruins and reavers alike. Mab's folk leave her alone, which is exactly why I hid ... my friend here."

Eddie's eyes narrow, impatient. "This is the friend who will help us get Jim out of the Baobab Tree. You hid him in the lair of a violent monster, the child-murdering queen of an older world."

"Yes," I say. It's more fun not to tell him everything I'm thinking. And his summary is basically true. At least, I hope it is.

"Lead on," Adrian mutters, "et cetera."

"Macduff," Mike volunteers.

"Actually," I say, "it's, 'lay on, Macduff, and damned be him who first cries "Hold! Enough!"'"

"You know your Shakespeare," Eddie says. It's not quite a compliment.

"I knew the man." That was well before I was Outcast, before humans started filling the Outside with all their machinery and Mab had to respond by constructing the Outer Bounds. In the Bard's day, mortals were more frequently guests in Mab's Queendom. There wasn't much of a boundary, back then.

"Well, I'm damned to start with," Eddie reminds me, "but lay on anyway."

I turn my attention to the shack.

It looks like a moldering boulder, moss and black decay like rot covering a heap of cracked stone with a thin gray-green film. One cavity, facing slightly away from us, is a window but looks like an eye. A second, pointing straight at us, is a door and a nasal cavity at the same time. A third hole, like another eye, faces skyward. Lazy, greasy smoke rises from it.

"I don't see her," I say. The fire makes me nervous.

Adrian pulls out his lens again and peers through it. "Nothing," he confirms. "What about the friend? What am I looking for?"

"I don't know how Rahab would see the doll," I tell him, and I hop the fence.

"What?"

The others hesitate, then follow me.

I want to be quick. Funny as she can be, Buzzard Betsy is a dangerous, destructive creature. She's not a queen anymore, but she's still a monster.

The grass in the yard is wiry and tough. Beetles scuttle across hard-packed earth, gnawing at the tough yellowish stumps that pass for a lawn. As I approach the hut, I hear a soft *bawk-bawk-bawk*.

"Oh," I remember to say. "Don't let the chickens bite you."

"Ow!" Mike hollers at that instant.

"Sorry!" I don't mean it. I also manage not to laugh, which is a good trick, since it's pretty funny.

Bang! Bang! Bang!

There is a moment of stunned silence. Mike Bass stands over the splattered bloody remains of one of the chickens. The others scatter for the far corners of the yard.

"Little *chingón* had teeth!" Mike looks shaken up and surprised. A chunk of fabric is torn from the ankle of his trousers, and he's bleeding.

"Hen's teeth." I grin. "Rare, those."

"Fangs!"

Hyoo-hyoo-hyoo-waaaaoooo! Bang! the Mockers take up the call. *Hyoo-hyoo-hyoo-waaaaoooo! Bang! Bang!*

"Oh, that's good," Eddie says. "That will help a lot." He scans the trees, and I think if he saw any of the Mockers, he'd shoot them. Fat lot of good that would do. They'd all just yell *boom* instead of *bang*, and the noise would be louder.

"Quick!" I vault in through the eye-socket window.

Crunch.

I land in bones. Not big bones like the shack is made of, but little bones. They're scattered all over the floor. As I land, a chicken scurries out through the front door, something clutched in her beak that might be a rib.

I want to laugh at this, because it's funny. But I can't, quite. And I don't know why.

Mike lands beside me with a louder *crunch*, and then Eddie Guitar.

"Hell, no," Eddie says, looking around at the bones. "Just … hell, no. How many damn kids … ?"

He's right. They look like children's bones, deep up to my ankles all over the bare dirt floor and in some corners drifting up to the height of my knees. Arm bones, leg bones, ribs, pelvises. No skulls. I smell rotting flesh, and I see gobbets of it scattered here and there among the bones, rotting so bad the chickens won't even touch it. Against one wall of the skull-shack is a heap of furs, and in the center is a smoldering pit of ash and coals.

"Tell me these are remnants of an older world," Eddie growls.

"They're remnants," I say softly. I'm lying. He doesn't believe me. "Funny, isn't it?" I don't quite believe myself.

Above it all, bolted into the ceiling with a nail that looks like a fragment of bone, hangs a cage. It's woven of twisted, thorny branches, and I guess from the size of it that it will probably hold two children.

"Son of a bitch," Adrian curses. He's come in through the door.

The Queendom isn't showing me bones, these are real. Buzzard Betsy ate the children whose bones these were.

I don't find that funny. Not anymore.

The other guys find it even less amusing. They all look sick and angry.

"Be grateful," I say. "When Rahab and the rider were defeated and thrown down into the sea from the First Mound, other things went with them. All the things meant to be excluded from mortal creation, and that included Buzzard Betsy. Bad she certainly is. She eats children and turns their skulls into her bird-creatures. Think how much worse she would be if she had free rein to come and go in your world."

"Let's get what we came for and get out of here," Adrian says. His eyes rove around like he can't bear to focus on anything.

"*Carajo*, yes." Mike starts digging into the furs of the sleeping pile. "What does your friend look like?"

"A rag doll," I say. "He has X's for eyes."

"What's a monster doing with a doll anyway?" Eddie asks. "Or is this just one more sign of how completely screwed up your native country is?"

"That's the easy question," Adrian says. "The better question is, 'Hey, Twitch, why are you friends with a doll?'"

"She hunts with it," I say. "It's a lure." Part of me wants to chuckle, and another part of me feels disgusted. "And Pulse hasn't always been a doll."

"Huh?" Mike is puzzled. He doesn't quite formulate a question, though, so I don't waste any time on an answer.

I show the falcon and swoop about the upper reaches of the room while Eddie digs into the bones. Adrian brings the Eye up and scans the room through it. His movements are stiff and forced.

There's no doll in the cage and nowhere else inside the shack to hide anything. And no Pulse, inside or outside his doll repository.

"Maybe she buried it?" Mike wonders.

"Maybe she lost it." Eddie looks angry.

"Maybe she ate it." Adrian looks bitter.

Hyoo-hyoo-hyoo-waaaaoooo! Bang! I hear a great flapping of wings in the oak trees outside, and I fly out through the eye socket in the ceiling. The Mockers storm this way and that through the trees. Something is disturbing them.

Or they're welcoming something home.

I drop to the roof of the shack and show girl. I'm on the lip of the opening, so I can peer down inside and see the guys scramble. They press themselves behind the wall and peek through the window to get a better look at the forest.

The flapping and crying noises reach a crescendo, and then an explosion of Mockers bursts from the trees. I found them funny once. Now the sight of them makes me want to cry out in objection. The Queendom isn't showing them, either. They're real. And they're horrible.

I hold my tongue for fear of what comes on their heels.

Mockers swarm about the bone shack. They shriek their all-too-human cries, some sounding like children weeping, some like children screaming. *No!* I hear, and *Please!* The Mockers whose cries sound like gunshots and birds are a relief.

I try not to look at them, but I can't avoid it. They swarm about me, press at me with gnarled and scaly claws. Their bodies might belong to eagles or large owls.

They have children's heads.

Only with no teeth.

I laughed at the Mockers on the day I first crept into Buzzard Betsy's shack to use her doll as a hiding place. I knew no Ranger would ever look there; Betsy was funny, but she was dangerous, and besides, Oberon likely hadn't told anyone exactly what I had. That would prove embarrassing. And Oberon himself wasn't going to go around knocking on the door of all the Queendom's worst monsters, asking after Pulse Lemur. I laughed at my cleverness, and I laughed at the silly bird-children and the chicken with teeth and at Betsy herself, because they were hilarious.

I'm not laughing anymore.

I can't say anything to the others below. Any word I utter will be repeated by the dozen bird-fiends clustered about me, scratching at me. Thank goodness for the leather clothing on my girl seeming, or I'd be bleeding badly by now.

I lean over the open hole to try to catch the eye of one of the guys, but pull my head back immediately.

Buzzard Betsy is coming out of the forest.

I quickly show falcon. My falcon doesn't look anything like the Mockers, who crowd around me *hyoo-hyoo-hyoo-waaaaooo-bang-*ing, but my girl, my boy, and my pony would fit in even less. I hop slowly on the top of the skull, claws scratching loudly at the bone beneath me, trying to stay behind the Mockers and at the same time keep an eye on Betsy.

She doesn't walk, she shambles. If there are legs moving beneath the rotting curtains that hang off her massive body, I can't see them. She wears a chain around her waist, which is something I don't remember. I smell blood and putrefaction, I see long nails and teeth filed to sharp, tiny points. I can almost feel the thick grease in the lank, knotted hair that hangs down Betsy's back. I see eyes that glitter, wedged in tight above a nose like a twisted tree root. The nose comes first, snuffling and wheezing, but, big as it is, the biggest thing by far about Buzzard Betsy is her mouth. It's hinged at the back of her toad-like head, about where I imagine her ears ought to be, though I don't see any ears. It's lipless, the flesh at its edges ragged and raw, sometimes exposing gums and sometimes showing teeth, and it's so big that I think it could swallow me in one bite, even if I were showing pony.

I get a good, long look at Betsy as she oozes across her yard, scattering toothed chickens out of her path. I see the doll under her left arm, and I think about diving for it, but I can't. As Betsy bends at the knees and sluggishly climbs through the door of her shack, I smell her and I smell my own fear, and I see Eddie Guitar, Mike Bass, and Adrian Keys all scooting out the window at the same moment. They have guns in their hands and looks of panic on their faces, and they press themselves to the outside of the shack, staying out of Betsy's view.

I should snatch the doll and run, I think. With Oberon's help, I can free Jim and we can be gone.

Only I can't shake from my mind the vision of what I saw tucked under Buzzard Betsy's other arm as she marched across her yard. Maybe it's because my ears are still ringing a little from the shooting in the Outer Bounds, or maybe it's because I don't want to hear the noises that were coming out of their mouths, but in my mind's eye the vision is silent.

A vision of three children, kicking and screaming and unable to escape as Buzzard Betsy carries them into her lair.

CHAPTER FIVE

I slide down the roof of the shack to join Eddie, Mike, and Adrian. Landing hurts, and no wonder. I ache from exertion alone, not to mention the splinters in my rump and the cracks in my head from the ceiling of the Silver Eel. I'm such a mess, it's almost funny.

I point to the Mockers staring down at us from the roof and circling overhead, and I cover my lips with a finger. The last thing we need is all the Mockers crying out together in a chorus of, *So, Twitch, what's the plan now?*

Eddie nods. He's staring through slitted eyes.

Adrian points at himself and Mike Bass and at the door. Then he points at Eddie and the window, then at me and the hole in the ceiling. That sort of looks like the beginnings of a plan, but it needs a little work.

I point at myself and then make a gesture with my hands to describe the cage, hanging from the ceiling. They frown and shake their heads. Do they not understand, or do they disagree?

"No! Please!" one of the children inside the shack cries. It isn't funny. They're real, they're scared, and they need help.

Hyoo-hyoo-hyoo-no-please!

Hyoo-hyoo-hyoo-waaaaoooo, no-please!

Mike cradles nothing in his empty arms and rocks it to sleep, then points at me.

I scratch my head, puzzled. Does he mean the doll, or the children? *Doll or children?* I mouth to him. He shakes his head back.

Eddie huffs, exasperated. He points at me and flaps his arms like wings. Yes, of course, I'm going to fly in through the ceiling, I get it, I can't very well burrow through it. But I don't know what they want me to do next.

Adrian kneels. He has a knife blade and he writes something in the dirt at his feet.

I try my best, but no amount of staring at the scratches allows me to read them. I shrug, flap my arms like wings, point at the ceiling and cradle an imaginary doll in my arms.

"Heeeeelp!" The scream is frantic, and the Mockers flurry about, agitated.

"Screw this!" Eddie pumps his boomer and walks to the door.

I spring into the air and show falcon. The Mockers pummel into me, the air is thick with them. A Mocker bites at my tail, but without teeth its bite can't hold me and I slip free.

Hyoo-hyoo-hyoo-screw-this!

Hyoo-hyoo-hyoo-waaaaoooo, screw-this!

Boom! Boom!

Through the flapping and writhing quasi-bird bodies about me, I can see the boomer's flash and smell its stink. He's hitting Mockers. I can hear their shrieks, and their agitation increases.

"Adrian!" Eddie shouts. "Can you clear these things out of the way?"

Then Mike begins to fire too. I can't see them very well, and I fight claw-to-claw to try to get free of the crowd. The Mockers butt into me and scratch me.

"*Aves repello!*" I hear Adrian shout.

That sounds like a good idea, I think, but only for a second. *Aves* means *birds*.

I'm a bird.

If I thought the Push was bad, the buffeting blow that whips off Adrian as he casts his spell makes it feel like nothing. I'm punched skyward along with all the Mockers. The rooftop of the shack and the yard around it are cleared of bird life out to a spherical perimeter marked at ground level by the tombstone fence. This means the chickens, too, and I almost laugh to see them hurled out like blown dandelion spores. They're so little, they keep sailing out past the fence and into the forest, and some of them get stuck in the Spanish moss. Chicken trees, that's funny, but I have to focus, and Adrian's spell is a problem.

The Mockers and I flap our wings and shriek in protest.

Hyoo-hyoo-hyoo-repello!

I can more or less watch the action unfold, forty feet directly below me. Adrian struggles at the window. He's holding up his candle and the Eye and trying to get off a spell, but he keeps catching himself against the side of the building. He's falling asleep.

Eddie advances into the shack, firing a blast off with his boomer at each step. Buzzard Betsy shrieks and flings aside the child in her hands, a girl in a nightdress. She bounces off the wall and hits the ground, still moving. Mike fires several bolts with his shooter and then he rushes in, running to grab the girl.

The other two children scream in the cage. I can't see Pulse.

I flap my wings but achieve nothing.

Adrian drags himself fully erect against the side of the house and gets off another spell. I don't hear the words over the shrieking of the Mockers and the gunfire, but I see the cage spring open. The children come spilling out, bony legs flapping pell-mell in all directions.

Mike grabs the girl at the side of the room and practically throws her out the window. Then he sees something and stops.

Betsy swoops down on Mike, jaws gaping. Eddie's boomer flashes fire into her side, but she ignores it, grabs Mike Bass, and clamps her vast mouth down around him.

Mike screams. It's a very high-pitched sound, considering how big Mike is. I laugh, but only a little.

Eddie lets his boomer drop to his side and pulls out his smaller weapon, a shooter like Mike's, only it can shoot very, very fast. He raises it, but Betsy snaps her head forward like a whip, spitting a projectile of Mike in Eddie Guitar's direction. Mike and

Eddie collapse in a tangle of rock and roll musicians and lie still. There's blood. A lot of it.

"Oberon's beard!"

They need my help. The thought of the impact makes me nervous, but I show pony—

And fall.

Buzzard Betsy can't hear me coming, I guess, but the whistle of my own meteoric descent is huge in my ears. She shuffles a lurching step across the floor of her shack and bends to grab one of the unconscious men—

And I plow into the top of her head.

I choose to stay in equine form as I hit her, even though ponies aren't famously good at falling. But the pony weighs more than the boy or the girl, and things aren't looking good for my comrades. I take the impact more on my chest and forelegs than anywhere else, and Betsy and I are knocked flying in opposite directions.

I'm stunned, but I manage to show the girl, and I sort of roll once or twice before flopping to a complete, inert stop against the wall of the shack.

Lightning stabs me in the ribs. My right arm hurts, but I can't even feel the left one, and it dangles at my side, useless. Top to bottom—literally, since my head and my rump are both injured— I'm beaten and sore.

But I'm not defeated. I pull out one of my fighting sticks.

"Mab's belly button, Betsy," I say. "I hope that's enough for you."

Betsy makes a sound that's part groan and part roar. She's covered in those moldering drapes of a dress, so I can't see much in the way of detail, but I can tell that she's moving.

I roll over and somehow land on my knees. Then Adrian's at my side. He slaps himself in the face with one hand and with the other he drags me to my feet. "Easy, sweetheart," he says in a gentle laugh.

I laugh at him. "Are you using your Glamour on me, Adrian?"

"If the shoe fits," he says, "or something like that. Get the kids."

He grabs Mike and Eddie and starts shaking them. He's chanting something in Latin, and I hope it's a healing spell for Mike. I walk away, risking that Adrian falls asleep and all three of them get eaten by Betsy in so many gulps, but Adrian seems awake and motivated. Besides, I won't go far.

And someone should check on the children.

The three of them huddle against the tombstones. On the other side, a fluffy wall of angry chickens snaps at them with stolen children's teeth, and overhead, a storm of child-faced feathered ghouls variously yells *Bang! Boom! Repello!* and *Mab's belly button!* It sounds like an entire madhouse accusing me in court.

I show a kindly mother. This is not one of my natural showings, but it's one I've had to practice with Adrian from time to time, so it's one I'm quite good at. I limp, and I still can't move one of my arms, but they won't notice.

"Can you help us?" the biggest of the three children asks. She's a girl.

The middle child is a boy. His eyes are as big as coconuts, and he doesn't say anything. Clean streaks from tears cut through the dirt all over his face.

"Did you see the horsey?" asks the smallest child, also a boy. "A horsey came from heaven and saved us!" He shakes uncontrollably, and his eyes roll back in his head. If we get him home now, he'll probably start his own religion.

"This is all just a dream," I comfort him.

"We can't get past the chickens," says the girl.

"Bad chickens," I chide them, and I whack two or three of them aside with my fighting stick. They spit out bloody teeth and flap away. The others get even angrier, but they back down.

I gather the three children under my good arm and look back. Eddie stumbles in my direction, Mike leaning heavily across his shoulder. They're both bloody, especially Mike's shirt. Behind them comes Adrian. He's slower than Eddie, and I worry that maybe he's falling asleep, but when I see that he isn't, I realize that the truth is even worse.

Adrian is walking backward. He has his own shooter in his hand, and he's pointing it at the shack.

Graaaaaaack!

The ear-splitting cry comes from Buzzard Betsy. I know it from the tone, though I can't see her, and from the angered, violated sound of it.

And then I hear her footsteps.

"Run, children!" I push them towards the trees and begin laying about me with the fighting stick. I'd like to show pony and carry them, or show falcon and harass Buzzard Betsy, but I can't do either. As a pony, I'd be lame. As a bird, I'd be grounded.

Even showing boy, I only have one usable arm, and that one hurts.

But it's enough to beat a path through the chickens and the Mockers. The flying bird demons buffet me, but I stay hunched over, and they can't do much worse than that. Then I hear guns behind me.

B-rap-p-p-p-p! B-rap-p-p-p-p!

Mockers fall left and right, shredded by the bursts fired into their midst. The boomer goes off too, and then I plunge into the Spanish moss. It's cold and slimy, and I need a place to go or else I'll just run forever and Buzzard Betsy will surely catch me.

I aim for the Outer Bounds. I don't have to aim for any place in particular, since everywhere in the Outer Bounds is really the same place at the same time. It's all just out from the center. This time, the Push is at my back, and I fly. The others fly with me but not quite as fast, and I have to be careful not to leave them behind.

The Spanish moss slaps me in the face one last time, and then it's gone and I'm in a swamp. I hear shooting behind me still, so I don't think I've lost anyone. The swamp looks like it goes on forever, like the Queendom always does, and every ten feet is a new puddle of reeking slime. A row of Greek pillars and a half-submerged marble rooftop tease me with a moment of substance, but I know they're just a remnant.

Poking out of each puddle is a head. The heads are all talking to each other, *chatter-chatter-chatter-chatter*, none of it in any language I can recognize. It's probably not a real language anyway, it's just something the Queendom wants to show me.

I step into the first puddle with the children, and it's as deep as my neck. They go underwater.

"Dammit!" Eddie yells. "She won't stop!"

"I'm shooting for the eyes!" Mike shouts.

They both turn at the edge of the swamp and throw themselves behind a bloated log that lies half in and half out of the stew. I plunge into the cold, stinking water. I wish I had the use of both my arms. And I wish those heads would stop telling me jokes, so I could concentrate.

Chatter-chatter-chatter. A head framed in wispy orange hair grins at me from only a couple of feet away, lips peeling back to bare perfectly white teeth as I go under.

I find one of the kids and pull it up. It's the biggest, the girl, and I throw her onto her back behind Mike. He'll give her the most cover. My arm feels like it's about to snap in two as I toss her, and I see that Adrian's crouching beside the others.

And he's got the doll. Pulse.

So we just have to survive Buzzard Betsy, do something about the children, and then we can go spring Jim out of the Baobab Tree. No problem.

Overhead, the Mockers circle thick and dark. They've picked up the call of the hilarious heads now, and the air is thick with the sound of rattling teeth and soft, fleshy, gruesome imitation of the same, raining down from the sky. At least the Mockers can't really bite. I slap a water serpent gliding at me over the scum out of the way with one hand. Again I dive.

I grab another body, flailing, and I pull it out. It's the littlest kid, the visionary excited to see the falling horsey. He spits cold mud from his mouth, he's crying but he can breathe, so I think he'll be okay.

Mike is reloading and sees me; he grabs the kid and pulls him ashore.

"I thought you were dead!" I snap at him.

"Maybe I am!" The blood runs down his side and into his pants. While he's under cover, he pulls a flask from his pocket and drinks.

Eddie fires shot after shot into Buzzard Betsy with his boomer. I don't think they're seriously injuring her, but each shot forces her to stagger back a step or two, and they do leave purple blotches. As Eddie reloads, Adrian fires off a burst with his much smaller gun. It's sheer physical force that is holding the thing back.

"Hurry!" Eddie snaps at me, reloading his boomer. He doesn't tell me to leave the last kid. I dive.

I feel around in the cold mud, and for a moment I can't find anything. Then, fingers. I grab the hand and pull it up. This time it's me spitting out the mud, and when I pull the hand out—

I see it has no flesh on it. Just bones.

Wispy-haired Redhead smiles at me. "Chatter-chatter-chatter," he says, and his bony fingers squeeze mine.

"Oberon's buttocks!" I toss the hand aside.

Bang!

The head splatters. It was Mike Bass's shot. He nods at me, grimaces. *"Fundillo,"* he says. "Get the kid." He turns around and shoots at Betsy.

Betsy's getting awfully close.

I feel like my one functional arm is almost detached from its socket, but I go under the mud again. It's cold and slimy, and that actually feels kind of good on my injuries. Especially the cuts on my head. When I feel body parts submerged in it, this time I check them for size. Wispy has an entire corpse under the surface, so it distracts me for a moment, but then I find the smaller body at its feet.

Smaller and still.

I grab the body and come back up. Filth streams off me and I hurl the boy to the bank. I fall to the ground next to him and the girl helps me. She pounds on the other child until he coughs and breathes again.

"Adrian!"

Mike kicks me with one foot and helps roll me over. I feel like a wet cat, and I resist the urge to shake myself and spray everyone. Instead, I run straight at Betsy.

"Twitch!" Eddie stops shooting and stands up from cover, exposing himself.

I jump straight for Buzzard Betsy's face. I raise my fighting stick as if the point is to hit her with it, puny little thing that it is.

Betsy's gray-green skin is mottled and veined even more than before. She looks like a bloodshot eyeball all over her body, with the red, ropy veins congregating in nexuses like bruises where, I guess, she's been shot. So she isn't having a very good day either. And she's pissed off.

Betsy grabs me with both hands. I'm expecting it, so the only surprise is how fast she is and how long her arms are. That's a big enough surprise.

She squeezes. I feel like all my ribs will shatter and my insides are going to burst. Maybe I've made a serious miscalculation. Betsy raises me to her mouth, her eyes glittering with rage and hunger, the raw flaps of skin around her mouth pearling her yellowish fangs with red.

I have a surprise for her.

I show pony.

Just for a second. I hurt even worse while showing pony than I do while showing boy, I feel like my chest is about to crack open. But in that second, just as Buzzard Betsy's face twists into a snarl of realization, I kick her right between the eyes.

Betsy goes down, and I show girl. I'm stronger when I show boy, but when I show girl I'm a little more resilient. And I roll better.

Still, the ground hits me like a humongous hammer.

Betsy makes a heavy gargling sound with a scream inside it. I feel like she's screaming for me, too, that's how bad it is. She clutches her face with her gigantic paws, and when she's able to get up, she'll be mad.

"The doll," I croak, and then clear my throat and try again. "The doll!"

Adrian heard me the first time, and he's already giving it to me. As soon as I hold it, I can feel Pulse. He jiggles a little bit inside. I wonder what it's been like for him. Not very comfortable, I guess, and he's had to see all the madness that Buzzard Betsy gets up to in her nasty shack.

Hopefully he's not too pissed to help me. I want Oberon to squirm.

"This way!" I cry. The direction doesn't really matter, but I pick a more cautious path, threading among the pools of muck and the babbling heads. I've put the fighting sticks away, and I carry the doll. Her misshapen mouth is funny, but it sort of disturbs me, so I turn her face to the ground and don't look.

The children follow me, then the others. Eddie is in the rear, saying hard words. Because he really wants me to believe him, he shoots one of the chattering heads just before we leave the swamp.

That's loud, but it doesn't matter. Betsy will know where we are because the Mockers are following us.

Hyoo-hyoo-hyoo-waaaaoo-boom!

Hyoo-hyoo-hyoo-waaaaoooo-graaaack!

We run through a field of tall grass, each strand as thick around as my finger and as stiff as wood. The meadow rattles as I crash through it, and I have to grab the middle child's hand to pull him through. The littlest fella has no problem and just charges straight ahead. A brook. A grove of pine trees on a hill, and we run down the other side.

And there's the wall, the Outer Bounds. It looms ahead of us, taller than anything, like it's actually holding up the glittering sky. And a gate. No Rangers in sight, but that's not so unusual. They'll be on patrol inside.

I push the children to Adrian. "Get them through the first mirror you can find that looks safer than here," I tell him.

"That shouldn't take long," he cracks, and puts away his shooter. "Come on, kids." He takes out the lens and squeezes it under his eyebrow as he drags the three of them into the Outer Bounds. They look at me with big eyes, like chipmunks, and then they're gone.

"Yell if you meet Rangers!" I call after him.

"I don't like your home, Twitch," Mike tells me. He's filthy and wounded, and he looks rattled. His breathing sounds like a bellows in need of oil and more than a few patches. I'm sure I'm no better, and I don't even have a good answer for him.

"Now what?" Eddie asks. "We aren't making progress."

"Aren't you the one in charge, Eddie?" I ask with my best innocent grin.

"Yeah," he says. "I order you to come up with a plan."

"I see. Okay, here it is."

Grrrraaaaaaaaack!

The wooden grass clatters, and a second later, Buzzard Betsy charges into view. She's even more mottled now because she's taken hits from the landscape as she's run through it, but she has a head of steam built up, and she doesn't stop. An unfortunate sapling in her way, my height and as thick around as my leg, explodes instantly into moist toothpicks as she charges through it.

"We take her down," I say. It's a joke, but they don't laugh.

"*Chingado.*" Mike sags, dropping to his knees.

Adrian emerges from the gate as Betsy rushes down upon us. He has the Eye in his hand, and he grins.

"I knew you guys would get into trouble without me." He laughs, squints through the Eye, and raises a stub of candle that he always carries in his pocket.

"*Per Volcanum ...*" He yawns.

Betsy barrels closer.

Mike slaps his hands at Adrian, tries to pinch the wizard.

"*Per Volcanum ignem ... Per ... Per ...*" Adrian sways on his feet.

Boom! Boom! Eddie fires shots at Betsy, but she's coming downhill at us now, she's mad, and the boomer isn't strong enough to knock her off her chosen path.

"You can do this, boyfriend," I whisper to Adrian, and I show him confident girl. It isn't easy showing him that, with my arm gimped at my side, my ribs most likely shattered, and my head nearly caved in.

Adrian nods. "*Per Volcanum—*"

He's still awake, but he can't get out the words.

"*Ignem mitto!*" I shout. Not a spark.

Buzzard Betsy is upon us.

CHAPTER SIX

Maybe your friend can help!" Eddie snaps.

He fires over and over with his boomer. The empty shells from his weapon spin out into the air and rain around me. Mike fires too, but I think he's missing every shot.

"Aim low!" Eddie shouts to the big guy.

We can't stop her. Can we get away?

"Adrian!" I tuck the doll under my arm and slap the wizard. I'd shake him, but it would hurt my ribs too much.

"Volcanus …" He rubs his face with his hands. He's struggling.

"Forget the firebolt!" I cry. "Let's get out of here!"

He perks up a little. "Leave the Queendom?" he asks.

"Abandon Jim?" Eddie barks. "No way!" He fires again.

"No!" Betsy rushes down the hill as fast as an automobile. "We'll just come back in a different way!"

Eddie slams out the last of his boomer shells, and it looks like he finally hits Buzzard Betsy's feet. She collapses, slamming into the moist earth like a bomb. Dirt flies up in all directions, and she plows a furrow wide and deep enough to plant hippopotami inside it.

"Ha!" Mike lurches forward onto his hand and empties his shooter into Betsy's back as she rumbles to a halt.

Eddie grimaces and pushes more shells into the boomer. The sword still dangles from his torn jacket. It looks wrong on him.

"Maybe we don't need to run," he suggests.

Betsy raises her head. She spits mud from her quadruple-wide maw, vomiting out a croak as loud as thunder.

"*Huevos*!" Mike falls to his side.

"Into the Outer Bounds!" I shout, and I back through the gate. Mike tries to stand, his face twisted.

"Turn my head!" says a voice. It takes me a moment to recognize it. "I can't see all the fun!"

Adrian hears it too, and stares. He puts the Eye over his face and stares closely at the doll. Mike staggers towards me, reloading his shooter. Eddie steps deliberately, shooting all the while.

I hold the doll up and point the X's on her face towards Betsy.

"Oh, yeah," Pulse chuckles. "You're in for it now."

"Unhelpful git," I call him.

"Where's your sense of humor?" he chides me.

Betsy lurches to her feet, springing out of the furrow her vast bulk has dug in the earth. She lands with her legs wide apart and her arms spread. The nails on her fingers shine, greasy and ragged, and they look like they're all pointing my direction.

"Dammit," Eddie grumbles. "I coulda sold cars for a living."

But Betsy doesn't attack. She hangs in the air and quivers. Her beady eyes glitter and her jaw works, snapping open and shut and spraying fetid slobber each time. The Mockers above her circle and cry out.

"Here's one!" Adrian calls from behind me. "Opens into an empty restroom!"

And Betsy turns and shambles off. Her pace is strange, different from the shamble we've seen from her before. She seems to pull back with her shoulders, like the upper part of her is resisting something, and she leads with her vast belly. Her steps are ragged and irregular.

She's being pulled, is what it looks like.

Eddie raises his boomer to fire at her again, but doesn't.

"Son of a bitch," Adrian says.

"Chicken!" Pulse yells. "Come back here, you coward!"

Betsy turns her head and growls wordlessly at us, but she pushes through a stand of pine trees and is gone. The Mockers linger a few moments longer than their mistress, spitting bitter blame upon us.

Hyoo-hyoo-hyoo-waaaaoooo!

Then they, too, disappear.

"Booooooooooring!" Pulse howls.

Eddie pumps his boomer and presses the firing end of it to the doll's forehead. "I haven't known you long," he snaps, "but I think I can already tell how I feel about you."

"Ah," Pulse purrs. "This one's funny, Pony. No wonder you stayed away so long."

"I stayed away so long," I remind him, "because I was thrown out of the Queendom."

Eddie lowers his gun. All three of the rock and rollers stare.

"Did you say you put the kids in a restroom?" I ask Adrian. My head is spinning a little.

He shakes his head. "A daycare center. I'm not sure, but I think it might have been in Texas."

Eddie takes a roll of white tape from one of his packets and commandeers Mike's flask. He goes to work on Mike's injury, sloshing it with whisky and then bandaging it. Eddie was a soldier. He knows what he's doing.

Mike leans against stone and submits to being treated. "Why doesn't it have a tail?" he gasps. "Don't you all have tails?"

Pulse cackles. "Listen to the big Outsider!" he jeers. "He thinks I'm Pulse Dolly!"

"You are," I tell him. "The rest of you is barbecue."

"And I was such a handsome lemur," Pulse laments. He sighs. This is just a sound, of course. The doll isn't Pulse's body and doesn't move at all. "You could have taken me with you, you know."

"And carry a child's doll around with me everywhere I went?" I ask. "Or a skull?"

"You're already carrying a tail everywhere," Pulse points out. "How much worse would a doll be?"

"Worse," I insist.

The guys scratch their heads and make dubious faces at each other.

"That's not the real reason, though, is it?" Pulse Lemur never was a fool. No matter how stupid some of the things he did were. There's no point lying to him.

"I needed you to be hidden," I agree. "You were my insurance. *Our* insurance."

"Oberon was going to kill you!" Pulse's cackle sounds worse coming out of the doll's head.

"He was," I say. "Until I told him that killing me wouldn't save him. If he killed me, you would tell everything and he'd still be in trouble. Then he agreed to make me an Outcast instead."

"This is really charming," Eddie butts in. "Would you care to explain?"

I sigh, but Pulse leaps right in.

"Once upon a time," he says, "there were three friends. Hilarious, slap-each-other-on-the-back friends, all of them Rangers and one of them a King."

"Oberon," Adrian says.

"Shush!" Pulse says. "And these friends, they did things together that were truly funny. Fires and droughts and plagues and all the best things to induce a good belly laugh."

"Ha, ha," Mike says slowly. He isn't laughing. "*Cagado.*" Eddie finishes with the tape and hands Mike back the flask. Mike drains what's left.

"And one day, the King tells his two friends that the Queen has a visitor. 'Oh, is it like that?' the friends laugh. 'No, it isn't like that,' he tells them, 'she has a fancy, important visitor from another court, they're scheming together big, schemy plots, and the King and his Rangers are supposed to arrange a parade and a chariot.'"

"Belial." Adrian remembers.

"Belial, very good, one of the biggest Princes of Hell, sits right on the Infernal Council, and he needs a ride because his own beasties don't travel so well in the Queendom."

"Because of the light," Mike guesses.

"Because of the light," I tell him. "Some of the folk of Hell take it fine. Others are burned at the touch, like the Baal Zavuv."

"Stop interrupting me, Pony!" Pulse snaps. The doll's smile is fixed and greasy. "So these three friends plan a little joke, and it's going to be a good one because the more people who are upset and the more important those people are, the funnier the joke. The chariot's going to be pulled by six white horses. Or ponies. And the King doesn't have but the one shape, but his two friends can both show horse."

"Pony," I say softly.

"I thought you said you were a lemur," Adrian interrupts. "Isn't that like a monkey? Or a raccoon?"

"I can show a lemur," Pulse admits. "And also a big warhorse, a destrier."

"With a lemur's tail," Mike says.

"And proud of it."

"Not anymore," I remind him.

"I told you to stop interrupting. So the King and his two friends have access to the chariot and all the horses, you see? And they're Rangers, so they can move around in the Outer Bounds without anyone thinking anything about it. So the three of them make a quick trip through to the Outside, and they collect beans. Bushels of beans."

Mike snickers.

"Hell," Eddie curses. "You're like children."

"Beans, beans, the musical fruit," Adrian chuckles. "You know …"

Eddie snorts. "I'm surrounded."

"And when the chariot team is eating, to get their strength up, an hour or so before the chariot ride, the friends make good and sure that the team eats lots and lots of beans. The friends tell them that it's special food, a reward for their special and very important duty. And the horses' stomachs aren't used to beans, naturally."

"Naturally," I say.

"Why not?" Mike asks.

"Because they're not Mexican fairies," Adrian sneers.

Mike looks annoyed. "Lots of people eat beans."

"Yes," I agree, "but not fairies. Beans are a human food, like maize or Twinkies. The Queendom doesn't have such innovations. Mab's subjects mostly eat fruit, nuts, and meat. Their bellies don't handle human food any better than human bellies can take the food of the Queendom."

Eddie laughs sourly. "You're all paleo."

Pulse laughs with audible glee. "We were paleo before there was a paleolithic! And so we meet him at the Crossroads and carry him across the Queendom, and right there, on the Avenue of Stones leading to the main gate of the Shadowless Palace, it happens."

"Trumpets," I say. I don't mean to, but I chuckle a bit. It's funny, after all.

"Trumpets!" Pulse yells. "Great blasting farts—and worse—from bellies unable to handle legumes, all aimed at blobby, tentacle-faced Belial, and the horses can't even turn away to be discreet about it because they're all in harness, and me and my friend Pony here right in the back, right in front of the Infernal, hooting away!"

He cackles. I laugh too. It's hilarious. I guess we laugh too long, because Eddie Guitar cuts us off.

"Then what?" he asks.

Pulse is silent for a moment. "Show him."

"You sure?"

Pulse says nothing. Then he snaps. "What? I nodded yes, didn't I?"

"No," I say, "you didn't nod. You can't nod anymore, remember?"

I pull apart the stitching at the back of the doll's head. It's tricky work with just one hand, but I do it, and then I reach inside and pull out stuffing so I can remove Pulse from his container. I toss the doll aside and hold up Pulse Lemur.

Pulse is just a skull. A smallish skull, like a child's, though a human scholar would puzzle over it, note its lemur-like snout and front teeth, and pronounce it a new species of pseudo-hominid, and congratulations to Charles Darwin. That funny old man gets credit for us all the time.

"*Carajo,*" Mike says.

"What happened," Pulse continues, his jaw not moving at all as the sound of his voice clearly emanates from the bone, "is that Belial blasted me."

"Chaos," I add. "Everyone bolts, the chariot is overturned, Belial falls off the Avenue and kills a hundred people in his thrashing about."

Pulse laughs. "Unbelievably hilarious. The funniest day the Queendom has ever seen."

"And we get in trouble," I add.

"Two of us get in trouble," Pulse corrects me. "The two lowly Rangers. Or rather, the one, you, since you immediately rush me off and hide me in the shack of old Funnybones there."

"Sorry," I say.

Pulse giggles. "For what? I've been laughing nonstop since you left!" As if to demonstrate it, he cackles long and loud. The laugh bothers me, and it reminds me of the bones scattered on the floor of Buzzard Betsy's shack.

"Oberon blamed us," I say to the band. "He was going to have me executed, only he knew I had Pulse's skull, and he was afraid if he killed me, Pulse would tell."

"Which I would have," Pulse said, "because that would have been hilarious. Can you imagine how pissed off Mab would have been?"

"Only it was something of a bluff," I finish, "because Pulse was hidden, and no one ever would have heard from him again. But Oberon didn't know that, and we had a standoff, and we resolved it by him pleading with Mab to just exile me."

"That's serious." Pulse's voice sobers up. "No one's been exiled in a century or more. No wonder I haven't heard from you."

"None of this explains what good this skull is going to do us," Mike complains. He looks a little pale, but give him credit, he's on his feet.

"Sure it does," Eddie contradicts the bass player. "We're going to blackmail Oberon, the King of the fairies."

"You make it sound so tawdry," I object.

"I don't think it's tawdry," Pulse says. "I think it's very funny."

I'm not surprised.

"Unless anyone has a better idea ... ?" I leave the possibility out there for a few seconds, but no one volunteers anything.

"Now's a great time to squeeze the little pimple," Pulse giggles.

"Yuck." Mike puts away his shooter.

"Really?" Adrian asks. "All we've been through, and the word *pimple* makes you uncomfortable?"

"I can think something is gross without feeling uncomfortable."

"In this band," Eddie says, "that's a necessary skill."

"Why is now a great time?" I ask. "What's going on?"

"Something big." Pulse's voice is animated.

"How do you know?" Eddie says. "You've been stuck inside a doll."

"Yeah. Why the doll anyway?" Mike asks.

"I knew that even if it occurred to anyone that Pulse might be hiding inside Betsy's doll," I say, "nobody would want to be the one to go and check." I consider, and without meaning to, I shake Pulse around in my hand.

"Hey!" he snaps.

I laugh. "Not so funny?"

"No, it was funny," he admits.

"So something's going on with Betsy." I think about that some more. "But Betsy's not the sort to make big plans. What's the chain about, then?"

"Got it in one!" Pulse hums. "But I don't know what the chain does."

"You must have seen who put it on her," Eddie says.

"Do you sleep?" Mike asks.

"A man in a funny hat," Pulse says.

Adrian grimaces. "Isn't that how *Curious George* starts?"

"That's the man in the yellow hat," Eddie reminds him. "I can tell you never had kids."

"Never really even *was* a kid," Adrian admits. The raw, dry sound in his voice reminds me of the children's bones on the floor of Betsy's shack, and I shudder.

"Funny how?" I ask. "Did the hat kill people?"

"Funny like out of place. Funny like a cowboy hat, only not really, and it has tails. Funny like in all the years I spent looking through mirrorgates at the Outside, I don't ever remember seeing a hat quite like this one."

"And it was a man," I repeat. "Not one of Mab's children."

"A man, and an old one."

"An old man in a funny hat." Eddie guffaws. "It isn't Curious George; it's Gandalf."

"And then what?" I ask. "Am I right to think the chain makes Betsy do things?"

"I still don't know," Pulse insists. "The man in the hat put that chain on her. Occasionally, out in the trees, Betsy runs into other Wild Things with chains on them."

"Wild Things?" Mike asks.

"Like Betsy. Monsters from before the Queendom. Things that don't bow the knee to Mab and are dangerous. And a lot of them have chains on now."

This news makes me feel uncomfortable, but it probably has nothing to do with us. "You sure it isn't Mab's doing?"

"How could I ever be sure of that?"

"Jim," Eddie reminds me. "A Baal Zavuv got Jim, remember?"

"We're going to the Baobab," I tell Pulse.

"You don't look like you're in any shape to do that," he points out.

"You can see too?" Mike asks.

"I have no choice," I tell the skull.

"That'll be fun, then." The skull doesn't move, Pulse can't move, but at this moment his teeth still give me the impression of a slightly insulting grin.

"Suddenly I'm not so anxious to go," Mike says.

"Adrian," I say, "I think I can get us to the Baobab if you can get me around the Push again."

"Easy as falling," Adrian says. "As they say."

"Everybody ready?"

Eddie pumps his boomer. Mike runs his fingers through his hair. Adrian squints through the Eye. I turn to face away from the Outer Bounds, and the stiffness and sharp pangs that lance through my body remind me that I'm hurt. Bad.

"Here we go."

I can't run, and I certainly can't show pony and gallop, but I jog as fast as I can manage. Adrian chants, and the Push slides off my body again.

We run over the top of the dune and through the pines, but now the other side of it is covered in desert. Mirages of camel trains, tents, and date palms fade in and out of my vision. Needle-thin, tree-tall columns of rune-speckled stone jut accusingly at the sky here and there across the dry landscape. Atop a mountain-high dune stands a giant with a serpent head, a kilt about his waist, and a huge curved scimitar in each hand. The ground is a red-hot iron pan, and it burns my feet. I ignore it like I ignore the man-tall cacti that sing at me, the carpets of scorpions slithering quietly under all the rocks, and the eyeless newts skittering over the sand, belching tumbleweeds. I ignore it, and then it's gone, replaced by grasslands, the grass of which is taller than me and the earth of which is covered in ice-cold water up to the middle of my calf.

Then that's gone too, and I stop running. I'm standing beside the Hedgerow, a thick, dark-green wall of ivy. The others step to ground beside me, and I show Adrian grateful girl.

"Well done," I tell him. I mean it. I hurt all over.

He grins. He looks totally awake. "No sweat."

Eddie and Mike examine our surroundings suspiciously. We're in a small forest glade, totally bounded on one side by the Hedgerow.

"Is it my imagination," I ask the sorcerer, "or is your curse getting easier?"

He shrugs. "Some, I guess. I feel like I'm working some things out."

"Holy crap," Mike mutters. He's pressed his face against the Hedgerow to peer through it. "Not *that* guy."

"Aha," Pulse says. "This is where things get really funny."

I press my face up to the Hedgerow to take a look.

CHAPTER SEVEN

The Baobab towers over everything within the Hedgerow, but I can barely see the great knobbly disks of its foliage, high overhead and parallel to the ground. What I see at first is an explosion of color.

Tents and flags. The biggest, fanciest tents are over by the tree. I can see the gold and purple cloth of their flaps and Rangers standing guard around some of them. Nearer the Hedgerow are plainer tents, and swarming around the tents are more of Mab's subjects. Throughout, there are tables laden with food—berries, haunches of meat, roasted squash.

"Don't even think about it, Mike," Eddie hisses.

"What?" Mike grumbles.

"I'd kill for a coffee myself," Eddie says, and spits on the ground. "But don't even think about it."

"Think about it, both of you," Pulse whispers. I tuck him away and out of sight so I'm the only one who can hear him finish his thought: "It'd be hilarious."

"I got a candy bar anyway," Mike says, and pulls snacks from the Silver Eel's green room out of his pockets. "Want one?"

Eddie shakes his head. "Too solid."

Adrian shakes his head. "Too heavy."

"Suit yourself." Mike munches on a bit of chocolate. He trembles a little as he eats it. He needs the energy, even aside from the fact that Betsy bit him.

The Mockers circulate among the tents, picking flesh off platters at the banquet tables with their toothless mouths. Their cries mix into a general cacophony that is muted by the thickness of the Hedgerow. I see Buzzard Betsy too. She stands in a trodden-down circle of earth, shifting slowly from one foot to the other and muttering.

And there are others, many of them. Crawlers with odd numbers of legs and gigantic, needle-filled mouths. Slitherers with heads at either end and tongues that drip saliva, each drop burning a smoking hole into the ground. Shamblers like Betsy, overgrown and moldering. A creature with six lizard-like legs, no tail, and a bobbing, wiggling lump of flesh hanging on an antenna in front of its mouth. The lump of flesh looks like a human baby. Bellowers, leapers, dancers, creepers. Every Wild Thing in the Queendom has been rounded up and stands around the Baobab. This is unnatural. They should be killing each other and killing Mab's children and running amok, but instead they fidget like children made to wait too long.

Every single one has a chain around its waist.

"Mab's knobby knees," I mutter.

"What is this?" Eddie asks.

"I can't be sure," I tell him. "But if I had to guess, I'd say it's a council of war."

And then I see the man Mike was talking about.

He sits at a table on a low rise close to the tree. Half the hill has been scalloped away, leaving a gentle slope terminating in a cliff. Seated around the table are various parties I know. I see Belial the Scabrous, the big tentacle-waving, scale-encrusted, semi-gelatinous Prince of Hell. Beside him is a Bearer of the Word I recognize, the whiny, treacherous archangel Raphael. They stand at the bottom of the cliff so they can participate at the level of the table despite being many times bigger than all the others. Around the table at the top of the hill, seated on carved wooden chairs, are Mab and Oberon and the man Mike noticed.

It's the man in the funny hat, the funny hat being a round- and flat-brimmed piece of red headgear with tassels behind it. He wears a red half cape, too, and I've seen him before. We saw him on top of a meatpacking plant in Dodge City, Kansas. I recognize the Legate of Heaven immediately, even without the four golems and the red palanquin resting at the bottom of the hill.

"Where's Jim?" Eddie asks.

"He's got to be inside the Baobab," I tell him. "You'll see him when we get closer."

Eddie is silent for a moment. "I just don't see how that can happen," he says. His voice sounds heavy, maybe heavier than it ever has before, which is saying something. Eddie is not a cheerful man.

I show him cute girl. Not too cute, I don't want to irritate him, just cheer him up a little. "Keep your chin up, darling," I tell him. "We'll think of something."

Eddie looks away.

"Oberon," Mike reminds me. "That's the plan, right?"

"And what else would it be?" I show Mike the same cute girl, and he looks flustered.

"I can get us inside," Adrian says. "A ward of seeming is no big deal."

"Easy for a sorcerer like you," I agree.

"But then what?" he asks.

"Can you make us look like Queen's Rangers?" I ask. "With leather jerkins and greaves and spears?" I encourage him by turning up the cute girl. "The tree and the lightning bolt?"

"Sure." He grins. He holds up three long hairs, and I remember that he took them from the tail of Flit Fox. "I can even give you a face Oberon will recognize."

I grin back. "And what will happen to the spell you put on her, sealing her mouth?"

Adrian shrugs. "There's a risk it goes away," he admits. "But do we have a choice? If you're going to walk up to that table, don't you need to be someone Mab and Oberon know and trust?"

"Do it!" I say.

"Oh, this will be good!" Pulse cackles, close against my body where no one else can hear him.

Adrian tucks the hairs into the pocket of my jacket.

"Copping a feel, cheeky boy?" I wink at him.

He chuckles and then marks each of us with a chalk glyph on our foreheads, including his own. He hesitates. "Pulse?" he asks.

I pat the bulge where I've tucked away my friend. "He'll stay with me."

"*Per Mercurium facies muto!*" he incants, and then we all look like Queen's Rangers. The others still have their own faces, though, or at least narrowed, tighter, smaller versions of their own faces. And Eddie looks like he's been bleached.

"How do I look?" I ask.

Adrian sways a bit on his feet, and I put my hand on him and show him sexy grin to strengthen him. He snaps out of his wooziness and winks at me.

"Like Flit Fox," Eddie says.

"Let's not waste it," I suggest.

"Lay on, Macduff."

You can't walk around the Hedgerow because it grows in a complete circle. It only has one gate, too, and that's far away around the perimeter, leading off to the Avenue of Stones. Besides, any self-respecting fairy wouldn't walk around to the door—she'd fly over the Hedgerow or climb through it.

We'll have to improvise.

"Eddie," I say, "do you have a knife?"

Of course Eddie has a knife. In two shakes, he's cut a pair of branches out of the Hedgerow, creating a narrow passage through it. I lead, keeping Adrian close behind me. Mike follows, and then Eddie brings up the rear. He looks like a small, elfin black man with all the color sucked out of him, holding a wooden spear. I'm pretty sure that under Adrian's ward of seeming, the spear is really Eddie's boomer.

We emerge from the Hedgerow behind a mud pit. In the mud, things shaped like worms and as big as horses roll over each other and gnaw each other's rubbery flanks with toothless mouths. They're chained, too. I've never seen such a sight as these chains on all the Wild Things, and I wonder what the chains do.

And why Mab is letting the Legate of Heaven go around in her Queendom, chaining up all the Wild Things. And why she and the Legate are sitting down to a picnic at the Baobab tree with Belial, the ugliest Prince of Hell.

I grin at a couple of Rangers standing a gluttonous watch over a trio of ostriches roasting on a spit.

"Flit Fox," they nod.

"Wiggle Emu," I nod back. I nod again to the other, whose name I don't know.

"Pony, you clever clogs, you," Pulse murmurs. "Wouldn't it be funny if I started yelling right now?"

"It would," I agree. "It'd be so funny, I'd have to smash you to tiny pieces on the spot, before I even tried to defend myself or get away. And that would be hilarious too."

"Yes, it would," Pulse agrees, but his enthusiasm is a little more muted.

I make a beeline. I look officious, like I have an important task. I can't very well go slinking around trying to avoid notice and then walk up to Mab's table, so I go bold as brass. Also, walking fast means no one invites me to eat and no one makes any serious effort to engage me in conversation. This ruse won't work if someone has just seen Flit and knows she's under a spell—or thinks Flit is missing in action and wants to ask me questions about it. I return waves and salutes and call out names when they occur to me.

Walking fast does hurt quite a bit more than walking slow, though. I try not to limp visibly. I probably fail.

We approach the bluff. I pass the corner of a boxy tent full of spears and leather greaves and stop a moment at the sight of the Baobab tree.

A baobab of any sort is a strange-looking tree, with a really thick trunk and a shallow canopy of branches arrayed at its top like a collection of lily pads on the surface of a pond, each lying parallel to the ground below. This baobab, *the* Baobab, is particularly strange. It has open woody knots all about its barrel chest, and the knots are stained with blood. Its roots part from its trunk ten feet above the earth and explode down like a skirt of wooden snakes, plunging into the ground only inches apart. The roots quiver when touched, and only part upon the command of Mab or Oberon. Which makes the space underneath the Baobab's trunk a sort of prison cell.

Jim stands in the cell, glaring out at the world.

"Look at that stubborn son of a bitch," Adrian says. He means it as a compliment. "If he only called for his dad, don't you think he'd be rescued in a heartbeat? But instead he just stands there wearing *pissed off* all over his face."

"That's rock and roll for you," Eddie says. "Arm up."

Eddie hands out spears from a dried elephant's foot like an umbrella stand. That's smart. I take one. Even if I can only use it with one arm, the thing has a sharp point on it, unworked enough that it will poke a hole through any of Mab's children.

"*Mierda*," Mike mutters. He's staring at the Baobab. "Is that thing a tree or a monster?"

"It's a tree," I say. "A tree that eats flesh and can move."

As if it's heard me, which it clearly hasn't, the Baobab's trunk shudders.

"Is it a ... a Wild Thing?" Mike asks.

I cock my head and consider for a moment. "I don't know," I admit. "I think it's like Rahab. Old like the Wild Things, but sort of a special case. The tree doesn't wander around in the Queendom, it stays here. The Baobab serves Mab."

"This is nuts."

"True," I admit. I'm just glad the Baobab isn't wearing a chain around its trunk.

"Let me see!" Pulse hisses.

"Once." I take him out and give him a good long look.

"Hey!" he cracks as I stuff him back inside. "It's just about to get really good."

"Don't worry," I say, "you'll be in the thick of it."

"You going to bring Oberon over here, then?" Eddie asks.

I look around the edge of the clearing and nod a direction. "Get as close to the tree as you can without getting into trouble. I'll bring him to meet you."

Eddie pumps his boomer. It looks like he's holding two spears and stroking one of them. "What makes you worry I'd get into trouble?" he asks.

I show him a dazzling groupie, though I don't know how much of it he can see through Adrian's wards. "That's rock and roll for you," I tell him.

I leave them and walk up the hill. A few steps along, I am challenged by a sentry, but when I growl at him, he shows dormouse and backs down. I hear music playing over all the monstrous and bustling sounds of the council, and I see that on the far side of the bluff stands a little band, playing to entertain the table. There's a harpist, and also something that looks like a guitar but has a really long neck and only three strings, a pair of kettledrums, and a tambourine player. For a crazy moment, I want to walk away from my mad plan and simply sit down with the band and play.

Just for a moment, though. Then I get control of myself and focus on the table.

Mab is resplendent. She's tall and thin with hair like gold, and oak leaves ring her about the ears. Oberon looks like he's her match, like he might have hatched out of the same nut, even, same height and build, though his hair is jet black. But he's wrapped in that tailed coat and trousers that she chose for him, and he's got an expression on his face like a servant or a dancing monkey, eager to please. Mab's the one who wears the skirt in the family.

The Legate looks ageless, though he feels old, so old he can't be human, I think to myself. I don't look at him because when Mab and Oberon are entertaining others at their table, a Ranger would be careful not to molest the guests. I don't look at the Infernal or the Angelic, either, though they both practically scream at me, begging to be stared at. Belial looks like an octopus upside-down in bloody aspic, and he sounds like cars being torn apart with metal snips. Raphael burns white. There are meat and wine on the table in front of them, but no one appears to be eating.

I feel strange as I approach. I try not to think about my feelings, but they poke through anyway. Do I miss this place? Do I want to be here? This is my home, isn't it? Isn't this why I'm fighting to get Jim into Hell and force Azazel to do us favors—so Azazel will forgive any affront I caused to Infernal dignity and insist that Mab take me back?

But what is Belial doing here again? And with the Legate, a man who schemes against Hell in order to be able to scheme against Heaven?

Is my quest misguided to begin with?

"I want to see," Pulse mutters. I rap him on his bony forehead, and he shuts up.

Now is not the time to ponder and re-ponder.

I stop an appropriate distance from the table and bow. The Legate pauses in midsentence and waits. Oberon sees him waiting and turns to look at me.

"Yes, Fox?"

"My Lord," I say, "there is a disturbance in the Outer Bounds that may require your attention."

"Again?" Oberon rolls his eyes and climbs to his feet. "Pardon me, ma'am," he says to Mab, kisses her hand, and then flops in my direction. He's wearing the long, pointy-toed shoes of state to go with his formal tails, and they slap loud on the grass behind me as he follows me away from the table.

I feel a burning at my back, which might be the angel Raphael, or the Legate's stare, or worse.

"Far enough," Oberon whines, and flaps to a halt. "What is it, Fox?"

I want a little information before I tell him anything. "You heard about the scuffle?" I ask. I am careful to stand so that he is between me and the parties at the table. "The resistance put up by the Outsiders?"

"Yes," he says, and points to Jim. "The Baalim delivered bar Azazel to Belial, who turned him over to us. I'd heard you were missing, and I'm happy that isn't true."

I see Eddie, Adrian, and Mike. They're standing around a fire pit with Queen's Rangers, warming their hands and doing a credible job of looking like bored soldiers. They're not as close to the Baobab as I'd like, but they're within a short sprint.

Jim still glares out at the clearing.

"But you see, Obie," I tell my King, my one-time friend, and the First of the Queen's Rangers, "Flit Fox *is* missing."

I take Pulse out and hold him between us.

Comprehension slowly dawns on Oberon's face.

"Mab's shiny belly!" he hisses.

"Don't let her hear you say *that*," Pulse warns him.

"Well, I can't very well curse by *Oberon*, can I?" He glares at me.

"Why not?" I smile. "I do."

"Hello, Obie," Pulse says. "It's been a long time."

"How do you look like Flit Fox?" Oberon asks me. He stares close, at me and at the spear. "How are you showing me this?"

"It's a secret," I said. "Learned it in the Rangers!"

"Liar!" Pulse gasps.

"Not that I'm anxious to see you again," Oberon whispers. "Especially not here and now." He hops from one foot to the other, like he's about to show a crow. Which he can't do. Oberon can only ever show Oberon. Right now he's showing surprised, uncomfortable, edgy Oberon.

"Unfortunately," I tell him, "it isn't my choice. I need a favor from you, and I need it now. And in fact, I need it right here."

"When you say *favor* ..."

Pulse laughs.

"I mean that you're going to do what I tell you, or I'll march over there with my friend Pulse and we'll tell Mab and Belial exactly who was responsible for the Avenue of Stones." I smile flirtatious teeth at Oberon.

Oberon's pale face grows paler. I can see wheels spinning inside his head, and I wonder what they're churning. I take a guess.

"It looks to me like now might be a particularly bad time for this news," I say, looking over Oberon's shoulder at the table. "Mab getting all cozy with Belial like that, she might have to throw you overboard to stay on the tentacled fella's good side."

Oberon snarls. "What do you want?"

"My friend," I say, and as I say it I realize that I'm saying something important. Something true. I nod at Jim. "Jacob bar Azazel. Tell the Baobab to let him go."

He looks stunned.

"It can be discreet," I suggest. "Tell it to just part its tails ever so slightly in back, and Jim will be on his way and gone long before anyone realizes."

Oberon looks over his shoulder, making sure no one can hear us. "You're mad!"

"Yes, she is!" Pulse agrees. "And I'm bored. I haven't seen a child get eaten in ages. So let's quit this nonsense and get to it!"

"Get ... get to what?"

"You choose, Obie," Pulse says. "Either way, you might make Mab really, really angry with you." He chuckles.

"Are you afraid of being caught?" I ask, and my own question makes me curious. "Can the Baobab tell on you?"

"Yes!" he snaps, then recovers himself. "The Baobab will tell Mab that I ordered the prisoner released."

I enjoy his squirming quite a bit, but I'm afraid it might be too hard for him. The end objective, after all, isn't to make Oberon uncomfortable, it's to get Jim out of confinement. "I'll make it easy," I say. "Tell her I tricked you. You saw Flit Fox, loyal Ranger, and he told you that a rescue attempt was going to be mounted on behalf of the prisoner Jacob bar Azazel. To prevent the rescue, you ordered Ranger Fox to move bar Azazel to the Shadowless Palace. You had no idea that Flit Fox was really the notorious Outcast Twitch Pony in disguise, and you're shocked to hear it."

Oberon hesitates. I think I've got him.

"Aw, that's no fun," Pulse complains. "What is there to laugh at if no one gets hurt?"

Then something scurries across the grass behind Oberon. It's quick and it's red and I try not to look at it, but I must glance at least briefly, because Oberon turns his head to see what's happening.

It's Flit Fox. He's running flat out for the table, and as Oberon and I look at him, he starts barking at the top of his lungs.

I bring up my spear, but I'm not fast enough. Oberon punches me in the jaw. The blow sends me reeling, and I drop Pulse onto the grass.

The skull laughs uproariously. "Now, *that's* hilarious!"

CHAPTER EIGHT

I lose my grip on the spear and roll through the grass. An enormous bellow rings off the shimmering vault of the sky from the hilltop, but I can't pay it any attention. I try to slither away, and Oberon picks up the spear.

He comes after me. He stabs for my head and misses, then for my chest and I roll aside. A third time he aims right at my belly, and I don't have time to move—

At the last second, I show falcon. The point of the spear rams down through the long silver hairs of my tail. It pulls hairs out, and that smarts, but I'm not injured.

I pull out one of my fighting sticks. Oberon rears up, spear raised over his head in both hands to thunder down upon me and impale me like a bug. His face is stormy, roiling and flashing lightning.

I throw the stick, and it hits him between the eyes.

Oberon falls back. "Mab's knuckles!" he howls, clapping long fingers over his face where I've pounded him.

I cast around for anything I can fight with and find Pulse.

"Ha ha ha ha ha!" he cackles. I don't find it very funny. "You've pegged him right in the nose, Pony! How does that feel, Obie, my lad?"

I shove my fingers through Pulse's eye sockets and drag myself to my feet. Oberon bends to pick up the spear he's dropped, and I see that behind him, confusion explodes at the table on the bluff. Belial rolls slowly out from behind the cliff, and Raphael is running in my direction.

Oberon charges.

"Tell everything!" I yell, and I throw Pulse.

The pain of throwing him knocks me back to my knees.

Oberon swings the spear like a club over his head, trying to knock the skull out of the air as it whizzes past him. He misses, and Pulse goes tumbling mandible-over-occipital towards Mab and the Bearer of the Word.

"Oberon did it!" I hear Pulse wail. "The Avenue of Stones! Oberon put beans in the horse trough! Oberon was the mastermind!" He laughs as he yells, obviously highly amused.

I don't know if Mab can hear him, but Raphael, whose course has him running right towards Pulse, frowns, perplexed.

Oberon's not amused. He spins, grabbing at the grass and earth to keep himself upright, and then he goes galloping back towards the bluff.

The Legate rushes for the palanquin, his four golems bending at the knees to pick up their poles as he climbs in. Raphael streaks across the grass toward me. I'd love to show falcon and leave him in the dust, but I can't fly. But then Oberon dives for Pulse's skull and throws himself under Raphael's feet. They both go down in a tangle of green and flaming white.

I get up and run.

Eddie, Mike, and Adrian are at the Baobab. Eddie has his boomer out—it still looks like a spear—and is guarding the others. Adrian incants and wiggles his arms at the Baobab.

It isn't going to work. That tree is one of the oldest and most permanent things here. It preceded the Queendom, it's the tree on Mab's coat of arms, you can't just cast a little spell on it and expect it to open up for you.

Not that I have a better plan.

I run scattered, limping in irregular wheels and gasping from the pain. Belial oozes across the grass towards the tree, and

Raphael is on his feet again, heading the same way. Mab shouts orders to the Rangers around her, and they take to the sky in bird forms, winging to close in on the Baobab.

The band is still disguised, but they've been identified.

At least we're within the Hedgerow. On fixed, permanent points, Mab's power is lessened.

I'm getting closer. I ought to reach them about the same time as the Legate, who is obviously working up some sort of spell himself—I can see the gestures and hear his chanting as his golems run. I'll get there in time to die with the others, I think.

That's hilarious.

Adrian shouts in frustration and turns away from the tree. Eddie begins unloading his boomer at the sky. *Boom!* Pump. *Boom!* Pump. *Boom!* Rangers show boy and girl and fall, stunned. Of course, the fall will hurt them more than the actual shots from the boomer, but Eddie's shots aren't useless.

Mike supports Adrian and pokes him with a finger, though the big guy looks over his shoulder at the tree. Behind the Baobab's root tails, each as thick around as his arm and many of them even thicker, Jim glowers. He pounds and kicks at the roots, but this has no effect. I could have told him to save his energy.

The Legate has out a candle like Adrian's, and he raises a lighter to its wick—

But Adrian's spell goes off first, and it's his good one. A blast of flame rockets towards the Legate and his palanquin. He throws himself out, tumbling heavy to the ground and dropping his candle and hat. The golems stop when he falls. They stand still, enduring the pounding flame in silence for several long seconds, and when it's over, they appear unfazed. A little singed, maybe.

The Legate scrambles aside to get out of the way of Adrian's firebolt. He steps on his own hat and moves away from the palanquin.

Why not? I see an opportunity. It's worth a try.

I shuffle over as the Legate moves away, preparing another spell, and I climb into the palanquin.

Ugh, I hurt. But the palanquin is soft, and it smells like cardamom. It's surprisingly roomy, too, for one man. Two could lie on the cushions in here if they were friendly enough.

Adrian wavers but stays standing. He chants another spell.

And then Mike does something surprising. He's been looking over his shoulder at the Baobab every few seconds, and now he steps away from Adrian and takes something out of his pocket. I can't see what it is, it fits too well into his hand.

He pulls back his arm and throws.

I still can't see what the missile is, but it's small and colorful. Whatever the object is, it bounces off the knotted wood around one of the Baobab's mouths and falls to the ground. The tree's mouth twitches.

Belial and Raphael rush past me. Belial moves like a glacier in fast-forward, oozing across the ground. If he has a face, I can't tell where it is. Raphael runs with long, swooshing steps, arms floating out beside his body. Adrian hates the archangel. I'm not in love with him either.

Another firebolt. The Legate has raised some sort of arcane field, so it glances off the air around him, throwing up a wall of sparks. Belial slides sideways to get out of the way, though, and Raphael throws himself to the ground.

"Go!" I shout at the golems. It's a silly move, a reflex, but it works. They start moving forward at a quick jog. Into the fighting.

Mike throws something again. Again he hits the crusted outside of one of the tree's mouths.

Eddie pounds the roots of the Baobab with the butt of his boomer in between shots, but the blows accomplish nothing. Adrian slumps, but he's still standing. He looks exhausted. He raises his arms to cast a spell again, but nothing comes out. He weaves on his feet.

Raphael stands, laughing.

Mike throws a third time. And this time, he hits. Whatever it is he's thrown goes into the Baobab's mouth, which snaps shut.

And then nothing.

"That was pointless," I mutter. I can hear Pulse cackling somewhere far behind me.

The Baobab shudders. Its bark wrinkles like a face showing distaste, and it bends over. It opens its mouth again to spit. Out comes a long string of brownish-red goo, and the Baobab doubles over.

I realize what Mike has thrown into the Baobab's mouth. It must have been one of his candy bars. And the Baobab is reacting the same way I reacted to my first Chocodile—with complete systemic rejection.

Mike hauls back and pitches another one, this time right into the Baobab's open maw.

The tree flexes in the middle, sharp and sudden, and spits the candy bar back out.

Mike hurls another one, and this time the Baobab tree lurches backward. Its roots all pull from the ground as it cringes under Mike's assault.

Jim runs out of his prison.

All the while, the golems continue to bear me into the fray, full tilt.

Raphael is talking, but I can't hear his words. He's probably trying to use his Whisper of Eden on the guys, but Jim isn't having any of it. He rips his sword from Eddie's jacket, cutting through the tough green fabric, and hurls himself at the angel.

I'm not sure how much damage Jim can really do, but he vaults off the back of a Queen's Ranger showing hippopotamus and slashes at Raphael's face. The angel staggers back.

Adrian fights to stay awake, and Belial is almost upon him.

"That way!" I yell to the golems. I point at Belial.

The golems are bigger than humans, and they have long legs under their kilts. We charge at Belial, and we do it fast.

Something else hurtles past us even faster.

The golems stagger to one side, and it takes me a moment to realize what I've seen. Beasts thunder from behind the palanquin and rush into the fray. There's a scuttling thing with enormous burrowing paws and mouths all over the back of its gigantic head. There's something like a praying mantis with a shark's head. There's Buzzard Betsy, and there are others.

The Wild Things are rampaging.

The palanquin crashes into Belial. The big, slimy ball of tentacles topples to the ground, clattering and roaring, and the foremost golems back up and immediately ram into him again. I have to grip the palanquin pole with my one good arm to avoid being tossed out. They've got enthusiasm, I'll give them that.

Belial shrieks and snaps in my direction. Something like a mouth opens amid all the tentacles. Long greenish teeth gleam dully and then snap together, slamming shut over the head of one of the golems.

With a shiver-inducing, spine-shattering squeal, Belial pulls back. His body undulates, sliding back and forth as it wobbles.

The golem's head is gone.

The golems back up two steps and charge again, ramming Belial's flank and tipping him over. The impact rattles me from my scalp to my toes. The headless golem runs just as fast and seems to hit just as hard as it did before.

I see Mab through the corner of my eye. She's riding on a white horse and charging into the center of things, her golden hair floating around her like a cloud of burning sunlight.

I look at the center myself and point the golems into the mass of arcing and flailing bodies. "Run!"

Jim fights Buzzard Betsy. He's picked up a spear from one of the Rangers, and now he swings his sword to keep Betsy at arm's length so he can poke her again and again with the spear.

Mike has Adrian slung over his back. The wizard is groggy, but I think he's conscious. For now. Mike curses, his face pale and sweating, and he fires his shooter into raging Wild Things. Eddie slams shells into his boomer.

Raphael hangs back, laughing and watching the monsters go to work. Mab rushes towards the Baobab, which has settled its roots again into the earth, and I have the horrible feeling that I know exactly what she's planning. As soon as she can get within earshot, she'll have the tree smash us to bits.

At least we're in a fixed point; that slows her down. Mab is most dangerous out in the fluid parts of the Queendom, where the Queendom shows whatever she wants it to.

Then Betsy takes a spear thrust into her body and Jim loses his grip on the weapon. He falls, and she rushes forward, trampling on the singer.

Boom! Eddie is at his side and firing. This will only piss Betsy off, I think, unless he can manage to hit her in the ankle or the eye.

The golems run forward, past Belial, past Raphael. The Legate sees me and shouts something, but in response, Mike fires his shooter at the man. The Legate ducks low to the ground, working up further spells.

Boom!

Grrrraaaaaaack!

Betsy's cry is so loud and exultant, I look back at her again. She raises arms to the sky, howling and turning—

Her chain lies at her feet. Eddie has shot through the links, and the chain has fallen off.

Betsy roars and rushes. For a moment, I think she's running at me, and I brace myself to be overrun. But she pounds past me, shuffling at train-like speeds, and with extended claws, chases after her target.

The Legate.

He screams like a girl—*that's* funny—and runs.

And instantly, all the other chained monsters run amok. The Wild Things turn and savage each other with tusks. They bite into Belial the Tentacular and are bitten back. They trample the archangel Raphael under their feet.

Rangers scatter, throwing down their spears and cursing.

"Get on!" I yell to the band. Mike throws Adrian into the palanquin. The effort squeezes a sound out of him that might be a whimper, and then he jumps aboard, but Eddie Guitar and Jim Throat keep their feet. Eddie fires his boomer at Mab and her horse, forcing her to detour away from the Baobab.

That's good, but we still have to get out of here.

"That way!" I yell to the golems. Even the headless one hears me—I don't waste time wondering how—and they set off at a trot, slowed down only a little by the fact that they're now carrying many times more weight. To ease their burden a bit, I show falcon.

I bounce along in the palanquin, stunned and broken. Mike's bleeding through his tape, and his blood speckles my feathers red.

I crane my bird head and see Mab rise before the Baobab, shouting words.

Surrounded by rampaging Wild Things, the Baobab slowly lifts its roots from the earth and turns to follow us.

At that moment, Eddie breaks away from the palanquin, splitting off to the right. "Eddie!" I cry, but he only hears a bird's call.

Jim joins him, and I see they're running for the musicians. Mab's band has stopped playing, and when they notice Jim and Eddie bearing down on them, they scatter. Jim grabs the thing that resembles a guitar, and Eddie, cursing, grabs the tambourines.

Oberon races at them, spear in hand, and Eddie shoots him. The boomer knocks Mab's consort to the grass.

I hear screaming behind me. I show girl to move my head and look around easier. The Baobab tree lifts half its roots from the ground, and the trunk splits with them. I see reddish wood in the underside of the tree, and then the monstrous thing lurches in our direction. It must cover two hundred feet in a single step.

I've seen the Baobab a million times, and I've always known it could move, but I've never seen it do so before now. And it's staggering. It's like watching living geography, like seeing an entire landscape pick itself up and run.

WHAM!

The ground shakes as the Baobab slams into it. Earth and grass rise and fall in a literal wave from the shock, knocking Jim and Eddie both off their feet. Jim rolls, but Eddie loses the tambourines and scrambles to recover them.

WHAM!

Another giant step.

"Adrian!" I poke the wizard. "Do something!"

He stirs himself slightly, breathing deep.

"*Chingón!*" Mike curses at him. The big guy grabs Adrian by the hair and drags him upright, pointing behind us with the barrel of his shooter. "Big tree!" he snaps, face quivering. "You gotta help us!"

Adrian shakes himself like a dog coming out of water. He gropes around his person and finds the Eye and his candle stub.

Poor boy. But if anyone can help us at this moment, it's Adrian.

WHAM!

Dirt clods rain down on the palanquin's canopy. Jim and Eddie fall to the ground again. The golems are amazingly surefooted, which is a good thing. The earth rises and falls under their feet, and they keep running.

I can see the opening in the Hedgerow ahead. It's a simple gap, thirty feet across. Behind it, I can see the nearest of the Stones jutting out of the mist that always shrouds the Avenue.

A dozen Rangers crowd in it, spears braced against the ground and firmly pointed at us.

"That was too close!" I yell.

Mike looks ahead of us and fires his shooter. *Bang! Bang! Bang!* He manages to knock down one of the Rangers, but it won't be enough. They don't have to stop us, not really. All they have to do is slow us down for a moment or two, and the Baobab will stomp us flat.

Or maybe it will imprison us in its roots again, and we'll be at the mercy of the Legate and Belial and Mab.

"*Caray,* do something!"

Adrian wipes sweat off his forehead. He doesn't look good, he's pale and blinking.

"You can do this." I show him cute girl.

The Baobab's root-foot reaches the apex of its step, and I peer up at it. Roots dangle down like tentacles, writhing and poking at the air.

"*Per Volcanum ignem mitto!*" Adrian shouts.

The firebolt rips away the palanquin's canopy; Adrian is shooting up. I watch the bolt lance into the writhing nest of the Baobab's roots and splash like red-hot glowing liquid all along the underside.

Adrian collapses forward onto one hand. He's holding himself propped upright, but his breathing still sounds suspiciously like snores.

"I hope that hurts!" Mike hollers.

The Baobab totters on one foot, knocked off balance.

Behind us, a cadre of Rangers coalesces around Mab. Mab rides on our tail, spear in hand, and the Rangers follow behind her. With them comes Belial. Buzzard Betsy is still chasing the Legate around the field.

"What about in front of us?" I yell.

Mike swivels and fires his shooter at the Rangers in the gap again. Eddie, running at our side and slightly behind us with Jim, joins in with his boomer. They have no effect. The Rangers wait for us with flirtatiously bared teeth and sharp spears.

The Baobab totters overhead—

CRACK!

Something shatters, and I don't immediately know what it is.

Guns go off close to me, filling my vision with white flashes, but the Rangers hold their ground. Mab closes the gap behind.

"Jump!" I scream at the golems.

They jump.

An explosive shattering sound behind me turns my head as we sail through the air. I see a cloud of splinters snapping from the roots of the Baobab still in the ground, and I realize it's shattered its own footing and lost its balance. The Baobab begins to fall forward.

We sail over the heads of the Rangers in the gap, spears poking at the legs and feet of the vaulting golems.

Ahead of us, gray mists swirl, and several of the Avenue's Stones come into view. I look behind, and I can see the fury on Mab's face, framed in gold. The Rangers in the gap turn to stab at us as we fly over, and Jim and Eddie bowl into them from behind.

Rangers scatter in all directions, showing vole, spider, sloth, girl, boy, and ocelot. Jim and Eddie burst through and onto the Avenue. The golems land, light on their feet despite their bulk, and keep running.

CRASH!!

Behind us, the Baobab smashes to the ground, its long, arboreal body lying right through the middle of the gap.

CHAPTER NINE

The golems rattle up the Avenue of Stones.

The Avenue can be infinite if you let it. It only has two ends, but what lies at each of those two ends is entirely up to the traveler, within a range of choices. The Avenue doesn't go anywhere you could want to go in the Queendom, but it does go to the Baobab, the Palace, and the Crossroads, as well as a few other old, old places. The fixed places.

"The Push!" I shout to Adrian.

He nods sluggishly and sets to work on a spell, looking at me through the Eye and muttering. As he prepares, though the golems run at full speed, the ground shoots past beneath our feet and the Stones whiz by, the gap in the Hedgerow behind us doesn't get any further away. The Baobab thrashes, trying to get up, but it may need help—I've never heard of the Baobab falling over before, and I have a hard time seeing how it can stand. Still, it tries, bending in the middle and pushing off the ground.

"Come on," Eddie mutters. Jim runs, looking over his shoulder, pseudo-guitar in one hand and sword in the other.

Rangers begin to bound over the trunk of the Baobab. The fliers show winged forms and zip over the tree, bombarding the ground as boys and girls with spears. Others race beneath the arcing trunk on four legs, and some clamber over the top with hands and feet.

Boom! Bang! Bang!

Mike and Eddie open fire. At least we aren't in an enclosed space here, so I don't feel like my hearing is immediately and permanently damaged. Still, it's loud. I grab my other fighting stick and get ready to throw it. A magpie and a kingfisher bullet down in my direction, beaks snapping angrily.

"*Per Mercurium manum distraho,*" Adrian finally says, and the Push slides off me.

"Go!" I yell at the golems, but they don't need it. They're already running, and as the Push comes off us, we burst forward. I will us to the Crossroads.

Not before Squirt Kingfisher and Slouch Magpie hit the back of the palanquin, though. Slouch hits showing girl and stabbing with a spear, and Squirt shows monkey. He immediately jumps onto the face of the nearest golem.

I knock the first spear thrust aside with my stick. If I weren't beaten and crippled, I'd grab the spear with my other hand and throw Slouch off the ride. Instead I roll, pinning the spear under my body.

The move traps my arm under my own chest, leaving my head exposed, and Slouch takes advantage. She shows lobster, and big red claws clamp down on both my ears.

I scream.

Something heavy falls on top of me, squishing all the breath from my lungs. My ears feel tugged and torn—

Bang!

And then Slouch Magpie is gone.

Mike rolls off me. I'm even bloodier than before.

"Sorry," he says. "I didn't want to shoot you in the head by accident."

I'm afraid if I reward him by showing him pretty girl I might distract him. So I just smile, nod, and pat his arm.

I hear monkey howling and look back. Squirt Kingfisher has torn and bitten big chunks out of the golem's face, but it continues running, indifferent. Squirt roars his frustration and jumps again, not in my direction but at Jim.

Jim stops just for a moment and swings the guitar, holding it by the neck. Its body is heavy wood, and it slams hard into Squirt's face. With a loud *twang*, the instrument shatters. Squirt shows kingfisher and flaps in midair, dazed, which just gives Jim time to swing the neck back again from the other direction. He cracks Squirt square in the middle with a meaty thump, and the Ranger sails off into the mist.

Jim tosses aside the mangled instrument and runs again. He's behind us now, and Eddie is off to the side. Behind Jim come Rangers, and I can hear terrible shrieking and roaring sounds in the mist. Wild Things.

I continue to will us in the direction of the Crossroads. I can feel the unseen fingers of the Push sliding off my body as Adrian's interference continues to help. "Well done, Adrian," I tell him. He murmurs back to me groggily, no real words.

"Dammit," Eddie snaps. "Back to the tambourines again. I just can't get away from these things."

Mike struggles to situate himself on the bouncing palanquin. The conveyance was really built for one man in comfort, and the three of us are squashed too close. I show falcon, which helps, but Mike still has to be careful to avoid sitting on Adrian, who struggles to remain conscious. "Yeah, why the instruments, anyway?" Mike asks.

Eddie shakes his head. "Just a hunch," he says. "A terrible, terrible hunch."

"Get up, Adrian," Mike says. He prods the wizard and shakes him.

An earsplitting roar shatters the mist behind us. Dark shadows move behind the shrouding mist. They're too far away and too obscured to see any details, but the shadows are so wide and so tall that it's hard to imagine they belong to anything but the Baobab.

"Ah, hell." Eddie sees it too.

"How long until we get there?" Mike asks.

I huddle up into a corner of the palanquin and show girl. "We're almost there now," I tell him. The mist is thicker now. I can't see our pursuit anymore, though I can hear the animal cries of Rangers and the great, thudding footsteps of the Baobab. I can feel the Push on my body, reasserting itself. Adrian must be losing his battle to stay awake.

ROAAAAAAAARRRR!!!

That's a cry I've heard before.

"Rahab?" Mike asks.

"Rahab," I agree. "Herself. The great old dragon. Guardian of the Crossroads."

At that moment I also hear a loud buzzing sound.

"Maybe she won't see us," Mike suggests. "We can sneak past her."

"She'll see," I tell him. "Rahab has very good eyesight. If the mist works to anyone's advantage, it's hers."

"We have to go faster," Eddie says. He's panting with effort, so I don't know how he imagines that we possibly can. "We need to try to run past this thing as fast as we can before it can harm us. And get Adrian up."

Getting Adrian up is an excellent idea. The Push is painful, and I'm not sure if it's because his spell has failed or because something is strengthening the mechanism of my banishment. Either way, I want out.

The first Zavuv bounces off the palanquin's canopy and disappears into the mist, but the second dive-bombs Mike, sinking its mandibles into the leather of his jacket before he can get his shooter around and pointed at it. *Bang!* That fly, too, disappears, leaving behind it a faint, rotting stink that is made worse by the moisture in the air.

I stroke Adrian's brow and show him attractive girl. "Time to wake up, big boy," I murmur to him. He stirs. He's not asleep, but he's close.

Jim puts on a burst of speed and catches up. I duck, thinking he's going to charge right through the palanquin, but at the last second he jumps instead and lands on the back of a golem, riding it piggyback.

The golem doesn't bat an eye. It just groans a bit and keeps running, Jim's long black hair flapping out into the mist behind them.

Eddie is flagging, but he manages to follow Jim's example. He has to hold on with his elbows because one hand is occupied with his boomer and the other holds two tambourines. The instruments rattle noisily on the golem's chest as it runs.

"Faster!" I yell to the golems, and they speed up. The foremost runners plow through Zvuvim, shattering them into scraps of dusty-smelling black fiber. The chattering and buzzing noise becomes intense around us, but the golems don't slow down.

"Man." Adrian shakes his head and looks around at the palanquin bearers. "I gotta get me some of these things."

As he speaks, the Push lessens. He's reasserting his magic. Or maybe it just cheers me up to see him awake again.

Mike has a spear. I'm not sure where he got it—maybe it's the one Slouch Magpie was attacking me with—and he bats at the incoming Zvuvim with it. The Rangers disappear behind us into the mist, and the ground rises sharply beneath the golems' feet.

"This is it!" I snap. "The Eye, Adrian!"

Adrian looks through the Eye, and his body immediately stiffens in fright. "Son of a bitch!" he squeals. "Left!"

The golems obey him instantly, swerving off the Avenue of Stones and running across the hill laterally. The air-clotting swarm of giant flies around us immediately lessens.

A blast of light and heat hits the road we've just left behind. It isn't fire because it's white and smells like ozone. It's more like a bolt of electricity, like lightning has just struck the Avenue behind us. It smells of burnt flesh, and worse.

I hear the yelp of a dog and a soft sobbing sound.

ROAAAAAAAARRRRR!

"Rahab," I mutter to no one in particular.

Our path across the hill is taking us to the summit, behind one of the Stones that stand in a ring around the Crossroads.

"Adrian!" I slap the wizard. "Can you see the Crossroads?"

"I dunno about the Crossroads," Eddie shouts, "but I can see *that!*"

I look back to see what he's talking about. I'm jostled by the running golems, but another bolt of lightning shatters the sky, cutting the mist apart and blowing a crater in the packed earth of the Avenue. In its momentary blaze and the shining eye-echoes that follow, I see a huge, armless figure stalking up the hill to the Crossroads.

WHAM!

The Baobab's root-foot slams into the slope, and it draws itself up. About its flanks swarm flapping shapes that might be Queen's Rangers, fighting for space with the cloud of Zvuvim. At its feet run strange, undulating Wild Things, the baby-esca beast, worms, Buzzard Betsy, and worse. I see them for a moment, and then the flash is gone and they disappear again.

"Forget that!" Mike shouts. "The road—where's the road? Where do we go?"

The golems rush between two Stones twenty feet apart, and into the Crossroads.

"Stop!" I cry, and they do, like a machine.

Immediately in front of us, a clawed foot digs into the earth. Its talons are easily as long as my body, and as the beast steadies its balance by gripping, those talons dig furrows as large and as deep as graves. The leg sprouting out of the top of the foot rises into the mist and disappears. The leg is shackled, and I see the first few links before they're swallowed in the mist. Each is the size of an automobile, huge and black and clanking.

"*Huevos,*" Mike breathes.

Adrian claps the Eye to his face and looks around.

"Roads ..." he mutters. "There are tons of 'em. Roads in every direction. Roads going everywhere. This is the crossroads to beat all crossroads."

All I see is mist.

"Great," Eddie barks. "Find the one we need!"

The buzzing gets louder, and flies start to swarm around us again. Mike batters them away from the palanquin with his borrowed spear, and Jim and Eddie dismount.

"Quiet!" I hiss at them.

"Sooner rather than later!" Eddie adds. He shoves both tambourines around one forearm and swings his boomer like a club, knocking flies out of the air with its butt. The boomer *thuds* wetly into the Zvuvim, the tambourines adding a pleasing jangle to the blow.

"Water, water, everywhere," Adrian mutters. "You know."

Mike scrambles off the palanquin and attacks with his spear. He winces with each blow, but he kills flies. I hear hooting and roaring of beasts from the Avenue of Stones, and I want to help. I roll over and drop off the palanquin, wincing at the pain in my ribs, head, and arms as I hit the ground.

I'm unarmed. I can't usefully show a good fighting shape. What do I have to contribute?

The golems stand, impassive. I remember them fighting on the rooftop of the meatpacking plant in Kansas. "Attack!" I call to them. Nothing. I point to the cloud of giant flies and say it again. "Attack the Zvuvim!" Rahab's much bigger and scarier, but she doesn't appear to have noticed us yet.

The golems groan. The headless one takes one hand away from its bearer pole to pat itself around the stump of its neck. None of them attack.

I guess they're showing palanquin bearers right now, not fighting golems. Or something. I have no idea how golems work.

The buzzing of flies grows more intense. Humanoid shapes rumble towards us out of the mist, preceded by a shrill bellow.

Graaaaraaargh!

"Where there are Zvuvim, there's a Baal," I say to Adrian. "There's one for your collection."

"Too long."

"Twitch!" Eddie snaps, and he presses his shooter into my hand. "Use this!"

Then he raises his boomer to his shoulder and fires into the onward-shambling Baalim. Mike joins him, and Jim protects them both from the flies, slashing with his sword and ducking in and around the palanquin for cover. Zvuvim swarm over all four of the golems, biting and gouging. For all the reaction the golems show, the flies might as well not be there.

"I don't know how to use it!" I protest. It's something of an exaggeration. I've seen lots of TV shows in late-night motel rooms in recent months, not to mention the shooting I've seen in person from the other guys.

"Point and squeeze!" Eddie barks. "It doesn't have a safety; just point and squeeze!"

"That's good," I say, the earth under my feet shuddering. "The last thing I'd want now is safety."

"Over there!" Adrian points directly beyond the Baalim, past Rahab's earth-gouging claw.

I forget about the shooter for a moment. "You sure?"

He winks at me through the Eye. "I'm sure."

Rahab shifts, and it's like the earth spins. Her claw scrapes back as she adjusts her stance, battering both the Baalim. One flies back into the mist and disappears, and the other staggers sideways between two Stones and out of sight, squealing like a murdered pig.

Rahab's face looms large over us. It's the size of a bus. Fangs like spears gnash against each other, and slobber hits the earth, carving smoking pits with each gallon-sized drop. She's gold and blue and green, colored vaguely like the sea. Her chain rattles as she moves, a dark noise as loud as thunder.

"Gotta get me one of these, too," Adrian quips. He doesn't mean it. I can hear in his voice that he's fighting off sleep just at the sight of Rahab. That's not good.

Boom! Boom! Boom!

Eddie fires at the side of Rahab's muzzle. His shots do nothing but raise sparks as they glance off her scales. I've seen one of Rahab's discarded scales; it was larger than a dinner plate, twice as thick, and hard as steel. No surprise that the shots don't do anything, but I point the shooter at her and squeeze anyway.

I hit her right in the snout with the first shot, but I'm not expecting the force with which the weapon jumps in my hand or how quickly it shoots. After the first shot, a stream of projectiles goes high, glancing up Rahab's neck and then disappearing into the mist.

"Son of a bitch," Adrian mutters.

Rahab's jaws gape, but she hesitates. Adrian looks at her, and specifically at her eye.

He's seen it—the tiny, silvery flaw on the surface of her eye where, ages ago, her conqueror smashed out a little piece of Rahab.

And she's seen what Adrian's holding in his hand—a silvery fragment like a bit of polished glass.

Adrian looks through the Eye at Rahab the dragon, the source of much of his power. He sags.

Rahab raises her head and bellows. Lightning sizzles from her muzzle, blasting Zvuvim to nothing and scorching Stones black. She rears onto her hind legs, and her front claws jump into the air above us. I empty the shooter out into her belly, but I know it's a waste of time.

Eddie pushes Mike and me. He's cursing, trying to get us to move, but I can't hear his words. All I can think about is how enormous Rahab is and how powerful and beautiful she looks. And she's about to destroy us because the Crossroads is her place and we're not welcome here, and because little Adrian Pew has been carrying a piece of her around for years, and she wants it back.

CRASH!

Something plows into Rahab from behind. In the mist, I can't make it out, but it's so vast it must be the Baobab. Rahab falls sideways with the shadow pressing on top of her, lurching away into the mist, too big to disappear entirely.

But Rahab's movement has opened up the entrance to the Avenue. Gibbering shrieks and bloodcurdling howls bounce along the earth in our direction.

"Go!" I yell at Adrian. He snaps out of his reverie and scuttles across the Crossroads towards the path he's indicated. Mike and Eddie follow, and Jim grabs my arm.

He looks at me, quizzical.

"I'm right behind you," I say. He hesitates a moment, nods, then runs after the others.

I limp over to the palanquin and tumble into it. I see the Wild Things come out of mist. Buzzard Betsy is one of them, once again chained around her waist. There are wolves with multiple heads, too, and vast mouths without apparent bodies and snakes and insects and cats with no eyes, and if they catch me, I'm dead for sure.

"Run!" I yell to the golems, and I point at the Wild Things.

They sprint, and I immediately roll out of the palanquin.

"Mab's shiny belly, please let this work," I mutter as I fall. I have a vision of myself getting trampled flat by golem feet, so I cover the back of my neck with my hand to protect it and try to huddle into a ball.

The impact hurts, and I groan.

But the golems crash past me without pounding me, and without stopping.

I throw myself onto my feet and run. I spare just a glance for the Wild Things. They're confused by the palanquin, which is hilarious, and they all react differently. Some run. Some scamper out of the way. Betsy grabs a leading golem and tries to rip him to pieces. She manages to tear off one huge muscular arm with jaws, but the other clings tightly to the palanquin pole.

I keep running.

ROOOAAAARRR!

Rahab hurls the Baobab off her body and away from her. I hear a mighty and terrible *CRAAAACCK* as Stones tip over and shatter and the Baobab's vast, shadowy bulk disappears into the mist.

Lightning crashes, and I think it must be Rahab striking again. I smell scorched Wild Thing, but I don't slow down. Rahab's tail switches out of my way, clearing my path for the exit. I see a long, dark passage between two Stones. Eddie crouches at the edge of one of the Stones, taking cover behind it and firing his boomer at a Baal Zavuv, which has recovered from being thrown around by Rahab and looms up to threaten my companions.

Jim cuts down flies. Mike shoots them.

Adrian stands in front of them all, beckoning and calling to me. He holds the Eye in his hand, and he looks through it at me and at the dragon around whose feet I lurch.

"Come on, Twitch!" he yells. "Last one in is a—"

CRASHHHHHH!

A bolt of lightning slams down into the place where Adrian is standing.

Suddenly, he's gone.

CHAPTER TEN

I fall down. I hit the ground hard, pain jolting through my body and streaks of light flashing beneath my eyelids. I struggle forward on both knees and one shoulder for a few moments before I can again lurch to my feet.

Adrian's still gone.

I stagger forward. This isn't funny, but beyond that, I'm astonished at how much it hurts me. Adrian can't be gone. But if he's gone, he's gone, just another dead human, that's how they all go, and I shouldn't think twice about it.

Only there are tears running down my cheeks.

"No!" I yell, and I rush forward to where he stood.

There's a crater. And lying in the bottom of the crater, the Eye, in a pile of greasy ash. Greasy ash that used to be Adrian.

"No!" I yell again. I'm off balance, my mind isn't working. I should be running down the road with the rest of the band, headed to our planned rendezvous with the Infernal Princes. Eddie is yelling at me, waving at me to come running to him, but I can't. My ears ring. I'm deaf, I'm yelling, I don't know what words are coming out of my mouth or even what exactly I'm showing at the moment.

I bend down and pick up the Eye. It's hard to do, my muscles hurt so much.

As I straighten and look up, I see Rahab above me. She's enormous, far bigger than any moving thing has a right to be. I hold up the Eye and shake it at her.

"See this?" I yell. "I'm keeping it!"

ROAAAAAARRR!

She shakes her body, and her chains clank like school buses being chewed into shards. Coming around her flanks from behind her are onrushing Wild Things and Queen's Rangers. I should care, but I don't. Not enough.

"It was my friend's!" I shout. Which is crazy, because it was Rahab's first, and Rahab obviously knows it.

She rears back. The motion is like the movement of a mountain, a ripple of steely, scale-encased muscles back from enormous claws through haunches and flanks, the thrash of a tail that sends two of the Stones flying into mists and perdition. She's so tall, her head ought to disappear into the fog as she rises, but white electric fire crackles in her open mouth and eyes, and that fire cuts through the mist and keeps her visible.

"And now it's mine!" I shake it.

Rahab plunges forward. I'm going to die.

Clink.

A metallic jangle. Not Rahab's chains, but something much softer and yet more piercing. Rahab's chains rattle with the sound of darkness, but this is a lighter tone. One, and then another, and then a third, and then a rhythm springs into being that seems to bear with it a melody of gold and wind.

Eddie is playing the two tambourines. The tambourine—the timbrel—is an instrument so old it predates the throwing down of the dragon, the laying of the Crossroads, and the building of the Outer Bounds. It may be the first instrument, maybe as old as Herself is.

And Eddie's really, really good with the tambourine.

Rahab freezes. She hangs over me, nostrils big enough to crawl inside dilating over and over, exhaling a warm, wet miasma into my lungs. I stand beneath her fangs, and they're taller than I am. Her claw, suspended in midair over my head, is big enough to slice me open from crown to heel without slowing down.

But she waits.

Then Eddie starts to sing.

> *I will sing unto the Lord, for he hath triumphed gloriously:*
> *The horse and his rider hath he thrown into the sea.*
> *The Lord is my strength and song, and he is become my*
> *   salvation:*
> *He is my God, and I will prepare him an habitation;*
> *My father's God, and I will exalt him.*
> *The Lord is a man of war:*
> *The Lord is his name.*

I don't recognize the words, but they sound like Bible. Well, Bible language makes for terrible music, apparently. It doesn't rhyme, and it doesn't scan. It has no bounce or swing. Eddie is merely chanting. Still, somehow, the tambourines provide both rhythm and melody, turning his words into a song.

The dragon swivels her head and glares at Eddie Guitar.

I want to defy Rahab, but I can't. I want to attack her, but that's insane. All I am now is two legs that more or less work and one wounded arm. The rest of me is out of commission, and I've thrown away both my fighting sticks.

I shuffle across the toasted, furrowed earth, conscious of the vast girth of the primordial reptile beside and above me. All she has to do is shudder, and her bulk will squash me flat as a leaf.

But she doesn't shudder. She stares at Eddie, who keeps singing.

> *Thy right hand, O Lord, is become glorious in power:*
> *Thy right hand, O Lord, hath dashed in pieces the enemy.*
> *And in the greatness of thine excellency*
> *Thou hast overthrown them that rose up against thee:*
> *Thou sentest forth thy wrath, which consumed them as stubble.*

"What are you doing?" I ask Eddie as I reach him, but he ignores me and concentrates on his playing and on his words. He holds his head at an unnatural angle, looking steeply up, his eye fixed and glittering.

I follow his gaze, and see that he's staring into Rahab's eye. "Get moving," he grunts to me out of the corner of his mouth.

He doesn't miss a beat in the elaborate weave-and-rattle of his two hands. "They're almost on us."

A deep baying like the noise of hounds reminds me of the Wild Things. I turn and see Buzzard Betsy in the fore, shambling at high speed around Rahab's haunch. With her are the ugly thing with the baby-like appendage for a lure, a pack of headless, six-legged hounds with ragged mouths in their chests, and a snake with a human face.

Rahab snorts.

Eddie sings again. I shuffle past him as quickly as I can. I'm tempted to look through the Eye at what's happening, but something about that idea feels wrong in my own mind. Premature. Inappropriate. I curl my fist around the lens, imagining the wrath in old Rahab's heart at the sight of me.

> *And with the blast of thy nostrils the waters were gathered together,*
> *The floods stood upright as an heap,*
> *And the depths were congealed in the heart of the sea*

When Eddie finishes his song, he snaps both his tambourines rapidly several times in the direction of the Wild Things.

"Attack!" he barks.

It's his I'm-the-boss voice, the tone that gets Mike away from the bar and onto the stage and sometimes even wakes Adrian up ... *woke* Adrian up ... but it can't possibly work on Rahab the dragon. I limp faster and prepare to be squashed.

ROAAARRR!

Rahab whips around, and for a moment I think I am about to die. Her tail hurtles towards me through the air like an earthquake in corporeal form. Eddie and I both drop to the dirt, and I expect that the monster's next move will be to whip that same tail vertically into the sky and then slam it down on top of us, reducing us to paste—

But Rahab lunges forward, away from us.

She spits lightning, the crackling, white fire of it blasting a deep hole in the unruly mass of beasts rushing our way. The headless hounds are vaporized. Queen's Rangers and Zvuvim swarming among the beasts shriek as they are crushed or hurl themselves out of the way. Rahab smashes one of her forelegs down—*SPLAT!*—and the human-faced snake splits into two flailing halves.

Buzzard Betsy escapes their fate. Mockers shriek about her in a cloud, *hyoo-hyoo-hyoo-waaaaoooo!* She charges right over the crater where Adrian died. The mist swirls around and behind her like a cloak, and she lifts her talons high—

Eddie raises his boomer—

And Rahab's tail sweeps over our heads again. Big and strong as a train, the enormous whip of scale and muscle plows into Betsy. The monstrous queen, eater of children and once-custodian of my fellow prankster Pulse Lemur, *ooomphs* uncomfortably and achieves sudden liftoff.

Gracefully as any bird, with hair, dress, and limbs trailing behind her like the dust of a comet, she launches into the sky and is gone.

"Stop staring and run!"

Eddie jerks me by the elbow and drags me with him.

I can't run, but I hobble as fast as I can.

Zvuvim clack and buzz more intensely behind me. Those things only have any brains around the Baalim, I know, so at least one of the big, pig-faced lads must have recovered himself. Ahead of me, Mike's shooter flares in the mist, and Eddie's boomer barks beside me. I don't know what they're even aiming at; as we move away from Rahab, the mist thickens again, and I can't see a thing.

I hear hoofbeats behind me. I try, but I can't run any faster.

The air changes. A dark, warm blast hits me in the face. It sweeps mist away, ripping it into tatters, and I see that the Stones have changed too. They aren't the squat, thick menhirs of the Avenue and the Crossroads anymore. They're fangs, jutting up and curving inward over my head to sharp points. Dark lichen scabs them over, and a dim reddish light makes the lichen look like fresh black blood.

Sunset. The light is red because the sun is setting.

I've never been down this road. I'm just following Jim's lead, and Adrian's. I know where it's taking us, though—this was once the City of Ainok. Mud sucks at my ankles, and the track ahead of me winds down among jagged, spiky rocks to a stagnant sea and the gaping mouth of a cavern. Crumbling ruins, gigantic, moldering walls and columns, jut from the rotting sea and stand tall and lonely at the top of the hill above me. This was once a place of unspeakable beauty.

Giant flies buzz around us, and Eddie swats them away.

"Stop, Pony!"

The command is in Oberon's anxious whistle of a voice, and I ignore it, staggering faster. Eddie still drags me by the elbow. He shoots a glance over my head and keeps going.

"Stop!"

This voice is Mab's. Out of sheer reflex, the habit of thousands of years, my legs stop working and I almost topple forward into the mud.

Eddie turns with me to look. Oberon stands up to his ankles in mud, his bottle-green uniform spattered black. He holds a spear in both hands, and behind him, Mab sits astride a big black horse. The horse is one of her Rangers, of course, Duck Percheron, but he isn't going to show anything but big strong horse as long as the Queen's on his shoulders. The other Rangers haven't emerged from the mist swirling behind the royal couple. Maybe they're fighting Rahab and all the monsters. Mab's hands are empty, but she has something at her side that might be a spear.

And she's showing powerful, seductive Mab. And Eddie has noticed. His nostrils are flared wide, and his teeth are gritted.

"Eddie," I say, and I squeeze his hand. He doesn't squeeze mine back, but he does raise his boomer. It's a tentative gesture, only half-convinced.

I hear shooting and Spanish curses. Behind me, lower down along the muddy road, Mike struggles against the big flies.

"Surely," Mab says to Eddie Guitar, and she slowly blinks twice to tell him that she really means it. She's turned on the charm so thick that it almost overwhelms *me*, and I'm not even the target. "This wretched creature is of no interest to you."

She gestures at me. I'm the wretched creature, and it hits me in that moment that the Queendom is not my home. It hasn't been for a long, long time. I feel like a wretched creature right now, broken and run over and discarded. Still, I'm not dead yet.

I pull at Eddie's hand. "Come on, Eddie," I say gently.

He shakes his head and sucks in a deep breath. I'm not sure he's heard me.

Oberon takes a step closer. Duck Percheron snorts and raises a hoof in open threat. I wish I had something to fight with. If I weren't so beat up, I'd show pony and kick Mab's consort into jelly. I spit at Oberon, and he hesitates.

"Leave the caitiff," Mab urges Eddie. Her smile is rich, like an overgrown forest. "Bring the half-devil back with me, to the Queendom."

Caitiff, that's me. She's right. I'm not one of hers anymore. And this whole plan of mine to get Azazel to forgive me was misbegotten from the start. It was never Azazel who was angry with me. It was Mab herself, and maybe Belial. And nothing I've done in crossing the Queendom will endear me to either of them.

I could grab the hoof, maybe, and hand it over. But Adrian's dead and Mab hates me and the only family I have left are this nameless rock-and-roll band, so I'm not going to betray them to her.

Where is Jim anyway? I look around behind me and see why he and Mike are delayed. One of the Baalim is on the road, and Jim fights it hand to hand with his sword. Mike tries to cover his back against Zvuvim attacks, but there are a lot of them and he has only the one shooter.

I show pretty girl to Eddie, as pretty as I can. "Let's go, big fella," I say to him. It feels like a betrayal, but I can't figure out who the victim is—Adrian? Eddie? I pull on his hand and try to lead him back, away from Mab.

Oberon steps forward to fill the space, the pointy end of his spear held in my direction.

"You don't need Jacob bar Azazel," Mab says in a throaty voice. She's showing the most alluring Mab I've ever seen. "Everything you need is in the Queendom."

She raises her arm, and I'm stunned to see what she holds in her hand.

It's Azazel's hoof.

The thing we chased across the desert for, our ticket for negotiating with His Lowness. I'd assumed Jim still had it. He's been carrying it around taped to his belly since we got it. Of course, once they captured Jim, it must have been easy to take it from him.

But if Mab has the hoof, what is she after? And the Legate and Raphael and Belial—why did they hold Jim in the Baobab's roots, and why are they chasing us now?

Do they want Jim himself?

"Everything you need is with us," I say to Eddie. I'm confused and I'm desperate. I might be lying. I'm showing as pretty a girl as I know how, but I'm nothing next to Mab's glory.

Eddie scowls and yanks his hand away.

"Eddie ..." Mab smiles.

Eddie's eyes are glazed with madness. He points his boomer at Duck Percheron's forehead, and the big black horse shies back half a step.

"Everything I need," Eddie grinds out slowly, "is at *home*."

Mab's eyes flash fire. She opens her mouth—

Boom!

Eddie hits Duck right between the eyes. The boomer slugs won't kill him, but they won't feel pleasant, either. Duck falls backward, and in confusion and pain, he shows a fat brown quail.

Mab collapses on top of him. They hit the ground together, just as the Ranger flashes from quail to chubby boy. I think he's in an intermittent, unstable showing when his Queen squashes his head, forcing a sound out of his lungs that is part squeaky chirp and part strangled grunt.

Oberon spins around and gasps.

Eddie lunges forward, snatches the hoof from Mab's grasp. Oberon raises his spear over his shoulder to hurl it at Eddie.

I show pony. Only for a moment, because my ribs hurt and this showing is heavy. I show pony just long enough to bite Oberon on the back of his neck.

Hard.

"Ponyyyyyyy!" my former friend howls. His spear cast misses, and he tumbles into the mud.

I show girl and run. Stagger, anyway.

Eddie doesn't need any persuading to follow. He pumps out three quick shots with his boomer and then he's with me, sloshing through the mud, boomer swinging in one hand and the other clutching Azazel's hoof to his chest.

Just as we catch up to him, Jim disposes of the Baal Zavuv. He does it like a parody of a matador, standing in front of one of the stone fangs until the last moment of the Baal's head-first charge and then dropping flat to the mud. The Baal crashes into the stone and bursts both its own eyes, spattering black goo crawling with larval flies over the lichen, the stone, and Jim.

Jim stands and runs his long sword through the demon's head, putting an abrupt end to its frantic shudders.

"You forgot something!" Eddie barks to Jim. He waves the hoof.

Jim nods, but Eddie doesn't offer him the hoof fragment, and Jim doesn't ask for it.

The pain is so sharp I can barely see. I find myself leaning on Jim as we run. Flies buzz around us, but they're brainless and do us no harm. Behind us come things, an army, or maybe a wall of beasts. I don't look, I just hear the gigantic thumping of thousands of feet and hooves in the mud.

The orange-red light gives way to dark blue, and we drop down to the edge of the sea. I see a single star, brighter than any star has a right to be, above the open maw of the cavern on the seashore. The sea itself is sucking mud, strewn with the swaying carcasses of animals. Half-submerged skulls stare at me in accusation, fleshless limbs point.

We run, clattering over a beach of bones. Eyeless birds cry and swoop without aim. The mud feels like it has fingers concealed within it, trying to drag me down. I hold tight to the Eye. I don't know what to do with it. I don't know if we're going to make it. I don't have anything left to fight with.

The great sloping brow of the cavern shuts out most of the twinkling stars. Out of the mud, we rise haggardly on stone steps worn deeply in the center. We're covered in filth, and we stink of death. Every step Jim takes bounces my head on his shoulder, and at the top of the steps, he sets me gently down.

Gently, but I gasp in pain.

And fear.

"You!" I hiss.

At the top of the stairs is a double door. The doors are enormous slabs of cold iron, maybe thirty feet tall and twenty feet wide together. I tremble at the thought of how much that iron door would hurt if it fell on me. Knockers wrought of similar iron, each five feet across, hang fifteen feet off the ground; each knocker is shaped like a skeletal human ouroboros, twisted in a ring of pain to seize itself by the ankles. The skulls' mouths are open as if to scream.

Standing in front of the door, holding the reins of her meat-eating horse in one hand and an old black shooter in the other, is the Marked Woman. Her face tattoos swirl at me menacingly, as they did when she burned and tortured me in the restroom in Kansas.

She smiles, and I can't read it. "You guys get around."

Jim snaps mud from his arms and chest and snorts. "Twitch," he says to me, and points up at the knockers, "this is the sort of thing I'd ask you to handle. Ordinarily."

"Ordinarily," I say, "I'd be happy to handle it. But I've had a bad day, and I can't really fly right now." Quite apart from the fact that the doors and knockers are made of unforged iron.

"I can," the Marked Woman says, and she steps like she's going to remount her horse.

"I got it," says Eddie. He pumps his boomer once and shoots the doors.

The doors ring with a deep *GONG!* The sound hangs in the air like snow. I turn to look at the road behind us.

Mab and Oberon ride, the queen on Duck Percheron and her consort on a zebra I don't recognize. Beside them stomp four scorched, tattered golems, one of them headless, one of them missing an arm, together bearing the palanquin in which rides the Legate of Heaven. He looks really irritated, and I wonder if he's particularly upset with me. Maybe he's mad that his golems got so banged up, but I don't really feel like that was my fault. Not entirely. Finally, bringing up the rear, come Rangers and Wild Things in two loose columns, bristling with spears. The Queendom is marching to war—spattered in mud, wounded, bedraggled, and completely pissed off.

Above them shines the bright star I noticed before. It looks enormous, almost like a tiny moon.

"*Mierda.*"

Behind me, I hear a scraping sound, and then I feel a warmer, drier wind on the back of my neck. I stumble out of the way, Mike Bass and I leaning on each other for balance, as the great double doors of the main entrance of Hell swing open.

A doorkeeper emerges.

He's beautiful. He's almost tall enough to fill the doorway, and he looks like a human. Like one of Homer's old Greeks, actually, with curving helmet, greaves on his legs, a breastplate, a kilt, and a spear. He has hair like mine, long and white, and just a hint of a smile on his face. Other than his size, the only thing about him that looks inhuman are the enormous birdlike talons that sprout out from the bottom of his greaves and grip the stone floor fiercely, gouging out chips at each step.

"Welcome." His voice is deep and grave. I don't know who he's talking to, but he bows, and a long cape sweeps out behind him. "You are expected."

That isn't funny. That isn't funny at all.

ROCK BAND FIGHTS EVIL #6

THE GOOD SON

CHAPTER ONE

The Ruins of Ainok and the Gate of Hell

The End of the Age of Pisces

When life gives you lemons ..."

The fairy Twitch stood surveying the horde of champing, snarling enemies on their heels. Queen Mab, the hideous Belial with beak and tentacles snapping, and the Legate of Heaven, that conniving old weasel, stood at the head of the wild hunt. Behind them, Queen's Rangers fidgeted, Wild Things bellowed and roared, and demons of Hell raged. A cloud of swarming Zvuvim buzzed all about them, almost obscuring the shroud of mist from which the pursuers and pursued had all emerged in a pell-mell race from the Crossroads of Rahab and Mab's own Queendom. A white glow among the giant flies might have marked the presence of Raphael, the renegade Bearer of the Word.

Behind Jim was the open gate of Hell and its doorkeeper, Baraqyel. Around him, almost unrecognizable after millennia of decay, were the ruins of his birthplace: Ainok, City of the Free. Beside him were, if he could be said to possess any such thing, his friends. His *surviving* friends. Also Jane, who had been Qayna, who had killed Jim once, and the flesh-eating horse she rode.

For all the crowd and the chaos, he felt profoundly alone.

Monsters in front and monsters behind. Things were about to get crazy.

Check that; things had been crazy for a long, long time.

"I don't actually know how the saying ends." The fairy's voice was strained. It had taken a real beating in Kansas City and in the Queendom, and it looked like it was barely still on its feet. "I never heard him finish it."

"Lemonade." Mike supplied the deficit. "You make lemonade."

"Yeah," Eddie grunted. "Only life hasn't handed us anything as nice as a lemon. And precious few people want to drink a tall, cold glass of shit." Eddie held his shotgun and Jim's father's hoof clipping. He hadn't offered the hoof back to Jim after recovering it from Mab.

Maybe he didn't trust Jim anymore.

Probably he shouldn't. Still, Eddie and the others had rescued Jim from Mab's Baobab-root prison cell and fought through to successfully carry out Jim's plan of crossing to Hell under the feet of Rahab the Dragon. They'd done it at the cost of Adrian Pew's life.

Maybe that was the moment when Jim had lost Eddie's trust.

"The Council sits." Baraqyel the Fallen called out over Jim's head at the army before him. Jim didn't look back, but he heard rustling and scrabbling sounds that had to be the mustering of Hell's defenses. "Will you join the other Princes, my lord Belial?"

Belial surged forward. He was more like a plant or a squid than anything humanoid; he'd been more radical than many of his fellows when they had begun altering themselves. Not that Jim had been there to see it, but he'd heard the stories. Belial had been one of the first to join Jim's father in the experiment and one of the least restrained.

He'd wanted power, he'd taken a great risk, and he'd paid a serious price. He looked more like a talking, tentacled avocado-worm with a beak than like the angel he'd once been. That beak and those tentacles had tortured Jim through many a fragmented dream.

"I will!" Belial's voice rang like twisting steel in the reddish-black gloom of the ruins of Ainok. He drew himself up to his full height, towering even over Baraqyel, who was several times the height of a man. "Stand aside."

Jim tightened his grip on his sword and ventured a look back. A thing like an enormous toad squatted immediately behind him, claws dug into the stony ground. Its maw gaped open, mephitic fumes rising from the rotting flesh of its tongue. It had to stand with its mouth open, though—the creature, one of the thousand nameless demon-things of Hell, had every one of its hundred unblinking eyes embedded in the slimy gray meat of its uvula. Behind the toad waited others of his father's minions, implacable, ready.

"Certainly, my lord." Baraqyel didn't blink, but the doorkeeper did keep the point of his spear angling generally in Belial's direction, poised to defend if he had to. "Dismiss your armies, and you are welcome to take your seat."

"Armies?" Belial shook as he laughed, a horrible, rumbling sound with wet tearing noises within it. "These are my friends."

"As you say, my lord. But your friends have no right to sit in the Council, unless they are invited in by carried motion."

"And the whelp?" Mab demanded. She held a spear, too, shaped like a lightning bolt. Slow, plodding *booms* in the distance reminded Jim that the great defender of her Queendom, the Baobab Tree, was free and mobile. From the sound of the booms, it might be coming this way.

At least Rahab was chained.

Jim smelled brimstone. A Hellhound. He almost smiled, and wondered if it was Phthonos again. The mindless affection of his father's hounds was almost enough to ease his sense of solitude. Almost.

"The whelp has a right to be here," Jim said. He gestured expansively at the tumbled megaliths, the rubble, the crater, and the lake with the dead birds floating in it. "This is the whelp's home."

His eye fixed inadvertently on the lone visible star in the sky, and he had to tear it away.

"Whether he appreciates it or not," Baraqyel said smoothly, and Jim remembered that he had offended the gatekeeper at their last meeting.

"And your friends?" Mab stared at Jim with fire in her eyes. "Will you leave them here to entertain us?"

"I got a right!" Eddie waved Azazel's hoof in his left hand.

Belial's tentacles tightened in unison around an imaginary cone pointing in Eddie's direction. The monstrous Prince of Hell had no discernible eyes, but he seemed nevertheless to be looking quizzically at Eddie. "*Do* you?"

Eddie held the shotgun by the pump in his other hand, and with one quick motion he shook it up and down. The ejected spent shell clattered across the stone and plopped into dead water. "And I got a counterargument for anyone who disagrees."

"Attack!" Belial howled, and surged forward.

In a burst of sulfuric flame, the Hellhound shot past Jim and into the fray. Eddie leveled his shotgun and fired.

◗ ◆ ◗

Crannock Castle, the West Country

English Civil War

BOOOOOM!

The guns on the wall of Crannock Castle roared, defying the rabble of Roundheads surrounding the moldering old fortress. At the parapet stood Elaine, hair unbound and blowing free in the wind and the smoke. The torchlight made her long blonde hair shine like a heaven-flowing river of gold, and her eyes glittered.

James shifted uneasily, eyeing the flints on both his pistols. The rain had stopped, but his powder was still wet and useless. He lay concealed on a wooded hill within earshot of the castle's gate and the crowd in front of it. The Roundheads had slack defenses, maybe indicating that they knew the fate of Matthew Taylor's men. That, the darkness, and the careful slitting of a few throats had let James slip this close.

"Stand aside, girl!" yelled Sir John Horsham. He sat astride a big horse, clad in neck cloth and mail, the rolls of merchant's fat around his neck no doubt making it hard to breathe. He was armed like a warrior, at least, with a brace of pistols and a basket-hilted broadsword hanging from his sash. Around him were his senior aides and other leaders of the Parliamentarian force besieging the castle. They all looked like burghers and aldermen, but James knew they were soldiers to be feared. More so, given the armed masses of buff-coated men at their backs. "Let us speak with the master of this place!"

Elaine laughed, and James fell in love all over again. Her laughter was fierce and free. It was the way a hawk might laugh, mocking pursuers and defying all the world to catch it or show it cause. James could be free with a laugh like that, alone together and free together, forever. He sighed.

Where was the old man? James wondered.

"Why, Sir John!" Elaine called to the Parliamentarian leader. "'Tis good of you to come all this long road in person, but I fear that we are already well supplied with Cambridge wool! But if you wish to give any of your wares as gifts to your king, leave them at the gate, and I shall see that His Majesty receives them!"

The pork-faced burghers harrumphed and snorted.

"You are encircled!" Sir John waved at the banks of glaring guns rolling into place in a circle around Crannock in the surrounding wooded hills, the ranks of cavalrymen ready to mount, and the musketeers. "Is that all you have to say?"

Elaine rotated in the breeze, looking at the armies about her ancestral manse and her own pitifully small cluster of men, bunched in their green livery all along the castle's battlements like so much moss. When she had taken it all in, she turned back to her attacker.

Surrender, James willed her. *Surrender or stall.* If they blasted her off the wall with cannons, there was nothing he could do. If they settled in for a siege or took her prisoner, he might still stand a chance.

"I do have other things to say to you, Sir John!" Elaine Canning admitted. "But I would not wish to scorch the ears of your delicate lady companions, and I do not know if you own a goat!"

Her own men laughed uproariously, though they stayed hunkered down behind the stone walls. The East Anglians and Kentishmen standing at the gate looked considerably less amused.

"Your father!" Sir John snapped. From his vantage point, James saw blue veins standing out in the increasingly ruddy flesh of the man's face. "I will speak with your father!"

"Will you?" Elaine called. "I have not spoken with him for days! Or rather, he has not spoken to me."

Sir John faltered. The feeling of dread in the pit of James's stomach matched the expression on Sir John's face. "Where is he, witch?"

Elaine disappeared behind one of the wall's crenels. The men at the gate shifted uneasily in their saddles for a moment, but then she reappeared, stepping lightly into the crenel between the merlons.

"Here he is!" she cried, and held something up.

It was her father's severed head.

The Roundheads backed their horses, gasping and cursing. A tall, bony Parliamentarian with stringy black hair leaned over and vomited on the ground.

Sir John shook his fist at his enemy on the wall. "As you brew, hag, so shall you drink!"

"Oh, Sir John!" she snapped back. "That is surely true of all of us. It was true, for instance, of my father!" She leaned back to get maximum leverage, then hurled her father's head at her foes.

The Roundheads saw the macabre missile coming and didn't wait for it. Wheeling, they bolted back for their lines. The head of the former lord of Crannock Castle thudded off the green grass just behind the hooves of the last of their horses and rolled, coming to a stop face up and looking across the battlefield-to-be at James.

"God's wounds," James muttered. "This takes a dark turn."

▬ ◗ ▬

The Ruins of Ainok and the Gate of Hell

The End of the Age of Pisces

Two of Mab's Rangers bounded forward, flashing in and out of their animal forms and barreling for Jim. Looking at the shimmering ocelot-puck-goose and hippopotamus-brownie-cobra coming his way, Jim felt tired.

It was almost over now, he told himself. Soon he would be with her.

Still, he was happy when Eddie blasted one of the Rangers sideways with his shotgun. The squirming hippo splashed loudly into the oily waters of the lake and vanished.

Jim grabbed the goose around the neck. When it honked, he squeezed, cutting off the protest. The goose slithered into an ocelot, and he punched it in the face with the basket hilt of Sir John Horsham's sword, battering it silly. He threw the hapless Ranger aside, into the deadly waters.

There were too many. Jim heard guns going off at his shoulder, but the bullets wouldn't inflict much harm on the fairy warriors or the Wild Things. Grenades or plastic explosives would have come in handy, but if the band had any left, they were in the crumpled wreckage of Eddie's old Dodge van back in Kansas City. A good firebolt from Adrian Pew would've been handy too.

Only Adrian had died at the Crossroads, incinerated by the oldest enemy of order itself.

Rangers swarmed over Jim. He was buffeted back and forth, but when he saw three of the fairies piling onto Twitch, he kicked his way through the mass of Mab's children and grabbed his drummer by the shoulders.

The fairy felt like paper under his touch, and it looked up at him with liquid eyes.

"Adrian," Twitch said.

Jim batted away a spider monkey and tried to think of something to say. He had nothing, and then a ram knocked him sideways and off balance. Brass hooves flashed over his head from something that looked like a wolf but had mandibles and antennae like an ant.

Bang!

Another gun fired.

Jim felt his mind slip. He grabbed for it but missed, and then it was gone.

The hooves above him melted away like July snow. A Valkyrie crashed over his field of vision, black wings spread wide, her mount's body stretching into a long leap, and fire pouring from her hands. A screech like the world was splitting apart pounded through Jim's head like a sonic nail. He thought he might be screaming, though he couldn't be sure.

A dark creature in his hands spat blood at him and hissed, showing long fangs. Jim stabbed it—

And then something fast and green hit him, knocking him down. He raised his sword, but the green bolt kicked it aside with hard hooves. His assailant loomed over him, tall and black with a twisted, demonic face and skinny arms. It pointed a rod at him, a scepter of fire and death.

Jim pushed off the ground with his ankles. His body pivoted upward on his ground-rooted shoulders, and he kicked the demon in the back of its head. It stumbled forward and off of Jim.

Jim rolled to his feet, looking for his sword.

The demon kicked it further away.

The screeching sound shredded Jim's eardrums. The spitting black thing sank teeth into Jim's hip. Somewhere, something called him. This all seemed wrong. Something bad was happening, something Jim couldn't quite understand, though he tried to force his mind to it.

He rammed his shoulder into the wand-wielding demon, knocking it back. As it fell, it kneed him in the face and he tumbled away.

He groped for the sword but couldn't find it. The biting thing scratched at his head and neck, and he grabbed its neck with his off hand.

Wand-demon kicked Jim in the gut. The force of the blow lifted him off the ground an inch, and he flipped over onto his back, spread-eagled. Wand-demon rose to its full towering height, bellowing and pointing the wand at Jim. Above the demon, the sky swirled in yellow and green streaks that coruscated and shifted in sync with the scratching, whistling sounds in his head.

Jim's outstretched hand found the hilt of his sword. He snatched it, pointing it up at Wand-demon—

And a wave of cool air snapped across him.

For a moment he thought he was in the hills of the West Country. Elaine ran before him, holding up her long skirts the color of the cool grass over which she ran. He grabbed her arm, pulling her to himself.

"Stop!" Eddie shouted.

There was no Wand-demon and no Elaine; there was only Eddie Marlowe, cursed family man, ex-Marine, and mediocre guitar player. Eddie stood over Jim and leaned forward, pointing his shotgun down.

"I don't want to have to shoot you, Jim!" Eddie yelled. "But I will if I have to! Let Twitch go!"

Jim looked down at himself. He held his sword in his right hand, but the fingers of his left were clenched tight around Twitch's neck, squeezing the fairy's throat so hard that its choke was silent and breathless. Twitch scrabbled at Jim's arm with limp, weak hands, and its eyes bugged out.

Jim released his drummer.

"Sorry." He climbed to his knees.

"Drop the sword!" Eddie shouted.

"I'm fine," Jim told him.

"What?" Eddie was still bellowing.

Earplugs. The madness that had taken Jim hadn't touched Eddie because he was wearing his earplugs.

Qayna. Crow Jane, they had called her in the trenches of the Great War, where death and madness rode in her wake. The bullets of her cursed gun could kill immortals, and the report when she fired tortured the minds of everyone in earshot.

He dropped his sword and raised his hands in surrender.

"You sure know how to show a girl a good time," Twitch muttered. It stood, but it didn't straighten its back out of a crooked hunch.

"I didn't mean it," Jim said.

"It's okay. I was pretty sure you were Buzzard Betsy."

"What's that?"

The fairy shook its head. "Does it matter?"

Clopping hooves cut the conversation short as Qayna returned. Her big black horse dripped blood from its sharp teeth.

Jim looked beyond the rider. A pair of Hellhounds wrestled with a chain-belted ogress, a heavy thing with talons and a lipless mouth. The Infernal toad-beast tore into a knot of fairy Rangers. The Legate's golems, burnt black and missing parts but still moving, harried Baraqyel and kept him at bay. It looked like a stalemate, though a fragile and thrashing one.

Another heavy *boom!* rang out, this one accompanied by a faint trembling of the earth under Jim's feet, reminding him that the Baobab was coming.

"You're here for the Council," Qayna said. It wasn't a question.

Twitch shuffled sideways, away from the mounted woman. Eddie spun to deliver a roundhouse kick that knocked a baboon off Mike's back. The baboon hit the ground in the shape of a fat spider and scuttled away up the road. Eddie dragged Mike to his feet.

"*Mierda.*"

"Yeah, enchilada to you too." Eddie scooped Mike's dropped pistol off the ground and dragged him back towards the open gate.

More chaos-formed, mutilated, twisted things spewed forth from the gate; others trickled down the hill. With a blast from his shotgun, Eddie knocked back something with three legs and an open mouth facing downward at the mud.

"Which ones are on our side?" Mike yelled, his voice hard to hear in the din.

"When in doubt," Eddie hollered back—*boom!* His shotgun shredded two buzzing Zvuvim into black paper.

"Yes," Jim admitted to Qayna. "I'm here for the Council. And you?"

"This is the Liminal Year," she said. "All things are possible."

"The cosmos shifts gears," he agreed.

"Besides." Qayna looked around her, keeping her seat easily as her horse kicked away a writhing knot of serpents. "When there's only one game in town ... where else you gonna go?"

Jim's laugh sounded harsh to his own ears.

Baraqyel slammed his immense spear through three of the golems in a single blow. The spear sank several feet into rock, pinning them. As the Legate scampered forward, raising his hands in some arcane gesture, Baraqyel grabbed the fourth golem—the headless one—by its legs and picked it up off the ground. He swung the golem like a club.

The Legate danced back, knocked off-balance, and Baraqyel hurled the golem over its master's head and into the lake.

"Go!" Baraqyel called to Jim, taking a step back from the advancing mass and letting a Hellhound rush past him to do some of the heavy lifting for a moment. "Your father is expecting you!"

"He is, is he?" Jim couldn't help curling his lips into a tight sneer.

Eddie dragged Mike. The big bass player looked shocked and disoriented. Qayna offered a hand to Twitch and, after a moment's hesitation, the drummer took it. Qayna pulled the fairy onto the front of her saddle and urged her horse forward, past a stream of slavering troll-creatures.

The iron gates loomed huge around Jim as he passed through. Within, two faceless giants stood, each grasping a ringed grip with both hands.

Jim turned to take one last look at the winking star whose arrival signaled the Liminal Year, and at Baraqyel and the faithful hordes of Hell, battling the armies of the Mirror Queendom, the Legate of Heaven, and the rebel minions of Belial. The lake's waters rippled, and a gray arm—a golem's arm—surged from the depths. It clawed at the dark air twice, fingers closing over nothing, and then fell beneath the surface again.

Was *dragged* beneath.

Qayna trotted in through the gates and past him, followed by Mike and Eddie.

The Baobab loomed out of the mist, a sudden skyscraper of charging tree.

"The door, Baraqyel!" Jim snapped, but the Fallen didn't turn his head.

It was a hell of a time to show pique. Jim shouted a word of command in Infernal, and the blank-faced giants threw their bodies into the effort. With an immense grating sound and a final *BOOM*, they slammed the gate shut.

CHAPTER TWO

The City of Ainok

The End of the Age of Gemini

"I did not intend this."

Jacob bar Azazel looked up at his father. Jacob was as small as any of the children of men, wiry and strong but little. He was just a boy, though his father was a titan and a Prince. His father was Azazel, first of the Fallen. Though with sorcerous operations Azazel had reformed his body, he had kept his original Heaven-given stature. He had been a Bearer of the Word, and he still towered over his son, his goatlike legs and bat wings casting a shadow that covered the entire platform at the top of Ainok's central Tower.

Jacob didn't want goat legs or bat wings or a Princely title. He wanted to be with his father. He had never known his mother, and the fact that he was his father's son isolated him from those around him. He could not be proper friends with his father's rivals or his subjects or his slaves. He and his father were alone, but at least they were alone together.

253

Azazel, first of the Princes of Ainok, looked out over his City of the Free, and his son turned and followed his gaze.

The city was sluiced by its great canals. They brought bright, clean water over sparkling stones from the Rivers of Eden in an immense spiral that touched the very middle of Ainok. The water made a single twist around the Grand Plaza in the city's center and then spun back out again, a second spiral within the first that carried the city's filth out and away to the foul, swampy lake to its south. From the ground, the canals appeared to be an impenetrable maze of long, curving main branches and shorter tributaries, some of clean water and some inexplicably foul. From above, the pattern of running water looked like a gigantic flower.

The plain was almost perfectly flat. Enchantment made the water flow.

The canals crossed broad plazas and ran along wide boulevards. Every building in Ainok was squarely framed of dark wood and white stone, and everything sparkled. Ordinarily, that sparkle would have been complemented by the incessant bustle of a people about its business. The boulevards were wide to accommodate wagons and caravans, and the plazas left plenty of space for merchants' booths. Now, as the first burning stink of the smoky trails of the falling Bearers of the Sword reached Jacob's nostrils, the Free People fled. They jammed the city's gates and streets, trampling each other and staining the streets red with their blood and the blood of their animals.

The Fallen ran too, trampling the smaller folk under hoof and claw in their flight.

"They came in tents at first," Azazel continued. "They had heard of my rebellion, and though I raised no flag, they came to me anyway. *I* was their flag. Some of them wanted to be powerful. All of them wanted to be free." He turned and looked at his son, and his eyes were warm. "Everyone wants to be free. Not everyone understands the price."

"What's the price, Papa?" Jacob asked. The top of the Tower felt intimate, warm, and safe even though the wrath of Heaven fell from the skies all around them and Azazel's people massacred itself in the streets below. Everything but the platform was remote and unreal, not urgent. His father would protect him.

Azazel turned again and looked down at the city. "When you are free," he rumbled, his voice like a lion's warning growl, "you must bear all the consequences of your actions alone."

Jacob considered this. "What do you mean?"

His father sighed. "I mean that the city of tents became unlivable. We walked in our own excrement. We ate and breathed flies, and our own flesh hosted their eggs. I could not sleep for the sounds of rutting and murder about me at all times."

"Did you stay because of me?"

Azazel laughed and knelt. Standing at his father's knee and under his wings was as good as being inside a building. Jacob grinned as his father gently mussed his hair. "I would have," the Prince of the Free agreed, "but you did not exist then. I had not even met your mother."

Jacob didn't know his mother. He nodded, eager to hear the story though he didn't understand it.

"I built this city." Azazel stood again, his heavy hooves clicking loudly on the white flagstones that paved the Tower's platform. He stretched an enormous arm to point as he spoke. "I barred access to this plain while I worked, and I began by flooding it to clean it of the filth that was here. I dug the canals myself. I plowed the guiding lines into the ground, and I laid the incantations by my own hand. I marked out the Grand Plaza and the Palace, but the first building I raised was this Tower, and here I finally planted my banner. And then I opened the roads again."

"And they came, Papa."

Azazel nodded solemnly. "They came. They gathered in the Plaza and heard my rules, and they agreed to them. We would be rebels, but we would rebel together, and our burdens would be shared. I did this, you understand, for myself."

"And also it made other people happy."

Azazel shrugged. "Yes."

"And now?"

Azazel looked to the horizon. Bearers of the Sword strode across fruited fields, igniting them with their fiery white touch. Jacob trembled to look at the vengeful angels, faces entirely hidden behind platelike visors and tree-sized swords dripping liquid fire on the ground, but his father looked calm. Resolved.

"Now," Azazel said slowly, "I wonder if I have taken full enough account of what the consequences and the burdens really are."

The first of the Bearers of the Sword reached the wall. It raised its enormous weapon overhead and swung it down like an ax. Masonry exploded on contact with the sword, blasting out over the fleeing crowds and leaving bloody furrows behind.

Azazel turned suddenly, looking down. He guffawed, a sound like an earthquake's groan but joyous. Jacob looked at the Grand Plaza but didn't see what his father was laughing at. Then Azazel snatched his son, held him close to his chest, and vaulted into the air.

The world flashed about them, but Jacob didn't close his eyes. His heart thrilled to be this close to his father. He was an only son, but his father had many women and many courtiers and rivals and allies on Ainok's Council, so he had little time, generally, for Jacob. He wondered if their separation made his father feel lonely too. The height and speed of the movement didn't frighten Jacob, and he tightened his arms against his father's enormous body and enjoyed the trembling, vibrating feeling of flight.

They alighted with birdlike grace, and Azazel set his son down. A woman stood there—a woman to Jacob's scale rather than Azazel's. She had long black hair, skin as brown as a nut, and anxiety written on her face as plainly as the blue tattoos that covered and identified her. She held a knife in her hand. There was something otherworldly or shifty about her; she continually squinted left or right, as if seeing phantoms invisible to others.

She was Qayna, the Marked Woman. She was a frequent visitor at Ainok; she had some history with his father, and Jacob didn't understand quite what it was. But he knew that Qayna had done something Heaven didn't like, and as a result she had been cursed to wander the earth forever.

He wasn't sure if that made her like his father, or his opposite.

She looked at Jacob, and he looked back.

"You must take Jacob and flee."

"The Swordbearers are here!" Qayna said. She waved her knife in a big circle, as if to show that they were surrounded.

Azazel smiled gently, but Jacob thought his father was keeping strong emotions bottled up. Jacob had a feeling, and he couldn't quite tell himself why, that his forced departure was another of his father's ... consequences. Burdens. "Must I repeat myself? I took you in when you had no place else to go, Qayna. Will you not repay the favor?"

Qayna took Jacob's hand, and then a whirlwind of action exploded around them. Jacob watched with feelings that were half-sickness and half-detachment as his father fended off a rough challenge from the brutish, pig-headed Semyaz, mocking and then leaving his rival buried in rubble. And then Jacob and Qayna were running past a snake-headed giant and into the glittering city.

She dragged him along by main force. A Bearer of the Sword nearly killed him when Qayna ran down the wrong alley. Jacob didn't cry. He wondered what would happen if the big flaming sword that reduced stone buildings to smoking rubble hit the Marked Woman. Would it kill her, or would her curse protect her?

And what if the sword killed Jacob? It surely would if it hit him. What would be the cause of that consequence? Whose choices would have been the cause of Jacob's death?

Ainok was the only home Jacob had ever known, and he watched it blasted, smashed, and burned around him as they ran. He was a little surprised when the tough, dense hardwoods burned, but he was shocked to see stone itself burst into flame. The Free ran without coordination, and they died alone, ten thousand horrible, mangled deaths, as Jacob and his bodyguard rushed unnoticed among them. Then, as the Marked Woman dragged him along a canal, its murky, waste-bearing waters now slightly darker with the blood that sluiced into it from the city streets, he saw his father again.

Azazel stood on the other side of the canal. Jacob had run across most of Ainok only to be within yards of the father he'd left. The Prince of the Free was now surrounded by multiple Bearers of the Sword, along with a single Bearer of the Word.

Jacob didn't know any of the agents of Heaven personally because they never came to the Free City. They had never come, anyway, until today. But this figure was the height of his father and drifted slightly off the ground, lifted by six wings that rarely actually moved. It was like he floated, and occasionally fluttered his wings to give the floating direction, which was very different from the muscular, animal flight of Jacob's father. The Bearer of the Word burned white.

This was how Jacob's father had looked before he had chosen to look otherwise. Of course, Jacob had never seen him like that.

"Have you come to spout more defiance?" the Wordbearer demanded. Jacob tried to stop, though he had no way to intervene and no hope of standing against Heaven's armies. It didn't matter; Qayna dragged him along, all his resistance amounting to nothing.

"What defiance?" Even his father's surrender looked proud and noble. "I am defeated, and I have come for punishment. Leave the others be. They harm no one. They only wish to be free."

Was he laying down his freedom for his son only? Jacob wondered. Or did Azazel really feel the benevolence towards his subjects as he claimed?

Qayna yanked Jacob's arm and dragged him on, but he kept watching as she ran.

"For you, there is no punishment."

"No?" Jacob thought his father looked amused. The Swordbearers closed in around him.

"Punishment is for violations of the law. What you did was so unthinkable, it was against no law. It was inconceivable until you did it."

Azazel laughed. "If I have broken no law, what are you doing here? If I have broken no law, how can there be a Writ for the Bearers of the Sword to execute? Or is Heaven now breaking its own laws?"

One of the Bearers of the Sword put away his weapon with a deep, shuddering rasp. From some unimaginable place on his person, he produced a long, silver-blue, shimmering length of chain.

"Your choice—your action—is to be erased." The Bearer of the Word smiled. The expression chilled Jacob to his bones. "Undone. Blotted out. This is the Writ that has issued. This is what the Bearers of the Sword have come to do."

"Heaven eliminates its rivals." Azazel laughed. "And then it tries again."

Qayna shuddered to a halt, and Jacob bounced off her hip. He didn't see why she had stopped; he couldn't take his eyes off his father. The Bearers of the Sword and the Word wrapped chains around Azazel, Prince of the Free. Jacob felt tears sting his eyes.

"You are not Heaven's rival," the Bearer of the Word sneered when the chains were in place.

Jacob was dimly aware that Qayna was trading words with bearded, armed, and armored men beside the canal. He couldn't see them through his tears, and he couldn't focus hard enough to make out their words.

"No?" Azazel thundered. He drew himself up to his full height. Even with glittering chains pinning his wings to his shoulders, he looked mighty, fearsome, and dangerous. The Bearer of the Word shriveled slightly and shrank back under the assault of Azazel's glaring eyes. "Then what am I?"

Qayna dove into the water, dragging Jacob with her.

He struggled. He didn't try to get away from her, but without thinking about it, he reached to grab his father as he fell and drag Azazel with them. Of course he missed. He was so far from his father it might as well have been leagues, and he kicked in rage as the cold, filthy waters swallowed him.

He continued kicking, angry and uncomprehending, as he felt the walls of Ainok pass over his head. He kicked as thick river bottom weeds wrapped around him and Qayna and she cut them away to carry them both on. And as cold needles stabbed deep into his brain and robbed Jacob bar Azazel of consciousness, he kicked one final time.

In that last moment, looking up through the silt- and blood-laden water at a shimmering curtain of daylight, he would have sworn he saw a figure looking down at him. A figure whose name he didn't know, but whom he recognized as one of the Princes of

Ainok—a shapeless, tentacled figure with a snapping beak.

Then, blackness.

"Do I have a choice?"

Jacob opened his eyes, and the monstrous figure was gone. He saw fire through water.

At first, he thought in his disorientation that he was looking down into a bowl of water and that beneath the gently-rippling concentric rings on the bowl's surface, someone had placed diamonds full of fire. He had seen more than enough sorcery at his father's court not to find that astonishing.

But then he realized that he wasn't hanging facedown. He was faceup. And that realization did astonish him.

Because it meant that he was still lying beneath water. Not Ainok's canal any longer, but a large font or bowl. The rings he saw were above him, not below, and the brilliantly burning gems were outside the water.

He wasn't breathing, but the needle in his brain was gone.

"Yes," said a second voice, and Jacob realized that the first voice he'd heard belonged to his father. The second was deeper, which barely seemed possible. "You have always had choices."

Jacob tried to inhale but couldn't. His lungs wouldn't move. He tried to stretch forth his hand and touch the surface of the pool, but he couldn't do that, either.

Am I dead? he wondered.

"But doesn't that make a mockery of everything you've just told me?"

A long silence.

Jacob focused on his body, trying to reassure himself that he hadn't lost sensation. It was hard to tell without being able to move. He didn't feel warm, but he wasn't cold either. His eyelids seemed to be the only thing he could move, and all they could do was slowly blink open and shut.

He heard Azazel speak again. "'A choice between two opposites,' you said. 'Light and dark, good and evil, and the inevitability of cause and effect,' you said."

More silence. Jacob strained his concentration, trying to will his muscles to push his legs beneath himself so he could stand. He had no idea what he'd see if he succeeded, but in the end, it didn't matter. His limbs refused to obey his command. More sorcery.

"A house is built in stages. A plan unfolds one step at a time."

Jacob wondered who his father was talking to. It wasn't a voice he recognized, and his father's words had an uncharacteristic sound to them. They were ... restrained. Calm. Meek? He didn't think that could possibly be the right word, but he didn't have another. His father addressed someone who was not his subject and who was maybe, just maybe, his superior.

"So I just accept that this is another stage of the gradually self-revealing plan?"

"The plan is not self-revealing."

"No?"

"*I* reveal it."

"I stand corrected. How long will the revelation take?"

"Until the end of time."

This time it was his father's turn to be silent. After long moments, he asked, "So ... forever?"

There was no answer.

"What is the alternative for me, then?" Azazel continued. "Life and death, corruption and incorruption, happiness and misery ... if I do not accept this burden, what horrible end awaits me?"

"There is a true exile."

"You say that as if it were a curse. But I chose as I did thinking that I *was* choosing exile in truth. I didn't expect this audience. I certainly didn't seek it."

"There are consequences for the child too."

Another long silence followed, and then a visible form appeared above Jacob, blocking out some of the burning lights. Jacob couldn't make out details on the silhouetted shape, but when it suddenly stretched enormous, batlike wings and revealed a human-shaped head and shoulders, he knew it was his father.

A small disturbance dimpled the surface of the water. Then another.

Then Azazel, First Prince of Ainok, knelt. In the changed light resulting from his movement, his son saw his face and saw that his cheeks glistened.

More disturbance of the surface above.

Tears, Jacob realized. His father wept.

"You force my hand."

"No." The answer was immediate but gentle. "There is compassion for you too."

"Only after you break my spirit with punishment."

"No punishment. Cause and effect. Consequences."

"The difference eludes me." Another shadow crossed the surface of the water, wavering, and Jacob realized that it was his father's hand, stretched forth and hovering just above the water. He longed to reach up and take his father's hand, but he couldn't.

"I don't choose the consequences. They are necessary. In the end, they may be for the good."

Azazel sprang to his feet, the near-clarity of his face again fading into remote shadow. "That is the essence of it. I deny that I have any choice in this matter, but I accept what is forced upon me. I will bear this burden."

"It will be a long and hard road."

"I will do it for my son."

A pause.

"Now he is my son too."

The words didn't sound like a welcome, though. They sounded like a sentence.

CHAPTER THREE

Palestine

The Waning Years of the Age of Aries

Jacob bar Abbas smiled and said nothing. He knew it would make the Roman mad. Being angry made people stupid. So did being greedy and eager. And he wanted the Roman to be stupid.

"When does the Liminal Year begin? Is it this equinox?"

The Roman was a paunchy man, prematurely bald, with a vicious sneer in the proud hook of his nose. He crouched in the dungeon before Jacob, illuminated by a single torch in a bracket set into the wall, looking into his chained prisoner's eyes for any sign of recognition or surrender.

Behind him stood his two kilt-clad, deaf-mute assistants. They were tall, as tall as Jacob, though where he was as pale as ivory even after years in this dusty desert crossroads, they were as black as black could be. Abyssinians, he guessed from their faces. He was broader in the shoulders than they were, but they were fat and muscled, and Jacob's frame had wasted away in the holding cell. The Roman wouldn't use his own men for this interrogation—he wouldn't want them to learn the secrets he was after. So instead, he used these slaves. He'd probably kill them when he was finished. He'd kill all three of them.

That might be interesting.

But really, it was better that Jacob just escape before it came to that. Also, it was better that he not give anything away. He had no way of knowing whom the Roman might serve. He also had no way of knowing where his sorcerer friend had gone. Why hadn't Ishbaal rescued him yet? Was there another wizard at work here?

He laughed. He was perfectly capable of matching the Roman's cosmopolitan Latin, but he deliberately spoke in rough, tribal tones. "You tell me, Roman. You seem to know much."

In the interrogation's pause, the chanting of the crowd outside became louder. "Bar Abbas, bar Abbas, bar Abbas!" they rumbled. Jacob repressed a grin. The fact that the window through which the sound came was fifteen feet off the ground was not a problem. The fact that the window was barred and Jacob was chained to the wall with iron links was a real obstacle.

The Roman stood, chewing his lip. He moved away and gestured to one of the Abyssinians. The big man stepped in close to Jacob and knotted his fingers in Jacob's long black hair. The Roman took a short, leisurely stroll once about the vaulted cell while the African pounded Jacob repeatedly in the mouth.

Jacob fought to keep his grin plastered on his face. The blows smarted.

When the Roman returned, the Abyssinian tossed Jacob to the ground and stepped back.

"The soldiers who cornered you in the Golden Gate reported that you were a Scythian. You're no Scythian."

"I smell too nice?" Jacob grinned. The taste of his own blood filled his mouth.

"You smell too bad." The Roman frowned. "You positively stink."

"So bathe me."

"I know that the Council meets at the opening of the Liminal Year. *Always*. And also at the close."

"Yeah? What Council?"

"On Earth as it is in Heaven. When the sky shifts, we enter the Age of the Fish—a new heaven and a new earth."

Jacob scratched himself and grunted.

"We approach the Liminal Year," the Roman continued. "Hence, the wonders in the sky. The monsters on Earth and spewing up from the deep. Two-headed babies, fish that walk upon the land, new stars … all mark the impending time of great change. And in the Liminal Year, during the transition, all bonds are loosened, all pacts are void, all things are possible. The Council sits to elect a new First Prince, a new Accuser."

"Council?" Jacob yawned. "Prince? I thought you were a prefect or a governor or something."

The Roman laughed. "And you, Jacob *bar Abbas*, are clearly no Scythian."

"I never said I was."

"Thank you for dropping the bad accent."

"What accent do you think I should have?"

The Roman shot a quick sidelong glance at one of his Abyssinians and narrowed his eyelids. "A much … *older* accent."

Jacob looked from one Abyssinian to the other, slowly examining them. "I assume you've taken these men's tongues."

The Roman nodded. "Of course."

"How certain are you of their deafness? Can they read lips? Can they read and write?"

"What are you suggesting?"

"I'm suggesting that if I had anything interesting to discuss with you, I certainly wouldn't want to risk it becoming public."

The Roman looked smug. "I trust these men."

Jacob leaned forward slowly, eyeing the two slaves skeptically. "Are you even sure they're the men you think they are?"

The Roman looked startled. "Do you mean … sorcery?"

"What else are we talking about?"

The Roman leaned close. So close he was within reach, though the Abyssinians watched like vultures. "Do not toy with me, Jacob bar Abbas." His breath was heavy with cumin and fish sauce. "I mean to have power."

"So do I, Pilate," Jacob lied.

"Bar Abbas, bar Abbas!" the crowd rumbled.

The Roman stood. "Leave us!" He flung his arms at the door in a gesture of command.

The Abyssinians ducked subserviently and padded out.

Standing at the door behind them, Pontius Pilate muttered an incantation. *Sumerian*, Jacob thought, *grammatically rough but serviceable.* So there *was* another sorcerer in the mix. Jacob's mental wheels ground a little more, and he felt something like hope.

"A powerful magician like you," he said. "I can't imagine what you need me for."

"I don't need you to lock a door, Jacob *bar Azazel.*" Pontius Pilate paced closer but still well out of Jacob's reach. "I need you to get me into the Council meeting, which none may attend but by right or by invitation."

Jacob nodded slowly. "You're right, I am bar Azazel."

"Lucifer's son, heir to the Morning Throne. In exile among the lowly mortals of this world. A falling out with your illustrious father?"

"I'm here by choice." Jacob watched the Roman carefully and ignored the upwelling emotions within him. It was true, he was something of an exile. After Jacob's death and return, his father had never looked at him the same way again. Unable to explain or understand, and unwilling to tell his father what he had seen beneath the water in the pool of his own death, Jacob had instead taken to wandering. "I can go back any time I want to. I just save it for important occasions."

"Good. That's just what I need. A short trip home with a new friend—me—is clearly an important occasion."

"I can't help you."

Pilate screwed his face into a suspicious fist. "I'm glad you drop the pretenses. Now, if you can let down your maidenly reluctance, perhaps we can get to business."

Jacob chuckled and leaned back. He rested his shoulders against the base of the cell wall, his sandaled feet sprawling out on the floor. "I lost my shyness centuries ago, Roman. The problem is that it isn't possible."

The Roman arched an eyebrow. "If that's really true, then I have no use for you and will have you executed."

"And piss off the mob?"

Pilate snorted. "I am a Roman and a soldier."

"Exactly."

Pilate put his hand on the dagger belted at his waist. "The only thing keeping you alive at this moment is the fact that I don't believe you, bar Azazel. I suggest you choose your next words very carefully. A retraction and offer to do what I want *will* suffice. An alternative suggestion *might*. Anything else signs your own death sentence."

Jacob sighed. "Here's how it is: When were you born?"

The Roman furrowed his brow. "Why do you care?"

Paranoid bastard. "I don't. But I assume you're less than a century old."

"Go on." Pilate's voice was cold, but held a note of curiosity.

"You'd have to be thousands of years old to be admitted. Not as a policy. As a matter of simple physical fact."

"I'm in no mood for riddles," the Roman snarled, but the snarl was halfhearted, and the narrowing of his eyes suggested that a riddle might be exactly what he was in the mood for.

"How long have you been in Judea, Pilate?"

"I'm tired of the questions, darkling. Time for answers."

Jacob nodded and sighed, holding up his hands in surrender. Pilate shuffled half a step closer. Jacob explained, "The Jews have an old story in their book of Judges. The Gileadites had defeated the Ephraimites and were guarding a ford on the river. They wanted to make sure none of the Ephraimites got through. 'When those Ephraimites which were escaped said, Let me go over; that the men of Gilead said unto him, Art thou an Ephraimite? If he said, Nay; Then said they unto him, Say now *Shibboleth*: and he said *Sibboleth*: for he could not frame to pronounce it right. Then they took him, and slew him at the passages of Jordan.'"

Pilate cocked his head and released his grip on his dagger. "A password."

"Exactly."

"I can say *Shibboleth*, bar Azazel."

"True. But you don't speak Infernal."

"You can teach me."

"You're not capable of learning."

The Roman put his hand on the dagger again. "Are you insulting me?" He stepped another half step closer.

Jacob shook his head. "More ancient stories. Really, you're never going to get anywhere unless you learn the true history of the world."

"So tell me," Pilate growled.

Jacob sighed. He carefully kept his eyes fixed on a point on the floor between his knees. "A long time ago, a group of people wanted to get to Heaven. Without permission, you understand? They wanted to force their way in, get a heavenly name. I'm still not sure their plan made any sense, but what they did was build the world's tallest tower. Ever."

Pilate snorted, but his eyes flashed. "Jewish nonsense."

Jacob shook his head. "I was there. It might have been nonsense, but it wasn't Jewish. It was long before the world saw its first Jew or even its first Hebrew. I don't know whether they would have succeeded; Heaven didn't let them finish anyway. It shattered the tower, and it cursed the entire race with the Confusion of the Tongues."

"Idiotic. This is an old fable. You're telling me that after this ... this *construction project gone wrong*, mankind spoke separate languages."

"That's one thing that happened," Jacob agreed. "Another thing that happened is that they forgot the original languages. Not only forgot them, but their descendants born into the Confusion forever after lost the ability to speak them, remember them, or even hear them clearly."

"Original languages?"

"Adamic was the original human tongue," Jacob said. "Angelic and Infernal are closely related."

The Roman hesitated, then rocked back a step. "I don't believe it."

"If I told you the password a thousand times," Jacob shrugged, "you wouldn't be able to remember it."

"Liar." But the Roman looked convinced.

"Ten thousand times. You probably wouldn't even *hear* it."

Pontius Pilate bared straight white teeth. "Try me."

"You're an idiot." Jacob said it in Infernal.

A flicker passed over Pilate's face. "I said try me," he repeated himself. "Say the password."

Jacob laughed. "I did."

Pilate frowned and stared. "Liar."

"I'll do it again." Jacob shifted to Infernal. "You're an idiot. You're a flyblown, goat-humping moron."

The Roman shook his head. "You're just moving your lips silently."

Jacob ran his fingers through his hair. "No, really, I'm not. This is the problem, you see. I tell you the password, and you can't even hear it. You never will, no matter how often I say it or how loud."

"Shout."

Jacob looked at the door. "Really?"

Pilate nodded. He muttered more Sumerian, gesturing over his own face. Then he stepped closer, leaned forward, and cupped one hand around his ear. "Shout it as loud as you can."

"Okay." Jacob cleared his throat. He hollered, again in Infernal, "You really are just too damn stupid to live!"

The word *damn* in Infernal ruffled the hair around Pilate's ears, and the Roman's eyes widened in surprise. As his mouth split into a grin and he started to say something, Jacob kicked him as hard as he could in the crotch.

Pilate rose into the air, his eyes growing even wider. His arms flapped wide like wings, and as he came down, Jacob caught him with both hands, one around Pilate's throat and the other gripping the Roman by his fighting wrist.

"Mrump—" Jacob choked the Roman's words into silence, then twisted and slammed his enemy to the floor. Before the sorcerer could do anything but arch his back in pain, Jacob was on top of him, chains clanking heavily as he drew the other man's dagger and pressed it against his throat.

Jacob's toes *hurt*.

"I know," Jacob hissed savagely into Pilate's ear, ignoring the throbbing in his feet. He didn't have any attention to spare for the door; he just had to act fast and hope for the best. He pushed the dagger hard enough to draw blood from under the Roman's jaw. "This wasn't how you expected things to go. But that's a toga for you—no protection where you need it."

Pilate's eyes bugged out of his face. Hungry, battered, and anxious for his freedom as he was, Jacob still had to laugh.

He shook his chained wrist, knocking heavy links against the Roman's face. "I, on the other hand, feel that the night is finally headed in the right direction. The next thing that will happen is that you're going to use one of your spells to unlock me."

Pilate arched his thin eyebrows skeptically. Jim relaxed his grip just a hair, and the Roman snorted.

"Here's the thing," Jacob continued. "I understand Sumerian, believe it or not, because I was once a camel driver in Sumer, and I heard you cast your spell locking the door. So I know you can do it, and I know more or less what the spell will sound like. So you're going to cast the spell I ask— *exactly that spell*, and nothing else—or I'll simply kill you."

"And then?" the Roman croaked, hard put to squeeze air through Jacob's grip. "After I cast the spell?"

Jacob shrugged. "Then you have to hope I won't kill you."

Pilate looked from Jacob's face to the chain and back. "Agreed."

Jacob relaxed his grip another few degrees but compensated for it by pressing the knife deeper into Pilate's skin. Blood trickled down onto the Roman's chest.

"You've cut me."

"I never yet saw a spell ruined by the addition of a little blood," Jacob growled. "Do it now!"

"My hands ..."

Jacob stood, dragging the Roman with him and slamming the man firmly against the wall. He again pressed the dagger to the Roman, this time to his eyeball. Pilate slowly brought his hands up. Not taking his gaze from the dull gleam of the weapon in Jacob's hands, he duly chanted an opening spell, touching the chains.

Which promptly fell away.

The *Clang!* of the iron on the floor was louder than Jacob was expecting. "Again!" he snapped.

"Again?" Pilate cowered against the wall, shrinking back from the touch of the dagger. "What are you ... do you mean the door?"

"Idiot!" Jacob nodded upwards. "The window! Open the window!"

"I ..." Pilate looked up. "That will be harder."

"You're not the first wizard I've known, Roman. Do it now."

Jacob heard thudding and clanking sounds from the hall that might be soldiers approaching. So did Pilate, and he shot a hopeful eye in that direction.

"Now!" Jacob stabbed through the lobe of Pilate's ear, pinning him with a forearm across the throat in the same move.

Pilate chanted and waved, and the bars in the high window vanished.

"Prefect!"

The voice came from the door. Jacob didn't waste time looking.

He spun the Roman around by brute force and slammed his head into the stone. Pilate collapsed forward into a stunned crouch, grabbing at the wall for support, and Jacob took two steps away.

He turned and launched himself. As he heard keys rattling in the lock, he stepped onto Pontius Pilate's back, planting his feet right between the man's shoulders. He jumped, angling not at the open window, which was too high, but ninety degrees away from it, at a blank wall.

"Stop!"

Shoulders slammed into the door.

Jacob touched the wall lightly—his smashed toes *hurt*—and sprang away from it again, extending his body into the fullest stretch he could after long days of crouching in chains. The dim light of the night sky flashed before his eyes, and he feared for a moment that he was going to miss his catch—

But he jammed his left hand into the open window—

Wham!—

And held.

He swung sideways until his body was nearly parallel to the floor, his one hand straining to bear the impact, feeling the mortar crumble under the pressure. Then his swing hit maximum extension, his arm did not quite rip out of its socket, and he slid back again, under the window, still clinging.

The door imploded inward, and Jacob saw red uniforms out of the corner of his eye. The guards would have pila or javelins or something capable of reaching him.

"Kill him!"

Jacob hauled himself up with both hands. He skinned his knuckles, and the force with which he had to throw himself into the small space of the window made him bang both shoulders painfully.

Beyond the window was a drop of ten feet to a baked tile rooftop.

Pain seared the flesh of his buttock. Someone had stabbed him. But that was one thing; a spell from Pilate might do much more harm.

Jacob toppled forward.

He held the dagger out to one side as he dropped, to be sure he didn't impale himself on the stolen weapon. *Whoomph!* He hit the terra-cotta hard and felt tiles shatter under him. He slid down the roof, hands, shoulders, buttocks, and toes all in pain, uncertain of what his next step was. Whatever happened, he had already fixed on one certain resolution: he was going to start wearing boots.

At the edge of the ceiling, he crossed over a lead rain gutter, grabbed at it, missed, and fell.

Another ten feet, and he hit the ground. Dirt. Hard-packed dirt.

Jacob staggered to his feet, sucking thick air into his battered lungs and looking for a horse. They'd be after him in a moment, but he had the advantage, and he knew now he'd get away.

He was free, but he was alone, and that made him uncomfortable.

Time to go find Ishbaal and his men.

CHAPTER FOUR

Palestine

The Beginning of the Age of Pisces

Get us up to the mount," Ishbaal gasped. He looked bad under the exploding lights in the sky, his white tunic and cloak soaked in blood as he leaned against the wall of the alley. Most of the blood was his own, and his dark desert complexion was drained and lifeless. His bent nose and thick, unruly hair didn't help, nor did the heavy feeling that preceded him wherever he went and crowded into his wake—the sense of perdition, gloom, and foreboding that came from the little man's surfeit of corrupt and sorcerous bargains.

"Wait here." Jacob set down his spear and stepped out into the street.

Even the street was narrow, a winding, cobbled path that climbed up to Herod's Temple between dusty yellow-brick walls.

Half a dozen paces downhill from Jacob, on a small plaza, a staved-in door gaped open. A woman's cries came from within. This morning, such cries would have meant cannibalism. The drained and depleted defenders of Jerusalem's walls were weeks beyond the ability to perpetrate anything so vigorous as rape, but as the food supplies had gone, the powerless had begun to disappear. Babies first, then children and the old, and eventually even adults.

No one talked about where they went, but everyone knew.

But this evening, under the vicious leer of the evening's first star—the last evening star of the Liminal Year—the walls had fallen, and the Romans had entered the City of David.

The Romans and their Infernal allies. With the falling shroud of night had come the Zvuvim again, and other, darker, nameless things. They had shattered the defenses with a mighty final blow, and now they chased the Judeans from door to door in the city, sparing none. Strange fire and the foul smoke of charred flesh filled Jerusalem as the powers of Hell—*some* of the powers of Hell—did their worst.

All of Jacob's men, defamed as robbers and worse, had fallen. All but Jacob himself and the mage Ishbaal. His men had fought and died for their own reasons, which included loyalty, money, and hatred of the Romans. Jacob had fought out of self-defense and a strained loyalty to his remote father—the Romans and their darker allies were after Jacob, and Jerusalem was a defensible city.

Had been a defensible city.

The three horses and the single Roman soldier standing outside the door told Jacob that the reason for the woman's screams was rather more prosaic than cannibalism, if just as sordid.

"*Ave!*" he called to the soldier as he approached. He affected a good Italic accent in his Latin and a friendly tone to his voice; that and the darkness should throw the soldier off, he thought. He just needed to get close enough to be able to kill the man quietly—

"Alert!" the man shouted. "We're attacked!"

He threw himself at Jacob.

Jacob cursed and stepped aside. The soldier pressed his assault, shouting and stabbing with his short gladius.

An answering shout from within the building reminded Jacob that there was no time to mess about. He hesitated a moment to present a better target, and when the soldier attacked this time, he let himself fall directly back.

The gladius whistled overhead—

Jacob hit the loose cobblestones and bounced—

He swept with his long legs, kicking the soldier's feet out from under him.

"*Mentula!*" the soldier cursed, and then Jacob took his own sword from the soldier's hands and stabbed it into big-nosed Roman face, right between the iron cheek guards of his helmet.

"Jew!" shouted a second man, appearing the doorway with sword in hand.

"Guess again," Jacob snarled. He rolled over the body of the dead man, coming to a seated landing with the freed gladius in his hand. The second soldier charged, evidently aiming to take advantage before Jacob could stand.

Jacob hurled the gladius.

It was long for a throwing weapon, but its tip was sharp and Jacob knew how to throw a knife straight. The gladius sank into the soldier's throat with satisfying ease, and he ran past Jacob blind and stunned, slamming into the wall on the other side of the street before finally falling to the dust.

Jacob rolled to his feet. He ached, but he had always had an excellent, athletic physique—an inheritance from his father, he thought. Ignoring the pain, he vaulted into the saddle of one of the shying horses, grabbing the reins of another as a lead rope.

A third soldier appeared in the door, bloody sword in his hand. Jacob noted with disgust that the woman's cries had ceased. The soldier stepped forward, but in a flash of light from fire streaking across the sky he met Jacob's eyes.

"You!"

Jacob charged his horse at the man. The soldier stumbled back into darkness within the building. "*Fossa!*" he swore. "Help! The northerner, bar Abbas! He's here!"

No time. Jacob turned and crossed the little plaza to the alley. "Ishbaal!" he called.

No answer.

Jacob dismounted and wrapped the horses' reins around a spar from the wreckage of what had once been some sort of merchant's tent. He ducked into the alley and found his comrade unconscious, slumped on the ground.

Bleeding and in a bad way, but alive. That was good. Without Ishbaal, Jacob had no way of opening the gate that Ishbaal was so certain was on the Temple Mount and no other way to get to the Council in time—the nearest Masseboth were leagues away, with thousands of irascible Romans blocking the path. His father worried that some of his own allies might back Semyaz's play to stay in power beyond this Liminal Year. Azazel needed Jacob's vote.

They were distant, Jacob and his father, but not so distant that Jacob wanted Semyaz on the Morning Throne.

He bent to pick up the wizard and heard a low growl.

Jacob looked up slowly. Deep in the alley, down a steep flight of uneven steps, he saw glowing eyes. Dozens of them.

Cursing, Jacob threw Ishbaal over one shoulder and grabbed his spear with his free hand. It was a good thing that the sorcerer was a small man. Two steps brought him to the mouth of the alley; he flung the little Egyptian across the back of one of the horses and jumped onto the other.

He whirled to meet the enemy.

They would have been baboons if they'd had heads. But green eyes glowed on their chests, and ragged teeth gnashed and snapped in mouths set into their bellies. They came at Jacob, bounding off the walls and leaping down from the rooftops.

Jacob charged, swinging the spear like a staff. He had to make himself a big target, he thought, and a juicy one, and not let these creatures become interested in Ishbaal. He battered one Hellbaboon against the wall, trampled two under the horse's hooves, impaled a fourth, and punched his fingers into the left eye-nipple of a fifth.

The horse screamed in panic and pain as the demons attacked it, but it had nowhere to go but forward.

Jacob flung himself backward, somersaulting over his mount's rump and landing squarely on both feet. He cracked the spear in his hands like a whip, hurling the impaled demonling off the end of it and into the body-face of a baboon that leapt at him off the wall. Another attacker he kicked twice, once between its green eyes and a second time in its backside as it turned, sending it skittering down the alley after its companions.

The rest of the monsters attacked the horse.

Jacob ran, grabbing the reins of Ishbaal's animal and leading it up the hill and away from the scene. The screams of the dying horse followed him for several minutes, and when they cut off abruptly, he guessed he was far enough away that the Hellbaboons would find some closer, easier prey than him.

He crossed through a gate into the Upper City, wishing he had some way to bar it after him. The Lower City behind and below him burned. Gigantic shadows moving from building to building and flashes of animal limbs on enormous humanoid bodies told him that some of the Fallen had personally joined in the attack.

Not the Princes, presumably. They would be at the Council. But their minions were here to catch Jacob.

For a moment, images of the fall of another city, ages earlier, flashed before his eyes.

"Not the palace, you idiot," Ishbaal murmured. He could barely raise his head off the horse's flank to look about and see where they were, and his words sounded like the distant whistle of a breeze in the trees. "The Temple."

"The other roads are blocked," Jacob said.

They crossed the aqueduct. Bodies floated in it, which didn't bode well for the path ahead of them. Even when they'd fallen to eating each other's flesh, the Jerusalemites had been smart enough not to pollute their water source.

Ishbaal slumped against the horse again. Jacob passed the old Hasmonean Palace and spared a glance for Herod's larger, newer home against the western wall of the city. The Idumaean's gaudy arriviste statement was already on fire, but the family home of Mattathias's sons lurked black and empty, looted weeks ago.

Another gate, and then long, stone stairs. Smoke thickened the air and deadened the sound of the horse's hooves clopping on the stairs. The walls around the temple precinct—where this whole doomed stand had started—loomed high and spectral, flickering green and blue and silver as sorcerous fire shattered various quarters of the city.

At the top of the stairs stood someone Jacob hadn't seen for decades.

"I know you," he said, tightening his grip on his spear while trying not to look bellicose.

"You may have known me as *Saul*," said the other man. He wore a Roman uniform and held a long club in both hands, resting it on his shoulder. It was an improvised weapon, maybe a laundryman's tool; his sword's sheath was empty.

Behind the laundryman stood a dozen Roman soldiers with swords and spears.

"No," Jacob disagreed. "That wasn't it."

Pontius Pilate's eyes flashed fire. "I'm *Paul* now," he said. He moved down one step, closer to Jacob.

"The city's on fire, *Paul*," Jacob said slowly. "Let's get out of here."

"Agreed. We'll go *your* way." Pilate stepped to one side and gestured to the Temple behind him.

"I can't," Jacob said without thinking.

Pilate's eyes flashed fire. "Fool me once," he said.

Jacob sighed. "I didn't mean it like that." He pointed at Ishbaal. "My sorcerer's dead. I don't know how to open the gate or where it is. At this point, I'm just running." He looked back at the fires below. "I don't have a plan."

"The Antonia burns," Pilate said. "But I think we can get out by the Pool of Bethesda." He stepped closer. "But first, let's get rid of this dead weight."

"No," Jacob started to say, and moved to put his body between Pilate and Ishbaal—

Pilate swung the club.

Jacob was caught by surprise. He was tired, he had fought too much already this evening, and above all, he expected any attack from the Roman to land on Ishbaal. Instead, Pilate attacked Jacob. The laundryman's club was hard and heavy, and as it slammed into Jacob's leg, he felt the bone break.

Jacob fell backward, landing hard on the stairs and sliding down. He let go of his spear in the fall and heard it clatter down the stairs and out of sight. His borrowed horse, its reins suddenly falling free, neighed and drifted upwards.

The soldiers jeered.

"Just in case you had any idea that you might want to … *kick* me."

"Wait—"

Pilate advanced, raising the club again.

"No more lies, Jacob bar Azazel," he snarled.

"Oh, yeah … *Paul?*" Jacob struggled to right himself, but the pain in his broken leg was excruciating.

"A man who lives a long time," Pilate said slowly, "may find it convenient to take many names over the years." He paused to smile, his face flickering red in the light of Herod's burning palace. "Don't you think?"

He swung his club down again, battering Jacob's other leg.

Jacob cursed in Infernal, the force of his words and his pain snapping back the Roman's kilt for a moment. Both his legs were broken beneath the knee. He wouldn't be walking anywhere for a good long time.

"I've given you your two warnings, bar Azazel." Pilate raised the club a third time. "The Liminal Year ends. The Council meets again. I *will* attend. Or you will die."

The Roman's club burst into flame. For a split second, Jacob thought that the fire was the Roman's own doing, the conversion of his mere stick into a sorcerous and even more dangerous weapon.

But Pontius Pilate shrieked and threw the club down, staring in dismay at the palms of his hands.

Jacob didn't wait for another opportunity. He hurled himself forward on knuckles and knees, grabbed Pilate by the kilt, and threw the other man down the stairs. Pilate screamed louder, but on the third bounce his scream cut off.

Jacob turned to the terrible work of dragging himself up the stairs.

The soldiers, after a moment's shock, shouted and charged.

Ishbaal leaned forward over the horse's flank, muttering something in his native Egyptian and fluttering the fingers of one hand. With the other, he slapped distractedly at the horse's tack, trying to secure himself—he slowly slid forward—missed his grab—

The Romans rushed him—

A blaze of light erupted from Ishbaal's fingers, fanning out like a blade and smacking into the entire squad at chest level. Ishbaal hit the stairs head first and crumpled. Romans flew left and right off the stairs, disappearing into the shadows under the Temple's walls.

The light snapped off.

"Ishbaal!" Jacob dragged himself to his sorcerer's side. En route, he found a pair of Roman javelins and took them with him. The rumblings and fire of Jerusalem's fall seemed remote. Ishbaal, frail and broken in his arms, was very real and immediate.

"Not dead yet, bar Abbas," Ishbaal muttered. He coughed and spat blood, as if to cast doubt on his own words. "Get me on the horse."

Jacob was relieved. He knew that the feeling of darkness around Ishbaal was something most people couldn't see. Only him. And, he thought, his father. It was the Left Hand, a seal or a claim. Ishbaal had promised himself to Hell and damnation somehow. When Ishbaal died, Jacob wasn't sure what would happen, exactly, but the man's soul would join the damned in his father's realm. "To Hell with the horse. I'll carry you."

"To Hell with the horse? That's funny. You get that sense of humor from your father?"

Jacob remembered that his legs were broken and laughed. "It isn't humor. It's stubborn pride."

"It's a fine line."

Jacob dragged himself up the side of the horse and dragged Ishbaal with him, leaning on the javelins for support. The animal objected sharply but stood still for the mounting.

"Where'd you get the horse anyway?" Ishbaal asked, bouncing slowly on the animal's back as Jacob directed it back up the stairs. The sound of Roman soldiers calling to each other as they regained their senses made Jacob nervous, but he ignored it. "I thought we ate the last one weeks ago."

"It's a Roman horse. I guess they still have cattle to eat."

"Or maybe they had a lot more horses than we did."

Jacob laughed. "And yes," he said as the horse clopped unsteadily through the gate leading into the Royal Porch, "I did get my sense of humor from my father. With his job, maybe he needs it."

"He could change jobs."

Jacob chewed on that. "I'm not sure he can." He thought again of the moment of his own death and underwater resuscitation, and the conversation he'd overheard between his father and ... someone else, and his failure to ever discuss the moment with Azazel. He felt tied to his father and doomed, held at arm's length and sucked in at the same time.

What he wanted was to be free. Free and not alone. He wondered if those two states could coexist.

Ishbaal raised his head and pointed. "Deeper," he said. "Inside."

"Inside the courtyard?"

"All the way ... all the way inside." Ishbaal's breathing grew shallower by the minute, and the pain lancing through Jacob's calves forced him to guide the horse by supplication as much as by use of the reins.

"You sure?"

Ishbaal nodded weakly.

"Centurion!" Pilate shouted behind them, outside the gate.

Jacob tried to make the horse go faster as they headed past metal warning plaques into the Temple courts. In the outermost gate, he risked a look over his shoulder. Beyond the Romans, in the flame-skeined darkness and chaos that Jerusalem had become, he thought he saw the familiar and loathsome outline of a tentacled Infernal.

So not all the Princes were already in the Council Chamber. He shuddered and pushed on.

The Gentiles' Court held nothing but scorched bones. Jacob felt a moment of peace crossing it, its high walls obscuring the fires consuming the city and allowing for a space of cooler air, a hollow protected from the flames and out of sight of the shadow that might have been Belial.

The Court of Women was entirely empty, and in the quiet, Jacob noticed something new and troublesome. The palpable darkness, the ill-omened feeling of trouble and sorrow that cloaked Ishbaal felt heavier. It felt closer, like it was invading Jacob's body too, into his lungs and blood and heart.

The Left Hand was stronger. Closer.

Up a few more steps and through the Gate of Nicanor, with its marble, its bronze panels, and its gilding above the door proper. He shut the Gate behind him, wishing again that he had some way to bar it. The Court of Israel, the Court of the Priests. Jacob spurred the horse as best he could with his knees, fearing the growing sensation of the Left Hand's grip and the sound of sandals in the courts behind them.

Herod's temple towered above them. There, between the altar and the door, stood a whip-thin, dirty rabble of the Zealous. Zechariah stood at their head, naked sicarius in his hand.

Jacob's heart sank.

With a dull *boom*, he heard the Gate of Nicanor open at his back.

"Are you a priest, bar Azazel?" Zechariah sneered. The Left Hand lay heavy on Zechariah, too. Heavy and ugly.

"I'm an angel," Jacob said. His legs screamed at him. "Today, we all are." He nudged Ishbaal, and the sorcerer twitched slightly in answer.

"Angels are not permitted to enter the House of the Lord."

"Herod's House," Jacob disagreed. "Soon to be desecrated and burned."

"True. And once it is nothing but a ruin, you may enter at will."

Jacob looked at the line of fanatics and felt the death of hope. They stared at him with glittering faces, hands and weapons twitching. They knew their end had come, and they planned to buy their places in Heaven with their lives. Jacob wondered if their plan would work.

He heard Roman boots behind him. He could feel the horse under him sagging from its double burden.

"Didn't David take refuge in the sanctuary and eat the Bread of the Presence?" he asked, trying one last time.

"I have no time to waste arguing with an ignorant, blaspheming foreigner." Zechariah spat on the ground.

Jacob hurled one of his javelins. It struck the leader of the Zealous in the center of his chest. He crumpled to the ground, looking surprised. The sudden increase in the strength of the Left Hand had made it feel as if Jacob were being pounded into the ground, but then, abruptly, it eased.

Zechariah twitched once, then lay still.

"Nor do I." Jacob stabbed the tip of his other javelin into the horse's rump.

Zechariah's dagger-wielding followers rushed forward. Roman soldiers attacked from behind.

But the stolen Roman horse, exhausted, spooked, and in pain, bolted. It took a sword wound to the chest as it battered its way through the Zealous, leaped up the temple steps, and charged into the darkness within.

A first chamber flashed by, and then a long hall of darkness thick with the smell of myrrh. At its end was a curtain at the top of a short flight of stairs, ten cubits tall, maybe. Something glowed or burned behind the curtain, which shimmered gold and mysterious above Jacob, Ishbaal, and the galloping, frantically neighing horse.

Then the horse struck something.

Hot coals showered both men and the animal, and they fell down together. Jacob heard the snap of bones breaking, and then the horse began to scream.

Had he run into a censer?

"Ishbaal?" No response. Jacob rolled to his knees, scattered stinging, sweet-smelling coals from his body. His shattered legs ached and almost dragged him down again. He raised the javelin over his head to put the thrashing horse out of its misery.

"Stop!"

Jacob hesitated. "The horse is dead regardless."

"Yes," Ishbaal said slowly. He was a man-shaped outline of black crouching against a field of red coal-stars on the floor. "But it matters how it dies."

Jacob heard a *snick* of metal in the darkness. Outside, *clangs* and shouting. "Hurry," he said.

"I'm going to do this thing," the sorcerer told him. Jacob felt as if the Left Hand were choking the life out of him. "You get up there and through that curtain. The Morning Throne is behind it."

"It is?"

"It will be."

"I'm not leaving you."

Ishbaal chuckled. "Oh, you'll see me again."

Jacob hesitated.

"It matters how it dies!" Ishbaal snapped. "Get going!"

Jacob crawled. Every inch his mangled shins banged across the floor yanked another curse from him. He cursed Zechariah, Pilate, Belial, even his father, and certainly himself and his own damned fate. He was at the foot of the stairs when the horse's screams stopped. He was halfway up them when the Romans burst into the door at the other end, torches held high.

"Kill the Egyptian!" Pilate shrieked.

Ishbaal bellowed a defiant curse in his native tongue.

The Left Hand squeezed once, then ceased.

Jacob leaned forward and fell against the curtain—

It caught him and held him, firm as any wall. Behind it, the light pulsated, taunting him.

"Father!" he cried. "Father, if you can see me, I need help! Open this gate, or I will not make the Council!"

"Seize the Jew!" a Roman voice shouted, and sandal soles pounded across the tiled floor.

"Father!" Jacob cried again, and slammed his fist against the curtain.

The soldiers raced closer.

"Father!" Jacob's cheeks were wet, and he wasn't sure why. Was he weeping for Ishbaal? For himself? A profound terror, a sense of isolation, swamped him, blotting out the excruciating pain in both his legs.

He raised his fist to pound on the curtain a final time, and it suddenly gave way, pulling him through and into the light beyond.

CHAPTER FIVE

Hell

The End of the Age of Pisces

Within the gates, horror.

This was not home, it never had been. Jim (Jacob, then) had died choking in effluent in the canals of Ainok, and when he had reawoken, strange and unexplained dreams aside, he had been in this place. But in a quieter corner, ministered to by servants who were monsters but loyal and even loving.

Only later had he learned that his father's mansions were full of this new thing, the *damned*. Later still, he had come to hate the fact, and he and his father had parted. This train of thought saddened him, and he tried to force his mind down other paths. Learning to play the lute from Elaine on a rare sunny spring morning in the woods outside Crannock Castle. Warm sun spilling down her hair and dress, infinitely long and infinitely warm, a cocoon of laughter surrounding them.

"This place could really use some music," Mike said. "You know, drown out all the noise."

The noise was mostly ear-shattering screams, though if he focused closely, Jim could also hear low moans and gibbering beneath the falsetto shrieks. Beneath that, the fleshy sounds of wrestling and physical lust, the rasp of saws on bones, and the soft sucking sound of flowing blood.

The damned heaped upon each other, passionately, angrily, vindictively, greedily, two self-gnawing piles of flesh and venom split down the middle by a snaking path. It was Baraqyel's role, traditionally, to bring visitors down this path, but Baraqyel was occupied, and Jim knew the way.

The dead and damned, of course, came in by a different door and were led by minions whose presence was altogether more dispiriting.

"You're forgetting your basic principles," Eddie said. There was something different about the guitar player's face, but Jim couldn't figure out what it was.

"What?" Mike pulled a flask from his pocket and took a sip. He kept patting his pockets as he drank, like he was looking for something else. Probably forgot that he'd thrown his candy bars at the Baobab Tree. "Place gives me a baritone guitar feel. Just because Satan can't hear it doesn't mean I wouldn't feel better for a few loud chords right now. Loud and distorted."

"Yeah," Eddie admitted. "So would I."

Qayna dismounted and led her horse. Twitch swayed, then gripped the horn of the saddle tightly with both hands. Jim had never seen the fairy so battered. He wondered if it would die, but it continued to cling tenaciously to life and the saddle, staring wide-eyed around itself into the mounds of the damned.

"I knew your brother," Qayna told Jim as they passed under jagged stalactites into a new gallery. Other passages led off in various directions, but Jim stuck to the path he knew was the shortest route. All the caverns were lit with reddish-yellow light from no apparent source. Magic.

Jim suppressed a laugh. "Yeah?"

"Yes." The Marked Woman grew quiet. "I ... I killed him, actually."

Jim looked at Qayna and tried to keep a poker face. She had made the wrong inference. "I thought you were famous for killing your own brother."

Qayna, the first murderer, laughed. "I've killed a lot of people," she admitted. "Most of them on purpose. Your brother was an accident, but I'm sorry."

Jim shrugged. "I grew up an only child. I don't think my father holds anything against you. I certainly don't."

"Perhaps not. Still, I have not seen him for several millennia."

"The first kinslayer and the first rebel." It was Jim's turn to laugh, and his laugh was bitter. "Estranged."

"We've walked separate paths."

Jim heard his own story in her words, and it made him feel a little better. A little. "And now? Are you really here just for the fun?"

"No. He sent for me."

The wailing of the damned sounded louder.

"Does he want you to attend the Council?"

"I don't know." Qayna was silent for a moment. "I have once before, you know. A long time ago."

"Oh yeah?"

"I was asked to vote on … an issue."

"On who would be leader?"

She looked at him sharply. "How did you know?"

"President of the Infernal Council? Lucifer? Satan? Moloch? The Accuser, the Adversary? It's the thing they care about most. It used to be the only thing they debated, until they agreed new rules and restricted when the issue could be brought up."

"Restricted it how?"

"The Liminal Year between each Age begins and ends on an equinox. On each of those nights, the Council meets, and the position of Moloch is a permitted subject for motions and debate."

Qayna looked away into the writhing distance. "The Liminal Year, when all things are possible. The equinox is tonight."

Jim nodded.

Qayna exhaled, a silent whistle. "Of course."

"I gather you haven't been an avid follower of Infernal politics."

She shook her head. "I've been too busy trying to die. But why two consecutive equinoxes?"

"That's my father's idea, I think." They crossed a stone arch, a natural bridge over a pit full of bloodied children and adults, alive with the sounds of gnawing teeth. Jim couldn't tell who were the eaters and who were the eaten. "If the Council makes a mistake, it can fix it a year later."

"But if they don't fix it then, they're stuck for two thousand years."

At the end of the arch, Jim led them right and around the base of a rockslide of boulders the size of houses. The ceiling disappeared into glowing red infinity.

"Yeah, well, if you let them fix it any time they wanted ... again, they wouldn't talk about anything else."

"What would a mistake be?"

Jim laughed, trying not to sound bitter. "In my father's eye? Electing anyone other than himself."

Qayna hesitated. "I never knew him to be petty."

"Not petty," Jim agreed. "Supremely confident."

"Perhaps he has reason to be."

Jim nodded. "Semyaz held the Throne once, for a year."

"How did that go?"

Jim blinked away images of Herod's burning palace. "It was a rough year. Semyaz is a liar and a bully." He laughed. "Even more than the others."

"And what if the elected Satan dies?"

"The Fallen don't die."

"Is killed."

Jim steeled himself and managed not to look at Qayna's pistol. "There are precious few things capable of doing that."

"Precious few are not zero. What would happen?"

"I don't know, but there must be a lawyer around here who can answer your question. Why do you ask?"

Qayna looked around. "A lawyer?"

"After all, we're in Hell."

"I ask," she said slowly, "because I begin to wonder what I have really been called here to do."

They walked in silence for a while.

"I don't remember the road being this long," Qayna observed.

"Hell expands daily," Jim told her. "It probably *wasn't* this long the last time you passed this way. Damnation is a growth industry."

Eddie snorted. "That figures." Jim realized what was different about the guitar player: his bad eye, the one that always slid around crazy in its socket because Eddie had visions of Hell, wasn't bad anymore. It looked as fixed and normal as its mate.

"Where's Adrian?" Twitch asked. The fairy looked agitated.

"In this giant place, you think we have any chance at all of finding that poor son of a bitch?" Eddie sounded dismissive, but the way he looked over his shoulder as he spoke made Jim think he was uncomfortable at the thought of meeting the wizard's shade.

"In this giant place," Jim said, "if Adrian's here, it's probably inevitable that you'll meet him."

Qayna looked at him sharply.

"What do you mean?" The fairy licked its lips.

"That's the way Hell works." Waves of memories crashed on Jim's mind, and he struggled to ignore them. "If there's any possible way your past can torment you, it will shove that past in your face."

"You mean Hell will bring Adrian here to torment me?" Twitch asked.

"Or to torment him."

"Shit." Eddie adjusted his grip on the shotgun and looked around him.

"You surprised?"

"Not really."

"Unless Adrian's not here," Jim added. "Hell isn't for everyone."

Eddie stopped and looked around. "Where's Mike?"

Jim and Qayna stopped too. The cavern they were in was full of sliver-thin poles running from floor to ceiling. The poles ran through strings of human beings, impaling them like so many chunks of meat on shish kebabs. The people, naked and filthy, clawed and shouted and spat at each other, demanding space, trying to get higher on the poles, or resting elbows and knees on their neighbors.

No sign of Mike.

"Dammit," Eddie grunted. "It's like being the driver of the short bus. Every time I turn around, one of the kids is climbing out the window."

"The Mare will find him." Qayna patted her horse's neck and whispered something in its ear. The animal leaned forward and snuffled at the path with large nostrils.

"By smell?" Eddie gestured around him at the writhing, battling bodies of the damned. "In all this?"

Qayna cocked an eyebrow at him. "The Mare followed your van by smell from New Mexico to Kansas."

Eddie shut up and stood aside.

The black horse moved quickly, nose to the ground. Qayna followed at its shoulder, holding its reins gently, and Twitch clung to the saddle like a shipwreck survivor on a bit of flotsam.

The party moved back through a couple of caverns the way they'd come, and then the horse turned onto a different path. Past the pile of fallen boulders and the stone arch, it took them down a twisting gullet of green stone, through a room pocked with pits full of mud and scorched, howling souls, to a broad shelf of stone above an apparently bottomless chasm.

On the shelf, talking to another man, stood Mike.

The Left Hand had always been heavy on the bass player. It had never felt as heavy to Jim as it did know.

The other man was young, maybe a teenager. He had the lean, muscular look of a restless poor kid with no job, no likely prospects, and access to free weights. Like many of the other inmates of Hell, he dripped blood and his skin hung in tatters.

And he looked a lot like Mike. He could've been Mike's son.

Qayna stopped the Mare. "What is this?" she asked Jim.

"I don't know." Jim considered. "Wait a moment."

They watched, Eddie cursing under his breath. It was a good thing Eddie didn't speak Adamic, Jim reflected. He'd shatter the windows in every storefront he passed.

Mike offered the damned man his flask. The man refused and spat blood on the stone. Mike nodded, said a few soft words with a sad expression on his face, and tried again. The weight lifter crossed his arms and stared. Mike nodded again, slowly. He set the flask on the floor between them and opened his arms wide.

The weight lifter hesitated. He stared more. Then he stooped, picked up the flask, and took a long drink.

He wrapped his arms around Mike in an embrace.

And then the weight lifter was gone.

The flask fell to the ground with a rattle. Mike's arms squeezed around his own torso for a moment, and he stumbled. When he regained his balance, he looked around, shaking his head as if coming out of a deep sleep.

He saw the flask.

He bent over, picked it up, and hurled it into the crevasse.

"Holy shit," Eddie commented. "What the hell just happened?"

"Holy shit indeed." Jim stared at Mike.

The Left Hand was gone.

So it was possible. His father had lied. Jim's heart beat faster, and he took deep breaths to calm himself. His plan wasn't insane.

Mike walked over to rejoin them. His steps were unsteady, and he looked at his own arms and belly over and over.

"You okay?" Eddie asked.

Mike's eyes ran a little wild in his head. "Get me out of here," he said.

"First things first!" Eddie snapped. "Don't you want to get your own back? Help your brother?" He waggled Azazel's hoof fragment at the bass player as a reminder.

"*Hijo de putas*," Mike swore. "*Maricón que seas*, I guess I got no choice."

"Spoken like a true brother," Eddie harrumphed. "Now let's go get a seat at the table."

Jim turned them back to their previous path.

Far away in the bowels of Hell, a *CLANG* echoed. In its wake came the roaring of beasts.

The gate had fallen, Jim realized. He wondered how Baraqyel fared.

"What's the plan, Jim?" Qayna asked. She looked unconcerned.

"What's *your* plan?" he countered.

"I don't know. I think I'm here as witness."

"Witness to what?"

"To whatever you're going to do."

Jim laughed. "I don't know what I'm going to do," he said. "I know what I want, and I know what cards I have to play."

"The hoof?"

"Jim doesn't have that anymore," Eddie shot at her. "*I* do."

Jim nodded. He didn't think he needed the hoof anymore. Really, the hoof belonged to a different plan, one that had ended only hours earlier but now seemed centuries away. The plan had always been what he'd told the band: get the witch in Chicago to summon Jim's father and strike a deal.

Only once he'd found the hoof fragment and put it into play this close to the beginning of the Liminal Year, his father's rivals had jumped into action. They'd wanted it like they'd wanted him—for the leverage they could get at the Council's meeting tonight.

At a blasted-out bar called the Silver Eel in Kansas City, Jim had turned the tables.

But the hoof might be enough to get Eddie admission, and maybe that would still work to Jim's advantage.

At a pair of roughly-carved stone columns, their surfaces creeping with animal figures and Primal glyphs, two figures waited: Ishbaal the sorcerer and Zechariah, leader of the Zealous.

Each with a dagger in his hand.

The roaring grew louder.

Ishbaal grinned. "It's been a while, boss," he said in Latin.

Zechariah slashed the wizard across the throat with his knife. Blood spattered the gravelly path, and the wound quickly closed again to Ishbaal's natural, nut-brown skin.

"Shut up!" the fanatic shouted in Aramaic. Ishbaal plunged his own dagger into the other man's belly. Again, the gout of red sputtered quickly to a trickle and then shut off, neat as any spigot.

"Aw, Hell, no," Eddie complained. "This is *not* gonna work for me."

"I thought you were used to seeing the damned," Jim said.

"Yeah. What I don't like is the private conversations. Especially not here."

"What do you want, language lessons?" Jim asked him. "All my wizards are dead."

"Tell them to speak English," Eddie grunted.

Jim arched an eyebrow. Eddie shifted from one foot to the other, looking nervous. "These guys have been dead two thousand years, Eddie," Jim pointed out.

"I can do this." Qayna muttered a quick incantation in Adamic and blew into her fist. She then rapped once each on the foreheads of Eddie and Twitch. When she moved to rap on Mike's face, he pulled back.

"*¿Qué me haces, chucha?*" he snapped at her.

Eddie looked at his bass player through slitted eyes.

"This will make you understand," the Marked Woman said.

"Yeah? That'd be a good trick." But he dropped his resistance and let her knuckle his forehead.

"You're here for the Council," Ishbaal said. He raised his dagger, a hooked and recurving thing of Nilotic provenance, in an attempt to parry the coming blow. He failed, and Zechariah shoved his sicarius into Ishbaal's eye.

"Don't talk." Jim raised a hand. "Yes, of course."

"She's waiting for you, defiler." Zechariah's leer was made more gruesome by the blood that spattered his chin as Ishbaal shoved his recurved blade into Zechariah's belly.

"Stop talking!" Jim motioned to the band members and Qayna. "Go," he told them. "Get past these ... men."

"How is understanding this *mierda* supposed to help me?" Mike whined. "*¡Ándate a la chucha!*"

"No kidding." Eddie eyed both dead men with suspicion and clutched the shotgun and the hoof fragment tightly as he walked between them. "I'm feeling pretty good about not taking Latin in high school now. Or whatever language this is."

When the others had passed between the pillars, Jim raised his hands in admonition again to the two damned men. "You guys," he said, shaking his head at the futility of his own gesture but feeling compelled to make it anyway, "go easy on each other. There's no damnation but what you make."

It wasn't true, of course; the two men were damned and in Hell. But maybe, Jim thought, they could show each other mercy and make it just a little bit better.

The roaring was louder; his enemies were catching up to him. Jim looked over his shoulder and saw only damned souls.

"Defiler!" Zechariah spat.

Ishbaal sliced off the priest's ear.

Jim slipped between them and into the next cavern.

The last, he realized immediately. Beyond the sea of damned souls in this last chamber was the spiral staircase leading up to the arched hall and, beyond that, the chamber where the Council met. At the foot of the stairs stood guardian minions of Hell in black plates of armor like beetles, Phthonos and Misos cracking their forked tails from side to side behind them. But the thing that made Jim quake was closer to him than that.

Every damned soul in the room—if there really were multiple souls here, and not some sort of trick of Jim's perception—wore the same face.

Every single one of them was Elaine Canning, wrapped in glowing, red-hot chains.

"Jim," he heard Eddie say. "Jim, you okay?"

He wasn't okay. He was staring.

"You are returned!" the damned Elaines hissed, sadness in their thousand eyes. "Come back to free me, have you? Come back to see your handiwork? Come back to join your efforts with those of your father's million minions?"

Jim couldn't tell if it was a joke. Was she teasing him or torturing? "Elaine," he murmured. "Is this really you?"

CRASH!

The explosion came from behind Jim, and dust and fragments of rock blossomed all around him. The Baobab, he thought, or some of the larger Wild Things. They were so big, their passage through Hell was bringing down the roof.

"Who else?" Elaine snarled, and all traces of humor dropped from her voice. "And you? Are you real or another phantom image of salvation, a mouthful of water spat at the feet of the woman dying of thirst? Is this the moment of deliverance you promised me, or have you come to put your hand to damnation's plow?"

CHAPTER SIX

Crannock Castle, the West Country

English Civil War

James lingered in Elaine's arms, letting the fruited scent and taste of her kiss lull him into a sense that the moment was eternal. She enveloped him in her voluminous sleeves, her long skirt, her golden hair. Elaine would live forever with him, and he would never again be alone.

The soldier at the door cleared his throat politely.

"I must go," James said.

"He will not speak with me." Elaine's eyes were limpid and bottomless. "I have not heard a word from his lips since he learned of my love for you."

"But he listens. And perhaps he will listen to me, too."

Elaine nodded and kissed him a final time. Something dark brooded behind her eyes, but only a single tear showed on her cheeks. Reluctantly, James left her arms, passed through the door as the soldier opened it, and faced the man he would have for his father-in-law.

"I am master of this house, sir!" Harold Canning bellowed like a bull as he entered, but the roar was sluggish and wet, and he swayed on the creaking chair. He fixed bloodshot, jaundiced eyes on James and thrust out his lower lip, making his walrusoid whiskers quiver. His doublet was frayed and stained with the signs of incontinence, and his hose was more noticeable for its holes than for the flesh it covered. Behind him, the green curtain rustled, and James shivered. Drafty old pile of stones, Crannock Castle. The soldier closed the door behind James, shutting him in with Elaine's father and two other armed men in Canning green.

"You are," James agreed. He was dressed for the highway, with broad hat in one hand and sword and two pistols through his sash. He pulled his riding cloak back behind his elbows to keep it out of his way. "You are master of this house, and your daughter will succeed you."

Canning harrumphed.

"You should speak to her. It is not worthy of you to hold your tongue."

The old man ignored him. "Even if my whore daughter stoops to embrace you, you'll not have it. I would no more give this house to you than I would to a turd she had squatted to lay in the street! You are a man of no inheritance and less consequence!"

James sighed. *If you only knew,* he thought. He carefully kept his hand away from the hilt of his sword so as not to provoke the old man. It was an effort, given the vitriol the baronet poured out upon his own daughter. "I do not want the castle."

"No? Ha!" Sir Harold sat up several inches taller and leaned back, head cocked to one side and eyes rolling. "No, you want the *land*, do you not? I would sooner see it burned to the ground than in filthy, heretic hands like yours."

"I do not believe in the divine right," James said quickly. Too quickly. The old man squinted at him with suspicion in his eyes.

"You are a Stuart man, are you not?" His hand twitched on the arm of his chair, and James was acutely aware that behind him, at the door, stood two musketeers. "I should have had you hanged the day Charles rode into Parliament with his warrants."

"I pray you, sir, stay calm." James let his hand drift slightly closer to the weapon. He shifted his balance slightly, preparing to leap sideways at the sound of boots on the wooden floor behind him.

"You think I fear you?" Sir Harold smiled, and the curtain behind him *swished* softly. James thought for a moment that he saw something fleshy moving beyond the curtain, but he ignored it. Imagination. "Because you learned to play at swords from Frenchmen and Italians?"

He was mad, James saw. He wasn't damned, though; James could clearly see that Canning was free of the taint of the Left Hand. "Taught," he corrected the old man. "*I* taught *them* to play at swords. I learned to fight with a sword well before I ever saw a Frenchman." *And well before any such thing as a Frenchman existed, in fact.*

"Whether I speak with my daughter is none of your business, interloper! And my family has been in this castle," Sir Harold choked, "since before there was a France!"

Touché. "I do not want the castle."

"Do you know what my name means?"

"Harold?" James decided to risk a joke; it might defuse the heaviness that came with the stab and thrust of this conversation. "Is it not the name of the angel who announced the birth of the Lord?"

"Impertinent blasphemer!" Canning spat. "*Canning* is *cyning.* Did you know that?"

James had heard it before and nodded, trying not to let his weariness show in his face.

"That is *king* in the good old tongue! My ancestors were lords of Mercia, did you know that? They ruled from the Dyke to Watling Street, and no permission asked, not of Alfred, not of the Danes, and certainly not of any nameless Norman bastard who wanted to marry their daughters!"

"I am not a Norman. Or a bastard. Or nameless."

"Ha!" Canning collapsed back into his seat, foam flecking his lower lip. "And yet you would have me hold out. You would have me risk my life and my inheritance for the Stuarts who squeeze me dry. They say Charles is a skilled maker of bastards. Perhaps you're one of his."

"You call yourself a king," James ground out between clenched teeth, struggling not to grab his sword, "and yet you would throw open your doors to a rabble of costermongers and gong farmers who would saw the head off their own sovereign."

Sir Harold stared, cocked his head again, and finally lurched to his feet. He moved like an awkward marionette, like a madman whose body only caught up to the motions of his mind several seconds late. "It is not your affair!" he roared.

James exhaled smoothly to control his rage. "Elaine will not leave her home. The safety of that home is therefore my concern. Sir John does not care about you or her or your people. He will kill you or turn you out to have command of this place."

"You are not her lord. I am, until she marries."

"She would marry me." The argument had become muddied, and James regretted it. The conflicts between the two men—over the war, over James's love for the old man's daughter, and over the old man's sheer obstinate dislike for James—and Harold Canning's madness were a bad combination for clarity of communication. The urgent need was for Canning not to open the gates to Sir John Horsham's advancing Roundheads, and James opened his mouth to venture another plea—

"She'll marry a horse first, and swive me up a stable of centaur brats."

James whipped his sword from its sheath. "Withdraw your words, sir!"

Sir Harold stumbled back, knocking his chair over sideways and falling to his knees. "Take him!"

James spun sideways. His fighting reflexes, honed by centuries of conflict, wheeled him directly between Canning and his two guards at the door. The older of the two, a paunchy man with a grizzled beard, held his fire and instead drew a sword. The younger, a blond boy with a nose like an onion and beetling black eyebrows, had less discipline. He pointed his wheel lock pistol at James and fired.

James dropped to the ground as the spring-pushed wheel slammed the bit of pyrite home, showering sparks into the firing pan.

Bang!

"Aagh!" Behind him, James heard the baronet yelp in displeasure or pain. *Let it be pain*, James prayed silently, and then he hurled himself off the floor and to the attack.

The older musketeer eased forward, sword warily in front of him. The younger struggled to jam his pistol back into his sash and stumbled back.

James wasn't worried about facing two men at the same time—especially not two backwater soldiers like these—but their odds of getting in a lucky blow would decrease dramatically if he could knock one of them out of the fight.

Bad luck for the younger guardsman, who was still reaching for his sword.

James flung his hat straight for the face of the older man. He stepped back, ducking under the flying object and batting it aside with the tip of his blade.

James sank his sword into the younger man's chest. He didn't mean to disarm himself, but the guardsman reacted badly to being stabbed. He flailed and kicked, and in the moment of death, he pushed himself forward onto James's own blade.

The remaining soldier rushed James, swinging his blade.

James spun again. Out of the corner of his eye he saw Canning, who was not dead and was dragging himself back across the worn floorboards towards the green curtain. James didn't know what passage might be concealed behind the curtain; it was not his home, and even Elaine didn't know all the nooks and niches of Crannock Castle. He only hoped the old man didn't have a brace of pistols behind the curtain.

The guardsman swung for James's neck—

James twisted and jerked with his arms. By sheer force of muscle—physical strength was one inheritance he did have from the father he was reluctant to name to Sir Harold Canning, or even to his daughter—James raised the still-twitching body of the younger guardsman and used the corpse itself to parry the attack.

"God's blood!" the paunchy man snapped. He stabbed again, aiming over his friend's shoulder and trying to skewer James's head.

James shifted the body up slightly, batting aside the second attack.

"Devil's spawn!"

Of course, the old soldier knew nothing. Still, his words irritated James, and as the guardsman stepped to one side and moved to slash for James's leg, James hurled his flesh-and-bone shield straight at him.

The guards tumbled back together, the dead man bearing down the live one like a battering ram carrying away a door, and James yanked both pistols from his sash. He'd gone into the room expecting resistance and maybe worse, so the guns, both of them shiny new flintlocks, were loaded, primed, and fitted with fresh flints.

He aimed at the soldier struggling under the corpse.

"Stop!"

The door to Harold Canning's audience chamber burst open behind James, and he paused. He knew it wasn't an attack, but he also knew it wasn't a call he could ignore.

The voice was Elaine's.

James nodded. "Throw aside your sword, sir," he instructed the guardsman.

"Kill him!" shrieked old Canning. His heart pounding and his breath racing in his lungs, James imagined that the crazed old man was shouting at him.

The soldier hesitated.

James raised one pistol and pointed it squarely at the other man's head.

"James," Elaine pleaded. "Will you shed blood in my house?"

"Your father's house. Your father's choice." James pulled back the hammer of the pistol. "Always your father's choice."

The guardsman tossed aside his sword and raised his hands in surrender.

"Coward!" Sir Harold disappeared into the curtain behind his toppled chair.

James hesitated, considered hunting the old man down in his own house. If he hadn't been Elaine's father, he'd have done it. Even if Elaine had simply not been physically present, James thought, he might have been willing to give chase.

He sighed and lowered both his pistols.

Elaine grabbed the hilt of James's broadsword and braced one slippered foot against the dead man's shoulder. "Poor Andrew." She straightened out her back and slid the weapon from the dead body that sheathed it. "Not exactly Excalibur and the stone, is it?"

James scooped his hat from the floor. He'd need it. "You would make a singularly fair Arthur."

"You would make a singularly large-handed Guinevere." Elaine pushed him out the door, wiping his blade in passing on her father's curtains and pressing the weapon into James's hands.

"I would be Guinevere for your sake."

"For my sake you must fly. You tried, but he will not bend his will. We shall open our doors to the Cambridge mob."

"Should I fear your father?" They jogged down dark wooden steps. James knew where they were going, but dreaded the thought of parting and shut his mind's eye to the inevitable.

"You should. He has money, men, and hatred in his heart."

"Fly with me."

"I cannot." Elaine Canning stopped on a landing. She looked into her lover's eyes and shook her head. "This is my home, and he is my father, and whatever part of my heart does not lie with you must always lie buried here."

"You talk like a witch."

Elaine laughed and continued their descent. "Am I not one?"

"Milady?" asked another soldier at the front door of the manor house. "Sir Harold?"

They passed him without stopping. "Sir Harold commands that he not be disturbed," Elaine said firmly, and the soldier bowed his head and stepped back into his place at the top of the stairs.

Elaine led James to the stables. Rain drizzled bleakly in the courtyard, the droplets falling so slowly to earth they seemed suspended, as if the thick mud were generating itself. "I had hoped to avoid this," James said.

"And yet you dressed to ride." Elaine tapped the brim of his hat. She was not dressed to ride or even to be out of doors, but James still struggled with an urge to simply throw her across the back of his horse and kidnap her.

"I ride for aid," James told her. "Matthew Taylor's men are encamped at the head of the valley. If you will not leave Crannock, I will not leave you."

Elaine shook her head. "You risk yourself," she said. "Better to ride north, be free of me and Crannock and all things Canning."

"I can never be free of you." James studied her face as she pushed him into the shelter of the stable. "I would not wish it if I could."

"Then fly north," she insisted. "Hope for a short war and a quick reunion."

"I must protect you."

"*I* must protect *you*." Elaine jabbed a finger into his chest. "I shall tell my father you have fled into Cornwall. He'll believe it, 'royalist' that you are."

"I do not care a fig for Charles." James grabbed Elaine's hand in his.

"Nor do I. But I care many figs for you."

She kissed him, and then somehow, in a daze, James was on his horse and riding out under the portcullis of Crannock Castle. He spurred the horse without mercy, hoping he could get to Taylor's men in time, hoping they were not otherwise committed, and hoping he could get back to Crannock with reinforcements— *unwanted* reinforcements, but still—before the Roundheads arrived.

He rode into the rain- and night-darkened woods, daring robbers and Roundheads alike to look askance at him. He needed allies. Crannock was too well-placed, commanding its valley and the crossroads below it with its horsemen and guns, for Charles's friends to casually let it fall to the Parliamentarians. Matthew Taylor and all his guns would come running, and Sir John Horsham would have to withdraw.

As he rode, James also called invocations into the night.

They weren't magic. He didn't know sorcery, at least not beyond the rudiments. He could recognize spells and wardings, and maybe tamper with them slightly, but he had long ago cast his own die as a swordsman. James had seen his father's route, remaking himself and the world in the image of some dream in his mind's eye with sorcery, and in the long centuries of their estrangement, James had more than once attempted to dabble in the arts of enchantment. But James simply didn't have the gift for it. He liked to keep a wizard by his side when he could—he felt naked now without one—but he himself was not a sorcerer.

But Azazel, First Prince of the Infernals, was. James had no easy gate into Hell or to the ruins of Ainok, whence his father once ruled. A wizard, when he had one, might be able to take him there in spirit by incantations or could summon one of the Infernals, including James's father, to attend. Mab's folk had other roads they could travel, though the Queendom had long ago turned its back on Hell. There were gates—places on Earth that lay especially close to Hell—but none of them was near Crannock Castle; the nearest usable henge was leagues and leagues away.

But however many years might separate them, James was Azazel's only son, and Azazel kept an eye on him. Some power in the chief of the Fallen, or perhaps in his position, title, or Throne, gave him a far-ranging ear, and that ear often fell on James.

He begged for the attention of that ear now. "Father," he begged with chattering teeth into the cold spray on his face, "help me!"

Animals thrashed in the wet forest on either side of the road, and James pushed on. His fingers grew numb and his mount neighed bitter complaints, but he continued.

"Father!" he roared.

Wet flapping sounds in the darkness raised momentary hopes. In his imagination, he saw his father's gigantic form settling onto the road before him, batlike wings snapping to shake off the water like a whip cracking open the night.

No such thing happened. Silvery-black night, wet and cruel, stared James in the face and filled his road.

"Father!"

James reached the head of the valley hoarse and shivering. Steep hills on three sides created a gentle, bowl-shaped vale with narrow passes leading out north and east.

"No lights," he muttered. Something was wrong.

Had Taylor moved his troops?

James reined his horse to a stop. He drew a pistol and hunched over it, squinting into the cold drizzle. Dark shapes bulked immobile in the bowl. They might have been tents. Had Taylor ordered fires put out because there were Parliamentarian troops nearby? But if the camp were still occupied, some sentry should have challenged James to give a password, and there had been none.

The camp must be abandoned. Might it be a trap, an ambush?

And set by whom?

James stroked his horse's neck gently, feeling its pulse hammer through its cold hide. The animal whickered a faint objection but obeyed when James urged it left, around the edge of the forest and still within the cover of trees. Silence. The smell of wet leaves and the smushy, sloppy sound of hooves plowing through the wet carpet of the forest floor.

He'd have given a lot for a decent moon.

The horse balked.

"Easy, girl," James urged it. He was about to direct the horse to move around whatever had caused it to pull back when he saw a dull glint of metal on the forest floor. The animal whinnied in distress.

James dismounted, taking the horse's reins in his free hand and keeping the pistol in the other. Probably useless, he thought, except as a threat or a club. The firing pan had to be flooded with rain by now.

He crouched low and eased the pistol forward, prodding the darkness until he hit something that rocked when he touched it. Flesh, he thought.

"I am armed," he whispered.

Nothing.

Damnation. James shoved the pistol back into his sash and reached forward with bare hands, carefully not letting go of the horse's reins. The last thing he needed was to be chasing a skittish and abused animal about in the dark. His fingers met resistance but were so numb it took him a moment to detect anything about what he was feeling.

Flesh. *Human*, he judged as he found the corpse's fingers, *and cold*. James looked nervously out into the grayer blackness of the vale, wondering if it was full of dead bodies. *Elaine*. He had come here for allies to head off the Roundheads and defend Elaine. If Matthew Taylor and his army were all dead, he must remount and return immediately.

Then he felt the first blister. He didn't recognize it immediately for what it was, but it burst as he squeezed it, coating his fingertips with viscous ooze. And then he felt another, and, as his touch became more ginger, a third.

"Father," he muttered again. "Please help. Not for me. For her."

The horse at the end of its lead snorted, but Azazel made no apparent answer.

The body was dead, but he had to know why. James tore a strip from the dry part of his shirt and filled it with powder from his horn. Under the shying horse and the canopy of the trees, he found a spot free of dripping water, wiped dry his pistol's flint, and slammed a shower of sparks into his gunpowdered nest of cotton.

The powder flared, the cotton caught fire, and James held up the little light to see. The horse neighed and pushed back; Jim pulled the rein tight and kept the animal in check.

The extreme mutilation meant he had no idea whether he knew the dead man or not. Blisters covered the corpse's skin wherever it was visible, rendering his face a mass of pus-filled sacs, and James choked back the urge to vomit. From the midst of the dead man's face sprouted a beak, and though they ended in hands and fingers, his arms were rubbery and boneless. More like tentacles, James thought.

As if someone had used sorcery to warp and destroy the man's body, turning it into something ... inhuman. Something Infernal, in fact.

A grotesque replica of a very specific Infernal.

James's light snuffed out.

"Belial."

CHAPTER SEVEN

James lay on the wooded hill and scanned Crannock Castle. The Roundhead leaders, spooked by the sudden aerial assault of Harold Canning's head, galloped back among their ranks with much less dignity than they'd had when they'd ridden forward.

"God's wounds," James cursed again.

He'd ridden in silence back from the head of the valley. His earlier shouting for his father had left him with a hoarse, scratchy voice and a low heart. There had long been distance between them, but now he was truly abandoned when he most would have wanted aid. His father would not help him, and his lover would not leave her home—in which she was now trapped.

Trapped and maybe damned, James thought. He had seen far too many damned souls in the mansions of his father to be spooked at the thought, but endless torment was not a destiny he had ever wanted for Elaine Canning. He was too far away to tell for sure whether the Left Hand was upon her and much too far away to be able to help.

He needed to get closer. He needed to get into Crannock Castle.

"Sir!"

The voice came from behind him, and as it spoke, James heard the metallic *click* of a gun being cocked.

His sword lay pinned beneath his body. His guns were wet. He had no idea how many men stood behind him. Even if he avoided death, the sound of a gunshot would alert other soldiers, who would come running. He was defeated.

"Stand, sir!"

But that would leave Elaine alone. James's brain thundered through possibilities but found nothing it could firmly grasp. And what was Belial's role in this? Was the Infernal the guiding power behind Cromwell and his troops?

Did it matter?

"I said *stand!*"

James drew his knees under him and climbed slowly to his feet. He raised his hands beside his shoulders and wished he had a dry gun, loaded and primed.

"You are not in uniform."

"I serve no lord and ride with no army," James said. "I am a mere traveler, here by chance."

"And the men with their throats slit at the base of this hill, are they victims of chance?"

"I know nothing of them," James lied.

"Spies and assassins do not wear uniforms."

"Neither do fishmongers and cobblers."

"Are you now a fishmonger?"

"I am a traveler, as I said."

"Turn around."

James turned slowly. A Roundhead soldier in a buff coat stood in the trees, leveling a pistol at James. His coat and boots were mud spattered and stained from long use, and his hair hung down to his shoulders. He was alone, and James felt a spark of hope.

"You are no Puritan," James said, nodding at the long hair. The man didn't have the Left Hand upon him, either.

"Piss off. Look to your own faith, whatever comfort it may provide."

James nodded amiably. He wanted the man as distracted as possible when he made his move. "Please take me to your commander so I may vindicate myself."

"Give me your weapons."

"Yes, of course." James lifted his sash off his shoulder. He did it awkwardly, deliberately letting the pistols both tumble to the ground.

The Roundhead snorted his derision—

And James snapped the cloth forward.

It was an insane gamble, but James had superb reflexes and a steady hand, and in his position, anything he did was crazy. Throwing himself upon the mercy of the bloody-minded, inflexible Puritan leadership would have been the most insane risk of all.

The Roundhead squeezed the trigger of his gun—

James's sash snapped onto the top of the weapon and slid down it—

The hammer slammed home onto the frizzen, but the cotton of the sash deadened the blow, and there were no sparks.

No sparks meant no shot and no noise.

James dove forward, pulling both ends of the sash with his body as he fell. The soldier's pistol slapped into the mud beside James's shoulder as James moved from a leap into a roll, and then James kicked his heels against the man's temples and crashed to earth sitting astride his man, ankles beside the Roundhead's ears.

"Murmmph," the Roundhead objected, dazed.

James didn't trust any of the pistols or the Roundhead. The knife in his boot fairly leaped into his hand, and with a quick snick across the Adam's apple, James killed the scout.

"I hope your faith gives you comfort," he said, and he thought that maybe it would. James knew from sad experience that a mortal who died with the Left Hand on him suffered in his father's mansions. What happened to all the rest, he had no idea. He had no grudge against the Roundhead soldier and vaguely hoped the man was in Heaven.

James squeezed into the scout's buff coat and sash, throwing his own aside. Carefully scraping damp powder out of both his guns, he loaded them with dry powder, tamped in a ball, and primed the firing pan. For good measure, he added the scout's pistol to his own, checking its powder to be sure it was dry. His own hair was as long as the soldier's, so he crept to the foot of the hill and stole the helmet from one of the dead sentinels, tucking his hair under it to hide it. A genuine Roundhead scout could afford to stand out from other Roundheads; James didn't want to attract any attention at all. At least, not until he couldn't avoid it. And then he'd want his head covered.

James eyed the gate of Crannock Castle once more. Elaine stood above it, staring defiantly at her enemies. The Roundheads were close. Were they too close?

And what had happened to her father?

No time to dally. James threw the dead man over his saddle and mounted. The horse moaned, and James wondered if the exertion and stress had already doomed the animal. No time to care. He rode down the hill.

Gray predawn light seeped across the narrow road beneath the knoll, turning the mud black. James joined the road and headed around the hill, away from the portcullis and the bulk of the Roundhead army.

Two men in buff coats nodded at James, and he raised his head in friendly greeting. Then they were past, and he turned off the track into the trees again. His horse shook but obeyed.

He came in sight of the men on the parapet and heard jeers. Good for them.

Crannock Castle had a moat. It wouldn't stop James from swimming across, but it would slow him down, which was what moats were designed to do. Slow him down and make him an easy target. Jumping into the moat would also end his disguise. He had to rely on the besiegers' fatigue, on his crafted deception, and on the fundamental logic of the siege: the Roundheads were here to take the castle. They'd care about lone men trying to get out because those might be messengers who would go for assistance, but they wouldn't expect a single man to try to slip inside.

James rode alongside the moat. The Roundheads were disposing their long guns in range of the walls. They worked quickly, no doubt trying to get the siege weapons into place before the sun rose and made them easy targets for the men on the walls.

James saluted Sir John Horsham and his knot of men as he passed and got only a casual perusal in return. He turned and crossed the bridge over the moat. He looked up as he rode, hoping to catch Elaine's eye without having to say anything. She stared north, though—up the valley in the direction in which he'd departed. *Looking for any sign of Matthew Taylor or me,* James thought.

He took a chance and removed his helmet. Still, she didn't look.

He reached the inner bank of the moat. The portcullis was down, its fangs slammed into the earth. Behind the iron bars was a thick wooden door, also shut.

"Here now!" called a voice behind James. "What are you doing?"

"Elaine!" James shouted. He spurred his horse forward and felt its knees buckle as the animal finally collapsed.

"Seize that man!"

Bang! Bang! The Roundhead ranks fired, and James heard the snap of bullets as they chewed through the air around his head.

He hit the ground hard and rolled, trying to stay behind the body of his horse. "Elaine!" he yelled again, waving. He was beneath the parapet now and couldn't see what she was looking at, didn't know whether she'd heard him.

The horse writhed, twisting and threatening to come back upright again. "God's breath," James barked. He drew the Roundhead's pistol and fired between the animal's ears. The horse collapsed, still.

Bullets punched the castle wall behind James, stinging his face with stone chips. He grabbed the Roundhead scout's body and heaped it on top of the dead horse to make a low wall. "Elaine!" he shouted a third time, and then he leaned across the hedge of dead flesh to return fire.

"James?"

He looked up and saw her peering over the edge of the wall. He paused, not surprised at what he saw and felt, but still horrified. Dread squeezed his chest, and a cloud of impalpable darkness shrouded his eyes. The Left Hand was upon Elaine Canning.

She had murdered her father.

The dead man under James shook from the impact of bullets, and he sank down for protection.

"The gate!" Elaine cried to her men, and disappeared.

James looked over his meat shield again and saw two horsemen galloping over the bridge in his direction.

Two was just the right number. Two was the number of loaded pistols James still had.

James shot the first horse between the eyes. It crumpled in a wave of brown muscle and hide, spraying blood on the bridge and on the inner bank of the moat. Dimly, James realized that he could now see the blood as red, which meant that the light was improving. Morning was imminent.

Behind him, the portcullis machinery *groaned*, an enormous sound that James could feel in his bones.

He couldn't spare a glance at it yet. He let the second horse charge past the first and get nearer, dangerously near, before he shot it in the chest. The animal hit the ground like a cannonball, plowing across James's improvised shooting wall and knocking it all askew.

The rider screamed as the horse's body ground his leg beneath it. Without standing, James reached over and ran the man through the neck with his sword. The spurting blood looked redder than red. *Why is she damned and not I?* he thought. *I have killed many men. What has happened in the hours of my absence?*

"He's a Cavalier spy!" Sir John Horsham shouted. But he stayed behind a cannon and a low wooden palisade wall, waving at his men to attack. Roundheads left their big guns and raced forward.

James grabbed the dead horseman's pistol. The other rider rose to his feet, gun in his hand—

Bang!

James's shot threw the man's dead body into the moat.

"Run!"

The voice belonged to Elaine, and James turned and sprinted towards the portcullis before even looking. The iron grating was raised a foot and a half off the ground, its sharp spikes glaring menacingly at the earth beneath it. Behind the portcullis, inside the open door, stood Elaine Canning, a smoldering old snap matchlock in both hands.

"James!" she cried.

He hurled his sword ahead of him, then threw himself at the ground without slowing. Bullets popped in the air about him, *thunking* angrily into the wood of the castle's door. He slid on his belly, rolled, and finally tumbled to a stop beside the door.

"Drop it!" Elaine called inside, but the portcullis was already crashing down.

Jim lurched up into a crouch. Partly by the tired springs in his legs and partly by Elaine's hand on the collar of his coat, he fell through the open door and then collapsed again to the ground as Elaine slammed the door shut.

Crannock Castle's courtyard spun for a moment while James caught his breath.

"James," Elaine said, cradling him as he half rose. "I begged you to flee."

"I would have," he said, putting on his best devil-may-care grin, "only you would not come with me."

Outside the castle, cannons began to fire. Chunks of stone and mortar ripped from the parapets rained down inside the courtyard, and the manor house within lost its first window to a high-flying ball. Soldiers in Canning green rushed for the steps up to the ramparts with muskets in their hands. A few lingered, watching Elaine as if waiting for a command.

"James." She looked into his face, and her hard, brilliant eyes wavered and filled with unexpected tears. "I have done a terrible thing. Your heart may not bear it."

The morning's sun began to creep over the parapets with the gunfire, but the darkness of the Left Hand hung about Elaine like a shroud. "I saw your father's head fly from the ramparts," he said, and shrugged, trying to make light of the burden he felt. "I nearly took it off myself earlier."

Elaine laughed, a sound that lifted James's heart with hope. "He was going to send his men after you, James. He knew where you'd gone. I had to kill him to save you, and I would do it again a thousand times. That is not all, though," she added softly. She had a sudden sadness in her voice James hadn't heard before.

He sat upright. "What is it?"

"A trade, Jacob."

The voice came from behind Elaine, and it wasn't human. It sounded like large sheets of metal being torn apart, and James recognized it instantly.

"Belial!" James grabbed his sword and jumped to his feet. The ground under him shook as a cannonball plowed into the portcullis, only a few feet away.

Belial, ugliest Prince of the Fallen, moved out of the shadow of the castle's wall and into view. He was scabby and unearthly, a mass of quivering, blistered flesh that split and split again into tentacles. He had no visible face, only a fierce beak. He looked like a cancerous octopus standing on its own head, a sentient, mutated, moving eggplant.

"Your woman has damned herself."

James ground his teeth. "Your status as a Prince of Hell limits my choice of satisfying profanity."

Belial groaned in laughter. "You could tell me to go Heaven."

"What do you want?" James scanned the tentacles closely, calculating where he'd hit the Fallen if he had to. *Inside the open beak* was the only tactic that struck him as at all plausible. The rest of Belial was just too big and soft and undistinguished looking to seem worth attacking.

"You have a right to sit on the Council, Jacob."

"I prefer to be called James now. And you have the same right. For that matter, anyone who attends the Council meeting can vote."

"But not anyone can attend the meeting. Participants must be entitled or admitted by vote."

Elaine laughed again. "I did not imagine Hell to be so much like Parliament."

"Does it not seem fitting?" James grinned at her. Another ball smashed into the front of the manor house, throwing a plume of smoke and ground-up stone across the castle's yard. The entire scene was unreal to James. He struggled to keep despair off his face.

"I have agreed to help the woman," Belial said. "She has agreed to my price."

"Price?" James hesitated. "Will you remove the Left Hand from her?"

The tentacled thing quivered in what might have been a negative gesture. "Perhaps Moloch may do that, perhaps not. I am certainly not able. But I have promised to save this place from its enemies for the price."

"What is the price?"

"Your vote, James."

"On what?" James pushed Elaine to one side gently, fearing that combat was imminent. A pall of gunsmoke scudded over the castle yard like a lid on a pot, and he struggled against the sound of the explosions to keep his thoughts in good order.

Belial was silent for a moment. "On the only thing that matters."

James snorted. "The Throne? You speak of a vote hundreds of years from now."

"I will have your word today."

James nodded to the Canning troops who stood aimlessly behind Elaine. "Take her away from here," he said. "Into the manor, somewhere safe."

"Milady," said one the soldiers. They had no reason to obey James other than fear and the astonishing input of their own senses. Those were enough. Elaine jerked an elbow away from one soldier, but two others grabbed her, dragging her away from the confrontation, loyal enough to risk her wrath.

"A new bargain," James suggested. He paced to one side, circling around Belial and putting himself between the monstrous Fallen leader and his lover. "And a new price. You leave my woman in peace, and I will leave you alone."

Belial trembled. "You do not understand. The spell has been cast, the pact made. If you will not pay the offered price, there is an alternate tariff, and your woman will pay it."

James heard disturbance in the courtyard but could pay it no attention. He continued to circle.

"I cannot vote against my father. Without him, I am alone."

"You are alone because you have power. Friendship is for the weak. Only the downtrodden have need of cuddling."

James advanced. "Undo your pact, Infernal."

Belial laughed, a sound like a burning house. "And then what? Will you sing to her in the houses of the damned to ease her pain?"

"If I must." James slashed experimentally at the tentacle nearest to him, slicing off a length two feet long.

Belial didn't bleed or cry out. He reared up, tentacles curving up and back like a scorpion's tail poised to strike. "Choose now," the Fallen hissed. "The pact is binding. The choice is upon you."

"Leave him alone!"

The voice was Elaine's, and she was shouting. James looked up and was surprised to see his lover standing on the walkway of the castle wall. She held a short musket in both hands and pointed it at Belial. The sight of her defiant pose, dress and hair snapping gold and green in a morning breeze, cheered James's heart.

"Leave him alone!" she shouted again.

Belial ignored her. "Choose," he groaned.

James looked up at Elaine and smiled. He didn't know how he'd free her of the Left Hand, but he knew it must be possible. And he couldn't side against his father—not with anyone, and certainly not with this monster.

"Go to Hell," he said.

"Not I," Belial answered, his words grinding and pounding like a blacksmith at work.

At that moment, a cannonball crossed the parapet and sliced Elaine Canning neatly in two.

James's heart stopped, and time froze in a trickle of honey. Elaine's blood and broken body fell down upon him in a grisly rain.

He was yelling, he realized. He tried to stop himself, and found that he couldn't. The taste of Elaine's blood filled his open mouth.

When his howling and weeping ended, the wall was breached, and Roundheads poured into Crannock Castle to claim it.

Unhearing, uncaring, almost unseeing, James took his sword in hand and strode to meet them.

"Belial!" he howled.

CHAPTER EIGHT

Men fell to the ground left and right under James's merciless advance. They were soldiers and competent fighters, but competent at best, and unequipped to meet a warrior of James's experience.

There were very few other warriors with as much experience as James, son of Azazel.

He plucked a pike from the hands of an advancing soldier and hurled the long, heavy spear into the flank of a horse. When the animal and its rider tumbled into a squad of musketeers, James took full advantage of the confusion, wading in with heart roaring and blade singing. Ears, throats, hearts, and more felt the bite of his sword and sank with their owners to the rocky dirt on the castle yard's floor.

Then James was through the gap and advancing into the oncoming wave.

"Canning and Mercia!" someone behind him yelled. The voice might have been a million miles away for the remoteness of the sound, and James strode inexorably forward. He snatched loaded guns from the hands of dead and wounded men when he found them, firing off shots into the Roundhead forces elsewhere on the castle wall.

He crossed the moat on a bridge of corpses, grinding dead faces beneath the heels of his riding boots.

He looked beyond and above the men he fought, his body mechanically doing the job it had trained for centuries to do without the need of any conscious input, not against this cannon fodder. His eyes and his mind ranged elsewhere, searching for the Infernal who had wrecked his life, who had stolen Elaine from him.

The morning sun was bright, but the trees grew thick around Crannock Castle, and James could not be sure of what he saw. But he thought a rustle beyond the knot of men that was the Roundhead command might be caused by the retreating Belial.

So be it. They wanted him a Cavalier and a threat, he would be a Cavalier and a threat.

"Canning and Hell!" he shouted, not sure what he even meant, and leaped into the saddle of an abandoned horse.

He wheeled the animal around and charged, catching Sir John's eye in the process. John Horsham looked surprised, and then perhaps a little pleased, to see one of Crannock's defenders make such a counterattack. James thought he heard more of Elaine's soldiers thudding across the dirt behind him, but he paid them no attention and lunged forward.

BOOM!

A cannon thundered to James's left, and he only noticed it among the hail of gunfire because at the same moment his horse exploded under him like a bladder full of blood slammed against the earth. He hit the ground awkwardly but managed to turn his movement into a forward roll that brought him into a slightly dazed crouch.

James shook his head, wiped blood from his face, and then realized that the weight of the weapon in his hand had changed. He looked at the sword and found the blade snapped off halfway along its length.

"God's wounds," he cursed. His head rang like he was standing inside a bolt of lightning. "It will have to suffice."

He stood and charged again.

Two men reloading a cannon fell to his half blade, slashed through the face in a single motion. A musketeer captain ordering his cadre to reload lost his throat, and his men fled. A burly Roundhead pushing a barrel of powder from a sheltered spot behind a knoll out to the cannons lost a hand to James's fury and fled, and then James leaped from the edge of a supply wagon into the air, vaulting onto the back of Sir John Horsham's own mount.

"Damn you, sir!" Sir John howled, drawing his poniard.

"Even so," James muttered grimly, and he slashed Sir John through his fat throat. *Damn me so I won't have to be alone.* The blubber around the Parliamentarian's neck left James uncertain about the effectiveness of his attack, so he slashed a second time and a third, and then Sir John stopped moving and James was certain he was dead. He tossed aside his own broken weapon, drew Sir John's sword from its scabbard, and hurled the Roundhead's body forward into the dirt.

Blood spattered him and the horse both. Gunfire rattled the air. A ragged wave of green was mown into nothing as it ran into the teeth of the incoming flood of buff, but James noticed none of those things. All he noticed were eyes—manic, wide, staring eyes in dozens of faces turned in his direction.

For a moment, he and the eyes all froze.

Then one eye squinted, and beneath it, a pistol raised.

"Ha!" James snapped the reins of Sir John's horse and yanked it around, turning the animal away from Crannock Castle, in the direction where James thought he might have seen Belial escaping.

He left the battle at a gallop.

Not fleeing, he told himself later, as the horse's hooves pounded over wet plain's grass. *Pursuing the enemy.*

He didn't see Belial in the pursuit, though. Nor did he see any track or other indication of the Infernal Prince. And as the sun reached its noon zenith in the sky and he heard the rumble of gunfire and the squeal of bugles from other battles, unseen behind wood and hill, he realized that he was running for the henge.

He reached the stones in the early evening, his heart still racing. A lesser man, a more ordinary mortal, would have died from the sheer adrenalin rush that continued to rage through James's body. He shook it off, released the grateful and exhausted horse, and stepped inside the standing stones, his pistols and Sir John's sword in his sash.

His knees buckled, and he almost fell.

"Baraqyel!" he roared, catching himself against an upright column like a jagged fang. "Open up!"

The scene around him changed. The sunny plain of southwest England with its faint tang of distant gunpowder on the breeze disappeared, and in its place rose two towering doors with iron knockers, opening to release Baraqyel, his father's gatekeeper.

The Infernal's birdlike feet scratched furrows into the stone as he walked forward.

"Jacob," Baraqyel said.

"James. Let me in."

"Your father is expecting you." Baraqyel didn't move out of the way.

"I wager he is. Stand aside."

Baraqyel hesitated, leaning on his gigantic spear like a staff. "You know that I can't bar the way to you," he acknowledged. "But do you really think this is wise?"

"Entering my father's house?"

"Entering your father's house angry."

James was not in the mood. "The next time you offer me unsolicited advice as to the wisdom of my actions, doorkeeper," he growled, "I will teach you the folly of yours. *You are a servant.*"

Baraqyel nodded, his long silver hair bobbing gracefully over James's head, and he stepped aside. "I am a servant," he agreed. "But remember this: I serve of my free will. I am no one's slave— not your father's, and not yours."

James trembled in rage. He almost apologized. He almost slashed at the Infernal's face as he bowed low. In the end he did neither, and walked into the throat of Hell.

He found Elaine. Hell brought her to him in a melting, brownish grotto at the end of a path of upright nails. She wore an elegant formal dress, her hair bound in wire, and her entire body was wrapped in chains that glowed red-hot like iron in a blacksmith's fire. The stench of scorched skin sizzled in James's nose, and he had to fight not to look away.

Beside Elaine in the grotto stood her father, Harold. He, too, was dressed as if for an invitation to the Palace of Whitehall, in unblemished stockings, doublet, and a vaguely crownlike cap, as James had never seen him in life. His head was reattached and animated, and like his daughter, he was wrapped neck to ankle in smoking red chains.

Both had their arms free of the bindings. Each held, in his or her hands, the dangling end of the other's chain.

Held and pulled, teeth grinding with exertion and pain.

"Elaine," James heard himself moaning.

She looked at him, eyes glassy with pain. "James."

"I am sorry."

She didn't meet his gaze. Were those eyes blinded? "I chose," she said. "I was forced to it, but we are all forced to choose, and none of our choices is good. That is the terrible truth of the valley of the shadow of death. I do not regret that I had to choose, for I do not regret being human."

"Elaine," he moaned.

"Nor do I regret what I chose. I murdered my father, yes. I had to do that or let him murder my love. I gave my soul in pawn to the devil because I thought I could have my family's home."

"Belial," James rumbled.

"I do not regret that, either. I chose the deed; I accept the punishment."

"Someone else," James said, trying to formulate an objection. "Someone else could ..."

"But I do regret, love, that I cannot be with you."

James grabbed Elaine's hand, tearing it away from the red-hot chain. Blackened, scarred flesh, pus, and patches of uncovered bone stared up at him for a brief moment before she snatched her hand away again and seized the chain. As if in rebuke, her father groaned and yanked harder on his end of the chain.

"I will undo this," James said. "By my self, by my soul, by my life and my father's life, I will free you from this terrible burden that I placed upon you."

"Do you not see, James?" she said, and for a moment her eyes cleared and focused on his face. "I *chose* this burden."

James stumbled away, tears streaming down his face.

"I *chose*, James!" she called after him.

James stumbled blindly among the damned, ignoring their howled regrets and their bitter reproaches. He clung to Sir John's sword at his hip like to a lifeline, though here it would do him no good. Did he imagine he would attack his father with it? His sense began to return. But he kept the sword and the pistols and doggedly ran on.

Coiled in the heart of Hell lay the Infernal Palace and a warren carved out beneath the Palace that had once sparkled at the heart of the Free City of Ainok. It was separate from the Abyss-mounted chamber where the Council met and shielded from the writhing mobs of damned souls by trusted servants.

"Phthonos." James greeted the Hellhounds at the front door reflexively. "Misos."

They growled back at him with affection, blowing jets of flame from their crocodilian nostrils that shook smoke up from their broad leonine backs in rows of black wisps, and then settled back to watching as he passed. One of the damned, a bent old man repeatedly nailing his own feet to the floor with a mallet and then ripping them out again, stumbled sideways and within Phthonos's reach as James passed. The Hound batted him away effortlessly, its massive paw knocking him head over heels back into the howling mob.

"Father!" James roared, and he filled both his hands with pistols.

Eyeless imps, many-legged crawling things, and slugs with gaping mouths scattered out of James's way. Hell was not Ainok, with its hundreds of fair concubines, its bustling markets, and its spiraling canals. Hell was howling, grim-faced servants and the business of inflicting pain.

"Father!" James pounded on the doors of the Audience Hall with the butt of one pistol.

"I'm here, son." At the end of a long hall to James's left, Azazel appeared, massive and scene dominating even with his wings furled. He beckoned to his son, then retreated under an arch that James knew opened onto a balcony in the Abyss.

James followed, wiping blood away from his face and hands again.

Azazel stood waiting for him on the balcony. The stone platform jutted without warning from the wall of the Abyss for the length of several hundred yards and then, just as abruptly, ended. It was as wide as a boulevard and had no railing. Azazel needed no railing; he had wings.

But if James fell into the darkness, he wondered, what would happen? Would he ever hit the bottom? He didn't know whether the Abyss even had a bottom. It looked like it fell forever.

What it did have was light. Sunk into the walls of the Abyss here and there in uneven patches were crystals, gems, and fungus. Trogloditic creepers, white, eyeless, and relentless, also skittered upon the face of the rock face in all its apparently infinite directions, and the troglodytes as well as the stones and the lichen glowed with reflected light.

As he had done a thousand, thousand times before, James looked up. He saw no sun, no source of light, no ceiling or end to the Abyss above any more than there was a visible end to it below. The wall glittered and glowed in patches, but it was all reflection, and James couldn't tell what was being reflected.

Thud.

Azazel tossed something onto the floor between them. He stood with his wings close in to his back, which made him as small as he was capable of appearing. His posture felt like a humble stance, despite the fact that he towered over James.

"What is that?" James asked, curiosity getting the better of him even as he looked for himself.

It was a saddle.

"You were deceived," his father said.

James knelt to look at the saddle. It was an ordinary-looking saddle, his size, and the sort he had spent many years riding. "I don't understand."

"You were deliberately ensnared."

James replaced the pistols in his sash. He turned the saddle over, still trying to figure out what his father was getting at. On the underside of the leather, a network of scratches sketched out a ward that he couldn't activate, but he recognized the Infernal glyphs and guessed at their use. "Silence," he said.

"It's your saddle," Azazel told him.

So it was. James almost laughed. "Belial," he concluded. His heart began to rise within him. His father was showing him cordiality, welcome, even warmth. Was the stiffness between them over? Surely his father would help Elaine.

"He had also warded the castle. I had no idea, and I couldn't hear you."

James dropped the saddle and stood up. "This is outrageous."

Azazel shook his head. "It is normal. The Princes of Hell play a very rough game."

"I am not a Prince of Hell."

"You are." Azazel cracked a faint grin. "You are a Prince of Hell of a different sort, perhaps, but nonetheless … you sit in the Council by right, and you are my son. To Belial, this makes you fair game."

"A game is played with rules."

"Not this one. Or at least, not very many rules."

"To attack my love … ?"

Azazel turned and looked into the glittering Abyss for a long time. "What do you think happened to your mother?"

James had no answer.

Azazel looked long into the shaft of light that pierced the center of Hell.

"You handled Belial perfectly," he finally said. "You did not tie yourself to him as he wanted. He would have had you oathbound to serve him at the Liminal Council, to vote to depose me. Your refusal was the right choice, son. If you made it for my sake … I must thank you."

"Was it the right choice?" James's head spun, and he took deliberate steps away from the edge of the balcony and the Abyss. "But I damned her."

"The alternative was worse."

James leaned against the cold stone wall of the Abyss. He ignored a glowing white centipede that crawled over his hand and tried to think.

"Why?" he asked.

"This office carries a lonely burden." Azazel spoke slowly. "None of my rivals understands that, none of them is ... suited."

"Not suited because Belial doesn't understand?" James flailed. "Understand what?"

"Consequence," Azazel said. "Remorse. Wisdom. Hell is not just punishment."

"Elaine now suffers the consequence of my failure!" James snapped. "This is a perversion! What will she regret—love? Will that make her *wise*?"

Azazel studied his son. "Perhaps she will regret murdering her father. Perhaps she will regret choosing pride in her ancestral home over life." He shrugged. "Perhaps, even, she will regret consorting with one of the Princes of Hell."

"I am not a Prince of Hell!" James roared.

His own voice echoed back at him from the Abyss, progressively more hollow at each fainter return.

"What will you do?" he asked his father when the echoes had died down.

"I have already created a nasty snare and lodged Belial in it. He finds himself in the fragmented wilds of Mab's Queendom in a labyrinth of my making. I think it will take him some years to escape, and if he encounters Mab's folk, he will learn to his regret that they are not fond of trespassers."

"And for Elaine?" James's heart hammered large and loud. "I have stood by you against your enemies. Will you stand by me? What will you do for Elaine?"

Azazel, First Prince of Hell, sighed. "For Elaine, I will fulfill my appointed role."

James ground his teeth, biting back disappointment and rage. "What does that mean? You'll torture her?"

"I'll allow her to torture herself."

James shook his head. "And then what? What is the end?"

"I don't know," Azazel admitted. He turned and looked pointedly out into the Abyss, infinite above and below and sparkling with mysterious light. "Perhaps there is no end."

"That's no answer!"

"It's the only answer I have. I'm sorry. If you are looking for the mechanic of the universe, the great engineer who understands the entire system and knows its purposes and final states, you are in the wrong palace. I am a lawbreaker—not the first to break the law, but the first to willfully rebel, and I am here to serve out my sentence as best I can." He gestured at the arch behind James and the damned beyond. "I do it because I must, and I do it … for them. I will do it for her."

"Release her from damnation."

"I cannot."

James pulled his pistols again. Fury pounded in his temples, and the guns felt ridiculous and tiny in his fists, but he pointed them at his father anyway. He wanted to tell him about lying under a pool of water, frozen and dreamlike, seeing fire and hearing his voice. But he couldn't. "Impossible."

"But true."

"You sit on the Throne. You're Lucifer, first of the Princes of Hell. Moloch. The Adversary and all that."

"I run this part of the machine, no more."

"Free her!"

"Son …" Azazel reached forward gingerly.

"No!" James pointed the trembling pistols at his father. "You release her, or I won't come back as your son."

"Don't do this."

"I'll be done with you. Not cordial, not estranged. I'll be your enemy. If I am a Prince of Hell, I'll act like one. I'll come back with an army, with weapons and power, and I'll make you do what I want."

"But I can't. I don't have the power." Azazel's words echoed softly off the rock face.

"I'll make you!" James was blind with fury, and he had no idea what he was saying. All he could see in front of him was Elaine, bound in red-hot chains and blaming herself for what he had done to her. "I'll make you, or I'll do it myself!"

Bang! Bang!

James fired both pistols into his father's chest, knowing he could inflict no injury, and hurled the guns to the ground. Azazel's great brow furrowed into a thick knot as the gunsmoke blew about his face. He opened his mouth as if to speak but then closed it again.

And looked down at the ledge on which he stood.

James turned and stormed out of the Palace and then out of Hell.

CHAPTER NINE

Hell

The End of the Age of Pisces

It's not Elaine, Jim told himself. *If it were, she'd be here with her father.*

He didn't believe it, but it didn't matter. She was somewhere in his father's mansions, and in any case, the roaring and crashing behind him meant he was out of time.

He pushed past her, his own flesh stinging at contact with the hot iron of her chains. Qayna came with him, urging her monstrous horse into a trot, Twitch still clinging to its saddle. Eddie and Mike scrambled to keep up.

Two minions in beetlelike armor at the foot of the stairs scuttled aside and turned the blades of their pole arms away to let Jim pass. Beyond them, the dozens of similar guardians thronging the steps rustled left and right, parting like a curtain of chitinous armor. A sharp click behind Jim as he leaped up the first three stairs told him that not all his companions had been allowed through.

He turned.

"No right," one of the guardians hissed. The foremost of them held their halberds low and between them, crossing to block the way to Mike, Eddie, and the Marked Woman.

"I'm invited," Qayna said, and she brushed aside her long black duster to show the pistol at her hip and the knives strapped to her legs. Jim remembered the shots she'd fired at the surrounding Bearers of the Sword on the rooftop of a meatpacking plant in Dodge City and the red blooms like blood that had spouted from the impossibly wounded angels, and he himself flinched.

The sentinels either didn't recognize the weapon or they were braver.

"The Child of Mab has no right." A dry, rotting smell wafted from their mouths as the guards spoke, and Jim thought he saw mandibles twitching at the margins of their faceplates. These were minor minions of Hell, and he'd never seen one of them out of its armor. If they had names, he didn't know them. For all he knew, they didn't exist out of their armor.

Twitch looked up at the rider and then at Jim. "Please," it said, face pale and twisted with pain. "You can't leave me."

Jim looked beyond Twitch at the thousand damned Elaines and forced himself to steel his heart. "Take her," he said to Mike, ignoring the fairy's plea.

Mike did it, the fairy looking small and frail in the bassist's arms. His face cycled through emotions Jim couldn't read, and then he looked up at the singer. "Me too, huh, *maricón*? You just gonna leave me like a piece of shit on the sidewalk? You guys said come along, and now you're just gonna screw me worse than I was already screwed?"

"Don't worry," Jim said. "I get what I came for, I can help everybody." It was at least half a lie. The Left Hand that had hung around Mike since Jim had first met the bass player in New Mexico was gone, and Jim wasn't sure Mike needed help anymore. "It won't take long, and besides, nobody's after you. Just get in a corner and keep your head down."

Mike spat on the ground, but he stepped aside. Phthonos growled at the chunky bass player, jetting smoke from the nostrils on the top of its leathery snout.

"You leave your churls with me?" Elaine shouted at Jim in astonishment, the words echoing from dozens of mouths. He tried not to look at her. Soon, somehow, he would give her solace. He had to believe it. Mike himself was the proof. Mike was a thumb in his father's eye, a refugee from damnation.

It must be possible for others to escape the Left Hand.

"I ain't staying behind." Eddie raised the hoof fragment in his hand and stared at Jim. "I got a right too."

"No right," hissed the sentinels.

Qayna raised an arm and pointed at the back of the hall. "You have bigger problems, soldier."

CRACK!

Chunks of stone as large as Jim's head burst from the far wall like popping kernels of corn, hurtling into the room. Qayna yanked the reins of her horse and turned the animal, sheltering Mike and Twitch from the rubble with her mount's broad, black flank. Jim and Eddie ducked, and Jim staggered as the cloud of rock slammed into him. A wave of stink rushed into the chamber, hotter and more fetid than the air already inside, and with it came buzzing demonic flies the size of wolves.

"Go!" Eddie shouted, and he leaped forward.

Beetle soldiers grabbed him and hurled him to the ground.

Jim hesitated, taking in the scene.

Qayna whispered to her horse and slapped its rump; the beast followed Mike as he carried the battered fairy into the corner of the chamber. Eddie kicked and punched like the champion hand-to-hand fighter that he was, but the demonic guardians of the Infernal Council's privacy were relentless and willing to take large amounts of pain. They piled onto him, grasping, biting, and pummeling with the butts of their pole arms. Eddie howled in wordless irritation.

Phthonos and Misos leaped forward, through the scattering mob of damned Elaines. As the wall facing them sagged and collapsed, the invaders rushed in. Beaked Belial and the glowing white Raphael loomed above the ogres, Baalim, and warped beasts around them, but towering ever higher than them, frustrated in its attempts to enter by the lowness of the cavern, was the Baobab.

Only its mobile, leg-like roots were visible, but it slammed repeatedly into what remained of the wall, shaking rubble down out of the ceiling.

Below the giants came Mab, regal and angry with spear in hand. Oberon sprinted beside her in the dust, bounding on all fours like a rabbit with long green coattails flapping out behind him. Rangers accompanied them, ragged and battered but doggedly shifting shape and trading blows with Azazel's minions. Pontius Pilate, the Legate of Heaven, rode something that might have been a millipede but for its size and the scabby, featherless wings that stretched left and right above and behind him, sheltering him from the worst of the chaos. His galero had been knocked off somewhere in the bowels of Hell, and the dusting of powdered stone over his red robes made him look pink. In a less turbulent moment, Jim might have laughed at the sight of him.

Around them all, in a chittering angry cloud, swarmed the Zvuvim.

"Run!" Qayna yelled at Jim. She grabbed his elbow as she sprinted past him, pivoting him on his heels and turning him in the direction of the top of the staircase. Beetle-esque fighters rushed down the steps past Jim, and behind him he heard Misos and Phthonos barrel into fiery action.

ROAR!

"Jim!" The yell was in Eddie's voice.

Jim turned to look. Eddie was bloodied and covered with swarming Infernal warriors, but he wasn't beaten. The shotgun had been ripped from his hands, and he fought now tooth and nail— the nail being the fragment of Azazel's hoof, which he slammed left and right like a sharpened fighting staff, shoving it into slotted visors and up beneath chin plates to wound his attackers.

"Jim!" Eddie called again. He jerked his head to one side to avoid a crashing bootheel, and his wild, staring gaze caught Jim's eye.

Jim felt like a snake. He would help Eddie, he told himself, he really would. He had intended to all along. Eddie wanted the Left Hand lifted from him, and once Jim knew how to do it for Elaine, he'd do it for Eddie, too. But he had to get to the Council meeting to do anything, and he couldn't get bogged down. The hoof had once been the linchpin of his plan, but he had never been all that certain it would work—his father was a powerful sorcerer—but Jim had a better tool now.

"Jim!"

Belial surged forward, the blobby, wormlike avocado bulk of his sorcery-twisted body hurling Misos aside and plowing through beetle soldiers and buzzing Zvuvim alike. Mike huddled in the corner with the shattered fairy Twitch. The bass player had his pistol out and pointed it around wildly, but the gun wasn't what kept him safe. The Marked Woman's flesh-eating horse reared up over them, lashing out with its front hooves at any creature, Infernal, fairy, or other, that got too close.

Jim turned his back on the band and ran.

Up the stairs on Qayna's heels he rushed. The infinite caverns of Hell spewed minions from holes in the walls he couldn't count, pouring along the walls, onto the stairs, and even scuttling across the rough-hewn ceiling. They rushed, weapons first, towards and past Jim, parting around him. He encouraged them with his broadsword, knocking aside any armored Hell-thrall that threatened to get under his feet. They hurled themselves on the flies, at the Rangers, and under the crushing bulk of Belial and the Wild Things.

At the top of the stairs, Qayna turned and kept running.

At the edge of leaving the large cavern thundering with the sounds of battle, Jim paused.

The Marked Woman's boots thudded heavily down a colonnaded hallway that Jim had walked down thousands of times. The arches let in the glowing, million-sourced light of the Abyss, some of it crosshatched by gratings or tinted by colored, translucent panes. The hallway was free of the minion-fueled chaos that raged at Jim's back. The feeling that stopped him wasn't fear, exactly … it was something more subtle than that, something he had a hard time putting his finger on.

When he had entered the Council chamber before, he finally realized, it had been as his father's son, to cast a supporting vote to try to keep Semyaz away from the Morning Throne, and then again, when that had failed and Hell and Earth had both suffered a tumultuous year under the heel of the boar-headed Fallen, to cast him out of it. The tightening in his gut that paused him now was a sense that he was about to do something drastic and that everything was about to change.

Drastic, and maybe rash.

CRASH!

Jim threw himself aside as something slammed into the wall beside him. He backed against the wall, sword out to defend himself, and found himself standing beside the lion-sized body of Phthonos, one of his father's hounds—the one that had nearly caught up with him in Dudael, New Mexico, in fact.

Phthonos whimpered. Black, blue, and red jets of flame and curls of sulfurous smoke twisted up from the beast's scaly hide, indicating continued life, but it lay with its back unnaturally twisted. A dog in that position, Jim thought, would be dead.

A stray Zavuv descended on the fallen Hound, and Jim kicked it, smashing it against the wall.

"Jacob!" roared Belial. The Fallen surged through beetle soldiers towards the stairs. He nearly crushed Eddie, but as the beetles parted and ran, the guitarist was uncovered, and a split second before he would have been crushed flat by the giant's bulk, he rolled aside. "Jacob, wait!"

The Fallen reached the stairs.

Eddie rose to his feet and glared at Jim across the tempest and through an intermittent cloud of flies.

Jim turned away again. He leaped over Phthonos and ran into the passage.

Qayna waited for him, breathing hard. She held Gabriel's Horn in her hand just in case, but for the moment, at least, no one followed, not even the Zvuvim. The beetlelike minions must be doing their work.

The Marked Woman had a strange look on her face, insight mixed with curiosity. "How does this work?" was all she asked.

"What do you mean?"

She pointed with her gun back the way they had both come. "What stops just anyone from coming down this hall and interrupting the Council? And voting?"

"Besides the goons on the stairs?" Jim shrugged. It was a good question, really, and one he wished he had the answer to. A bad answer to the question could disrupt his plan now. "I don't know the details," he admitted. "I never cared until it was too late to ask, and no one has ever invaded Hell before. That I know of."

"There's some kind of warding, right?" she pressed.

"Something like that," he agreed. "I think this passage might not appear except for people who have a right to attend the Council."

"The passage appears for me."

"I don't know what your right is," he admitted. "Do you?"

Qayna lowered the pistol. "I came here once before. I was invited to come here again today. Does either of those count?"

"Maybe they both do." Jim turned and continued up the passage. Each *crack* and *boom* echoed down the hall from the entrance like a physical attack. "I think I have a right. I think I'm one of *them*."

Qayna was silent for a bit. "You mean the Infernal Princes. Do you not want to be one of them?"

Jim thought of the cannonball that had cut Elaine in half on the wall of Crannock Castle. He shook his head sadly. "I can't change my birth. But I'd like to rise above it."

"I'm not sure everything is quite what it seems. Maybe you don't *need* to rise above your birth. I know there's nobility in your father."

"Is there?" Jim laughed bitterly, thinking of the red-hot chains around Elaine's soul.

"Do you think he sees himself as evil? That he wants suffering?"

The passage ended in an arching span of stone, threading out ahead of them into the infinite up-and-down space of the Abyss. The catwalk ended against the side of a vast stalactite in an unrailed balcony and a tall door. Jim stopped and looked over his shoulder. "He at least permits it."

"More than *permits*. He inflicts it."

Jim snorted. "And you ask me if he wants it? What kind of game is this?"

It was Qayna's turn to shrug. "I don't know. A complex game, where not everything is as it seems and not everyone truly fights for the banner under which they march. Whatever game it is, I don't think I'm playing it anyway."

Jim stalked across the catwalk, shoving Sir John Horsham's sword into its scabbard at his belt as he went. "I'm done being a witness," he told her. "I'm done standing by. I'm going to act."

She didn't ask what he meant, and followed.

"Snocker," Jim said to one of the guards at the last door, and nodded to the other. "Chask."

Chask dragged his tongue off the floor and into his long, toothy mouth to titter a wordless reply. He ogled Qayna with mismatched eyes and tittered louder.

"Don't think I've forgotten you," Qayna told the doorkeeper, and suddenly she had knives in both her hands. "And don't think you can touch."

Snocker clenched his four hands together innocently and bowed, turning to grapple with the door.

"Why is everything in your father's kingdom so ugly?" she asked.

"I don't know if it's ugly," Jim said, "so much as it's *homemade*."

"What, Heaven has all the factories?"

Jim nodded. "Which means that Hell has a punk aesthetic." Snocker got the door open and shuffled aside. The minion's perpetually bleeding knuckles had left orange smears on the stone of the door. "Do it yourself, you know? There's a reason rock and roll is Hell's music."

"I thought it was the rebellious attitude and the moral decadence." Qayna grinned.

"Nope." Jim walked into the Council Chamber. "Earth has the lock on moral decadence. Everyone in Hell toes the line. They have to."

He shut the door behind them.

The Council Chamber was immense. It seemed larger than the stalactite it occupied, though its preternaturally perfect acoustics meant participants had no difficulty hearing each other. The vast room was dominated by a circular table surrounded by Fallensized seats, one of which was larger than the others. The seats buzzed, hooted, and cracked with the shuffling, uneasy motion of their occupants. Not all the seats were occupied, but most were, and they were filled with the Princes. Jim saw Ezeq'el, her eyes downcast and liquid, rage-bubbling Semyaz, and Yamayol with flared taurine nostrils.

The single larger seat was the Morning Throne, and its occupant was Jim's father, Azazel. He looked across the Chamber at his son with unreadable eyes, and his posture was poised—relaxed but impeccable. He looked ready, at the slightest challenge, to crack his titan's whip and launch himself into the air with flapping wings. He had come prepared for a fight. A fight he had fought before, and a fight he had been expecting for an age.

Literally.

Qayna stopped at his shoulder. "Everyone?"

"Except the Princes," Jim conceded. "Of course."

"Call the question!" Semyaz screamed. Jim looked the pig-headed Infernal in his beady eyes and nodded. Semyaz gnashed his tusks back at Jim. The Fallen was furious but had no choice.

"Seconded," Jim said. His legs were tired, but not so tired that he couldn't leap from the floor to the outward-curving leg of the nearest chair, and from there into the seat itself. He stood rather than sitting, which made him nearly the same height as the Fallen ranged around the table. He looked around at them, recognizing them all, hating them for what they represented, hating himself because he was no different.

Across the table, Qayna similarly clambered into an empty chair.

"You don't know the question," sneered a Fallen whose head looked like it had originally come from or been inspired by a snail. *Jomjael*, Jim thought. A turtle shell crusted over her back, and each enormous hand had seven fingers, all drumming on the stone table.

"Don't I?" Jim stared at her until she flinched.

"Belial isn't here," she mumbled, looking down at her feet, which, Jim remembered though he couldn't see them, were horse's hooves. "There isn't a quorum."

"There's a quorum." Ezeq'el's eyes burned holes through Jim. Half of him wanted to laugh out loud, and the other half flinched, hoping the binding held.

Azazel nodded and thumped a heavy fist on the table. Jim forced himself to look at his father's face. He expected to see fear there, or at least uneasiness, but he didn't. He wasn't sure *what* he saw, but it might have been resignation. "The question has been called—"

"I am here!"

The new voice clanged like tearing iron—Belial. Jim forced himself not to turn and look, though the Fallen's voice came wreathed in the buzzing of flies. Too bad. Belial's followers would have nominated him and voted the same anyway, but Jim would have preferred to have one less vote for the octopoid Fallen.

"So am I!"

At this last, Jim couldn't help it. The Legate of Heaven stood in the door, and beside him was Eddie Marlowe. They were both battered, bloody, and crusted in pulverized stone. Each of them clutched one end of Azazel's hoof fragment. Behind them, Snocker and Chask closed the Chamber door, and the sound of the Zvuvim cut out again.

Eddie stared sourly at Jim. "You left me. I had no other choice."

Jim was impressed, and he guessed that Pilate had used sorcery and the hoof to somehow finesse the Chamber's wardings. Still, he shook his head; the stubborn guitar player had no idea what he was getting into.

"Belial," Azazel said smoothly, his voice rumbling warm and loud in the Chamber. "Welcome. You're expected."

The worm-eggplant-octopus Fallen heaved himself to the table like a drunk bellying up to the bar, knocking aside an unneeded seat. "I am here by right."

"I am here by cunning, ruthlessness, and sorcery," Pontius Pilate said. He let go of the hoof fragment and dragged himself awkwardly up into an oversized chair. No one helped him or spoke, and he settled himself carefully against the back of the seat, spreading out his red skirts and punching the dust out of them. "But I am here nevertheless, and I intend to vote."

"Legate." Azazel nodded.

Eddie Marlowe said nothing. He climbed into the last empty chair, pumped his shotgun to chamber a round, and furrowed his brows angrily at the entire gathering.

"The question has been called," Azazel said again. "Who shall rule in Hell? Nominations are open."

"Belial!" shrieked the snail-headed Fallen, Jomjael. Yamayol the bull snorted in disgust, and others of the Fallen hooted in derision. The cacophony was deafening.

Jim shot a look at the Marked Woman. She stood on her chair, a tiny, inconsequential cowgirl in her hat and duster. He didn't miss the fact, though, that her coat was brushed back behind her hip and one hand hung low beside her cursed pistol.

"Seconded," said the Legate of Heaven.

This is the deal Belial forged in the Queendom, Jim thought. He had made promises to the Legate and to Mab.

"Azazel." The nomination was hissed by a kilt-wrapped Fallen with the head of a serpent.

"Seconded." The voice belonged to Baraqyel, and the word made Jim notice him for the first time. The gatekeeper of Hell leaned in the corner of the room, blood running down his birdlike legs and matting his long white hair. He leaned on his spear like a broken man on a crutch. Jim felt a pang of compassion and fought to stay focused.

Azazel nodded. He looked tired, Jim thought, and old. The First Prince of Hell turned to look at Semyaz, no doubt expecting the same motions from his boar-faced rival that he always heard.

"I have a nomination," Semyaz growled, jutting his tusks at Azazel. He sounded like he was fighting a stomachache, and every word spattered yellow drool on the stone table in front of him.

Azazel didn't smile. "Let's hear it."

Semyaz snarled, low and guttural. "I nominate ... Jacob bar Azazel."

A hiss ran around the table, turning heads as it went. Some stared at Azazel, some at Semyaz, and some at Jim.

"Seconded," Ezeq'el the centauress said sadly. The look on Azazel's face might have been shock.

Jim swallowed back a trembling feeling in his chest. "I move to close the nominations." He wondered whether he had enough support, even with all of Semyaz's crowd. He'd know soon enough.

Eddie stared at him across the table, uncertainty flashing in his eyes.

"Seconded," said Yamayol.

Adrian Pew's spell—his greatest spell, the one he hadn't understood that he was casting—had worked. The binding on the three Princes of the Fallen had held, and they had done as Jim had ordered.

So far.

"Very well." Azazel pounded the table again. He moved more slowly than usual, like an arthritic. "All in favor of closing the nominations."

A braying, screeching tumult of assent rang in the Chamber. Voting was by acclamation in the Council; the Fallen roared for the proposition they endorsed.

"All opposed."

Not a squeak. Eyes swiveled nervously about the room, astonished at the surprise attendees and the unexpected nominations; none of the Fallen wanted to add to the uncertainty they already felt and no doubt feared.

"Then we proceed to the vote."

CHAPTER TEN

The throng of beast-headed giants held its collective breath.

Jim looked at Eddie, the Legate, and Qayna.

Semyaz trembled, and his followers stared at him. Yamayol fumed, and Ezeq'el shed a single tear.

"Belial," Azazel said.

Belial himself emitted a sound like thunder, and so did all his followers. The Legate of Heaven raised his voice too, in a yell that was impossibly loud for a human throat. He was cheating, Jim thought, amplifying his voice with sorcery to make the acclaiming vote for Belial as loud as possible.

There was no point calling him on it. They had rules, and they all cheated.

"Azazel."

Another earsplitting roar. Baraqyel shot daggers at Jim with his eyes and pounded the butt of his spear on the floor as he yelled his approval. Azazel himself held his peace, and Jim squinted at his father. What was he doing?

"Jacob bar Azazel."

Semyaz howled the loudest, pounding the table before him, but Yamayol, Ezeq'el and all their faction threw in their animal screeches too. "Aye!" Jim shouted, and kicked the arm of the chair with his boot. Across the table, Eddie yelled something Jim couldn't hear and fired his shotgun at the ceiling.

Jim and the guitar player locked eyes briefly, and Jim nodded his thanks.

"Gaaah!" Semyaz shouted as the clangor of the vote died away, smashing his own forehead into the tabletop. "Curse you, bar Azazel!"

"You started it," Jim growled, remembering Elaine enslaved inside the shadow of the now-dead Adrian Pew. "You never should have made promises you couldn't keep."

"Trickery!" Belial shouted, writhing against the table.

"You don't have a leg to stand on." Jim spat on the table in the beaked Fallen's direction. "Literally."

"A tie," Ezeq'el said. Her voice held a hopeful note, and she looked across the table at Azazel.

"Not everyone has voted." The Legate of Heaven reached inside his robes and pulled out a folded, wax-sealed sheet of paper. He set it slowly on the table in front of him and turned to look at the Marked Woman.

Qayna stood perfectly still, but under the shadow of her broad-brimmed hat, Jim would have sworn the tattooed curses on her face were writhing.

"Qayna?" Azazel prompted her.

She looked at Jim, then back at his father. Was she, Jim wondered, really just here to be a witness? "I don't have a vote."

"You do." Belial's beak ground out the words like a machine. "All present vote. You are here." He trembled, and the immense table rocked back and forth on contact with his shapeless body. "You know what you are offered."

Qayna hesitated. Jim forced himself to breathe calmly, feeling the muscles of his shoulders tense into knots hard as metal.

"What is offered ... if it is not, in fact, a trick ... is slavery," she finally said. "I'm not here to vote."

"No?" Belial shrieked, rising up and half falling across the edge of the table. The stone slab skidded sideways, knocking over several Fallen on the other side. "Then why are you here?"

Jim's own chair toppled over, and he leaped nimbly onto the table. Settling into a poised, ready stance, he drew his sword.

Just in case.

"I was invited." Qayna shrugged. "It was the only game in town."

Eddie pumped his shotgun to chamber another shell, watching Jim warily. "What the hell happens now? You know, forgive the pun …"

Belial's tentacles wiggled like a tub of live bait.

"There is another vote yet to be cast," said Baraqyel. The doorkeeper of Hell staggered forward from the corner, leaning on his spear. His grin was tired but wide—the grin of someone who has won a long and close race. Beside him, the snake-headed giant hissed in pleasure.

"Azazel." Ezeq'el looked up from the floor, face beaming.

All heads turned towards Lucifer, Moloch, the Accuser, the First Prince of Hell, the occupant of the Morning Throne since there had been a Morning Throne.

Azazel stood. Jim's father stretched his wings out wide and then folded them neatly against his shoulders. He rested both hands on the table.

"I am tired," he said simply, "and I think the time has come."

Many voices hissed uncertainly.

Ezeq'el's eyes opened wide. "Azazel?"

"No riddles!" Belial barked. "No evasions! Vote, or there is no Satan!"

A faint smile curled on Azazel's face. "No Satan?" he asked. His cool eyes traveled around the table, touching on each attendee. They lingered, Jim thought, on Qayna and Eddie. They passed over the Legate without hesitation and came to rest on Jim. "What would that be like?"

"Don't you remember?" Jim asked his father. In his own mind's eye, he saw the spires of Ainok, the grand spiral of its canals, the glittering white stone and dark wood.

Azazel nodded and looked again at Qayna. "I remember," he said. "I remember … perhaps too much."

"Vote!" Belial squealed.

Semyaz pounded the table again in mute rage.

The other Fallen stared, uncertain.

Azazel nodded and looked again at his son. Jim tightened his grip on his sword. His father's hoof fragment lay forgotten in the corner; he prepared himself to leap for it. He could live to fight again another day, return to his original plan. He knew now that it was possible to free the damned, and he could—

"Jacob bar Azazel."

Jim heard his own name come from his father's lips, and it felt like the six syllables took an eon to pronounce.

His head swam. His knees buckled, and he fought to stand.

"Nooooooo!" Semyaz bellowed, and hurled himself forward onto the table.

Jim was stunned. He wanted to move aside, but he was exhausted, surprised, and off balance. Semyaz rushed at him like a train with a boar's head, roaring and slashing with ragged talons.

He had done it, Jim thought. He had taken the Morning Throne, and now he was going to die.

Bang! Bang! Bang!

Semyaz's claws missed, but his body plowed into Jim like a bus. Jim was swept away under a ton of pig's head and eagle's wings, off the table, and he smashed against the wall. He lost his grip on his sword. Blinding flashes of light filled his vision, and his breath was squeezed from him. Semyaz writhed on him in all his bulk like an elephant having an epileptic fit.

Bang! Bang! Bang!

A final shudder.

Bang!

Stillness. Jim felt very, very small and flat.

This was death, then.

But Semyaz lay on him like a fallen log, not finishing his attack.

When air returned to Jim's lungs and the room stopped spinning, he felt and smelled hot blood pouring over him. Not his own; Semyaz's blood. And he saw that the former Prince of the Fallen had three neat bullet holes in his temple.

"Seven trumpets," someone murmured. He wasn't sure who.

He heard padding soles of combat boots on the floor, and then Eddie Marlowe dragged him out from under the dead giant.

Jim stood awkwardly and tried not to show the weakness and pain he felt. Qayna stood in the corner, pistol still in her hand.

"Qayna," Azazel said in a calm voice. "You have broken the peace of the Infernal Council."

"You call that *peace?*" Eddie muttered, but he hunkered down at Jim's side and didn't draw attention to himself.

"Will you punish me, Lucifer?" she asked. She raised her eyebrows as she spoke, like she was daring Azazel to do his worst. "Will you kill me?"

"It is not my place to punish you." Azazel stepped away from the Morning Throne. "And I am no longer Lucifer."

The Fallen were silent.

Jim stared in uncomprehending shock.

"Jacob bar Azazel," his father said, "Firstfruits of Ainok the Free. You are Moloch, greatest among the Princes of the Fallen. Take your Throne."

Jim staggered to the Morning Throne. It was a simple gray seat, hewn from the natural stone of the Chamber, and he kept his eye fixed on it as if the image itself would hold him up. When he reached it, he lurched up its steps and collapsed onto the stone, warmed by his father's immense body.

Energy rushed through him.

Jim gasped, looking up at his father standing beside and above him. He couldn't decipher Azazel's expression. Jim tingled. He felt alive and strong. The Throne quivered and sighed beneath him like a living thing, and a rush of sound like tumbling waters filled his ears. In the rush, he thought he heard a million cries, a million whispers, and a million peals of laughter, none of it originating in the Council Chamber.

He sat upright and looked around the table.

Eddie and Qayna stood in the corner beside the corpse of Semyaz. They looked tiny, and their guns looked even tinier. The Legate furrowed his brows at Jim, his folded paper swept off the table and hidden away again. Yamayol sat back in his seat, stunned. Ezeq'el and Baraqyel wept openly. Belial gnashed his beak and trembled.

No one spoke.

Azazel turned and walked away from the Morning Throne. He hesitated near Qayna for a moment, but neither of them said anything. In the open door, he stopped and turned.

"There is one other item of business," Jim said.

He hadn't planned this, but he saw now that it was possible. He saw that the Princes would vote for it—enough of them, anyway, for the motion to pass. His accession was the thing that would make them accept it—they would choose formless, unknown opportunity for their ambitions over doubt about what Jim's rule would entail.

And he had some votes in his pocket already.

"Name it," Yamayol huffed. The bull-headed Fallen gripped the edge of the table, his massive knuckles white.

"I move to disband the Council. Free us all. Empty Hell."

Stunned disbelief on giant faces.

"Is this wise?" the Legate of Heaven asked, frowning.

Azazel started forward. "But the damned ..."

"I free them," Jim snarled.

"You can't." All eyes stared, shifting back and forth between Jim and his father.

"But I *do*!"

Jim slammed his fists on the arms of the Morning Throne and willed it. With the force of his mind, and with the energy in the seat beneath him, he threw open the gates of Hell and cast all its minions and prisoners out. He seized Hell in his mind and bent it against itself to break it. He felt power flow through him like a hurricane through a bottle's neck, stripping stone off the canyon walls and flesh and life out of his chest. The rushing in his ears grew to a ringing yell. Pain wracked him, and he gritted his teeth against it, staring at his father.

KRAAANGGG!

The Council Chamber split down the middle as if struck by a hammer. A continuous crack snapped into being all along the floor, two walls, and the ceiling, and one half of the room dropped six inches. The table groaned loudly and then it, too, split along the middle and collapsed.

Far away, outside the Council Chamber, clangs, booms, crashes.

He didn't know what he'd expected, but his expectations hadn't been that ... loud. Jim sucked in air. Already tired and pounded by Semyaz, he felt drained of vitality by the Throne now, too.

Azazel bowed his head and shoulders. "I didn't know you intended this."

"I *didn't*." Jim stood slowly. His knees trembled and he looked over the room. "Now get out. All of you."

He didn't watch them go. He couldn't; he was too broken. He held himself erect between the Throne and the table, the departing Fallen a blur before his eyes. When the Chamber had emptied out, he collapsed back into the Morning Throne. This time, it had no energy to give him. The rushing-water sound of voices was gone. He closed his eyes and felt physical comfort in the cool stone.

"What the hell, Jim?"

Eddie. Jim opened his eyes. The guitar player and Qayna the Marked Woman were the only ones left in the room with him. They looked like children next to the oversized seats of the Infernal Council, or dolls.

"This wasn't quite what I planned," Jim said weakly. He felt smashed flat.

"No shit. It wasn't what I planned, either."

The Left Hand still rested on the guitar player. As Jim looked at him, Eddie's bad eye slid sideways, and he shuddered.

"I ..." Jim gripped the arms of the seat. He had freed the damned, hadn't he? He had meant to free Eddie. "Hold on."

"You owe me." Eddie stared at Jim fiercely, sawed-off shotgun trembling in his hand. "You owe Mike and Twitch. You didn't get here alone, damn you. Hell, you owe Adrian, if you can find the poor son of a bitch."

Jim closed his eyes and tried to feel his way into the Morning Throne. It lay inert under him, cool and lifeless.

"Jim?"

He opened his eyes. Eddie's face was full of blame, but Qayna's was curious.

"You're Jacob," she said.

Jim stood, nodding.

"I killed you," she continued.

He staggered away from the Throne and towards the door. "I died," he admitted. "I wouldn't have said you were responsible."

"Jim?" Eddie called, and they both followed him out.

Jim lurched because he couldn't run. Snocker and Chask were gone, and the bridge connecting the Council Chamber to the rest of Hell lay silver-lit and cold across the Abyss. The crack that had split the Chamber ran along the bridge as well, and as Jim and the others reached the far side of the slender span, the bridge finally cracked. Jim didn't look back, but the immense crashing sound of the Council Chamber's stalactite slipping into the Abyss and taking the bridge with it chilled him.

Jim half-expected Zvuvim to harry their path, but the flies were gone. Emerging from the arched hallway, he found Phthonos. The Hellhound still lay whimpering, its back twisted. It looked up at Jim with mournful eyes, and Jim staggered past.

In the rubble he found Elaine.

Only one of her, standing, and with her chain still wrapped about her. No sign of her father.

As he stumbled down the stairs, Mike rose up to intercept him. "Hey, *maricón*, when the hell are we getting outta here?" Twitch lay on the ground beside Mike, staring up with battered eyes.

Jim ignored them. "Elaine!" he called.

She whimpered. "I would not complain, love," she said. "But I hurt."

Jim grabbed the end of the chain and gasped at its heat. He willed it to fall from her, struggling at the same time to unwrap it.

"No," she moaned.

"Jim!"

Eddie and Qayna arrived on the stairs at his back. Jim turned, trembling, seeing blame and anger in their eyes. Eddie had again picked up his father's hoof clipping, forgotten by those who had chased so eagerly after it in the chaos of the Council's meeting. Forgotten by Jim.

"I know!" Jim screamed, wiping blinding sweat from his face. "I screwed up!"

"Yeah?" Eddie's face was ashen.

"I thought I could save you." Jim sank to his knees, wasted. "I thought I saw a chance to grab the Throne from my father. I *did* see it. I thought I could free you—free you all. But the Throne just opened the doors and let everyone out. It didn't save anyone."

"That wasn't our plan," Eddie growled. "There was no Throne in our plan. Our plan was trade the hoof to your dad for what we wanted, and if that didn't work, use the hoof to force him. When the hell did you get big ideas?"

"Kansas City." Jim tried to stand but couldn't. The size of his failure overwhelmed him.

"Semyaz and the others. They agreed to vote for you."

"I forced them. Adrian forced them."

Eddie sat on the steps and sighed. "Now what?"

"Help me," Elaine whimpered. Her chain rattled on the floor.

"It must be possible." Jim looked up. "I know it's possible to remove the Left Hand."

"Yeah?" Eddie looked skeptical. "How do you know that?"

"Mike." Jim pointed. "I don't know how he did it, but he lost the Left Hand since he came in here."

The both looked at the bass player.

Mike scowled and snorted. "*Concha de tu madre, pendejo.* Why the hell do you think I'm *Mike?*"

Eddie frowned. "Sounds like he ain't gonna be much help. Where does that leave us?" He shook the hoof fragment. "Your father again? Chicago?"

Jim struggled to his feet again. He felt tired and very, very old. He looked at Elaine.

She groaned. "Help me."

Jim sobbed. "I can't."

Eddie looked away, embarrassed or disgusted.

"They came for your beat-up friend." Mike jerked a thumb at Twitch and brandished his pistol. "Me and the horse chased 'em off."

Jim looked at Twitch. "Who came?"

"Mab," the fairy croaked. "And her Rangers. The Mare of Diomedes frightened them off, but they'll be back. My exile is over, and I've been condemned to death."

Jim shook his head, feeling beaten. "And Raphael?"

"I last saw him fighting off a Hellhound and a Baal Zavuv," Eddie said. "He didn't look too happy that the old guy made a deal with me."

"What deal?"

Eddie fixed one eye sternly on Jim while the other slid off in random directions. "You think you got a right to know?"

Jim sagged. "No. And it doesn't matter."

Twitch closed its eyes slowly. "Death might be better than this, don't you think?"

Eddie whistled through his teeth slowly. "No deal," he said. "Or anyway, no deal that isn't over and done. I shared the hoof with him, he got me through the door."

"Help me," Elaine said again.

"I can't free you," Jim admitted. "I thought I could do it. I'm sorry. Maybe ... maybe my father."

"She's not asking to be freed." Qayna finished refilling the clip of her famous pistol and snapped it back into place.

Jim turned to Elaine again. His love's face burned, and the smell of her roasting flesh and melting hair stung his nostrils. "Help me, James."

Jim stood uncertain. "How?"

"She needs you to punish her." Jim wasn't sure whose voice had spoken. He was too distracted by the sight of Elaine before him, burning and crying.

"No." His lips felt numb.

Elaine groaned.

"I can free her. I ..." Jim looked about him at the rubble of his father's mansions. "Help!" he hollered, and his voice echoed back at him without mercy.

"James ..."

"I'll do it."

He grabbed the dangling end of Elaine's chain with both hands. The iron was hot, and his hands burned, but he held tight, ignoring the stench of his own flesh scorching along with hers.

"Please ..."

He pulled. The force of his arms jerked a sob out of his own chest and he thought he felt her bones breaking, but the sound that slipped from Elaine Canning's beautiful lips was a grunt of relief.

Jim held the chain and wept.

"How do we get out of here?" Eddie asked later. The pain broke Jim's sense of time, and he wondered how long he'd left the guitar player standing there.

Jim stood. "I can't come with you."

Eddie's face was hard. "Fine. Show me the way out."

Jim nodded. "I'll lead you. One last time."

"One last time."

He dragged Elaine with him through the empty caverns of Hell. She resisted, and sighed and moaned with relief every time he had to yank to pull her along with him. At some point in the dimming red darkness of the vaults, he began to sing.

> *A cold north wind is blowing*
> *Down along the range*
> *The man with the banjo and the three-legged mule*
> *Drifts across the plain*
> *The snow piles up in lonely humps*
> *But you won't hear him complain*
> *He just thinks of her and how*
> *With a song of unspeakable sorrow*
> *He broke her heart*
> *He broke her heart*
> *He broke her heart*

It was one of his, written for her during the cold nights of the '49 Rush.

Every step was agony for Jim's body and soul, and neither the song nor their arrival at the gates gave any solace.

The doors hung on one hinge each. Myriad claw and bite marks in the metal told the tale of the doors' opening.

"What's out there?" Eddie asked, thumbing more shells into his shotgun and stuffing Azazel's hoof fragment inside his torn green jacket as he caught up. He sniffed and wiped one eye, and

Jim wondered dully if he was emotional. Behind him, the Marked Woman led her horse, carrying Twitch on it. Mike walked muttering to one side.

Jim shook his head and shrugged. "I'm not the doorkeeper. *Outside* is out there. It could be the ruins of Ainok, it could be Missouri, I don't know."

Eddie peered through the shattered doors. "Missouri, huh?" A hot wind blew smoke in through the ruined gate. "Missouri's changed since I last saw it."

Jim felt nothing but the pain in his hands and the hammering of his heart. He pulled on Elaine's bindings and she moaned gratefully. "Yeah?"

"Yeah," Eddie said, and he pumped his shotgun. "It's on fire." The guitar player turned over his shoulder and called to the others. "Come on, then. I'm still damned and I still aim to do something about it. This ain't over yet."

Jim stared after the broken remains of his rock band as they staggered out into the burning night in the company of Qayna, the Marked Woman. Then he saw that Elaine cringed back from the light and the heat.

"Come," he whispered to her, and pulled again on the searing chains that bound her ... the chains, he realized, that bound them both.

He led her back through Hell with the last of the dying Infernal light, singing.

> *The drunks are up the gangplank*
> *Staggering pair by pair*
> *The woman with too many late nights in her eyes*
> *Flips a final chair*
> *She knows the flood is coming soon*
> *But she just shakes out her hair*
> *She thinks of him and how*
> *With a song of unspeakable sorrow*
> *He broke her heart*
> *He broke her heart*
> *He broke her heart*

As the red glow finally faded into nothing, he saw a glimmer ahead. Picking their way through rubble and over corpses, Jim brought his lady love past the Audience Hall to an unrailed balcony where once he had confronted his father.

The Abyss was still brilliant with light.

Elaine moaned piteously, and he pulled the chain harder.

"I love you, James," she whimpered.

"I love you, too."

The smell of the burning flesh of his own hands clogged Jim's nostrils, and the searing pain nearly knocked him to his knees. He dragged Elaine Canning closer to him and held her, feeling the burn across his chest as well as in his palms.

He looked up the endless tunnel of light and felt tears begin to fill his eyes.

What had he done?

ABOUT THE AUTHOR

D.J. Butler (Dave) is a novelist living in the Rocky Mountain northwest. His training is in law, and he worked as a securities lawyer at a major international firm and in-house at two multinational semiconductor manufacturers before taking up writing fiction.

Dave writes speculative fiction for all audiences. In addition to his steampunk, urban fantasy, and science fiction novels published with WordFire Press, look for *The Kidnap Plot* (Knopf) and *Witchy Eye* (Baen).

Dave is a lover of language and languages, a guitarist and self-recorder, and a serious reader. He is married to a powerful and clever woman, and together they have three devious children.

Read about Dave's writing projects at:

http://davidjohnbutler.com

IF YOU LIKED ...

If you liked *Road to Hell*, you might also enjoy:

Samantha Kane: Into the Fire
Patrick Hester

Another Girl, Another Planet
Lou Antonelli

Prospero Lost
Jagi Lamplighter

Other WordFire Press Titles by D.J. Butler

City of Saints

The Buza System

Crechling,

Urbane

Rock Band Fights Evil: Band on the Run Omnibus 1-3

Rock Band Fights Evil: Earth Angel 7

Our list of other WordFire Press authors and titles is always growing.
To find out more and to see our selection of titles, visit us at:

wordfirepress.com